Mark Billingham is a stand-up comedian who appears regularly at the Comedy Store, as well as being an award-winning television writer. He lives in north London with his wife and two children. His first novel, *Sleepyhead*, is available in Time Warner paperback. You can visit his website at: **www.markbillingham.com**

Critical acclaim for *Scaredy Cat*

'Billingham confirms his promise and delivers an assured and shocking thriller that shows his American counterparts a thing or two about menace' Maxim Jakubowski, *Guardian*

'An incredibly dark, brilliant thriller' *Evening Standard*

'Mark Billingham is the new-wave leader . . . like the best of British and American crime writing rolled up together and delivered with the kind of punch you don't see coming' Lee Child

'A cunning variation on the serial-murder theme . . . with well-observed characters and first-rate dialogue' *Sunday Telegraph*

'Taut, gripping and stylish . . . unputdownable' *Time Out*

'Scary, pell-mell, cliff-hanging thriller . . . [a] confident follow-up to [his] excellent first novel. Billingham has hit the ground running' *Literary Review*

'A tight, witty writer with [a] near perfect grasp of pace and rhythm' *Big Issue*

'Mark Billingham is one of my favourite new authors. Highly recommended' Harlan Coben

'Billingham writes with a deft hand about violence intruding on the every day. *Scaredy Cat* is an incredibly satisfying and engaging thriller' Karin Slaughter

An extract from Mark Billingham's exciting new thriller *Lazybones* can be found at the end of this book.

Also by this author

SLEEPYHEAD
LAZYBONES

Scaredy Cat

Mark Billingham

A *Time Warner* Paperback

First published in Great Britain in 2002 by Little, Brown
This edition published by Time Warner Paperbacks in 2003

A CIP catalogue record for this book
is available from the British Library.

ISBN 0 7515 3395 5

Typeset in Plantin by M Rules
Printed and bound in Great Britain by
Clays Ltd, St Ives plc

Time Warner Paperbacks
An imprint of
Time Warner Books UK
Brettenham House
Lancaster Place
London WC2E 7EN

www.TimeWarnerBooks.co.uk

For Katharine and Jack. But not yet.

And in memory of Vi Winyard (1925–2002)

ACKNOWLEDGEMENTS

As always, a great many people have helped, cajoled, suffered . . .

Special thanks are due to DI Neil Hibberd of the Serious Crime Group for his patience and informed creativity and also to Pauline O'Brien (Senior Press officer) and Selina Onorah (Office Manager) at the Metropolitan Police Area West Press Office, for their time and considerable trouble.

For invaluable advice on their own very different subjects, I must thank Jason Schone, Glenda Brunt, Yaron Meron and, as always, the correctly spelled Phil Cowburn.

At Little, Brown special thanks are due and in some cases overdue to: Filomena Wood, Alison Lindsay and Tamsyn Berryman.

There are those whose names, for many reasons, are destined to appear on this, and the corresponding page of all books to come . . .

Hilary Hale and Sarah Lutyens, obviously; Mike Gunn, for his past and his present; Alice Pettet, for notes and a name; David Fulton, for digging me out of a hole; Paul Thorne, for being unconvinced; Howard

Pratt, for knowing most things; Wendy Lee, for missing nothing . . .

And especially Peter Cocks, whose eyes and ears are sharper than most and whose instincts are rarely wrong.

And Claire, for being both Dave and Carmela.

Scaredy Cat

Knock hard, life is deaf.
– Mimi Parent

PROLOGUE

KING EDWARD IV GRAMMAR SCHOOL
FOR BOYS

14 August, 1984

Mr and Mrs R. Palmer
43, Valentine Rd
Harrow
Middlesex

Dear Mr and Mrs Palmer

Following an extraordinary meeting of the board of governors, it is with a good deal of regret that I write to confirm the decision to expel your son, Martin, from the school. This expulsion will come into effect immediately.

I must stress that this course of action is highly unusual and is only ever taken as a last resort. It was, however, deemed the only measure appropriate considering the nature of the offence. Your son's activities have been of concern for some time and are all the more disturbing considering his excellent academic record and previously reserved character. The most recent, repulsive incident is only the latest in a catalogue of unacceptable behaviour and flagrant breaches of school regulations.

As you are aware, your son is not the only pupil involved, and indeed, you may take some comfort from the fact that your son was almost certainly not the main perpetrator and has, in my opinion, been to some degree led astray. That said, however, he has shown little remorse for his actions and is unwilling to implicate his erstwhile partner in crime.

In order that the high educational standards of this school are maintained, I feel that similar standards of discipline must be enforced. This being the case, behaviour such as that engaged in by your son cannot be tolerated.

I wish Martin the best of luck in his new school.

Yours sincerely

P.H. Stanley

Philip Stanley, A.F.C., M.A. Headmaster.

Rectory Road, Harrow, Middlesex, MA3 4HL

PART ONE

EIGHT SUMMERS, ONE WINTER

2001

```
Date: 27 November
Target: Fem
Age: 20-30
Pickup: London railway station (Int or
Ext)
Site: TBA
Method: Hands only (weapon permitted to
subdue if necessary)
```

Nicklin watched, unblinking, as the two of them walked hand in hand towards him across the station concourse.

She was perfect.

He was still clutching the book he'd presumably been reading on the train and she was finishing a sandwich. The two of them were chatting and laughing. They kept moving. They looked straight at Nicklin but didn't see him. They weren't looking around for anybody. They were not expecting to be met.

He was sitting and sipping from a can of Coke, gazing casually towards the departure board every few minutes. Just another frustrated traveller monitoring the delays. He turned his head and watched them as they passed him. They were probably heading for taxi, bus or tube. If they were getting a cab then he'd settle back and wait for someone else. Annoying, but not the end of the world. If they were planning to continue their journey by public transport, he would follow.

He was in luck.

Still holding hands, the two of them stepped on to the escalator leading down to the underground. Nicklin put his half-empty can on the floor beside him and stood up, hearing his knee click loudly. He smiled. He wasn't getting any younger.

He reached into his coat pocket for the chocolate bar he'd bought earlier. Moving the knife aside, he took the chocolate out and began to unwrap it as he moved towards the escalator. As he stepped on behind a backpacker, he took a large bite, and after checking that the two of them were still there, twenty feet or so below him, he glanced out through the vast windows towards the bus depot. The crowds were thinning out now; the rush hour nearly over.

It was just starting to get dark. On the streets and in houses.

Inside people's heads.

They took the Northern line south. He settled down a few seats away, and watched. She was in her early thirties, he thought. Tall with dark hair, dark eyes and what Nicklin thought was called an olive complexion. What his mum might have called 'a touch of the tarbrush'. She wasn't pretty but she wasn't a dog either.

Not that it mattered really.

The train passed through the West End and continued south. Clapham, he guessed, or maybe Tooting. Wherever . . .

The two of them were all over each other. He was still looking at his book, glancing up every few seconds to grin at her. She squeezed his hand and on a couple of occasions she actually leant across to nuzzle his neck. People in the seats around them were smiling and shaking their heads.

He could feel the sweat begin to prickle on his forehead and smell that damp, downstairs smell that grew so strong, so acrid, whenever he got close.

They stood up as the train pulled into Balham station.

He watched them jump giggling from the train, and waited a second or two before casually falling into step behind them.

He stayed far enough behind them to be safe, but they were so wrapped up in each other that he could probably have walked at their heels. Oblivious, they drifted along in front of him, towards the station exit. She was wearing a long green coat and ankle boots. He was wearing a blue anorak and a woolly hat.

Nicklin wore a long black coat with deep pockets.

On the street ahead of him, with the gaudy Christmas lights as a backdrop, they were silhouetted against a crimson sky. He knew that this was one of the pictures he would remember. There would be others, of course.

They walked past a small parade of shops and he had to fight the urge to rush into a newsagent for more chocolate. He only had one bar left. He knew that he could be in and out in a few seconds but he daren't risk losing them. He'd get some more when it was all over. He'd be starving by then.

They turned off the main road into a well-lit but quiet side street and his breath grew ragged as he watched her reach into her pocket for keys. He picked up his pace a little. He could hear them talking about toast and tea and bed. He could see their joy at getting home.

He slid his hand into his pocket, looking around to see who might be watching.

Hoping it wasn't a flat. That he'd get some privacy. Praying for a bit of luck.

Her key slid into the lock and his hand moved across her mouth. Her first instinct was to scream but Nicklin pressed the knife into her back and with the pain came a little common sense. She didn't turn to try and look at him.

'Let's go inside.'

Tasting the sweat on his palm, feeling the piss run down her legs, she opens the front door, her hand flapping desperately, reaching down to her side for the one she loves. For the only one she cares about.

For her child.

'Please . . .'

Her voice is muffled by his hand. The word is lost. He pushes her and the boy through the doorway, hurries inside after them and slams the door shut.

The toddler in the blue anorak is still holding tight to his picture book. He looks up at the stranger with the same dark eyes as his mother, his mouth pursing into a tiny, infinitely confused 'O'.

ONE

A little after nine thirty in the morning. The first grey Monday of December. From the third floor of Becke House, Tom Thorne stared out across the monument to concrete and complacency that was Hendon, wishing more than anything that he wasn't thinking clearly.

He was, unfortunately, doing just that. Sorting the material in front of him, taking it all in. Assigning to each item, without knowing it, emotional responses that would colour every waking hour in the months to come.

And many sleeping hours too.

Wide awake and focused, Thorne sat and studied death, the way others at work elsewhere were looking at computer screens or sitting at tills. It was the material he worked with every day and yet, faced with *this*, something to take the edge off would have been nice. Even the steamhammer of a hangover would have been preferable. Something to blunt the corners a little. Something to turn the noise of the horror down.

He'd seen hundreds, maybe thousands, of photos like these. He'd stared at them over the years with the same dispassionate eye that a dentist might cast over X-rays, or an accountant across a tax return. He'd lost count of the pale limbs, twisted or torn or missing altogether in black and white ten-by-eights. Then there were the colour prints. Pale bodies lying on green carpets. A ring of purple bruises around a chalk-white neck. The garish patterned wallpaper against which the blood spatter is barely discernible.

An ever expanding exhibition with a simple message: emotions are powerful things, bodies are not.

These were the pictures filed in his office, with duplicates stored in the files in his head. Snapshots of deaths and portraits of lives lived to extremes. There were occasions when Thorne had gazed at these bodies in monochrome and thought he'd glimpsed rage or hatred or greed or lust, or perhaps the ghosts of such things, floating in the corners of rooms like ectoplasm.

The photographs on the table in front of him this morning were no more sickening than any he had seen before, but keeping his eyes on the image of the dead woman was like staring hard into a flame and feeling his eyeballs start to melt.

He was seeing her through the eyes of her child.

Charlie Garner aged three, now an orphan.

Charlie Garner aged three, being cared for by grandparents who wrestled every minute of every day with what to tell him about his mummy.

Charlie Garner aged three, who spent the best part of two days alone in a house with the body of his mother, clutching at a chocolate wrapper he'd licked clean, starving and dirty and screaming until a neighbour knocked.

'Tom . . .'

Thorne stared out into the greyness for a few more seconds before turning back resignedly to DCI Russell Brigstocke.

As part of the major reorganisation of the Met a year or so earlier, a number of new squads had been established within the three nascent Serious Crime Groups. A unit consisting entirely of officers brought out of retirement had been set up expressly to investigate cold cases. This unit, quickly christened the Crinkly Squad, was just one of a raft of new initiatives as part of a fresh and supposedly proactive approach to fighting crime in the capital. There were other squads specialising in sexual assaults, violence against children and firearms offences.

Then there was Team 3, Serious Crime Group (West).

Officially, this squad was devised to investigate cases whose parameters were outside those which might be investigated elsewhere – cases that didn't fit anybody else's remit. There *were* those, however, who suggested that SCG (West) 3 had been set up simply because no-one quite knew what to do with Detective Inspector Tom Thorne. Thorne himself reckoned that the truth was probably somewhere halfway between the two.

Russell Brigstocke was the senior officer and Thorne had known him for over ten years. He was a big man who cut a distinctive figure with horn-rimmed glasses and hair of which he was inordinately proud. It was thick and blue-black, and the DCI took great delight in teasing it up into a quiff of almost Elvis-like proportions. But if he was a caricaturist's dream, he could also be a suspect's worse nightmare. Thorne had seen Brigstocke with glasses off and fists clenched, hair flopping around his sweat-drenched forehead as he stalked around an interview room, shouting, threatening, carrying out the threat, looking for the truth.

'Carol Garner was a single mum. She was twenty-eight

years old. Her husband died in a road accident three years
ago, just after their son was born. She was a teacher. She
was found dead in her home in Balham four days ago.
There were no signs of forced entry. She'd arrived back at
Euston station at six thirty p.m. on the twenty-seventh
having been to Birmingham to visit her parents. We think
that the killer followed her from the station, probably on
the tube. We found a travelcard in her pocket.'

Brigstocke's voice was low and accentless, almost a
monotone. Yet the litany of facts simply stated was horribly
powerful. Thorne knew most of it, having been briefed by
Brigstocke the day before, but still the words were like a
series of punches, each harder than the last, combining to
leave him aching and breathless. He could see that the
others were no less shocked.

And he knew that they had yet to hear the worst.

Brigstocke continued. 'We can only speculate on how
the killer gained entry or how long he spent inside Carol
Garner's home, but we know what he did when he was
there . . .'

Brigstocke looked down the length of the table asking
the man at the other end to carry on where he had left off.
Thorne stared at the figure in the black fleece, with
shaved head and a startling collection of facial piercings.
Phil Hendricks was not everybody's idea of a pathologist, but he was the best Thorne had ever worked with.
Thorne raised an eyebrow. Was there yet another earring
since he'd last seen him? Hendricks was fond of com-
memorating each new boyfriend with a ring, stud or
spike. Thorne sincerely hoped that he would settle down
soon, before he was completely unable to lift his head
up.

Dr Phil Hendricks was the civilian member of the team. He was there at the beginning, obviously, as the discovery of a body was almost certainly what galvanised the team in the first place. The body that would yield to the knife; the story behind its journey to a cold steel slab whispered in secrets, revealed by its dead flesh and petrified organs. These were the pathologist's areas of expertise.

Though he and Hendricks were good friends, from this point on, in the context of the investigation, Thorne would be happy if he did not see him again.

'Based on when we know she got on a train from Birmingham, we think she was killed somewhere between seven and ten p.m. on the twenty-seventh. She'd been dead for something like forty-eight hours when she was found.'

The flat Mancunian accent conveyed with a simple precision the tawdry and banal reality of genuine horror. Thorne could see the unspeakable thought in the faces of those around the table.

What were those two days like for little Charlie Garner?

'There were no signs of sexual abuse and no indication that she put up any significant struggle. The obvious conclusion is that the killer threatened the child.' Hendricks stopped, took a breath. 'He strangled Carol Garner with his bare hands.'

'Fucker . . .'

Thorne glanced to his left. Detective Sergeant Sarah McEvoy stared down at the file in front of her. Thorne waited, but for the moment it seemed that she'd said everything that was on her mind. Of all of them, she was the officer who Thorne had known for the shortest time. And he still didn't know her at all. Tough, no question, and more than capable. But there was something about her that made Thorne a little wary. There was something hidden.

The voice of DC Dave Holland focused Thorne's thoughts again. 'Do we think he targeted her because of the child?'

Thorne nodded. 'It was her weakness. Yes, I think he probably did . . .'

Brigstocke interrupted. 'But it isn't really significant.'

'Not really significant?' Holland sounded thoroughly confused and looked across at his boss.

Thorne shrugged and threw him a look back. *Wait and see Dave . . .*

It was just over a year since Thorne had first begun working with Dave Holland and he was at last starting to look like a grown-up. His hair was still far too blond and floppy, but the features it framed seemed set a little harder these days. Thorne knew that this was not so much to do with age as experience. Wear and tear. The most wholesome and guileless of faces was bound to cloud a little when confronted with some of the things the job threw up.

The change had begun during their first case together. Three months in which Thorne had lost friends and made enemies, while Dave Holland grew closer to him, watching and absorbing and becoming someone else. Three months that had ended with the slash of a scalpel in a blood-drenched attic in south London.

Holland had learned and *unlearned* a great deal, and Thorne had watched it happen, proud yet saddened. It was an argument that he had with himself on a regular basis. Were they mutually exclusive – the good copper and the good person?

Learning a degree of desensitisation was all very well but there would be a price to pay. He remembered a warning poster he had seen in a dentist's waiting room: the graphic image of a lip bitten clean off by a patient 'testing' the local anaesthetic. You could bite and bite and not feel a thing, but it was only a matter of time until the anaesthetic wore off and then the pain would certainly begin.

The numbness would wear off too, for those colleagues who Thorne watched getting through their days inside their own brand of armour. Whether manufactured in their heads or from a bottle, it would surely wear off one day and then the agony would be unbearable. This was not Tom Thorne's way, and despite the bravado and bullshit that he'd learned, he instinctively knew that it wasn't Holland's either.

The good copper and the good person. Probably *not* mutually exclusive, just fucking difficult to reconcile. Like one of those things in physics that is theoretically possible but that nobody has ever seen.

A silence had settled briefly across what was laughably described as the conference room. It was actually little more than a slightly bigger office, with a jug of coffee and a few more uncomfortable plastic chairs than normal. Thorne considered what he knew about the man who had killed Carol Garner. A man who liked, who needed to be in control. A coward. Perhaps not commanding physically . . . Christ, he was starting to sound like one of those forensic psychiatrists he thought were so overpaid. What he *did* know of course, was that this killer was far from ordinary. Extraordinary, and with a greater *potential*, than Holland or McEvoy yet understood.

Then of course there was the *why*. Always the why. And, as always, Tom Thorne didn't give a flying fuck about it. He would confront it if it presented itself. He would grab it with both hands if he could catch the killer with it. But he didn't *care*. At least, not about whether the man he was after had ever been given a bicycle as a child . . .

McEvoy was shifting on the chair next to him. She had finished looking through her file and he could sense that she had something to say.

'What is it, Sarah?'

'This is horrible, no question . . . and the stuff with the kid, it's very fucking nasty, but I still can't quite see why it's us. As opposed to anybody else. I mean, how do we know she wasn't killed by someone she knew? There were no signs of forced entry, it might have been a boyfriend or an ex-boyfriend . . . so, why us? Sir.'

Thorne looked towards Brigstocke who, with the timing of an expert, lobbed another sheaf of photographs into the middle of the table.

Holland casually reached out to take a photo. 'I was thinking the same thing. I don't understand what makes—' He stopped as he took in the image of the woman on her back, her mouth open, her eyes bulging and bloodied. The woman lying among the rubbish bags in a cold dark street. The woman who was not Carol Garner.

It was a dramatic gesture and meant to be. Brigstocke wanted his team fired up. He wanted them shocked, motivated, passionate.

He certainly had their attention.

It was Thorne who explained exactly what they were up against. 'What makes this different, Holland' – he looked at McEvoy – 'what makes it *us*, is that he did it again.'

Now, it was as if the previous silence had been a cacophony. Thorne could hear nothing but the distant echo of his own voice and the hiss of the adrenaline fizzing through his bloodstream. Brigstocke and Hendricks sat frozen, heads bowed. Holland and McEvoy exchanged a horrified glance.

'It's the reason we know he followed Carol Garner from Euston station. Because as soon as he'd finished killing her, that same day, he went to King's Cross. He went to a different station, found another woman, and did it all over again.'

Karen, it happened again.

Please, let me tell you what happened. I couldn't bear it if you thought badly of me. I know that you can't possibly forgive or condone what I've done . . . what I'm doing, but I know that you'll understand. I've always thought that if I had the chance to explain myself to you, confide in you, that you would be the one person who would truly understand. You always saw me for what I was. You always knew what I thought about you. I could see it in that shy smile.

You knew that you had a power over me, didn't you, but I was never angry with you because of it. Part of me enjoyed the teasing. I wanted to be the one you teased. It felt like I was needed anyway. It just made you more attractive to me, Karen . . .

Jesus, though. Jesus. I did it again. What I was told.

She was alone and frightened of nothing. I could tell by the way she was walking when I followed her out of the station. Not a cocky fearlessness, just a sort of trust. She saw the good in everyone, I could tell that. It was dark and she couldn't see how weak and vile I was. There was no fear in her eyes when I spoke to her.

She knew though, what was going to happen, when she saw the fear in mine.

As soon as she knew, she struggled, but she wasn't strong enough. She was less than half my size, Karen, and I just had to wait for her to fade a little. She was scratching and spitting and I couldn't look at her. And when it was over, I couldn't bear it that her face, which had been so open and warm like yours, now looked like something behind glass, or frozen for a long time inside a block of ice, and I was the one who had made it like that.

And I was hard, Karen. Down there. While I was doing it, and again afterwards, while I was hiding her. I stayed excited until the hissing in my head began to die down and the scratches on my hands started to hurt.

I was hard like I never am, even when I'm thinking about the past.

I don't want to embarrass you by talking like this, but if I can't be honest with you about these things then there's no point to anything. I never really told you what I was thinking when I had the chance, so I'm not going to hide things now.

And I will never lie to you, Karen, I promise you that.

Of course, you're not the only one who knows what I really am but you're the only one who can see what's inside. I'm not making excuses, I know that I deserve nothing, but at the very least I'm being open about everything. Open and honest.

She was nothing to me, this woman from the station. She was nothing to me and I squeezed the life out of her.

I'm so very sorry, and I deserve what is surely coming.

I hate to ask a favour, Karen, but if you see her, the woman I killed, will you tell her that for me?

1982

The kids called it 'the Jungle Story'.

The victim was pinned to the tarmac with one boy holding down each arm and another sitting astride his chest. The fingers were the weapons – tapping, prodding, poking – jabbing out the rhythms of the story on the breastbone. The steps of each new animal marching through the jungle. The story was a very simple one; a straightforward excuse to inflict pain.

The wiry, black-haired boy leaned against the wall, his small dark eyes taking in every detail. Watching as the torment began.

When it was just the monkeys, or whichever of the small creatures the storyteller introduced early on, it was not really much more than a tickle. The victim would writhe around, telling them to stop, to get off; the fear of what was to come worse than anything. Then would come the lions and tigers. Heavier steps, the fingers jabbing harder, tears beginning to prick in the corners of the eyes. Everything, of course, leading up to the seemingly endless herd of elephants tramping through the jungle, the fingers slamming into the chest, the pain excruciating.

The big kid on the floor was screaming now.

The boy pushed himself away from the wall, took his hands from his pockets and moved across the playground to where the crowd of onlookers stood in a circle, jeering and clapping. It was time to intervene.

The one telling the 'story' was called Bardsley. The boy

hated him. He shoved his way through the crowd, which was not difficult as most of the other third formers were scared of him. He was, after all, the 'mad' one, the one who would do anything. The kid who would throw a desk out of the window or wave his tiny cock around in class, or let a teacher's tyres down. He'd had to suffer a great many detentions in his time to earn his reputation, but it was worth it in terms of the respect it won him.

He didn't care about geography or French grammar but he knew about respect.

He reached down, casually took hold of Bardsley's hair and yanked him backwards. There was a gasp from the crowd, which quickly turned to nervous laughter as Bardsley jumped up, furious, ready to transfer his aggression onto whoever was responsible for the terrible stinging on his scalp.

Then he saw who was to blame. The boy, far smaller and slighter than he was, stared calmly back at him, eyes cold and dark as stones frozen in mud, hands once more thrust deep into his pockets.

The crowd dispersed quickly into smaller groups. A kickabout was already starting as Bardsley backed away towards the changing rooms, promising some nasty revenge after school but not really meaning it.

The boy on the floor stood up and began to rearrange his dishevelled uniform. He didn't say anything, but eyed his saviour nervously while doing up his tie and dragging a sleeve across his snotty top lip.

The black-haired boy had seen him around but they had never spoken. He was a year younger, probably only twelve, and the different years didn't really mix. His sandy hair was usually neatly combed with a parting, and he was often to be seen in a corner somewhere, his pale blue eyes peeking out enviously from behind a book, observing the assorted games he had no part in. He was a big kid, at least a foot taller than most of the others in his year and brainy as hell, but he was slow in all the ways that counted. He probably hadn't done anything specific to piss Bardsley off, but that wasn't really the point.

The older boy watched, smiling as a brown plastic comb was produced and dragged through the sandy hair, dislodging pieces of playground grit. He had a comb himself of course, but it was a metal one; far cooler, and used mostly for the lunch-time comb fights of which he was the acknowledged champion. These fights were a more brutal version of 'Slaps' or 'Scissors, paper, rock' and could leave a hand dripping with blood within a few seconds. He was the champion, not because he was quicker than anybody else, but because he could stand the pain for longer.

He could put up with a great deal of pain when he had to.

The sandy-haired boy carefully put away his comb in the inside pocket of his blazer, cleared his throat nervously and produced a rarely seen smile. It quickly disappeared when it was not reciprocated. In its place, a hand, notably free of scratches and scabs, was extended.

'Thank you for . . . doing that. I'm Palmer. Martin . . .'

The wiry black-haired boy, the mad boy, the boy who would do anything, nodded. He ignored the hand and spoke his name with a sly smile, as if revealing a dirty secret.

As if giving a gift that was actually worth far more than it looked.

'Nicklin.'

TWO

'A few less questions, when it's all over, even *one* less than when a case begins, and you're doing all right . . .'

Thorne smiled as he carried his coffee through to the living room, remembering Holland's reaction when he had first passed on this pithy piece of homespun wisdom. It had also, he recalled, been the first time that Thorne had managed to get him inside a pub. An auspicious day.

Questions . . .

In the pub, Holland had smiled. 'What? You mean questions like, "Why didn't I study harder at school?" and, "Isn't there anybody else available?"'

'I think I preferred you when you were an arse-licker, Holland . . .'

Thorne put his mug on the mantelpiece and bent down to light the flame-effect gas fire in the mock-Georgian fireplace. The central heating was up as high as it would go but he was still freezing. *And* his back was playing up. *And* it was pissing down . . .

There were plenty of questions that needed answering right now.

Were the two killings genuinely connected? Apart from

the date and the fact that both women were strangled, there seemed to be no other link, so was the station thing just a coincidence? King's Cross threw up other possibilities. Had he mistaken the second victim for a prostitute? Why kill one at home and one on the street?

And the biggest question of the lot: did he kill twice on the same day because he was out of control, or was killing multiple victims actually the pattern? Blood lust or compulsion? Right now, Holland and McEvoy were earning overtime trying to find out, but whichever it was, the answer was not going to be pleasant.

In the eight months or so that the team had been together, they had only really worked on two major cases that were truly their own. Most of the time they'd been seconded – either individually or together – on to other investigations with other units, and then been reconvened when needed.

The aftermath of the terrorist atrocities of September 11 had seen the teams from Serious Crime involved in an operation unlike any before. Some had expressed surprise that repatriating bodies from New York should be down to them, but it made sense to Thorne. These were British citizens. They had been murdered. It wasn't complicated.

The phone calls had been the hardest: thousands of people eager to trace husbands and wives, sons and daughters who hadn't been in touch and who may or may not have been in the area. So far, of the hundreds whose missing relatives never did get in touch with them, only one had been given an identifiable body to bury . . .

Three months on, and the Met was still stretched – tracking down Anthrax hoaxers, monitoring possible terrorist targets, chasing their tails while street crime grew to fill the hole that was left. If suddenly phone-jacking didn't seem quite so important, there *were* still crimes, like those that Team 3 got handed, that needed to be taken very seriously indeed.

The two cases were both . . . unusual. The first was a series of gruesome killings in south-east London that bore all the hallmarks of gangland slayings. However, the bodies (when they'd been painstakingly re-assembled) were found to belong, not to drug-dealers or loan sharks, but to ordinary, law-abiding citizens. It quickly became clear that the murders were the work of one highly disturbed individual as opposed to an organised gang of them. Whether the killer – a happily married electrical engineer – had been simply trying to disguise his work, or had a psychotic fixation with the disposal methods of gangsters, was as yet unclear. He was still undergoing psychiatric evaluation.

The other case was the more disturbing, despite the lack of bodies. Guests in hotels were being targeted and robbed in their rooms. The minor physical assaults that were part and parcel of the thefts had soon begun to escalate however. Those that willingly handed over cash, Rolexes and other valuables were being tortured anyway. The knife was produced and the PIN number was demanded. The number was given and the knife was used anyway. Small cuts, nicks: wounding for pure pleasure. Thorne knew that this one liked the feel of a blade on skin, enjoyed hearing the intake of breath, and watching the thin red line fill out on the flesh and begin to drip.

The robbery was becoming something else: the robber, *someone* else. Behind his black balaclava, he was starting to enjoy his work a little too much and it was only a matter of time until people started to die.

That was when Thorne had been brought in.

With next to no physical evidence and no real description to work from, the case had quickly become hugely frustrating. Thorne, Holland and McEvoy, in an effort to trap this latent killer, this murderer-to-be, had spent nights in some very nice hotels but without success. Their efforts had evidently been noted and the individual responsible had gone to ground.

Two cases, one arrest. A fifty per cent hit rate, and the numbers would only get worse from here on in. Some had joked that the hotel case, given a few weeks, would get passed on to the Crinkly Squad anyway, but Thorne knew differently. Anybody who enjoyed inflicting pain to the degree this man did, would need to do it again. He would resurface somewhere. The MO might be completely different, but Thorne did not doubt for a second that one day soon he would be providing a pathologist somewhere with some overtime.

Thorne took his coffee across to the sofa and picked up the file on Carol Garner. He sat for a few minutes, not opening it, just staring out into the rain and thinking about the hundreds, the thousands of different people across the capital who owed their employment to the violent death of another. Thinking about the money generated by murder.

Thinking about the industry of killing.

Dave Holland stared over the top of his computer screen at Sarah McEvoy who was avidly studying hers. He thought about his girlfriend, Sophie.

The ongoing argument which they had been having in instalments for the past year, had flared up again. Sophie had a problem with Thorne. She had only met him once and had formed an opinion based entirely on what Holland himself had said about Thorne in the early days of their working relationship. So the man described by Holland over a year ago as 'obsessive' and 'arrogant' had become, in the strange folklore of Sophie's imagination, a pigheaded, self-serving lunatic whose refusal to follow procedure would one day cost him not only *his* career, but those of the people around him. *Those who didn't know any better . . .*

It wasn't that she didn't want Holland to do the job. She just wanted him to do it in a particular way; to be the sort of copper who keeps his head down and gets promoted, and who is universally liked. A copper who does just enough.

A copper like his father.

Once, she'd intimated that if he chose to go a different route then he would be going it alone. He had been furious at the threat and the ultimatum had been quietly forgotten.

At least, they both pretended that it had.

The arguments were never heated. The two of them were sulkers, bottlers-up. It was more a series of snipes and barbed comments, and the intensity had increased as soon as the new case had started. Yesterday evening, after a hectic day that had begun with the team briefing, Sophie had looked up at him across the kitchen table, smiled, and opened her account.

'So how many people did the great Tom Thorne piss off today then?'

He wasn't sure what upset him most about the whole thing. The assumption that as far as *his* career was concerned, she knew best? The lack of support? Or the fact that when it came to her assessment of Thorne, most of the time she was absolutely right?

McEvoy glanced up from her monitor and fixed him with bright green eyes. *Caught you.*

She was tall, 5´ 7˝ or 5´ 8˝, with shoulder-length, curly brown hair, a broken nose and full lips which smiled easily and, so it seemed to Holland, often. Right now, he reckoned the smile had at least three different meanings.

He didn't understand any of them.

'I heard something very strange today.' Despite the surname, she was pure North London Jewish. Her accent was flattish, hard. Sexy. 'A vicious rumour about the Weeble . . .' The nickname was a reference to Thorne's shape, to how hard people thought it would be to make him fall down.

Holland raised his eyebrows. *Another rumour?* When it came to Thorne, he'd heard most of it, but he enjoyed a good story or bit of gossip as much as anybody else.

'I heard that he likes country-and-western. Is that true?'

Holland nodded, as if confirming a terminal diagnosis. 'Yeah, he loves it.'

'What, all that yee-hah and Dolly Parton and stuff? Does he go line dancing?'

Holland laughed. 'I think it's a bit more obscure than that. He used to listen to a lot of techno and garage stuff as well, but I think that was just a phase.' He blinked slowly, remembering the almost hypnotic noise. Remembering the case it had helped to blot out.

McEvoy looked disappointed. 'Shame. He was starting to sound interesting there for a minute.'

'Oh he's . . . interesting.'

Holland believed *that* about Thorne, if he believed anything. If interesting meant unpredictable and stubborn. If it meant refusing to admit that you might be wrong. If interesting meant determined, and vengeful, and knowing the difference between right and wrong whatever the poxy rules said. And refusing to suffer fools. And possessing the kind of passion that would always make something happen. A passion that Dave Holland, whatever other people might want him to do and be, would have killed to have even the tiniest fucking bit of . . .

He thought about his father. A man who died a sergeant at sixty. Having done just enough.

McEvoy shrugged and her eyes dropped back to her screen. Back to the computerised catalogue of suffering and death from which the two of them were supposed, hopefully, to come up with some answers.

Holland had believed that relatively, London could not be *that* violent a city and that their search would not be overly time-consuming.

He had been wrong on both counts.

Looking for murders committed on the same day *had* sounded fairly straightforward, but Thorne was not a man who did things by half. Both time-frame and search criteria were broadening all the time. McEvoy and Holland had begun by looking for strangulations first and then widened things from there. They couldn't rule out assaults as they might be the work of the same man who had now perhaps graduated to full-blown murder. Even discounting domestics and gang-related attacks, it was a big job. To check thoroughly, to go back far enough to find a pattern – if indeed there was one – was going to take time.

Holland looked up at the clock. Another twenty minutes and they could call it a night. He tried to picture Thorne in a stetson and cowboy boots but the image wouldn't stick.

Thorne was too dangerous to be a figure of fun.

*

Johnny Cash made good music to read post-mortem reports by.

This, after all, was someone who once famously sang about shooting a man just to watch him die. Whether this was big talk or just a very bad case of boredom, he sang as if he knew a great deal about death. Thorne wondered, as he read the words Phil Hendricks had used to describe the manner of Carol Garner's death, how much he really knew. Now, the man with a voice like the long, slow tumble towards hell was singing about flesh and blood needing flesh and blood. Thorne certainly didn't require it, but the proof was there on his lap, right in front of him – the proof that sometimes, flesh and blood needed to *destroy* flesh and blood, too.

The body of the second victim, Ruth Murray, had been examined by another pathologist. Thorne had seen the initial report which confirmed strangulation as the cause of death and revealed that tissue had been removed from beneath the victim's fingernails for DNA-testing. He wasn't going to get too excited just yet. It sounded promising, but he would wait to see what Hendricks had to say once he'd carried out a second PM.

Thorne had once thought strangulation, as ways of dying went, to be a fairly soft option. It could surely not be as terrible as being repeatedly stabbed or bludgeoned. It was certainly not on a par with drowning, or suffocating or swallowing bleach.

He'd thought this, until he'd read his first PM report on a victim of manual strangulation. In many ways, the use of the bare hands to throttle – the flesh on flesh – made it the very worst type of killing. There was no weapon to separate killer from victim. In most cases the victim would lapse into unconsciousness quickly, but the damage inflicted could be massive, often leaving the victim as bloody and bruised as if they had been attacked with a hammer.

Carol Garner had died from asphyxia due to the compression of the carotid arteries, her body displaying virtually every classic trait consistent with violent strangulation.

The eyes were open, the eyeballs distended, the corneas and skin around the eyes showing signs of haemorrhage. The neck was a mass of bruises, some nearly an inch in diameter and there were bloody, half-moon-shaped indentations from the nails on the fingers and thumbs of the killer.

Thorne's hands drifted towards his throat. He closed his eyes.

Was that chocolate bar his, Charlie? Did he give it you to keep you quiet? Or did he produce it himself, afterwards, and eat it slowly, watching her, while you were crying?

There was massive bruising and abrasion to the floor of the mouth, the epiglottis and the lining of the larynx. The tongue had been all but bitten clean through. The crocoid cartilage was crushed, the thyroid cartilage virtually unrecognisable and the hyoid bone was fractured. It was this internal damage which most clearly indicated the severity of the attack which led to Carol Garner's death.

Did you see it happen, Charlie? Did he shut you out of the room, or did you stand and scream, and beat your tiny fists on his back and watch your mummy's eyeballs bulging out of their sockets?

Thorne leaned down to pick up the coffee that he'd left on the floor by the sofa. It was stone cold. He looked at his watch. He'd been immersed in the details of death for well over an hour. Thorne was as disturbed as always by this . . . capacity he had.

He'd tried reading crime fiction once but it had not suited him at all. He could barely read any so-called thriller for more than a few minutes without starting to drift away, and yet a jargon-filled description of ruined flesh had him riveted. He was confident that there was nothing overly perverse in this. He could honestly say that he had never enjoyed *watching* an autopsy.

The truth was that an intimate knowledge of real killers and real victims made him a difficult reader to please.

Thorne had seen enough wild-eyed gunmen and blood-ied blades, and soft-spoken, heavy-lidded perverts. He'd seen plenty of batterers and arsonists and smiling poison-ers. He'd seen more than his fair share of damaged bodies: some dead, and others more damaged still, left behind to remember.

He'd seen holes in flesh and holes in lives.

Thorne picked up his coffee cup and was heading for the kitchen to make another when the doorbell rang.

Hendricks was standing on the doorstep wearing a floor-length black leather coat and watch cap. He was brandishing a blue-striped plastic bag that was threatening to break at any instant thanks to the vast quantity of cheap lager it contained. The accent hardly suited dramatic declamation, but he did his best. 'Let us drink beer and talk of death.'

Thorne turned and headed back inside. Neither of them was big on ceremony. 'It sounds like you've already started on the drinking bit . . .'

Hendricks slammed the outer door and followed Thorne inside. 'I've been doing both, mate. I've been with

Dr Duggan most of the day . . .' He closed the inner door and moved into the living room.

'He the one who did the first post-mortem on Ruth Murray?'

'She. *Emma* Duggan. Very good, *and* very fanciable, if you like that kind of thing.'

Thorne shook his head and reached into the plastic bag that Hendricks was now cradling gently. 'Formaldehyde does nothing for me, sorry.'

'And I've spent the last few hours up to my elbows in Ruth Murray myself, so yes,' Hendricks said, dumping the bag on the sofa, 'I *did* have a couple on the way over.'

While Hendricks took off his coat, Thorne opened a beer and picked up the CD remote control. He switched Cash's *Solitary Man* back to the beginning. The guitar kicked in on 'I Won't Back Down'.

Thorne took the chair and Hendricks the sofa. It was a familiar and comfortable arrangement that, bar a few awkward weeks the year before, had been repeated at least weekly since Thorne had first moved in nearly eighteen months ago. He'd rattled around in the big house in Highbury for three years after his divorce, before finally taking the plunge and buying the flat. He still hadn't got used to the place. He *did* like the oatmeal IKEA sofa a lot better now it had a few beer stains, but though the place was at last starting to look worn, it had become no more welcoming.

The person responsible for most of the stains grunted, at home now and ready to talk about death.

'So . . . ?' Thorne was trying not to sound impatient.

'So . . . interesting.'

The phone rang. Thorne sighed, pulled himself out of

the chair and marched across to where the cordless phone stood, near the front door.

'Thorne . . .'

'Sir, it's Holland . . .'

'Nothing so far then?' He could hear the confusion in the silence from the other end. 'Don't worry, Holland, I can always tell if you're excited. Your voice goes up an octave.'

'Sir . . .'

'So, nothing at all? Maybe we need to widen things geographically as well . . .'

'There were a couple that looked likely, but there were arrests on both of them and the only other ones, two assaults . . . and two women stabbed on the same day in July, didn't pan out timing-wise.'

'Sure?'

'Positive. McEvoy double-checked. Couldn't have been the same killer who did both. Even if . . . you know, the times of death were a bit off . . . he'd have needed a helicopter to have done both of them.'

'OK, knock it on the head . . . like you weren't about to anyway. Tomorrow you might have more luck. I'm sure this wasn't his first time. You'll get something. Besides, you won't have any distractions.'

'Sorry?'

'I'm taking DS McEvoy with me to Birmingham.'

It took Holland a few seconds to work out why Thorne might be going to Birmingham, and why he would want Sarah McEvoy to go with him. Once he had, he was grateful that he would be the one stuck in front of a computer all day.

Then, after he'd hung up, Holland started to wonder what Thorne had meant by 'distractions'.

'Tell me about *interesting*.' Hendricks looked up at him
and raised an eyebrow. Thorne went on. 'Ruth Murray.
"Interesting", you said.'

Ruth Murray. 32. Married with, thankfully, no children.
Hers actually the first body to be found, wedged in behind
a large metal rubbish bin in a road behind King's Cross
station.

Hendricks had helped himself to the meagre contents of
Thorne's fridge while he'd been on the phone to Holland,
and his reply was broken up as he attempted to swallow an
enormous bite of a cheese sandwich. 'I'm writing it up . . .
first thing tomorrow . . .'

'I won't be here first thing tomorrow.'

'I'll have it on your desk by midday, all right . . . ?'

'Just give me the highlights, Phil.'

Hendricks wiped his mouth, swung his legs off the sofa
and turned to face Thorne. There were important things
to be said. 'OK, well first off, don't get too excited about
the skin under her fingernails.'

'Because . . . ?'

'Because most of it's probably hers.' He explained
before Thorne had a chance to ask him to. 'It's quite
common with strangulations. The victim often scratches
their own neck in an attempt to remove the ligature . . . or
in this case the killer's hands.' As Hendricks explained, his
hands automatically went to his neck and Thorne watched
them scrabbling at the flesh. 'She had good nails . . . made
a right mess of her neck. She might have scratched him as
well though, so it's worth looking at.'

'Carol Garner didn't have good nails?'

Hendricks shook his head. 'Badly bitten . . .' Thorne
wondered if she'd begun biting her nails after her husband

had been killed. Looking at her baby son and seeing his father. Never dreaming that the boy would be an orphan before his fourth birthday.

'But . . .'

'What?' Thorne leant forward, on the edge of his chair. Hendricks had been saving something up. Always the need to show off just a little.

'We might . . . *might*, have another DNA source. Duggan missed something.'

'But you said . . .'

'She was good. Yeah, she is. Just not as good as me.'

Thorne could not keep the irritation out of his voice. 'For fuck's sake, Phil, can we cut the Quincy crap?'

'All right . . . look, once it had been established that there hadn't been a sexual assault, Duggan didn't see any point in looking for bodily fluids. It was a fair enough presumption really, the body was fully clothed, same as Carol Garner. But I'd checked when I did the PM on *her*, so I looked anyway . . .'

Thorne held his breath. He could feel the excitement building in the same place it always did: at the base of his skull. A tingling, a buzzing, a low throb of excitement and revulsion in advance of the detail to come. He hated it when it was sexual. There was always a slightly higher chance of a result, but still, he hated it.

Hendricks was equally excited. 'It was Luminol and UV that did it in the end. Tiny patches all over her face and on her arms. It took me ages to work out what it was; it was actually more about working out what it wasn't . . .'

Thorne nodded. It was good news; if they caught him it almost certainly guaranteed a conviction, but it sickened him just the same. It was no consolation that the killer would probably have done it after Ruth Murray had been killed. If anything, it made it worse.

'Forty-eight hours then?'

Hendricks held up a hand. 'Yeah, hopefully. There's really only a minuscule amount of the stuff and to be honest, I'm not even sure we can get anything. There may be *some* cellular material, but I've certainly never heard of it being done . . .'

Thorne stood up. 'Hang on, Phil, I'm lost here . . . are we not talking about sperm?'

Hendricks shook his head. 'Tears, mate. Dried tears.'

Thorne's mouth actually fell open a little. Hendricks casually reached down for another can of beer. 'Fucker wasn't wanking while he was killing her, Tom, he was weeping.'

1983

Nicklin walked back towards the railway line, his right hand hanging awkwardly, cradling his clammy treasure. In his other hand was the last of a melting chocolate bar. He pushed what was left of it into his mouth, threw the wrapper onto the floor and turned around. He was twenty feet or so away, ready for his run-up, but Palmer had put the bat down.

Nicklin's face reddened. He had a good mind to stroll back and start smacking Palmer over the head with it, but he stayed calm. 'Come on Mart, pick the bat up. This is going to be brilliant.'

The bigger boy shook his head, squinting at Nicklin and raising a hand to shield his eyes from the sun. 'I don't want to.'

'Why not?'

'I just don't want to.' They stared at each other for a while. 'Why can't I bowl? You're much better at batting than me . . .'

'You can bowl next time.'

Palmer looked vaguely sick. 'Are we going to do it again? But how . . . ?'

Nicklin laughed. 'There's loads of them round here. Now stop pissing around, Martin. Pick the bat up.'

Palmer said nothing, thinking about the two more weeks until they went back to school.

The rails began to hum; there was a train coming. They watched as it rumbled past, a knackered old engine pulling a couple of rusty hoppers. Within thirty seconds, the only sound was a distant sizzle and the chirrup of a grasshopper from somewhere close by.

Palmer looked up. He saw the blue and pink splotches of cornflowers and foxgloves against the green of the embankment on the other side of the tracks. He saw mare's tails and periwinkles at Nicklin's feet. He saw Nicklin just staring at him, with the look that made his palms sweat and his head ache and his bladder start to fill.

Still, he didn't want to do this.

It always came down to something like this. Nicklin would find him and they'd spend half an hour or so down by the railway line, chucking stones at bottles or talking about football, until Nicklin smiled that smile and the games would change. Then they'd be dumping turds through letterboxes, or lobbing eggs at buses, or . . . this.

Palmer could hear a rustling in the long grass on the bank behind him. He wanted to turn around and see what it was, but he couldn't stop looking at Nicklin. Suddenly, Nicklin looked really sad. On the verge of tears almost. Palmer shouted to him.

'Look, it doesn't really matter does it? We can do something else . . .'

Nicklin nodded, tightening his fist, squeezing what was held inside. 'I know, course we can. I just thought . . . you were my mate that's all. If you don't want to be mates, just say, and I'll go. Just say . . .'

Palmer felt light-headed. A trickle of sweat was running down his back. He couldn't bear the thought of Nicklin feeling like this. Nicklin was his best mate. He would far rather he was angry with him than feel let down. He felt himself reaching down for the cricket bat, and was elated to look up and see Nicklin beaming at him.

'That's it, Martin. I knew you would. Ready?'

Palmer nodded slowly and Nicklin started running towards him, concentrating, his tongue poking between his teeth.

The frog spread its arms and legs out as soon as Nicklin let it go and for a second it looked as if it was flying. Nicklin began to cheer as soon as he opened his hand.

'Now Mart . . . now.'

Palmer shut his eyes and swung the bat.

It was a wet sound. Dull and sloppy. A small vibration up his arm.

Nicklin watched the whole thing, wide-eyed and yelling. His eyes never moved from the glorious blur of blood and green guts that flew gracefully into the nettles on the other side of the railway line.

He spun round, his black eyes bright in expectation of the sick, shit-a-brick look on Palmer's pale spotty face. The expression that he always saw afterwards. He froze and narrowed his eyes, focusing on something else: something behind Palmer and above him.

Palmer dropped the bat and turned away without looking at the stain on the blade to climb back up the bank. He stopped dead in his tracks. Next to the hole in the chain-link fence, the tall grass past her knees, stood a girl with long blonde hair. She looked the same age as him, perhaps a little older. Palmer had never seen anyone as beautiful in his whole life. The girl put two fingers into her mouth and whistled.

Then she started to clap, grinning her pretty little head off.

THREE

Both Thorne and McEvoy felt distinctly uneasy as they walked across the concourse at Euston station. Neither admitted this to the other and both later wished that they had. Both, as they bought magazines and papers, grabbed last-minute teas or cold drinks, imagined the eyes of a killer on them.

He had watched Carol Garner in this same place, and followed her. Perhaps he'd been standing where they now stood when he first saw her. Reading a newspaper or listening to a walkman, or gazing through the window of a shop at socks and ties. Thorne looked at the faces of the people around him and wondered if Carol Garner had looked into the eyes of the man who would later murder her. Perhaps she'd smiled at him or asked him the time, or given him a cigarette . . .

They walked towards the platform, past their own tattered posters requesting help and information from the public. There were similar posters at King's Cross and these had given them their only real lead thus far – a partial description. A forty-one-year-old prostitute named Margie Knight had come forward and told them about seeing a woman who she thought *might* have been Ruth Murray, talking to a man on York Way, a road running along the side of the station. She'd remembered because for a minute or two she'd thought it was a new girl muscling in on her patch.

It had been dark of course, but there was some light from the shop-fronts on the other side of the road. 'An ordinary kind of face really. He was a big bloke though, I can tell you that. Leaning over her, talking to her about something. He was tall. Not fat, you know, just big . . .' She'd claimed that the look she'd had was not good enough to make it worth her trying to do an e-fit. Helping the police was not something Margie felt particularly comfortable with.

Thorne stared at the poster. Carol Garner's death distilled into a single grainy photograph and a phone number. They'd shown a picture from the Railtrack CCTV footage on the local news and though there *had* been plenty of sightings, nobody had picked up on anyone who might have been following her.

They couldn't be one hundred per cent sure of course, that anyone *had* been following her. The station thing might yet prove to have been pure coincidence. The killer could have picked her up on the underground or on the walk home from Balham tube station.

Somehow though, Thorne was pretty sure that this was where he'd first seen Carol Garner. Chosen her.

He'd sat through that CCTV footage a hundred times, scanning the faces of the people around her, as she and her son walked blithely towards the escalator. Men with brief-cases, striding along and braying into mobile phones. Men with rucksacks, sauntering. Some meeting people or hurrying home, or hanging around for one of a hundred different reasons. Some who looked dangerous, and others who looked all but invisible. If you looked at them long enough you could see anything.

Except what you needed to see.

In the end, his eyes always drifted back to Carol and Charlie, hand in hand and deep in conversation. Charlie was laughing, clutching tightly to his book, the hood of his anorak up.

Thorne always found something horribly poignant about these CCTV pictures; these utilitarian clips of people in public places. The figures seemed real enough, close enough, that you could reach out and help them, prevent what you knew was about to happen. The fact that you couldn't, the fact that this recent past would inevitably become a terrible future, served only to increase the sense of sheer helplessness. The fuzzy, jumpy quality of the film touched him in a way that no album of treasured photos or home-video ever could. The jerky footage of Jamie Bulger being led away through that shopping centre to his death; or ten-year-old Damilola Taylor, skipping along a concrete walkway, minutes away from bleeding to death in a piss-spattered stairwell on a Peckham estate; or even a Princess – and Thorne was no great fan – smiling and pushing open the back door of a Paris hotel.

These pictures clutched at his guts, and squeezed, every single time.

The images of the dead, just before death.

Now, Carol and Charlie Garner strolling across a busy station concourse; relaxed and happy in a way that could only ever be captured on film when the subject was unaware they were being filmed at all.

Unaware that they were being watched. By a camera, or by a killer.

What should have been a ninety-minute train journey took closer to two hours, and nobody seemed hugely surprised. Thorne and McEvoy flicked through papers and chatted, and generally put the world to rights. The small talk was easy and enjoyable. It passed the time, and besides, each of them knew instinctively that they would not feel much like chatting on the return journey.

They were still an hour from Birmingham, and McEvoy was on her way back from the solitary smoking carriage for the fourth or fifth time. She caught sight of Thorne, his head buried in the paper, as she weaved her way down the carriage and it struck her how, from a distance, he looked like somebody you would try and avoid sitting next to. Up close of course, once you'd been around him a while, there was a warmth in the eyes; something that drew you in, in spite of yourself. But at first glance, he was, to say the very least . . . intimidating.

As she sat back down and picked up her magazine, Thorne glanced up and gave her the look of the reformed smoker – jealous as hell, but trying to be disapproving. She wondered what their fellow travellers made of the pair of them. They were both dressed reasonably smartly: she in a blue wool coat and skirt, and Thorne in his ubiquitous black leather jacket. She was carrying a briefcase, but she seriously doubted that anyone would mistake them for business types. Not Thorne anyway. Her minder perhaps. Dodgy-looking elder brother, or even her dad, at a real push . . .

'What's so funny?'

She looked up. Still smiling. *Maybe even her slightly older bit of rough.* 'Nothing. Just an article in this magazine . . .'

★

Robert and Mary Enright, Carol Garner's parents, lived a
few miles south of Birmingham city centre, in Kings
Heath, a ten-minute cab ride from New Street station.
Theirs was a purpose-built, two-bedroom house on a
modern estate, a short walk from shops and buses. The
sort of place that a couple in their early sixties might move
to. A quiet place where people like them could relax and
enjoy retirement, with little to worry about, now that their
children were settled.

Settled perhaps, but never safe.

Mary Enright, whose world had so recently turned
upside down, greeted them warmly and showed them into
a small and unbearably hot living room. She was a short,
contained woman. She produced tea almost instantly.

'Robert won't be long. He's taken Charlie over to the
park. There's a nice playground, you know, a roundabout
and some swings, it's very popular actually. To tell you the
truth, I think Robert gets more out of it than Charlie does
at the moment. He needs to get out of the house, you
know, breathe a bit. Things have been a bit tense to be
honest . . .'

McEvoy sipped her tea and nodded, full of understanding, or the appearance of it. Thorne looked around
the stifling room, happy to let his sergeant keep the conversation going. Both just waiting to see the boy. Both
dreading it.

The few child's books and toys, arranged neatly next to
the sofa, seemed horribly out of place among the orna-
ments, antimacassars and gardening books. The house
smelt of beeswax and liniment. It wasn't a place where a
child was at home yet.

Thorne noticed that there were already a few Christmas cards on the bookshelf in the corner. Greetings from those who didn't know. He wondered whether the Enrights would celebrate anyway, for their grandson's sake. Grief often came down to going through the motions.

And often, so did investigating the cause of it.

Charlie Garner had already been interviewed. As per procedure this had been done by specially trained officers under strictly controlled conditions. The interviews had taken place at a house in Birmingham owned and maintained jointly by local social services and West Midlands police. It was a simple modern house much like any other, except for the fully equipped medical examination suite and state-of-the-art recording facilities.

Charlie had been given toys to play with, and officers from the Child Protection Team had chatted to him while the entire process was monitored from an adjoining room. Thorne had watched recordings of all the interviews. Charlie had been a little shy at first, but once his trust had been won he'd become lively and talkative, about everything save what had happened to his mother . . .

Thorne wasn't sure he could get anything out of the boy. He didn't know if there was anything to get. He was certain that he had to try.

He was just summoning up the courage to ask if they might turn the radiator down a notch or two, when he heard the key in the front door. He and McEvoy stood up in unison and so quickly that Mary Enright looked quite alarmed for a moment.

Robert Enright shook hands and said, 'pleased to meet you', but his watery blue eyes told a different story. In stark contrast to his wife, he was very tall and had clearly once been fit, but where she was spry and alert, he seemed merely to drift, hollowed out and vague.

Death hit people differently. She was getting by. He had all but given up.

He slumped on to the sofa while his wife scuttled off to make more tea. 'Charlie's gone up to his room I think. He'll be down in a minute.' His voice was deep and gentle, the heavy Brummie accent lending a weariness to it that it almost certainly didn't need.

Thorne nodded. He had heard the *thump thump* of the boy's feet charging upstairs as soon as the front door had shut.

'Good time in the park?'

The old man shrugged. Stupid question. *Fuck off out of my house, away from me and my family.* 'It's starting to get cold . . .'

Mary bustled in, handed her husband his tea and attempted to kill the time until Charlie arrived with aimless chatter. She talked to Thorne and McEvoy about their journey up and how difficult their work must be, and how her friend had a son who was a sergeant in Leicester, and how she knew all about the pressures of the job.

Thorne thought: *it doesn't get any more difficult than this.*

The old man leaned forward suddenly and fixed Thorne with a hard look. 'What are you going to ask him?' Serious, unblinking . . .

Thorne turned to McEvoy, sensing that this would be better coming from her. This, indeed, was why he'd wanted her along. She picked up her cue. 'We don't nec- essarily need to ask him anything. We just want to get an idea of what he remembers really. Has he talked about what happened at all?'

'No.' Quickly.

'Nothing at all? I mean he might have said something that just sounded like a joke, you know, or a—'

'I said no.' Louder now, unashamedly aggressive.

McEvoy's eyes flicked to Mary, asking for help if she knew how to give it. She picked up her husband's hand and placed it on her knee. She took her hand away and held it up for Thorne and McEvoy's inspection. 'Bob worked in the Jewellery Quarter for forty years. He made this wedding ring in 1965. Made Carol's as well, four years ago. Sort of came out of retirement for it, didn't you?' She laughed and patted her husband's hand but he said nothing. 'See, we didn't have Carol until late.'

Thorne looked at McEvoy. He knew what she was thinking and he knew that she was wrong. These were not ramblings. These were fragments of a shattered picture that Mary Enright was holding up to the light in desperation, in the hope that Thorne and McEvoy might understand the whole. Might grasp the enormity of it. Now, she just shook her head and said it simply. 'Bob's taken everything very badly you see. Worse than me, really, or differently at any rate. It's often the way, I think, when something happens and there's two of you. One just muddles along, you know, gets on with things, while the other . . .'

Thorne could see them then. The old woman sitting in the corner of an overheated lounge, making jigsaws with her grandson or writing shopping lists, while her husband stands stooped in a back bedroom, shouting, his body racked with sobs.

He stared at Robert Enright until the old man met his eye, then he spoke. 'I want to find the man who did this thing to you. To your daughter and to you. Charlie saw him. We're here to let him tell us anything he feels like telling us. That's all.'

They all stiffened then, at the footfalls on the stairs. Thorne thought he saw Carol Garner's father nod, a second before the door flew open and her son ran into the room.

The boy froze on seeing the strangers, and lowered his eyes. He began to inch across to the sofa from where Mary reached out a hand and pulled him to her. He was perhaps a little small for his age, with longish mousy hair and brown eyes. He was wearing denim dungarees over a red long-sleeved top and his hands were covered in what looked like blue felt-tip pen.

'Some friends of ours have come to see you,' Mary said, her voice not much above a whisper. 'This is . . . ?' She looked across at McEvoy and Thorne, the question in her eyes.

'Sarah,' McEvoy volunteered, leaning forward with a smile. She glanced at Thorne. 'And Tom.'

Charlie looked up, appraising them. He rubbed his grandmother's hand across his cheek for a second or two, before dropping it and racing across to where his toys lay on the floor. He picked up a yellow plastic toolbox and emptied the contents on to the carpet.

McEvoy was flying by the seat of her pants. This was not the same as counselling a rape victim or trying to calm a battered wife. She'd noticed the hushed, almost reverential tone that Mary Enright had used when speaking to the boy and felt instinctively that this was wrong. At least, it was wrong if they wanted to get any information out of him. She knew that she had to gain his trust.

'Are you looking forward to Christmas, Charlie?' The boy picked up a thick, red plastic bolt and began pushing it through a hole in a tiny workbench. 'I'm sure Father Christmas will bring you lots of nice things if you're a good boy.' He pushed the bolt further in, his face a picture of concentration. McEvoy moved from her chair and knelt down, a few feet away. 'It looks like you're a good boy to me.' She picked up the plastic screwdriver and examined it, as Charlie furtively examined her. She tried hard to keep any hint of seriousness out of her voice. 'What would be *very* good is if you could tell me and Tom a little bit about when your mummy got hurt . . .' She glanced up at the Enrights. Mary's eyes were already filling with tears. Her husband sat motionless, his eyes on the floor.

Charlie Garner said nothing.

'What you could do, if you wanted, is tell your Nan about it. Do you want to do that?'

He didn't . . .

McEvoy felt herself sweating and it was only partially due to the temperature. She was beginning to feel out of her depth. She started to say something but stopped. She could only watch helplessly as the boy stood up suddenly, marched past her and plonked himself down at Thorne's feet.

Thorne gazed down at Charlie and shrugged. 'Hello . . .' Charlie produced a small squeaky hammer and began vigorously banging on Thorne's shoe. It might have been nerves or it might have been because the moment was, in spite of everything, genuinely comical, but Thorne began to laugh. Then Charlie laughed too.

'I hammer your shoe . . .'

'Ow . . . ow . . . ouch!' Thorne winced in mock agony, and

as the boy began to laugh even louder, he sensed that the moment might be right. 'Do you remember the man who was there when your mummy got hurt?'

The laughter didn't exactly stop dead, but the answer to Thorne's question was obvious. Charlie was still hammering on the shoe but it was purely reflexive. The intermittent squeak of the toy hammer was now the only sound in the room. Mary and Robert Enright sat stock still on the sofa, and Sarah McEvoy was all but holding her breath, afraid that the slightest movement could spoil everything.

Thorne spoke slowly and seriously. He was not following a different tack to McEvoy for any particular reason. There was no strategy involved. Instinct just told him to ask the child the question, simply and honestly. 'Can you tell me what the man who hurt your mummy looked like?'

A squeak, as the hammer hit the shoe. And another. Then the tiny shoulders gave a recognisable shrug. Thorne had seen the same gesture in a hundred stroppy teenagers. Scared, but fronting it out.

Maybe I know something, but you get nothing easily.

'Was he older than me do you think?' Charlie glanced up, but only for a second before returning to his hammering. 'Was his hair the same colour as yours or was it darker? What do you think?' There was no discernible reaction. Thorne knew that he was losing the boy.

Hearing a sniff, Thorne looked up and could see that the old man on the sofa was quietly weeping, his big shoulders rising and falling as he pressed a handkerchief to his face. Thorne looked at the boy and winked conspiratorially, 'Was he taller than your Grandad? I bet you can remember that.'

Charlie stopped hammering. Without looking up he shook his head slowly and emphatically. Thorne flicked his eyes to McEvoy. She raised her eyebrows back at him. They were thinking the same thing. If that 'no' was as definite as it looked, it certainly didn't tally with Margie Knight's description. Thorne wondered who was the more credible witness. The nosy working girl or the three-year-old?

Eye witnesses had screwed him up before. So, probably neither . . .

Whatever, as far as Charlie was concerned, it looked as though the shake of the head was all they were going to get. The hammering was growing increasingly enthusiastic.

'You're good at hammering, Charlie,' Thorne said.

Mary Enright spoke up from the sofa, she too sensing that the questions were over. 'It's *Bob The Builder*. He's mad on it. It's what he calls you sometimes, isn't it, Bob?' She turned to her husband, smiling. Robert Enright said nothing.

McEvoy stood up, rubbing away the stiffness in the back of her legs from where she'd been kneeling. 'Yeah, my nephew's always going on about it. He's driving his mum and dad bonkers, singing the theme tune.'

Mary stood up and began tidying things away, while Charlie carried on, the hammer now replaced by a bright orange screwdriver. 'I don't mind that,' Mary said. 'It's just on so early. Half past six in the morning, on one of those cable channels.'

McEvoy breathed in sharply and nodded sympathetically. Thorne looked down and brushed his fingers against the boy's shoulder. 'Hey, think about your poor old nan will you Charlie? Half past six? You should still be fast asleep . . .'

And Charlie Garner looked up at him then, his eyes wide and keen, the bright orange screwdriver clutched tightly in his small fist.

'My mummy's asleep.'

In spite of all the horrors to come, the bodies both fresh and long dead, *this* would be the image, simple and stark, that would be there long after this case was finished, whenever Thorne closed his eyes.

The face of a child.

It's been over a week now, Karen, and it's still on the television. I've stopped watching now, in case something comes on and catches me unawares when I'm unprepared for it. I knew that it would be on the news, you know, when they found her, but I thought it would die down . . . I thought it would stop, after a day or two. There always seems to be people dying in one way or another, so I didn't think that it would be news for very long.

They've got some sort of witness they said. Whoever it was must have seen me because they know how tall I am. I know I should be worried, Karen, but I'm not. Part of me wishes they'd seen me up close. Seen my face.

A police officer on the television said it was brutal. 'This brutal killing.' He said I was brutal and I really tried so hard not to be. You believe that don't you, Karen? I didn't hit her or anything. I tried to make it quick and painless. I don't really expect them to say anything else though. Why should they? They don't know me . . .

The other one, the one in south London, I can barely bring myself to think about that. It was horrible. Yes, that was brutal.

The scratches are fading, but a couple of people at work noticed and it gave them something else to use against me. Not as if they needed any more ammunition. It was all nudges and giggles and, 'I bet she was a right goer' or, 'did she make a lot of noise?' You know, variations on that theme. I just smiled and blushed, same as I always do.

Oh my God, Karen, if they only knew.

Sometimes I think that perhaps I should just tell them everything. That way it would all be over, because someone would go to the police and I could just sit and wait for them to come and get me. Plus, it might at least make some of them think about me a bit differently. Find someone else to belittle. It would wipe a few smiles off a few faces wouldn't it? It would make them stop. Yes, I'd like them to step back and start to sweat a little.

I'd like them to be scared of me.

But I'm the one that's scared, Karen, you know that. It's the way it's always been hasn't it? That's why I can't ever tell them. Why I can't ever share this with anyone except you.

Why I'm praying, praying, praying that Ruth will be the last one.

1984

They caught Bardsley just outside the school gates. He had a few mates with him but they took one look at Nicklin, at his face, and melted away into the background. Some of them were fifth-formers at least a year older than he was, and it excited him to watch them scuttle away like the spineless wankers he knew they were.

The two of them were on Bardsley in a second. Palmer stood in front of him, solid, red-faced and shaking. Nicklin grabbed the strap of his sports bag and together they dragged him towards the bushes.

The park ran right alongside the main entrance to the school. A lot of the boys cut across it on the way to school and back, and the sixth-formers would hang around with their opposite numbers from the neighbouring girls' school. It wasn't a nice park; a tatty bowling green, an attempt at an aviary and a floating population of surly kids – smoking, groping or eating chips.

Palmer and Nicklin pushed Bardsley towards the bushes that bordered the bird cages. He grabbed on to the wire of the nearest cage. It housed a moulting mynah bird which, in spite of the best efforts of every kid in school, resolutely refused to swear, producing nothing but an ear-splitting wolf-whistle every few minutes. Bardsley began to kick out wildly. Palmer clung on to the collar of his blazer, which was already starting to tear, and shuffled his legs back, out of the range of the boy's flailing Doc Martens. Nicklin stepped in closer and, oblivious to the pain in his shin as he was repeatedly booted, punched Bardsley hard in the face. Bardsley's hands moved from the wire to his face as blood began to gush from his nose. Smiling, Nicklin pushed him on to his knees, rammed a knee into his neck and pressed him down into the dirt.

After a nod from Nicklin, Palmer dropped on to Bardsley's chest and sat there for a few moments, breathing heavily, his face the colour of a Bramley apple.

Bardsley took his hand away from his face and glared up at the younger boy. There was blood on his teeth. 'You're fucking dead, Palmer.'

Palmer's face grew even redder as his big hands reached forward to grab greasy handfuls of Bardsley's dirty blond hair. 'What did you say about Karen?'

'Who the fuck's Karen?'

Nicklin was standing behind Bardsley's head, his back against a tree, his hands in his pockets, his foot pressed against the scalp of the boy on the ground. He pushed his tongue in behind his bottom teeth, opened his mouth and slowly let a thick, globular string of spit drop down on to the bloody face below. Bardsley flinched and squeezed his eyes tight shut. When he opened them again he was staring up at the pistol in Nicklin's hand.

Palmer and Bardsley moaned at almost the same time. Bardsley in terror at the sight of the pistol, and Palmer in disgust as the groin of the boy beneath him quickly began to grow damp.

'Shit . . . he's pissed himself!' Palmer jumped up and pointed down at the dark, spreading stain on Bardsley's grey trousers.

Nicklin giggled. 'Well turn him over then.' Palmer shook his head. Nicklin stopped giggling as the mynah bird let out a shrill whistle from the cage behind him. 'Fucking turn him over . . .'

Palmer stepped forward nervously. Bardsley glowered at him as he tried with some difficulty to scramble to his feet, one hand wiping away blood and spit and dirt, the other covering his groin. His voice was thick with rage and the effort of holding back tears, 'Dead . . . fucking dead . . .' But the fight had gone out of him and Palmer was easily able to yank him over on to his belly.

Nicklin moved round and knelt down next to Palmer at Bardsley's feet. 'Pull his pants down.'

Bardsley began trying to drag himself away until Nicklin leaned forward and pressed the pistol into his neck. Bardsley froze and dropped back into the dirt.

'Right, grab that side . . .' Nicklin took hold of Bardsley's waistband and began to pull. He looked at Palmer, who, after a second or two, did the same, and moments later, Bardsley's trousers and pants were around his ankles.

'He's got fucking blue pants on . . .'

'Stu, that's enough, isn't it?'

'Pissed his pants like a girl. I can smell shit as well . . .'

'Stuart . . .'

Nicklin handed Palmer the pistol. 'Stick this up his arse.'

At these words Bardsley was predictably energised, and his buttocks pumped rapidly up and down in his frantic attempts to get away. Palmer took a step back, staring at the ground, but Nicklin leaned in close to Bardsley, laughing. 'Go on Bardsley, you bummer, shag it. Shag the ground you fucking perv . . . only thing you'll ever get to shag, you spastic . . .'

Palmer turned the pistol over and over in his hand. Nicklin looked up at him, smiling, making certain that

Palmer was reassured by the smile before letting it slowly dissolve. Looking serious. Concerned. Shaking his head.

'He said he was going to do stuff to Karen, Martin.'

Bardsley tried for the last time to tell them that he didn't have a fucking clue who Karen was, but the words were lost as he dissolved into sobs.

Nicklin lowered his voice and spoke slowly. Things he didn't want to tell his friend; things he had to tell him. 'Dirty stuff, Mart. He called her names.' Palmer wrapped his fat fist around the butt of the pistol and dropped down slowly, his knees heavy on the back of Bardsley's calves. 'Said you'd done things to her . . . touched her tits.' Palmer pushed the barrel into the soft, pale flesh of Bardsley's buttocks and held it there. Bardsley whimpered.

Nicklin whispered. 'Go on Martin . . .'

Palmer looked down at Bardsley's soft, spotty backside, afraid to so much as glance at the boy next to him. Afraid of his friend's excitement. He could see the twin rolls of sweaty, girlish fat on his chest shudder as his heart thumped beneath them. He could taste the perspiration that was running into his mouth. He knew that he should throw the pistol away and get to his feet and run through the park, without looking back, down past the bowling green and up and across the playground, not stopping until he was home . . .

Nicklin put a hand on his shoulder and squeezed, and as the mynah bird screeched raucously behind him, Palmer pulled the trigger.

Bardsley screamed as the jet of compressed air fired the tiny lead pellet deep into his flesh.

FOUR

The train journey back to London had been half an hour quicker than the outward leg, but had seemed infinitely longer. For the first twenty minutes or so, Thorne and McEvoy had tried to make conversation, then given up. He picked up the newspaper he'd already read and she made for the smoking carriage.

Thorne had closed his eyes and tried, without any success at all, to go to sleep.

McEvoy hadn't bothered coming back.

It was after six by the time Thorne finally got back to Hendon. Becke House was in the Peel Centre, a vast compound that also housed the Metropolitan Police Training College. Hundreds of fresh-faced recruits buzzing about, learning how to put handcuffs on, learning procedure. Learning nothing.

A BBC film crew had been around for the past few months making a documentary on the new intake. Thorne had spoken to the director one day in the canteen, suggested that he might like to catch up with his subjects again in a year or two; see how those ruddy-cheeked recruits had matured into the job. The director had been hugely, stupidly enthusiastic. Thorne had walked away thinking: that'll be one show they'll need to put out after the watershed . . .

Thorne headed for the office. He decided he wanted to put in another couple of hours. It would be a good idea to save the drive back to Kentish Town until the rush hour had died down a little. That was the excuse he gave himself anyway.

Holland was the only member of the team there, still hunched over a computer screen. In spite of the day he'd had, Thorne didn't envy him. He'd been forced to attend *two* courses and was still a computer illiterate. The only things he could access with any speed were the Tottenham Hotspur FC supporters' newsgroup and the technical support line.

'Where's the DCI?'

Holland looked up from his computer, rubbing his eyes. 'Meeting with the Detective Super.'

'Jesus Christ.' Thorne shook his head. 'We've only just started.'

'Where's McEvoy?'

'Probably soaking in a long hot bath by now . . .' Holland nodded. Thorne noticed how tired he was looking. 'Go home, Dave. Start again in the morning.'

'Yeah, I'd better, before I get RSI. My mouse finger's fucked.' He stopped laughing when he pictured Sophie's expression as he walked through the door. 'I'll just finish what I'm doing . . .'

One week into it, and neither of them wanting to go home. Both afraid of looks on faces.

Thorne pushed open the door to the office he shared with Brigstocke, and waited for a second or two before turning on the light. The room looked a damn sight better in the dark. Who the hell could be expected to work efficiently in an airless grey box like this, or the even smaller one next door that Holland and McEvoy worked out of? Worn grey carpet, dirty yellow walls and a pair of battle-scarred brown desks, like two rectangles of driftwood floating down a shitty river. No amount of potted plants or family photos, or knick-knacks on monitors could stop this room sucking the energy out of him, blunting him.

There were moments in this office, when Thorne almost forgot what he did for a living.

He flicked on the light and saw a post-mortem report sitting on his desk.

When he *almost* forgot . . .

Sarah McEvoy consoled herself with a glass of wine, another cigarette and the thought that crying was easy.

She couldn't think of the boy in Birmingham as anything other than a potential witness and she knew that perhaps she should. She knew that there were feelings missing. Not maternal ones necessarily, or even feminine. Just human. She felt angry at what had happened to the boy's mother all right. Anger was always instant and powerful. It made her feel light-headed. Anger was enjoyable, but sympathy never came as easily.

It wasn't fair. She felt that her behaviour was being judged. Maybe right now, Thorne was telling somebody else, Holland probably, how . . . hard she was. There was no middle ground as a woman. She was used to it, but it still pissed her off. Frigid, or a slag. Girly, or one of the boys. Hard, or emotionally unstable. Actually, hard-*faced* was a favourite with female colleagues. Usually followed by *bitch* or *cow*.

She was sure that Tom Thorne wouldn't be crying about anything.

As it was, there had been quite a few times lately when she'd woken up and been pretty sure that she *had* been crying. She could never be positive of course, however puffy she looked, or fucked up she felt. She certainly wasn't going to ask whoever she might have woken up next to for the details. Conversation of any sort, by that point, would be kept to a bare minimum in an effort to get rid of them as fast as possible.

She knew what those at work who guessed at her domestic arrangements would make of them. For this reason she did her best to ensure that it stayed as guess-work only. She wasn't frigid, so there was only one other option wasn't there? It was a small jump for a small brain from 'sexually active' to 'sexually active with superior offi-cers'. There were still those who suspected that any woman rising through the ranks did so on her back.

Right. Lying on her back and staring at that glass ceil-ing . . .

It was nobody's business and it was her choice. A regular boyfriend was nice in theory and a bonus at parties, but in her experience it rarely meant regular sex, and she needed that. She needed to feel wanted, and if that occasionally meant *used* then that was fine, because it cut both ways.

All the time she was checking to see what was on TV and thinking about what she might eat, she knew perfectly well that she'd end up going out. She'd been thinking about it all the way back on the train. Staring at her own reflection in the blackness of the carriage window, smoking cigarettes down to the filter and wishing the hours away. She might even walk there. It was only fifteen minutes away. Following the path of the railway line all the way from Wembley Park to Harlesden.

She'd need to get changed first though. The people she was going to see, like those on the train earlier, almost certainly had no idea what she did for a living, but she didn't want to take any chances.

In the single pool of light from a desktop lamp, Thorne sat, trying to keep his mind on death, but distracted constantly by an image that was full of life. Much as he tried to concentrate on Ruth Murray's post-mortem report, he couldn't stop the animated features of Charlie Garner from intruding: staring up at him from beneath the gurney, or peeking around the mortuary door.

He had finally worked out what it was that had disturbed him so much when Charlie had looked up at him in that sitting room only a few hours before. He'd seen it instantly, but it took a while before he *understood* exactly what it was he'd been looking at when he stared into that child's eyes. There, in that face, in those shining brown saucers beneath long lashes, Thorne had seen doubt.

My mummy's asleep . . .

The smile had been broad and beautiful, but in those eyes had been the tiniest flicker of something like uncertainty. The smile hopeful, but the eyes betraying a knowledge Charlie Garner didn't even know he had. Who could blame him? Now, that child could never be really certain about anything ever again. It was too harsh a lesson and learned too early.

And each time Thorne saw that face, the flicker of doubt grew stronger . . .

When the phone on the desk rang, Thorne started a little, and on glancing at the page in front of him, realised he'd been staring at the phrase *blood-spotted conjunctivae* for the past half an hour.

'DI Thorne . . .'

'It's Phil. Have you read it?'

'It's right in front of me. I've . . . had loads of stuff to wade through.'

'How was Birmingham?'

Thorne exhaled and leaned back in his chair. He should have gone home much earlier. Even with a smooth run back to Kentish Town, it would be ten o'clock by the time he got in. Another couple of hours to wind down meant getting to sleep late and waking up pissed off. Hendricks, by contrast, sounded relaxed. Thorne could picture him, legs up on a piece of sixties' black-leather furniture, some skinhead in the kitchen making them both dinner.

'That bad?' Hendricks asked.

'Sorry?'

'Birmingham. Doesn't matter, tell me tomorrow. Listen, bit of good news. Catch the bastard, we'll put him away. There *was* plenty of Ruth Murray's own tissue under her fingernails, but loads of his as well. Profile should come through some time tomorrow.'

It was *very* good news. Now he would at least drive home in a good mood. 'No need to test those teardrops you were so excited about then?'

Hendricks snorted. 'Nah, tell you the truth it were a fuck of a long shot. We might have had a chance if he'd worn contact lenses.'

Thorne was intrigued. 'This sounds good . . .'

'Obvious really. A foreign body in the eye would cause

a certain amount of irritation so the tear fluid would probably have contained more cellular material. See? Even
better if he'd cried out of his nose actually . . .'

'I don't want to know . . .'

'It's all academic now anyway.'

'No chance of a Nobel prize just yet then?'

'One day, mate.'

Thorne folded up the post-mortem report and started
putting papers into his briefcase. 'Never mind, it told us
something about him anyway . . .' There was no response.
Thorne heard someone talking to Hendricks. He heard his
friend's muffled voice answering, then heard the hand
being taken off the mouthpiece.

'Sorry Tom, dinner's nearly ready.' Hendricks's voice
dropped to a whisper. 'Got myself a cracker here, mate.
Nice arse, *and* handy in the kitchen. Sorry, what were you
on about?'

'The tears. I'm not sure exactly *what* they tell us about
him, mind you.'

'Well, we know he was in a better mood than when he
killed Carol Garner.'

Thorne stood up and closed his case. He might make it
home by quarter to, with a following wind. 'Right . . .'

'No, I mean it. Go through the report, it's obvious. He
must have calmed down or something. Maybe whatever
the fucker was *on* had worn off. It's a very different attack.
The hyroid is intact, there's only minimal damage to the
cartilage . . .'

Then Thorne could feel the tingle. The small current
running up the nape of his neck. Making him catch his
breath. Almost sexy . . .

Something that had been nagging at him was coming

into focus, revealing itself. He sat down again, opened the case and pulled out the post-mortem report. 'Take me through this slowly can you, Phil?'

Opening the report now, tearing pages as he turns them too quickly, speed-reading, his breath getting shorter by the second as Hendricks turns their murder case into something altogether more disturbing.

'OK . . . externally, both bodies were much the same, Murray and Garner, but internally it's a different story. Ruth Murray died from a slower, more sustained pressure on the artery. Call it a slow, hard squeezing. Carol Garner was nothing like that. She had bruises on the back of her skull where he smacked her head on the floor as he was throttling her. That was . . . frenzied. With Ruth Murray it was different. Maybe he'd got the anger out of his system. Maybe that's his pattern. You tell me mate . . .'

Then, Thorne knew. No, not *his* pattern . . .

The tears. A big man's tears on a body, outdoors. A body less damaged, wept upon. Elsewhere, a child in a house, nuzzling what was once the sweet-smelling neck of his mother, now bruised, and bloody, and broken inside. The wrapper from a chocolate bar, discarded . . .

Was he taller than your Grandad?

And Charlie Garner slowly, defiantly, shaking his head.

'Phil, can I call you back . . . ?'

Tired as he was, Holland had *still* not left. Thorne's expression, as he burst into the office next door, was enough to wake him up in a second.

'The stabbings . . . tell me about the stabbings.' Thorne's voice low, measured, but with a scream of something – excitement maybe, or horror – lurking just beneath the surface.

'Sir . . . ?'

Moving across the cramped office, talking quickly. 'Two women, both stabbed on the same day. July, I think you said.' Thorne nodded towards the computer, trying to stay calm. 'Call them up.'

Holland spun the chair round and began to type, trying to recall the details. 'One in Finchley, I think. The other one . . . much further south if I remember . . .' The relevant documents appeared on his screen and Holland studied them for a second or two. 'Forest Hill, that's right . . .' He scrolled slowly through the document, shaking his head. 'No . . . no . . . it's not possible. He couldn't have done them both.'

Thorne nodded and glanced out of the window. His eye was taken by the sparks flying up from beneath a tube train passing below on its way south from Colindale; lolling heads in the brightly lit carriages, snaking away from him as the track curved round and out of sight.

'He didn't.'

Holland stared at him, waiting. Thorne stood stock still and spoke slowly, but Holland could see his fists clenching and unclenching at his sides. 'The knives used might have been similar, might not, I don't know . . . not sure it matters. The pattern and depth of the wounds though . . . in all probability the *number* of wounds, on each of the victims, will be at odds with each other. The . . . character of the two attacks will be completely different.'

Holland turned back to his screen and typed again, calling up SOC and pathology reports as Thorne continued. 'One of the women will have died from multiple stab wounds. Vicious . . . indiscriminate . . . savage. The other, probably one single wound, to the heart, I would guess, or . . .'

Holland spun round again. The look on his face told Thorne all he needed to know . . .

Brigstocke answered his mobile on the first ring.

'Russell Brigstocke . . .' The voice low, betraying annoyance.

'It's Tom . . .'

'DI Thorne . . .' Spoken for somebody else's benefit.

The meeting with Detective Superintendent Jesmond had probably turned into dinner. So much the easier.

'We're onto something. Tell Jesmond. Call it a breakthrough, he'll like that.' He turned to share the moment with Holland but the DC was studying the documents on his screen intently. Trying to make sense of it all. 'Tell him it's one hell of a good news-bad news routine . . .'

'I'm listening,' Brigstocke said.

'I don't think we're looking for one man.'

Thorne expected a pause, and he got one. Then: 'Are you saying that these murders might not actually be connected?'

'No I'm not. They *are* connected, I'm certain of that.' Thorne knew the look that Brigstocke would be wearing. Contained excitement, like trying to hold a shit inside. He wondered what Jesmond, no doubt holding a large glass of red wine and studying his DCI's strange expression, would be making of it.

Brigstocke was starting to sound a little impatient. 'So, what is it? A new lead on the killer?'

Thorne kept it nice and simple. 'Kill*ers*, Russell. Plural. There's two of them.'

1985

It was a moment he would always remember. Karen sitting on the bank, pushing a strand of blonde hair behind her ear, and Stuart smiling, mouth full of chocolate as always, his dark eyes focusing on something in the distance, searching for it, seeking out the source of their next adventure.

And him, looking from one to the other, nervous but happy, the sun in his eyes and a small cloud of gnats swirling in front of his face . . .

It was a moment that took him back to a day two summers earlier. That day with the cricket bat. The day when he saw Karen for the first time. That was when he and Stuart were at the same school of course. Before the business with the air pistol . . .

The two of them weren't really supposed to see each other after the Bardsley incident. Following the expulsion, efforts had been made to keep them apart, and for a while Palmer had been happy enough to go along with that. After all, the police had told their parents that it would be better for everybody if they were not allowed to be together. There had been talk of 'influence' and of 'geeing up'. He missed the excitement though, he missed the unpredictability, and he was delighted when Stuart, once they'd started hanging around together again, told him that he'd missed it too. Plus, he always felt better about being around Karen, if Stuart was close by.

Karen was older than he was, closer to Stuart's age, but

Stuart couldn't make her laugh the way he could. He'd always been the one that got her giggling, ever since that day when she'd crawled through the hole in the fence and seen the business with the frog. There were times, when he saw the two of them whispering, or smoking, or watched them walking ahead of him along by the railway line, that he would start to feel like he shouldn't be there. Then Karen would stop and smile that smile at him and ask him to pull some stupid face, or put on a silly voice or something and he would soon have her in fits. Sometimes he thought that perhaps she was teasing him a little, but he didn't really mind. He could see how important he was to her, and to Stuart. He could see the three of them together, friends for good, the long grass of the railway embankment becoming the carefully tended lawn of a college quadrangle and the back garden of one of the big houses that each of them owned . . . and finally, the rambling parkland of that Heath in London his mum had taken him to once, where the three of them would sit together on a park bench, with dogs, and perhaps children.

Palmer knew, as much as he knew anything at barely fourteen, that he was in love.

Karen stood up and looked around for a few seconds before half-running, half-tumbling down the bank. She pretended that she was going to crash into Nicklin, and he pretended to be frightened. At the last minute, she jumped and Nicklin staggered back as he caught her, shouting and laughing, one hand holding tight to her arse.

Palmer laughed too and, swatting the swarm of gnats aside, followed them as they each lit a cigarette and began walking slowly towards the small group of blackened, broken-down railway buildings in the distance.

Once inside the main building – a disused equipment shed – they did the usual quick sweep, searching for signs of habitation. Tramps slept here sometimes. The place still smelt of stale piss and strong lager. They'd found the remains of a fire a few times before now, and empty tins and syringes, and once, a used condom which Nicklin had picked up and chased Karen around with for a while. Today the place seemed even more deserted than usual. The usual fixtures and fittings. A mountain of fag ends, some old newspapers, a soggy, mouldering roll of carpet that had once been a dosser's bed.

Huge bluebottles flew around their heads as Palmer threw stones at the remaining slivers of glass in the rotting window frames. Nicklin stubbed out his fag and looked around for something, anything, to spark him off, and Karen wandered around singing the latest Duran Duran single, her light, high voice echoing off the grimy Artex walls.

'Let's go. Fuck-all in here.' Nicklin aimed a kick at an empty bottle. It skittered across the concrete floor and into the far wall where it smashed.

Palmer cheered. 'We could start a fire or something . . .'

'Let's all have a dump,' Karen said, ignoring him and leering at Nicklin. She began to laugh and Palmer turned away, blushing. He hated it when she talked like that. She would squat down in the long grass sometimes and he couldn't bear it.

'Boring,' Nicklin said. 'Fucking eggs for lunch anyway. Couldn't squeeze one out even if I wanted to.' He lit another cigarette from a packet of ten Silk Cut. Karen took a loose one from the top pocket of her denim jacket and moved over to join him. She took the cigarette from Nicklin's mouth and used it to light her own.

When Palmer turned round, Karen and Nicklin had gone. For a moment he was frightened, but then he heard them just outside, murmuring. He looked out through the broken window towards the embankment opposite. There was a housing estate at the top, where Stuart lived, and he'd seen people emptying their bins down there, using the grassy, green bank as a rubbish tip. Shitting in it, every bit as much as Karen or Nicklin did.

He still loved the place though. He knew where there was a foxes' earth hidden in the roots of a large oak tree. He'd once found a baby jay at the foot of the very same tree, bright blue and puffed-up, miaowing like a cat, calling for its mother. He knew where to find massive blackberries and which species of butterfly were attracted by the buddleia that flourished all over the place, and he knew where he could find slow worms and grass snakes nesting beneath rusting sheets of corrugated iron . . .

He was startled by a footstep next to him, the sound of broken glass being ground into concrete. He turned quickly to see Nicklin at his shoulder, smiling like he'd finally found something.

'Karen wants to do it with you.' His tone, matter of fact. Palmer said nothing. Nicklin took a drag on his cigarette, waited, shrugged. 'I'll tell her you're not up for it then, shall I?'

'Everything?' Palmer's voice, helium-high, his breathing ragged.

'That's what she said. She's had it with loads of blokes, done all sorts, it's not a big deal really. Probably suck you off as well . . .' He ran a hand across his head. His normally thick black hair had been cut suedehead-short for the summer.

'What does she want me to do?'

'Just fuck her, mate.' Then a snort and a laugh. Nicklin's voice high too, his movements jerky. Excited . . .

Palmer turned to look at him, his palm already pressing against the front of his trousers. 'No . . . I want to. I just mean, does she want me to go outside or will she . . . ? Come on, Stu . . . what?' Trying to force a smile. Mates together. Not scared.

'Just get it out. She's probably got her pants off already. I'll go and get her.' Nicklin flicked his cigarette into the corner and strolled outside.

After a few seconds, Palmer could hear him round the side of the building, whispering to Karen. He strained to hear the noise of clothing being removed, listened for the sounds that he always imagined he would hear before sex – a moan in the throat, a catch in the breath. The only breathing he could hear was his own; rapid, desperate, unsexy, as he loosened his belt and reached for his zip. He turned away from the doorway and stared at the wall, trying to calm down. Trying not to think of the things she was going to do to him. Someone had scrawled a cock on the dusty grey breezeblocks. He looked down at his own, far less impressive member and began to rub at the red marks around his belly where his waistband had pinched.

He heard movement in the doorway behind him. Her voice was almost enough to end it before it had even begun.

'Ready then, Martin?'

His hand had moved to his cock without him even realising it. He was moaning softly and stroking himself even as he was turning round to look at her, smiling . . .

Karen and Nicklin stood in the doorway, their mouths

open, clutching on to one another, waiting for the best moment to let the laughter out. Karen was the first to crack, but the laugh died almost as soon as it came out of her mouth and she looked quickly away. Nicklin began to howl, slapping his sides as Palmer had seen people do in films. Nicklin saw the look on his victim's face and spat out his scorn in between the laughs. 'Fuck, Palmer, it was a joke. I was joking . . .'

Karen glanced back. 'Jesus . . .'

Nicklin pointed at Palmer's crotch with a groan of disgust and Palmer's fist tightened instinctively around his soft, shrivelled penis.

Karen leaned against the doorframe. 'Jesus, Martin . . .'

'You've upset her now,' Nicklin said. Karen began to cry softly and the amusement vanished from Nicklin's voice in an instant. 'You really have upset her, you stupid bastard. Because you don't know a fucking joke when you hear one, you pervert . . .'

There was nothing left to do then but run, as he should have done that day in the park, and the summer before that, and a dozen or more times in between.

He ran without stopping to dress himself, clutching his trousers to his waist, bolting through the doorway, between the boy with the short black hair who was tugging with his teeth at the wrapper of a chocolate bar, and the girl in the blue dress who was sobbing.

He ran away towards the grassy, green embankment.

He ran, his head down, towards the housing estate. Wiping the tears away as he charged through the long couch grass and clattered across a rusting sheet of corrugated iron.

He ran far away from the nest of snakes.

FIVE

'How are they working together?'

It was the first question Brigstocke had asked him the previous night on the phone, and it was the first question he put to them now as a group. They were gathered in the bigger of the two offices. Brigstocke, Thorne, Holland and McEvoy. The core of an investigation that had been sizeable before and overnight had become the biggest that London had seen in a long time.

Thorne's answer now was the same as it had been a few hours earlier. He had no idea, but he hoped that together, they might come up with something, anything, that might point the hundreds of officers and civilians working on the case in the right direction. The hundreds working in the industry of killing . . .

'It seems likely that they kill alternate victims.' Brigstocke looked as though he hadn't had a lot of sleep the night before. Thorne hadn't had a great deal himself, but he hadn't had Jesmond giving him grief at the same time. Thorne looked at his DCI and saw, as if he needed another one, an object lesson in the benefits of avoiding promotion. He didn't need a lecture from a desk jockey like Jesmond. He knew full well that those wondrous, imaginary places where the buck stopped and where credit, if any, would be due, were a long way apart.

Brigstocke leaned forward, his fingers interlocked in front of him on the desk, his voice a little hoarse but crackling with urgency all the same. 'The evidence suggests that they are different types, psychologically as well as physically, but we need to know how they . . . interact. Do they attack their victims together and simply carry out the actual killing individually? Maybe one kills while the other keeps a lookout . . .'

'I don't think that's likely.' Holland was the first to speak up. Thorne was as impressed as always at the confidence, at how far he'd come in a year.

Brigstocke nodded. 'Go on, Holland . . .'

'Margie Knight's statement made no mention of a second man . . . of anybody else at all in the immediate vicinity as far as I can remember, and nothing that Charlie Garner has said would indicate that there was more than one man.'

'Have another word with Margie Knight,' Brigstocke said. His eyes met Thorne's.

'I'll give the Enrights a ring.' Thorne was already hoping that he would not need to speak to them again in person. At least not until he had good news. 'Holland's right though, sir, the boy's said nothing at any time about two men . . .'

One was bad enough wasn't it, Charlie?

'I think we're forgetting about the time element here.' McEvoy sounded as tired as Brigstocke. Thorne looked across at her and thought that she didn't look a whole lot better. 'They could have killed Carol Garner and Ruth

Murray together, or at least both have been present *when* she was killed, but the stabbings in July almost overlap timewise and they were miles apart. Each of them has got to be working on their own.'

'I agree,' Thorne said. It was about as much as he *was* sure of.

'OK, so the chances are that, even though they kill on the same day, they kill separately, but we have to presume that they plan these murders carefully. For Christ's sake, they must get together to work everything out, discuss dates . . .'

Thorne shook his head. 'I don't think we can presume anything.'

It was possible that the men they were after might never even have met. Thorne had read about a pair of killers in the United States who did their butchering separately but who got their kicks out of communicating with each other. They discussed the selection of potential victims by phone and over the Internet. They egged each other on and then compared notes after the event. They shared the experience but never actually clapped eyes on one another. Thorne shivered as he recalled reading that one of the murderous pair had used his last breath to send best wishes to his partner in crime, seconds before they'd administered the lethal injection. If it was true, at least financially, that when the USA sneezed, the UK caught a cold, might it not also be the case when it came to one of the biggest growth industries of all?

McEvoy took out a cigarette and lit it. 'You said that the killers were probably different psychologically. What about bringing a profiler in?'

Brigstocke nodded first towards the cigarette and then

the window. McEvoy sighed, stood up and strode across to the window while Brigstocke answered her question. 'I've already been on to the National Crime Faculty . . .' McEvoy opened the window and winced. Third floor, December, it was a little bit more than fresh air.

'Jesus . . .' Holland turned and grimaced at McEvoy. She took another drag, mouthed 'sorry' at him and blew the smoke out of the window.

Brigstocke continued. 'Both the profilers on the current recommended list are busy on other cases . . .'

Shivering, Thorne reached for the leather jacket he had slung across the back of his chair. 'Which kills you quicker, passive smoking or pneumonia? This is ridiculous . . .'

McEvoy took a last drag, flicked the butt out into the wind and closed the window. 'Bunch of girls,' she scoffed, moving back to the desk. As soon as she'd sat down again, she locked eyes with Brigstocke and carried on as if nothing had happened. '*Both* the profilers, you said. Are you telling me that there are only two of them in the whole country? Two?'

'Two that are actually recommended, yes.'

'That is fucking ridiculous.' Brigstocke shrugged. McEvoy shook her head in disbelief. 'Oh come on . . . profilers aren't like psychics, you know. It's a recognised science. Sir?'

She looked at Thorne for support. She'd picked the wrong man. 'I don't think now's the time to discuss the pros and cons of profiling, Sarah. Whatever any of us think, there isn't one available anyway.'

'Couldn't we find our own?'

Holland grinned at her. 'I'll grab the *Yellow Pages* shall I?'

Brigstocke brought the discussion to a close. 'Listen, if we find somebody ourselves, if we use someone who's not on the NCF list and we fuck it up, we'll all be ironing uniforms again the next day. Nobody wants that kind of bad publicity.'

Thorne looked up from the notepad in front of him. He'd been doodling.

Three pairs of eyes. Two drawn in thick black strokes, the eyes big, heavy-lidded, cold. One pair finer, the dark eyes smaller, long-lashed . . .

'Talking of publicity,' he said, 'what kind do the Powers That Be think we *do* need?' Thorne could guess, but the mischief-maker in him wanted to hear the DCI say it. Such decisions of course were not for the likes of him. He just had to worry about catching the people that generated the publicity in the first place.

Brigstocke answered in a voice that Thorne thought was no longer wholly his own. He'd mislaid it somewhere between the squadroom and the Detective Superintendent's office. One on one with Thorne, there was no problem, he would say what he thought, but with lower ranks present, Brigstocke's tone was unreadable. 'I spoke to Jesmond first thing and a press conference is being organised for this afternoon. I gather that he *will* be telling the press about this latest development.'

There was no such greyness in Holland's response. 'That's stupid. Surely we should be keeping this *out* of the press. Knowing that there are two of them is the only advantage we've got . . .'

A small part of Thorne was relieved that Holland could still be so naive. 'There you go again, Holland, thinking like a policeman. Detective Superintendent Jesmond, on the

SCAREDY CAT   81

other hand . . .' – Brigstocke smiled at this, in spite of himself – 'has his job to consider and he's realised, quite
cleverly, that to the great British public, two *separate* murderers sounds fractionally scarier than *one* pair of them . . .'

Even as he spoke, Thorne could feel an old, instinctive
dread beginning to settle over him. He was certain that
the two men they were after would prove to be a whole lot
scarier than any number of run-of-the-mill, bog-standard
murderers.

When the meeting was over, Thorne, Brigstocke,
McEvoy and Holland left the room in silence, each in their
own ways coming to terms with the importance, the
urgency of the job ahead. If there were plenty of unanswered or unanswerable questions, one thing was horribly
evident. They needed to catch these men quickly before
there were more bodies for Phil Hendricks to deal with.

Because he would be dealing with them two at a time.

Jane Lovell, a thirty-nine-year-old divorcee, had bled to
death on a warm July evening on a patch of wasteland in
Wood Green, N22, in the London Borough of Haringey.
That was why, five months later, on a bitterly cold Monday
afternoon, a long weekend of collating, of organising, of
sod all behind him, Tom Thorne was at the headquarters of
the Serious Crime Group (East). The teams based here
policed ten boroughs' worth of killing, Haringey included.

Thorne, freezing in a smoke-filled room in Edmonton,
sitting opposite one of the most arrogant little gobshites
he'd had the misfortune to encounter in a long time.

'Are you saying we should have seen a link? Christ
knows why. Buggered if I can see a link between your
two . . . what are the names?'

'Carol Garner and Ruth Murray. Sir.'

DCI Derek Lickwood nodded and spat out the smoke from his latest cigarette. 'Right. Yeah, well, it all seems a bit far-fetched to me, but that's your business.' He wore an expensively cut blue suit and leaned back on his grimy plastic chair as if it were a well-upholstered leather recliner. His hair was black and swept back from a face that was almost, but not quite, handsome. Both chin and nose were a little big, as was his Adam's apple, which bobbed furiously up and down as he spoke. He addressed his comments, curiously, to a point six inches above Thorne's head.

'When it starts becoming my business though, I get a bit nervous,' Lickwood said. 'I'm not mad keen on people who are supposed to be colleagues, strolling in here and intimating that maybe my team, and by implication, me, could have done a better job of something. That upsets me.'

Thorne, even after a cursory glance at the file on Jane Lovell, had realised that it would have been hard to have made a *worse* job of it. Everything that needed to have been done, had been, but no more. It was by the book and not from the heart. Two days after Jane Lovell had been stabbed to death, the case was as cold as she was.

Thorne could see that Lickwood's reaction was all pose. A typically spiky and defensive response from an officer who feared that his shortcomings were going to be exposed. Thorne knew that he wanted, very badly, to punch Lickwood in his smug mouth, and he knew that he would have made a very tidy job of it. He also knew that, if he was going to get anywhere at all, a little diplomacy was called for.

Call it diplomacy. Basically it was just bullshit.

'As far as Jane Lovell and Katie Choi, the victim in Forest Hill, go, sir, there was probably no link at all, other than . . .'

'Right.' Lickwood leaned forward and jabbed at the file on the desk in front of Thorne. 'We looked at the Katie Choi murder, of course we did, but she was butchered. Jane Lovell was killed by one single stab wound, clean. The Choi girl was virtually unrecognisable. He'd almost cut her head off. Why should anybody think they were connected?'

Thorne nodded. Connections. When 'sick' connected with 'warped' they gave the job to him.

'Ostensibly they aren't . . . weren't.' Thorne was picking his words carefully. 'The only link is the one we're now seeing retrospectively – the fact that they were killed by two people who, in all probability, are at least known to each other . . .'

Lickwood, eyes wide, parroting. 'In all probability.'

'There aren't so many murders in London that we can put it down to coincidence. Two women stabbed to death on the same evening. Four months later, two women strangled to death, both of whom had passed through main-line stations just before they were killed. I think the killers are narrowing their parameters as they go. Increasing the number of specifics . . .'

Lickwood looked at the spot above Thorne's head. 'Sorry, I'm not with you.' Thorne could guess what he was thinking. *Smartarse.*

'If it's some sort of game, it's as if they're trying to make it harder for themselves.' Thorne couldn't help smiling at Lickwood's nod. The tiny gesture, given to signal his understanding and agreement, indicated perfectly just how obtuse he really was. At that moment, Thorne would have been happy with just one quick right-hander. Break the fucker's nose. A small slap even . . .

'Where d'you want to start then?' Lickwood said, lighting up again.

Thorne had, in fact, started already. McEvoy and Holland were busy re-questioning all the key witnesses, notably Michael Murrell, who worked in the cinema at Wood Green shopping centre, which Jane Lovell had visited just before she was killed. Murrell had given a description of a man he'd seen hanging around outside the cinema who looked as if he'd been waiting for someone. After tracing most of the people in the cinema that night, this man could not be accounted for. An e-fit had been created, which was of course on file, but Thorne wanted to see what difference five months had made to Michael Murrell's memory. He also wanted to see what DCI Derek Lickwood had to say about one statement in particular.

'Tell me about Lyn Gibson.'

Lickwood blew smoke out of his nose in a dramatic gesture of exasperation. He clearly enjoyed using his cigarette as a prop, but he was hammy as hell. 'Mad as a cut snake if you ask me. I think she enjoyed the drama of it all, you know, maybe she had a thing for coppers. She was round here every ten minutes, hassling us, demanding to know what we were doing.'

'She was Jane Lovell's friend . . .'

'So she said . . .'

'She thought that Jane was being pestered by someone at work?'

'Pestered one minute, *doing* the pestering the next. Gibson couldn't make her fucking mind up, which made it obvious to me that she didn't really know much about anything. Basically, she thought that there was some bloke Jane worked with who we should be looking at, but she had no idea who he was. Jane never mentioned his name apparently, which was one more reason not to take it particularly seriously . . .'

'Did you not even check it out? Talk to the people she worked with?'

'It's in the file.'

Thorne knew full well what was in the file. He'd spent most of Saturday and Sunday ploughing through the reports on Jane Lovell and Katie Choi. Patterns of dried blood on wasteland. Stab wounds running into the hundreds. Another weekend of light reading.

He waited Lickwood out.

'Without a name it was a waste of time. It's not a small company. We asked around, got a feel of the place, looked at a couple of people, but short of asking if anybody there was harassing a woman who'd just been found murdered, there was bugger all we could do.'

Thorne was finding it hard to maintain even a pretence of respect for the man's rank. 'What about company politics? There's always rumours. Couldn't you find the office gossip?'

Lickwood leaned back in his chair again, striking a pose, only inches from tumbling arse over tit. 'Well, that was the problem, mate. We'd already found her, hadn't we? Dead as mutton, a hundred yards off the Wood Green High Road. As far as we could tell, Jane Lovell *was* the office gossip . . .'

★

Dave Holland rarely went to the cinema. He and Sophie were much fonder of a night in with a rented video, and if he sometimes wondered whether or not he was missing out on something, one look at the seedy, sticky-carpeted interior of the Odeon, Wood Green told him he was better off with Blockbuster.

Michael Murrell was a tall, unnaturally skinny black man in his late thirties, who coughed to announce his presence, brushed non-existent lint from the sleeve of his blazer, and announced curtly that he could give Holland five minutes of his time at the most. It took a lot less than that for Holland to realise that this man's job as Front of House Manager was pretty much all he had going for him. What he lacked in warmth he made up for in efficiency and an unparalleled knowledge of popcorn sales. He could doubtless have told him how many buckets of salty or sweet had been sold in the last calendar month, and whether men or women were the biggest consumers of cheese-covered nachos. Though not exactly charmed, Holland was relieved. Whatever the cause of this strange devotion to work, he guessed it made Mr Murrell a reliable witness. He still had, or at least claimed to have, a vivid memory of the man he'd seen hanging about outside the cinema five months earlier.

'*Pearl Harbour* with Ben Affleck and Kate Beckinsale. The programme started at eight twenty, the main feature at eight thirty-five and the audience began leaving at twenty past ten. I've got a good memory, Detective Constable, I can still see his face.' Murrell spoke matter-of-factly, staring at Holland from behind thick, oversize glasses. 'You see, what sticks in my mind is that he didn't look shifty or suspicious . . . as much as scared.'

★

Sarah McEvoy could smoke for England, but Lyn Gibson made her look like a lightweight. She worked for a small PR firm in Putney, in a building with a strict No Smoking policy. They'd been standing in the car park, freezing their arses off for twenty minutes and already there were cigarette butts scattered around their feet.

Lyn Gibson's were easy to spot. The ones with the bright red lipstick. Four of them.

The fact that her mouth was otherwise occupied was only one reason why she wasn't saying much to begin with about her friend's death. It was obviously still difficult to talk about in any depth. McEvoy knew better than to push. Five months was a long time in Serious Crime. A lot of bodies. To the friends and relatives of the dead, five months was a moment.

'Jane wasn't a saint, you know, but there was never any malice in her.' When Lyn did speak, she spoke slowly, in a series of disconnected statements, as if seeking some reassurance in this catalogue of *things that were true*, this solid analysis of her dead friend's character.

'She was always laughing. With me at any rate. I know she had a good old cry on her own sometimes though . . .'

It was only when McEvoy mentioned Jane Lovell's job that Lyn Gibson became animated. Then, she spoke passionately about a man that her friend had said was bothering her. Jane had admitted that she'd flirted with him, maybe even led him on a little, but it was only teasing. She'd never really been interested.

'Something about him worried her though. She could never really say what it was and when I tried to find out more she shut up, like it was something spooky. I never even knew the bloke's name. But you should try and find him. I know that wanker Lickwood thought I was some kind of nutter, but I knew Jane. You know . . . ?'

McEvoy was impressed. The woman was angry, but as far as McEvoy could tell, she had no axe to grind. There was a burst of throaty laughter as Lyn Gibson put another cigarette in her mouth, but as she lit it, McEvoy could see the flame reflected in the tears that were gathering, ready to drop.

'I told her to come and stay at mine, you know. Stupid cow was too fond of her own bed.' She laughed again, and the laugh became a cough. She took a deep drag and pressed the heel of her hand to an eye. 'I'll tell you the really stupid thing. The film we went to see that night. It was shit. It was a shit film . . .'

It was amazing how much a simple thing like the Christmas lights in Kentish Town could raise Thorne's spirits. They were a long way removed from the gaudy display of Oxford Street or Brent Cross, just simple strings of white bulbs stretching from one side of the main road to the other, but he found them bizarrely uplifting after two hours in the company of Derek Lickwood.

Thorne liked Christmas. He didn't get as excited as he had when he'd been a kid, but then who did? As an only child, it had always been special. Now, he could afford to be cynical when the decorations started appearing in shops sometime just after Easter, and marvel at how much money was spent, but he always hoped for a white Christmas, and a kids' choir singing *In The Bleak Midwinter* still made him teary.

This brief, early flowering of seasonal cheer was more than a little pissed upon when Thorne arrived home and opened his post to discover that his one and, thus far, *only* Christmas card was from the Bengal Lancer, thanking him for another year of custom. Now seemed like as good a time as any to thank them for their card-cum-calendar, by ringing to order a home delivery.

Moving to get the phone from the table by the front door, Thorne noticed the light blinking on the answering machine. He pressed play and then, a few seconds later, hit the *Stop* button as soon as he heard his father's voice. Thorne knew that the message itself would almost certainly be unimportant; just the latest in a long line of thinly veiled hints about his failure to ring.

Thorne took the hint and picked up the phone.

Since the death of his mother two and a half years earlier, the relationship between Tom and Jim Thorne had settled into one defined by the father's absurd, almost pathological fondness for pointless quizzes and stupid jokes, and the son's grim acceptance of blame for the fact that the distance between them was far more than the twenty-five miles from North London to St Albans.

Forced laughter and instant guilt.

It was usually the joke that came first. 'Tom, what is ET short for?'

'Go on dad . . .'

'Because he's only got little legs.'

Then the guilt, which tonight took the form of the annual amble round the houses to decide where Thorne's father was going to spend Christmas. He'd spent the last two with Thorne in London, *and* the couple before that, when there'd been three of them. The days when there had been *four* of them to exchange socks and perfume, eat dry turkey, argue over the Queen's speech and then fall asleep in front of *The Great Escape*, seemed like a long way away. The days before strokes and hospital visits and a grief that changed people for ever.

The days before affairs.

Now, there was just the father and the son, and it was as if the old man needed to be wooed, like a girl. He had a sister in Brighton, whose name would go unmentioned all year and would then be mysteriously dropped into the conversation around the same time that the first Christmassy Woolworths adverts appeared on television. Thorne knew his dad's 'I know you're busy, let's not bother' routine by heart. Like Santa, it came once a year and Thorne had started off believing it. Yes, he *might* go to Eileen's . . . maybe it would be easier for everybody . . . he didn't want to put anybody to any trouble . . . he promised to tell him as soon as he knew what he was doing . . .

Thorne was well aware that the old sod knew *exactly* what he was doing.

By the time two cans of Sainsbury's premium Belgian lager had washed down a plateful of Kentish Town's finest Kashmiri food, Thorne had stopped being pissed off with his father. It was time to catch up with McEvoy and Holland.

Holland told Thorne that he'd gone through Margie Knight's description with Michael Murrell, and even though they were similar, Murrell maintained that the man he'd seen had been wearing glasses. 'Right, let's get Knight *and* Murrell together,' Thorne said, 'Come up with something definitive.'

McEvoy confirmed that Lyn Gibson's story needed checking out. Something had gone on with somebody at Jane Lovell's office and it was worth looking into. After all, might not at least one of the killers have started close to home? Started with somebody he knew? Thorne had been thinking exactly the same thing and despite what Lickwood had said about it being a waste of time, he'd already decided to see what he could find out. He'd have done it anyway, whatever DS McEvoy had thought of Lyn Gibson, just to annoy Derek Lickwood. If he couldn't punch him, he could at least piss him off.

As he spoke to McEvoy, Thorne gathered up the take-away cartons off the floor. Elvis, his cat, squirmed around his ankles, yowling. He'd inherited her, stupid name and all, a year earlier in unpleasant circumstances, during the hunt for the 'Sleepyhead' killer. Elvis was a nervous moggy, but it never seemed to affect her appetite.

Thorne carried the rubbish through to the kitchen. He couldn't say that he actually *liked* his flat very much, but it was at least tidy, most of the time.

He scraped the dried remains of his dinner into the bin, thinking that it would be nice to hear a woman say how tidy his flat was.

Sarah McEvoy told Thorne that she'd see him tomorrow and switched off her phone. She smiled across at Dave Holland who, not two minutes before, had said and done exactly the same things.

The bell rang for last orders. Holland looked first at his watch and then at McEvoy. She nodded and reached for a cigarette as he picked up their empty glasses and began pushing his way through the crowd towards the bar.

Thorne sat thinking about the day, no crowds keeping *him* from drink.

It had been a day when sirens had wailed. When he'd been aware of the all too familiar noise, more so than usual; every few minutes, moving towards or away from him. The Doppler effect of one barely registering, before another took its place. Perhaps there'd been some horrible incident. A train crash. A fire in a tube station. Or perhaps it was just another day in a city Thorne loved and hated in pretty much equal measure.

Police cars, ambulances, screaming their way around the streets of the capital.

The sound of London.

Thorne stared at the television screen. He was thoroughly unengaged by the brash and jumpy images. Half past midnight, and the programme seemed to consist of a partially dressed woman shouting at complete strangers in the street. Thorne didn't connect with it on any level. He saw only a face that was vaguely familiar. A tired-looking, grey face, dimly glimpsed, floating behind the dusty screen, in the occasional, blessed moments of dark stillness.

Outside, it was cold enough for snow.

Inside, Thorne sat staring at his own reflection. Wondering what Charlie Garner wanted for Christmas.

1986

Even later on, when winter came, he knew that he would prefer to be outdoors. On the street. There were bound to be a couple of days, he knew that, a couple of those really bad days when the cold made your balls ache, when he would need to get into a hostel for the night. He'd heard a couple of the really old ones, the stupid old fuckers, the drunks, talking about nights when your trousers would freeze stiff and stick to your legs, and you'd have to piss in your pants just to thaw them out. Then, maybe, he might go back to the shelter, back for the hot soup and Jesus bit. Otherwise though, unless the snow was at least a foot thick, he'd be sleeping outdoors. I mean that was why they called it 'rough' for fuck's sake.

And he'd always been able to put up with plenty of pain.

This place was genuinely unique. A maze of walkways and underpasses and tunnels. A small city of concrete rat-runs for the human rats. It was only really at night that Cardboard City sprang fully formed to life. In order to appreciate the faces properly – the mad eyes, the running sores, the matted beards – you needed to see them lit by the glow from a fire burning in an oil drum. By day, the skateboarders had the run of the place, but when darkness fell they would pick up their boards and drift away, home for dinner, and then the vermin would come out. The vermin like him.

He'd only arrived here recently. At first he'd been content with a doss-house and had usually made enough each day for a night in the Endell Street Spike in Covent Garden, but he didn't believe in doing things by halves. Outdoors was best, and besides, it tickled him to live here, down below the South Bank, with the Royal Festival Hall and the National Theatre right above his head, in a city built from boxes and fuelled by strong lager and despair.

Begging would do for the moment. There was plenty of time to work out an angle, but for the time being, a couple of quid a day was doing him handsomely. Enough to buy a paper, and a can of something, and always the chocolate to give him energy.

He firmly believed in never doing anything unless you were going to give it absolutely your best shot. He was a very good beggar. He'd picked it up very quickly. He didn't just stand there looking like a puppy who's pissed himself, holding out his hand like some Ethiopian. He made an effort. Yes, he was brighter than most of the others, and him being only sixteen didn't hurt, but it wasn't rocket science was it? It was all about making the punter think that they had no other choice. Not by being aggressive, no; that was stupid and a waste of energy. It just needed to be real, and looking like you had a sense of humour didn't hurt. If I can afford to laugh about this, mate, you can afford to put your hand in your pocket, and if all you've got in there is a pound coin then you might as well toss it my way. Gawd bless you guv'nor . . .

These yuppie cunts could afford it anyway.

Leaving had been the best thing, he was certain of that now. Six months ago, chucking a few things in a bag, nicking the money he'd need to tide him over from his mum's purse. He'd not been a hundred per cent sure then, but he knew he didn't really belong there.

Had to go.

He still thought about Palmer and about Karen. Thought about them far more often than he thought about his mum. He dreamed about his dad, once, but tried not to think about him.

It was stupid really. He didn't exactly miss *them*, he missed the things he could do when they were there, and the feelings he got from doing those things. Palmer and Karen were just like his air pistol or his knives or his cricket bat. They were things he used.

It was a warm night. He lay back, his head on his bag, and stared up through the ramps and stairwells at the thing that flashed and moved on top of the Hayward Gallery. Somebody told him that the colours changed with the wind. Art, by all accounts. Wank, more like . . .

The moon was full above Waterloo Bridge. He could see figures moving slowly across, staring left and right, marvelling at the view up and down the river. Stupid tossers. The best view of London wasn't from up there. London was happening down where he was, among the dopers and the dogshit. It was a city that came alive the lower you went, and he was starting to fit right in.

Martin and Karen . . .

He pictured them, in that blackened shed by the railway line, or in the park or the shopping centre, or traipsing through darkening underpasses, following him, looking. Martin, his huge hands flapping in panic, needing to be soothed, needing to be coaxed. Karen, laughing at him, at his awkwardness and anxiety.

Nicklin drifted off to sleep and dreamed about fucking them both.

SIX

Baynham & Smout was a large accountancy firm whose glass-fronted premises on Shaftesbury Avenue nestled next to those of film companies and publishers, a stone's throw from Chinatown and Soho. If, having spent a hard morning number-crunching, an accountant wanted a bowl of hot and sour soup and a handjob at lunchtime, this was a fantastic place to work.

Thorne sat on a vast black leather sofa admiring the understated but classy artwork on the expansive white walls. He glanced at Holland on the chair opposite, leafing through the style magazine he'd picked up from the glass-topped coffee table in front of him. He wondered how much more it had cost to kit out this lobby than it had cost to furnish his entire flat. Probably more than it had cost to *buy* his flat . . .

He caught the eye of one of the two gorgeous young receptionists sitting at adjacent, walnut desks on the other side of the lobby. She smiled. 'Won't be much longer.' As the words echoed off the marble and glass, her colleague looked up and smiled as well.

Thorne nodded. One of them would only have been there for five months . . .

He closed his eyes and saw an image from one of the photos in his ever expanding gallery. She was lying on her side, her right arm trapped beneath her, and her left thrown high above her head, like a schoolgirl eager to get a teacher's attention. One high-heeled shoe was missing; it lay a few feet away, in a patch of nettles, and the dew glistened on her thin summer skirt. She was yellowy white, like the bone of some giant dog, gnawed and then forgotten. Her clothes hung on her like scraps of flesh, her hair like pale strands of gristle. The single patch of colour – the blood that had poured from the wound in her chest and dried overnight to the shade of old meat.

Thorne looked over at the two girls busy at their computer screens when they weren't answering the constantly trilling phones. He wondered which of them had replaced Jane Lovell.

'Sean Bracher . . . sorry.'

Thorne looked up to see a sharp suit, a proffered hand and a mouth with far too many teeth in it. Holland was already on his feet and Thorne stood up to join him. He picked up his battered leather jacket and moved to follow Bracher to his office, but Baynham & Smout's Assistant Director of Personnel was going to do his talking to the police right there in the lobby. He flopped into one of the chairs, tossed his mobile phone on to the coffee table and called across to the reception desk. 'Jo, a pot of coffee would be good . . .'

Bracher was in his mid-thirties, with rapidly thinning hair, which Thorne guessed he was not at all happy about. Clearly an Essex boy made good, he could probably turn on an acquired sophistication when it was needed. With Thorne and Holland, he'd obviously decided that matey was the way to play it: estuary vowels, laughter, innuendo. One of the boys.

The coffee arrived quickly, and Bracher said his piece. 'I can only really tell you what I told your colleague back in the summer. We're a big company and I tend to pick up on most things that are going on, but there's no way I can be on top of what the people here are up to in their own time. Having said that, there was no-one Jane had a problem with as far as I'm aware. I'm here for people to tell me stuff like that and Jane and I were good mates, you know, so, I think she'd have said something.'

Holland placed his coffee cup back on the table. 'I get the impression that Jane was pretty much the life and soul round here. That she liked to enjoy herself.'

There was a resounding raspberry noise as Bracher shifted on the leather chair. 'I think that's why what happened hit everybody here so hard. It can get a bit dull around here if you're not careful, and since everything went so bloody PC, some people can get a bit touchy if people try to . . . liven things up.'

Thorne glanced across as a motorcycle courier came through the revolving doors, took off his helmet and strolled towards the reception desk.

'Liven things up?' Holland said.

Bracher leaned forward, elbows on knees, fingers intertwined. He had a serious point to make. 'Seventy-five per cent, *at least*, seventy-five per cent of people meet their husbands, wives, or long-term partners at work. That's a fact. But if you so much as ask a woman out these days, you've got to be careful, you know? You used to be able to have some fun, men and women could wind each other up a bit, but now it's all got a bit po-faced. Nobody really talks to anybody else now, except for five minutes when they're making a coffee or whatever. "Water-cooler time" I think they call it in America. Anyway, Jane didn't give a toss about any of that. She just enjoyed a laugh, and if people didn't like it, then sod 'em, you know?'

Thorne watched as the courier pulled a package from the bag over his shoulder and handed it to one of the girls at the desk. She laughed at something he said . . .

'Was there anybody who didn't like it?' Holland asked in such a way as to imply that not liking it, whatever *it* was, would have been utterly stupid.

'Well, there's always a couple of arseholes anywhere isn't there? I bet you've got a few on the force haven't you?' Holland smiled, but only with his mouth. 'Yeah, there was the odd one, you know, couldn't see the joke, but we'd just take the piss. You've got to have a sense of humour haven't you? I mean, we're all fair game at the end of the day . . .'

Thorne tuned Bracher out. The courier and the girls on reception were still flirting. Jane Lovell might have been killed by a complete stranger, and she might have been killed by someone she knew well. A third option was that her murderer was someone with whom she was casually acquainted – someone she saw regularly without ever really knowing. A courier, a shop assistant, someone she met at the tube station every morning.

Call it a couple of thousand suspects . . .

'Jane was always up for it, you know? Up for the crack.' Bracher was still eulogising. 'As far as I know, she got on with almost everybody.'

Thorne spoke directly to him for the first time, his sarcasm undisguised. 'And, *as far as you know*, Mr Bracher, did she ever get *off* with anybody?'

Bracher reddened. He picked up a teaspoon and tapped it against the side of the table for a few seconds. 'Look, I'm here to make sure that people can work together. Who they're sleeping with is really none of my business.'

'Even if it's someone in the same office? I find that hard to believe.'

Bracher's mobile rang and he grabbed for it gratefully. As he murmured into it, he raised his eyebrows at Thorne, an apology for the tiresome interruption. Thorne looked at Holland. Time to go.

Bracher shrugged and stood up. 'I'm sorry, but unless there's anything else . . .'

As they all shook hands, gathering up jackets and over-coats, the thought crossed Thorne's mind that Bracher had primed a colleague to ring him after ten minutes, giving him an excuse to get away. As he and Holland pushed their way out through the revolving door, a second thought entered his mind. A question. Had he developed finely honed, razor-sharp instincts, or was he just a cynical bastard?

'What do you make of him, then?' Holland asked. They were walking along Shaftesbury Avenue, towards the Cambridge Circus NCP on Gerrard Street, where Thorne's F-reg Mondeo was busy lowering the tone. It was bright but freezing. Scarves and sunglasses weather . . .

'I think he was sleeping with Jane Lovell, or had been at some point.'

Holland nodded. 'Worth looking at d'you think?'

Thorne pulled a face. He *was* a cynical bastard, but those instincts he did have told him that Bracher, though an arrogant, unpleasant sod, was probably no more than that. He wondered how many more of them he was going to have to deal with before this case was finished.

★

Back at Becke House, Thorne walked past McEvoy who was on the phone in the Major Incident Room. She waved at him, indicating that she needed to talk. He nodded and carried on through to his own office.

He sat down at his desk, flicked the desktop calendar forward to Tue, Dec 11, and stared for a minute at the psychedelic screensaver that Holland had installed for him. The vivid colours swam and morphed and bled into one another, and he gazed at them until they began to blur and hurt his eyes. They were there, so he'd been told, to stop the computer screen burning out. Thorne wondered if they made something that could do the same for policemen.

He stood up and marched briskly out of the office into the Incident Room, not looking at anybody, not speaking, grabbing a chair and taking it with him.

He wasn't burnt out yet . . .

If he disliked his office, his feelings for the Incident Room were closer to pure hatred. There was so much more of it. A room of sharp corners and dead air. A long, dirty window, the light diffused through an off-white vertical blind, one blade permanently broken and crumpled onto the windowsill, where it lay among the corpses of a hundred long-dead bluebottles. A dozen or more desks. Sharp corners waiting to catch a thigh or tear the back of a hand. There was one in particular that caught Thorne several times a week, no matter how hard he tried to avoid it. The room was a feng shui nightmare. Not that he had any truck whatsoever with that kind of rubbish. The only rearrangement of furniture and personal belongings that he had *any* belief in, involved burglars and fences.

He dragged the chair across the room behind him,

steering well clear of the lethal desktop. He planted himself at the far end, in front of the wall, and stared.

Jane Lovell. Katie Choi. Ruth Murray. Carol Garner. Photocopies of photos on a tatty, cork pinboard.

And file names on a computer, sticky labels on jars in a mortuary . . .

Arrows and swooping lines marked in thick, black felt-tip pen on a wipe-clean chart. Lines that linked grainy prints of the four victims to lists of dates, times and locations. Beneath these was another batch of names in a row of wonky columns. Margie Knight. Michael Murrell. Lyn Gibson.

Charlie Garner . . .

Witnesses. Friends. Family. Figures at the periphery of the case diagram. Thorne stared at the chart. A few nights before, he had sat and thought about the hundreds, the thousands of those whose livelihood depended on killing. Now, he thought about the more unwilling participants. Those who had not chosen to play any part in the process – a process that ended with their names scribbled on a wipe-clean board.

Those hundreds of lives touched by a single death.

Jane Lovell. Katie Choi. Ruth Murray. Carol Garner. Four single deaths. Two twisted killers. Thorne stared at the names and pictures on the wall in front of him and felt it slipping away. The case was going cold. They were losing it.

Thorne turned at a commotion behind him and saw Brigstocke marching across the office in his direction. A step or two behind the DCI was a man Thorne recognised from the press conference a few days earlier. He couldn't remember the name . . .

'Tom, this is Steve Norman, our new Senior Press Officer.'

Norman, that was it. Soberly suited and suitably respectful as he'd welcomed the ladies and gentlemen of the media into the briefing room at Scotland Yard, and smoothed the way for Trevor Jesmond with a few easy jokes. Nothing that might compromise the seriousness of the investigation of course, or distract the attention of the cameras from their intended target. Clearly he was some-one who could tailor his demeanour to any occasion.

Thorne stood. Norman stepped smartly forward and reached for his hand. He was a smallish man, sinewy and energised. His black hair was gelled and swept back, and his dark eyes held Thorne's as their hands met.

'Pleased to meet you, Tom.'

There were perhaps forty people in the room – detec-tives, uniforms and civilian auxiliaries. The hubbub, the noise of phones ringing and printers whirring, was not inconsiderable. Thorne, for reasons he couldn't explain, felt forty pairs of eyes upon him and imagined that the entire place had fallen silent.

Brigstocke gestured towards the other side of the room. 'Let's go into the office shall we. You can't hear yourself think in here . . .'

Thorne led the way. Brigstocke and Norman walked a few paces behind, and despite his best efforts, Thorne could hear nothing of their murmured conversation. As he glanced back over his shoulder, he caught his thigh on the sharp corner of the deadly desktop.

'Fuck!'

The stab of pain was intense. He kicked the leg of the desk. The eyes of the woman behind it widened in alarm, her arms spreading to prevent a tottering tower of paper-work from collapsing.

When Thorne reached the door to his office, still rubbing the top of his thigh, Holland, who was on a coffee run, caught his eye. The DC's raised eyebrows asked the question. Thorne's tiny shrug gave the answer. *Your guess is as good as mine, mate . . .*

Once inside, Thorne poured himself into a chair and was a little disconcerted to see that Brigstocke was still standing and Norman was leaning casually against a desk. They were both looking down at him.

'It's clear that the media are not giving up on this until we've got a result . . .' Brigstocke said. It was the voice he usually reserved for superior officers. 'So it's important that we keep Steve up to speed with everything.' Thorne was hugely relieved that Brigstocke hadn't gone as far as mentioning the fabled hymnsheet that they were all supposed to be singing from.

Norman flashed the smile that Thorne had seen him use to such good effect when he'd introduced Jesmond at the press conference. 'Russell's already filled me in. I just wanted to introduce myself properly, and apologise in advance, because at some point I *will* become a pain in the arse.'

Thorne, who didn't doubt it for a second, did his best to summon up something like a smile in return. 'I'm sure I'll cope.'

Norman nodded, pushed himself away from the edge of the desk, strolled across to the window. 'If a media type says "off the record", my advice usually would be to shut the fuck up very bloody quickly, but off the record, Tom . . .' Brigstocke laughed. Thorne sort of joined in. 'Anything I should know about?'

'Impossible to say,' Thorne said. 'I don't know how many things you don't know.' Norman didn't turn from the window so Thorne couldn't judge his reaction, but Brigstocke's was clear enough. Thorne knew that he'd better play along. 'We'll make sure you're the first to know if anything significant breaks. We're chasing up a few leads . . .'

Norman turned from the window and looked straight at Thorne. 'Listen, I don't really expect to be the first person to know anything, but it's always a good idea to use the press. If you don't, give them a chance and they'll have you . . .' Thorne didn't bother even trying to think of a smart-arse answer, because he knew Norman was right. He'd seen too many good policemen eaten up. If the appetite was to be satisfied, he needed to tolerate people like Norman.

'Right now, they're getting a bit impatient,' Norman said. 'We've made a major breakthrough, no question about it, but we need to follow it up.'

'We should never have made it public. The fact that the killers are working together . . .'

Norman dropped the matey tone as if it was a turd. 'That was not down to me, Inspector, as you well know. My job was, and *is*, to implement the decisions taken at a far higher level than *this*, as far as they affect the Met's relations with the media.' He looked across at Brigstocke, cocked his head.

Was that clear enough?

Brigstocke took a few steps towards Thorne, put his hands on the back of the chair.

'Anything from the meeting with Bracher?'

Thorne was uncomfortable discussing the case *as it*

was actually unfolding with Norman in the room, but he understood that Brigstocke was angling for something, anything, that he might be able to throw to the press office.

'Not really.' He turned to look at Norman. 'But we should be able to let you have a definitive e-fit of the man we think killed Jane Lovell and Ruth Murray very soon.'

Norman seemed inordinately pleased. 'Great . . . that's great. Excellent. I'm going to get us maximum exposure. Every front page in the country, every major news and current affairs show . . .'

There was a knock and Sarah McEvoy stuck her head round the door. 'Sir I . . . oh sorry, I'll come back . . .'

Norman threw up his hands. 'I'm about done here, Russell . . .' He started walking towards the half-opened door.

Brigstocke beckoned McEvoy in. 'It's OK, Sarah.' McEvoy stepped into the room and stood aside as Norman walked past her. Thorne could see him sizing her up, checking her body over, before he turned at the doorway.

'Obviously a DNA match would have been fabulous, but just having a print is the next best thing. If you get him, when you get him, they'll convict him. Media relations can help you get him, Tom.'

Brigstocke nodded, looked at Thorne. 'I'll see you out, Steve . . .'

Norman said something to McEvoy, and Brigstocke said something to both of them as he and Norman took their time leaving the office. Thorne stayed in his seat and watched them go, his mind wandering. He span his chair round and gazed out of the window. A glorious view of the industrial estate on the other side of the A5. Stores with names like Carpet Kingdom and Shoe World and Dictatorship of Leather. Vast, American-style warehouses. Everything becoming more American.

Including the killings.

Thorne watched the little square cars passing the big square superstores. From the windows on the *other* side of the building, he could gaze down at the college parade ground, occasionally see recruits being put through their paces.

Either way, the view was depressing.

'Looked interesting . . .'

Thorne spun round. McEvoy was perched on the edge of his desk, waiting to be told everything. He couldn't be arsed with telling her much more than was blatantly obvious from his expression. 'Not really.'

McEvoy wasn't going to be fobbed off. 'Seemed like a slippery customer.' Thorne said nothing. She had one last crack at him. 'I was especially impressed by the subtle way he managed to give my tits the once over.'

Thorne laughed. 'It wasn't that subtle . . .'

'Trust me, it's relative. Is he going to be a problem?'

'I don't think so, as long as we let Mr Norman think he's keeping the massed hordes of the press at bay. Right now, I've promised him this e-fit as soon as. We need to get Murrell and Knight in here . . .' McEvoy edged herself off the desk. Thorne saw her eyes flick away from him for a second. Bad news. 'What?'

'That was actually what I needed to see you about.' McEvoy tried to sound matter of fact. 'We can't find Margie Knight.'

'*Can't find her?*' Thorne was shouting. He knew that heads would be turning outside the office door.

'Look, she must have freaked out after she talked to us. Maybe she's gone on holiday . . .'

Thorne stood up, stomped across the small office. 'For fuck's sake, Sarah. We should have brought her in here straight away, got an e-fit then.'

'She's a prostitute. She has a natural dislike for the police because most of the time we're trying to arrest her or stop her making a living. You reckon we should have dragged her across London, tied her to a chair?'

McEvoy was reacting aggressively to the anger born out of Thorne's frustration, but he knew that she was right. Co-operation had to be just that. Memory was an untrustworthy thing at the best of times. Never a reliable ally. The last thing it needed was to be forced.

'Couldn't we just go with Murrell's description for now?' McEvoy asked. 'Maybe give the press a couple of options. With and without glasses . . .'

'No.' Thorne knew only too well how much of a difference a description could make. He'd made costly mistakes before. Inaccuracies, inconsistencies, were unavoidable, but keeping them to a minimum could save lives. It was that horribly simple.

'Murrell's description is five months old. Margie Knight had a good look at this fucker two weeks ago.' He walked back towards his desk, stopping opposite McEvoy, making it very clear. 'I want to see the face she's carrying around in her head. We'll put it together with Murrell's and then we'll see what he looks like.' She nodded. He moved across to his chair and sat down. 'So, what are we doing?'

'I've called in a few favours at Vice and every uniform in the area is carrying a description. We'll find her.'

Thorne looked at her. Her face was often difficult to

read, but at that moment it told him that whether McEvoy found Margie Knight or not, she'd tear every dodgy sauna, massage parlour and tin-pot knocking shop in the city apart trying. He leaned back in his chair and tried to sound as if he was still a little pissed off.

'Go on then . . .'

The doubts swept over him with the draught from the door that McEvoy slammed behind her. For a minute or two with McEvoy, when the anger had taken hold, he'd sounded almost decisive. It had almost been as if he actually had an idea what he was doing. Two weeks since Ruth Murray and Carol Garner had died and they were going backwards fast. Scrabbling about for leads from two murders committed five months before that.

Thorne knew that he was going to spend the rest of the day working by numbers and fighting away two horrible thoughts. The first was that probably, no, almost *certainly*, the only thing that would help the case move forwards now, that could provide a springboard that might lift the investigation on to another level, was another pair of bodies.

The second was not so much a thought as a feeling; like a virus or an infection lurking within him, waiting to burst into life, clammy and clinging, and immune to treatment.

A feeling that they wouldn't have to wait too long.

The police came to the office today, Karen. Two of them, hunting in pairs. Like the men they're after . . .

They were just sniffing around really. It wasn't at all dramatic. There was no smashing down of doors or snipers on the rooftops opposite. It's difficult to know just how much they've worked out. I've been racking my brains ever since they left but it gives me a headache just thinking about it. They wouldn't have come if they hadn't made a connection between Jane and the other one, you know . . . Ruth, the one behind the railway station. They must know about that. But how much do they know about the others? About his? I can't work it out at all . . .

All the time they were here, I knew that I could have ended it with a word. It would have been so easy to fall on the floor in front of them and confess. This is complete fantasy, I know. If I hadn't been terrified of the police, I would never have begun this in the first place, would I? So, I'm left, as usual, confessing to you, Karen. I must tell you that your face, the face I see in my mind's eye as I'm confessing, is full of understanding, and warmth. Full of love.

My work's really starting to suffer now and people have noticed. I got a warning the other day. I don't think they'd ever sack me or anything but if I want to carry on moving up in the company, you know, the intimation was that I'd better buck my ideas up. How can I concentrate on anything, Karen? How can I think about anything, with what's in my head? I'm amazed that I can still breathe. I'm astonished, all the time, that I can eat, and walk and dress myself.

All I can see are open mouths and red eyes and spit on teeth.

All I can hear are grunts and gulps and the sound of blood bubbling out of holes.

All I can feel is dead flesh against my fingers.

This is not even the worst, Karen. There is something much, much worse. All this, the sensory memories of these acts, might fade I suppose, given time, but time is something I am not being given.

Two weeks, no more, only two weeks since I pushed that girl into the shadows and put my clumsy, great hands on her. It's

*only been two weeks, Karen. Fourteen days, that's all. Hardly
time to catch my breath and already there is a new set of . . .
instructions.*

Soon, I've got to do it again.

1989

He knew, even before he'd come, that this would be the last time.

He'd glanced down at the head of the man on his knees in front of him and seen the bald patch and the grease and the bits of scurf in his hair, and decided. This was probably as good a time as any to call it a day. He'd put enough money away in the last three years. Now, he could move on.

He'd only spent a short time begging, and even then he'd done it properly. He'd gone about things professionally. It was the same with this. He wasn't doing it to finance a smack habit like most of the other boys in the same line of work. His earnings were not wasted on drink or gambling. He used what he needed for the very minimum of food and shelter, and salted the rest away.

He'd made a lot of money in dirty hotel rooms and executive motor cars. He worked harder and more often than any of the others. He'd always been able to take a lot of pain and his disgust threshold was no lower. It had been easy. Half a dozen a day, ten on some days and all paying in cash. Seven days a week, rain or shine. His customers knew that they could always go to him.

He was like a 7-Eleven.

He had more than enough now, and he'd spent time getting to know the people who could help with the paperwork. Now it was time for all that effort to pay dividends. What he was planning to do made sense of course. He needed to do it to be on the safe side, to make sure they couldn't find him, but he also liked the idea because he was bored. He'd been the same person for far too long. After nineteen years, he fancied a change.

It was time to reinvent himself.

He pulled his cock out of the old man's mouth and started to moan theatrically. The old man gasped and opened his mouth. He had a yellow tongue and sharp incisors and his nice clean work shirt was plastered to his neck with sweat.

He came, and for once it was more than the pitiful spasm and spurt he manufactured for punters on demand. Suddenly, the moan from deep in his throat was long and loud and deeply felt.

He came . . .

Spunking away everything that was left of Stuart Nicklin. Out and away. Ridding himself of himself . . .

The sensation continued long after the ejaculation was finished. He was still moaning as he began to rain blows down on the head of the old man on the floor. He punched and he spat and he kicked, the effort causing sweat to run down between his naked shoulder-blades. He closed his eyes as he continued to lash out, and imagined himself re-made, a long way from where he was, and from who he was. It was comforting. It was everything he had ever dreamed about. He saw himself surrounded by people that liked and trusted him. He saw himself in a position of responsibility. He saw himself paid to control other people's lives.

The old man had stopped screaming.

He opened his eyes and looked down at the pathetic figure in a nylon shirt, curled up at his feet, spitting out blood and yellow teeth. He gave him one more kick for good measure and began to gather up his clothes.

He still had some way to go of course, before his vision became a reality. The paperwork was fairly straightforward, but there was training to do. It would not be handed to him on a plate, he would need to work for it. And he would work hard because he wanted it more than anything.

He pulled on his shirt and slammed the door of the dingy flat behind him. He jogged down the stairs and emerged, grinning, into the sunshine. Taking the first steps towards a brand new life.

Considering everything that had happened, it was ironic that there was only one job that he'd ever really wanted to do.

SEVEN

Thorne woke from a dream filled with fountains of blood. He could barely make himself heard over the roaring of the arterial gush, as he shouted at the man with the scalpel. He fought to stop the blood falling onto the face of the young woman in the hospital bed, but she lay there unable to turn her head away, the dark red spots slowly obliterating the pink of her face, like the spatter from a paint roller.

He sat up and waited for the dream to evaporate, which it did, quickly, leaving only the memory, which was far, far worse.

The phone was ringing. Thorne glanced at the clock as he leaned over to grab it. Friday night had only just become Saturday morning. He'd barely been asleep for an hour.

'Tom Thorne . . .'

'It's Russell. Wide awake? Or d'you want to grab a coffee and call me back?'

Brigstocke's tone cleared Thorne's head in an instant. 'I'm fine, go ahead.'

'Our friend in the hotel trade is back.'

Thorne had always known that he would be, eventually.

He guessed there would be bodies. He guessed right.

'A middle-aged couple in the Olympia Grand, been dead since early yesterday evening by the look of it . . .' Brigstocke paused, cleared his throat. For Thorne it was always a relief to hear colleagues hesitate to speak about violent death. A relief and a surprise. 'He tortured them, Tom. There are marks . . .'

'Who's picking this up, Russell?'

Another pause, for an altogether different reason. 'I was hoping you would.'

Thorne sat up, swung his legs out of bed. 'I don't think I like where this is going, sir.'

'Don't go off on one, Tom. There's nothing sinister happening, but this was our case and I just don't want strangers on it. Team Two are already down there but I'd like you to get across, see what you make of it. Hendricks is on his way. Go and give them a hand.'

'What about the Garner case?' He knew it then. He'd named it. Four women dead, but for Thorne it was the Garner case. All the murders distilled into one, the one which for a small child had taken away so much more than just his mother. The case would *always* be about that child, as the case a year ago had been about a woman in a hospital bed, unable to move.

The woman he'd been dreaming about.

'It's been nearly three weeks, Tom . . .'

'Seventeen days.'

'Look, I agreed to let you spend time looking for Margie Knight, to hold back on releasing the e-fit, but we're getting nowhere.'

'Sir . . .'

'I've backed every decision you've made on this . . .'

'Because they've been the right decisions . . .'

'Jesmond's getting fucking jittery, all right? Now, I'm not talking about winding it down, so don't panic, but progress *somewhere* would go down a storm right now.'

Thorne was off the bed, catching glimpses of himself in the wardrobe mirror as he stomped around the room. He didn't look at all happy. He knew that Brigstocke was right of course, but his hackles were up all the same. 'Does he think we're sitting on our arses?'

'The hotel killings will be all over the paper in the morning.'

'What? How . . . ?'

'The bodies were found by a housemaid who went to turn down the beds. She called the papers before she called us.'

'Jesus. Norman must be up in arms . . .'

'He isn't the only one. The couple were Dutch, from Amsterdam. Tourists, Tom.'

Thorne grunted sarcastically. 'Oh, *I* see . . .'

'I don't care *what* you think you can fucking see, Inspector.' The change in Brigstocke's tone was sudden, and shocking. Thorne felt a twinge of guilt. The DCI was clearly under some pressure. 'We could have a decent break here, so while we're waiting for the same thing to happen on the other case, I want you to see what you can do, all right? So get down there and have a look.'

Ronald Van Der Vlugt had spent a fairly unremarkable fifty-eight years on the planet, until the night he answered the door to a stranger in a top London hotel. Now, he lay naked in the bath, an inch of bloody water slopping around his lifeless body, trussed up like a defrosting turkey.

'What about the cuts, Phil?'

Hendricks was kneeling by the side of the bath, measuring wounds, and muttering into a small dictaphone. He grunted, and scratched his head through his distinctive yellow showercap. 'Stanley knife, looks like. Something very sharp and very straight. Dozens of them, all over the poor bastard. Face, torso, genitals. Same in there.' He gestured towards the bedroom where Mrs Van Der Vlugt lay stretched out on the bed, staring up at the ceiling, her body as sliced and chipped and stiff as a chopping board.

'No chance he did it post-mortem is there?' Thorne asked. The dead would stay dead, of course, but the living did no harm in searching for a crumb of comfort to offer the relatives. Thorne glanced down at the cuts on the mottled belly, the floating faeces, the brain matter caked across the overflow. He had no idea whether the Van Der Vlugts had children, or grandchildren . . .

Hendricks shook his head. 'Too much blood, mate. He cut 'em up for a while, then smashed the back of their heads in. End of story.' Hendricks switched his dictaphone back on and returned to work. Thorne turned and wandered into the bedroom, exchanging nods with a couple of the SOCOs who crawled and crept slowly around the room, pressing tape into carpet, dusting surfaces, collecting fibres and hairs; working in a silence broken only by the click of knee joints, the snap of evidence bags and the rustle of white plastic bodysuits.

Thorne stood at the foot of the bed and looked at Sonja Van Der Vlugt. She was younger than her husband, he guessed. Early fifties with a roundish face. Silver hair cut into a stylish bob, a well-kept figure. And torture marks.

Thorne had no evidence to support him, none whatsoever, but he knew without any shadow of a doubt that the man responsible had made each watch as he took a knife to the other; the muffled screams behind improvised gags and the straining against bonds exciting him as much as the feeling of the blade nicking the skin, the blood running.

The small safe in the bottom of the wardrobe had been opened; there might have been jewellery taken, watches and cash perhaps, but this wasn't about theft.

Not any more.

Walking across the lobby towards the manager's office, Thorne was struck by how much it reminded him of the one at Baynham & Smout. The killer must have been impressed by the marble and the leather. Impressed and excited by the expense. If he was going to steal, he'd want to steal from people that could afford the finer things in life.

Thorne knocked on the manager's office door, wondering if the killer was motivated by envy. Dismissing the thought. *No, not about theft . . .*

DI Colin Maxwell of Team 2 at SCG (West) had a wide, thin mouth which turned upwards at each end, giving the impression of a permanent smile, rather like a dolphin. His workmates would have laughed at this anyway, but the fact that he was almost always miserable made it even funnier.

'Tom.' They shook hands. Maxwell turned to the short, plump man standing against the desk. 'Mr Felgate, this is Detective Inspector Thorne.' Felgate stood up and Thorne stepped across to shake his hand. It was only then that he noticed the woman sitting in a chair near the door. 'And this is Mary Rendle, who found the bodies.'

At the mention of her name, the woman raised her head and stared at Thorne. She was in her forties, with short black hair and a scar across her chin. It was Thorne who looked away first.

'How much longer do you think it will be until the bodies are removed?' Felgate's question sounded matter of fact, as if bodies turned up in his hotel on a daily basis.

'We're working as fast as we can, sir,' Maxwell said.

'So . . .' Thorne waited until Felgate was looking straight at him. 'The Van Der Vlugts had ordered room service. Exactly what time was that?'

Felgate opened his mouth and looked at Maxwell. Thorne tried not to sound overly impatient. 'Sir?'

'I've already gone over all this with Mr Felgate,' Maxwell said. 'I'll fill you in later.'

For someone who, theoretically at least, had been sent to help, Thorne was not feeling particularly welcome.

It was a feeling he knew pretty well.

Thorne turned to look at Mary Rendle. 'Tell me about finding the body.' He caught her glance towards Maxwell and took a step closer to her. 'And I'm sure you've already *gone over* this with DI Maxwell.' Another step. 'Go over it with me.'

'I went to turn down the bed at about seven o'clock.' She had a smoker's voice, parts of the top range missing. 'There was no reply, so I used the pass key.' Her eyes flashed. 'It's perfectly normal.'

'Nobody's saying it isn't.'

'That's it, all right? She was lying on the bed, and he was in the bath. I don't know what else you want me to say . . .'

'You could start with why you didn't call the police
straight away.'

Thorne could have sworn she smiled slightly, as if this
was a question she'd been expecting. One to which she'd
rehearsed a good answer.

'They were dead, it was obvious. What difference was it
going to make? If they'd been alive I would have called an
ambulance, but they weren't, so I sat down and thought
about it . . .'

Thorne was gobsmacked. 'You sat down and thought
about it?'

She glared at him. 'I get three pounds sixty an hour to
pick up dirty towels and scrub toilets. I didn't have to think
about it for very long.'

Thorne and Maxwell walked across the lobby in silence.

Thorne was resigned to violent death. Most of his colleagues were, at the very best, resistant to its effects. Now,
members of the public were reacting in the same way, and
for the third or fourth time since he'd got out of bed,
Thorne wondered what it would be like to knock it all on
the head; to run a pub, or work in a shop, or maybe just sit
around doing fuck all, until concerned neighbours started
banging on the door.

They stopped at the lifts. Maxwell lit a cigarette, shaking
his head. 'Fucking unbelievable.'

Thorne shrugged. He hoped the newspapers had
agreed to give Mary Rendle a decent whack. She was
going to need something to tide her over. The look Felgate
was giving her as Thorne and Maxwell left the office told
him that she wasn't going to be picking up dirty towels for
very much longer.

Maxwell pressed the button to call the lift. He needed to go back to the murder scene. 'Listen, you'll be in on it when we get this fucker, all right?'

Thorne looked at the smiley dolphin face, unable to read it. The offer at least *sounded* genuine. 'Thanks, Colin. Anything you need, give us a bell . . .'

'The DCI's given us full access to the files, but you lot have done the donkey work, so it's only fair, you know.'

'Going at the staff first?'

They'd been convinced six months earlier, before the killer had gone underground, that he had to have some sort of contact with someone on the inside. Their best guess was that a member of staff at each hotel was feeding him information. They had no idea how he made these contacts, but they had to be telling him which guests were in their rooms, which had ordered room service, where he needed to avoid CCTV cameras . . .

Now, one of these contacts was an accessory to murder.

'Yes, I think so.' Maxwell nodded, but he narrowed his eyes slightly. Not liking to be told what to do. Not enjoying being patronised, however unintentionally or subtly Thorne was doing it.

The lift arrived and Maxwell stepped inside. 'Cheers then . . .'

Thorne stepped forward and put his hand against the closing door. 'Listen, has anybody looked into a drugs angle here? Just to be on the safe side. The torture, the Dutch connection . . . ?'

Maxwell moved back inside the lift, leaned against the ornately mirrored back wall. 'Ronald Van Der Vlugt was a rare book dealer. Over here for an exhibition of antique books and manuscripts at Olympia. My bet is, only drugs he ever took were sleeping tablets or laxatives. Viagra maybe . . .'

In spite of himself, Thorne laughed a little. He stepped back and waited for the doors to shut.

Maxwell was definitely smiling. His turn to patronise. 'I'm surprised at you, Thorne. Clutching at straws . . .'

Thorne looked at him hard as the doors began to close. 'Always, mate. Always.'

'You look like shit,' McEvoy said.

Thorne took a swig of coffee. 'So do you, and I've been looking at dead Dutch people all night. What's your excuse?'

It was just after nine o'clock in the morning and Thorne had been up eight hours already. He'd got back to the flat at quarter to five, failed to get any more sleep and come into work. The drive in, through the virtually empty Saturday morning streets, had been the best part of his day by a long way. Thorne was guessing that, by the time he got to bed again that evening, it still would be.

Now, he was utterly exhausted and in as foul a temper as he could remember. He obviously wasn't the only one.

'What I look like isn't really any of your business, sir.'

'What?' Thorne wasn't so wiped out that he couldn't start to get angry.

'Forget it.' McEvoy stared at him for a few seconds, her eyes cold and challenging, before spinning on her heels and marching out of the office.

'Jesus . . .' Thorne took a deep breath. He opened his desk drawer, stared blankly at the stapler for a moment and slammed it shut again.

He picked up the paper from his desk, leaned back in his

chair and read the *Tourist Slaying* story for the third time since getting to the office. It was predictable fare, hinting at the unspeakable horror in Room 313 while laying on the 'city no longer safe for visitors' stuff with a trowel. A smattering of gory detail, a heavy dose of outrage.

The newsprint began to dance in front of Thorne's eyes, so he closed them. It might have been a few minutes, it might have been an hour, when he heard Holland's voice.

'Sir . . .'

Thorne didn't open his eyes. 'If you've got fresh coffee for me, Holland, promotion's in the bag.'

'It's better than coffee.'

Thorne sat up as Holland dropped into a chair opposite him. It struck Thorne, looking at him, that maybe he'd had a rough Friday night as well.

'Margie Knight's turned up.'

It was the instant jolt of adrenaline that Thorne needed. 'Where?'

'Uniform found her last night. Noshing off some solicitor in a parked car on the Caledonian Road.'

If it was what Thorne needed, it might also be the bit of luck that the investigation needed. A simple piece of London business after dark. A woodentop with a torch, a working girl cleaning up on a Friday night and a brief who couldn't keep it in his pants. Cases had hinged on a lot less.

'Right, get her and Murrell in here today. I want pictures of this bloke on the streets as soon as possible. Let's move this thing forward, Dave.' Holland nodded and stood up. 'What's wrong with McEvoy this morning, anyway?'

Holland stopped at the door and turned. 'Sorry?'

'Somebody's rattled her bars. I made some crack about what she looked like and she bit my head off.'

'Right.' Holland looked away, shook his head thoughtfully. 'Probably just being over-sensitive. Maybe it's her . . .'

Thorne held up a hand to stop him. 'The mood she's in right now, Holland, if you so much as *suggest* that it might be her time of the month, I'm guessing she'll kill you on the spot.' Thorne was making light of it, but he sensed that it was more than just a bad mood. His original comment *had* been tit-for-tat, but there was no question, McEvoy did look rough.

'I'll try to find out if there's anything up with her.' Holland spoke as if Thorne had asked him to perform an autopsy.

'Are *you* OK, Dave?'

There was a long pause, and the few mumbled words that Holland managed before hurrying out of the office obviously did not come easily. 'Bit of trouble at home . . .'

Thorne had wondered about it before, but this was the first time that Holland had so much as hinted that things between him and Sophie might not be hunky-dory. His reticence told Thorne that now was probably not the time to dig any deeper. Whatever was going on, he hoped they could work it out quickly. Thorne had only met Sophie once; she had seemed nice enough.

Thorne glanced up at the clock. Nearly ten. Brigstocke was due back from a meeting with Jesmond any time, and chances were it would not have been a barrel of laughs. Thorne would bring him up to speed about last night and then give him the good news about Margie Knight's miraculous reappearance.

Take some of that pressure off.

McEvoy . . . Holland . . . Brigstocke. Thorne got up, left his office and walked across to the coffee machine, thinking that perhaps he wouldn't be the first one to crack up after all.

Duddridge always waited for the customer to leave before counting the cash. It was only polite. Besides, knowing that nobody ever tried to rip him off had made him fairly relaxed about payment. People were always told gently that if their accounts weren't settled to his satisfaction, he could find them.

Use some of his own stock.

The money was all in twenties. He counted it without even looking down. He glanced around the pub which was starting to fill up with the afternoon football crowd, the lads with mullet haircuts and loafers, gathering for the last Saturday before the Christmas break. They would crowd around the big screen TV, drink themselves silly and watch the Sky coverage of the day's games, each of them putting away enough lager to pay twice over for a satellite dish at home.

The money, as expected, was all there. Duddridge decided to have a celebratory drink. It had been a nice bit of business after all. A simple referral from someone he knew and a mug punter he could overcharge, one who had no idea he was paying over the odds.

He pushed his way to the bar and ordered a Jack Daniels and Coke.

He'd sold gear to all sorts over the years, but this one had been odd, no question about it. The bloke hadn't got a clue what it was he wanted for a start. It had all been written down for him, presumably by the bloke who'd referred him to Duddridge in the first place. He said he wanted it for protection of course, which was what they all

said, trying to make out like they were just responding to
the dangerous times they were living in, but just needing it
quickly and not wanting to piss about with licences and
stuff. Right, and people only did smack to see what it was
like, because they were writing a book about it.

Thing was, with *this* bloke, Duddridge could almost
have believed it. The fucking great idiot had looked scared
to death. Most of his customers were a little nervous, but
they weren't buying cornflakes, after all. The bloke who'd
handed over the fistful of twenties, one of which
Duddridge was now peeling off to pay for his drink, *he*
looked like he was going to shit his pants at any moment.

Maybe he *did* just want it for protection. Weirdo certainly didn't look like he could hurt anybody, or *want* to
hurt anybody, at least.

It always made Duddridge a little wary selling to people
like that. You never knew when it might come back at you.
The items he sold were completely untraceable – he had a
reputation built on that – but you could never predict
exactly what the people who bought them might do. A
simple job was fine, they were his bread and butter. He saw
himself as someone who sold quality tools to professionals.

But there was no accounting for nutters.

Duddridge felt the mobile phone on his belt vibrate.
Another customer. He downed his drink and began
making his way through the crowd towards the doors. He
pictured his last customer doing the same, just a few minutes earlier, moving awkwardly between the tables, clumsy
cunt knocking over a drink, one hand flapping for the door
handle, the other clutching on to his purchase for dear life.

He always made a bit more dosh out of the amateurs,
but he didn't really like doing business with them. You

could never be certain what you were dealing with. It was always the unassuming punters, the funny-looking ones, the ones whose neighbours were always shocked and amazed . . . who you saw on the news, their eyes like puddles of piss, shooting up a playground or walking calmly into McDonald's with an Uzi.

The thought reminded him. Uzis. He needed to talk to his contact in the States, see if he could get his hands on a few.

1999

He shut the door behind him, took off his jacket and slumped down behind his desk. From somewhere down the corridor he could hear raised voices, a door slamming. The temperature must have been well into the eighties; fans on all over the building, the place reeking of sweat and bad tempers. He stared out of the window, perfectly content. He had his own ways of coping with stress.

He reached into his jacket pocket, took out his wallet and removed a small, tattered, passport-size photo. Two young boys, on an afternoon much like this one, pulling faces in a photo-booth. Two boys he used to know, pissing about in Woolworths, more than fifteen years earlier.

Now, he bore only the faintest physical resemblance to the smaller of the boys in the photo. Just the eyes, really. He was a world away.

He was nearly thirty, and considering the somewhat bumpy start, had achieved a hell of a lot. Anybody would have to admit that. Life was good, he was still on the up, and in Caroline, he seemed to have found the perfect wife. She was someone suitable in every sense, the ideal person to have by his side. They'd met seven years before, during training, and clicked straight away. They found the same things funny, they each had their own interests, and in the five years they'd been married, he could barely remember a cross word.

Yes, he felt good about sharing his life with Caroline. Sharing most of his life.

She never questioned the late nights, or the time away from home, or the occasional lack of interest in the bedroom. Perhaps she'd already convinced herself he was having an affair. If so, that was no bad thing.

He was seeking excitement of course; it was what he'd always done, but he'd never have found what he needed in furtive liaisons, in the willing arms of some young tart or other. He needed a hit, a high, a buzz. He needed something far deeper and longer-lasting than he could find in simple adultery.

He wanted no part of anything consensual.

He'd always managed to get what he wanted, eventually, and this had been no different. It had become surprisingly easy actually. He was always careful – travelling widely, never repeating himself, taking no chances. Now, if he was being honest, he was becoming a little bored.

He wondered if perhaps it went in cycles. Exactly ten years before, hadn't he become bored with who he was? He'd made the decision then to start again, to change everything, to become someone else. Now, he was happy with who he was, who he'd become, but what he was doing, for pleasure, had started to excite him less and less. It was a drug to which he was rapidly becoming inured, and it was not acceptable. It was something that needed to change.

Happy with who he was . . .

There was a knock on the door and a colleague put his head round, pale-faced and sweating, to remind him he was needed elsewhere.

He pulled his jacket from the back of the chair and slipped it on.

He picked up his wallet from the desk and slid the small photo back inside.

He stared at the credit cards that carried his name. Not his real name, of course, but the name he'd been known by for more than ten years. His real name belonged to someone he'd last seen in a first-floor flat in Soho, a long time ago. If he was walking along the street now, and heard his old name, heard those two words being shouted at him, he'd know he was being shouted at by someone who didn't know him. Someone he'd been at school with . . .

He looked at his watch. Late for a meeting. His mind racing backwards and forwards in time. Remembering, imagining . . .

Moments later, striding briskly away down the corridor, he reached for his wallet a second time. Smiling, he took out the photo again, and looked at the two young faces.

Fifteen years was a very long time.

EIGHT

```
Date: 16 December
Target: Fem
Age: 20-30
Pickup: Pub, club, winebar etc.
Site: TBA
Method : Firearm (pref not silenced)
```

Sunday. Thorne's first real day off in nearly a fortnight.

Lunch with the old man had seemed like a reasonable idea at the time. A distraction, something to wash over him, a time-killer. Now, driving back down the M1, he really wished he hadn't bothered. Aside from anything, he was starving. Of his parents, it had been his dad who'd done most of the cooking. Once upon a time, he'd enjoyed it, but his enthusiasm for that, along with everything else, had waned at the same rate as his fascination for pointless trivia and old jokes had rocketed.

While Thorne had pushed a lump of overcooked chicken and a few pallid, underdone vegetables around his plate, his dad had waffled on at absurd length about everything and fuck all. He'd quizzed him about what he thought the five top-selling soap powders in the country were, and giggled through countless stories about men walking into pubs. In fact, he'd barely drawn breath for the entire time Thorne had been there, except for a few uncomfortable minutes when, in the middle of a story about nothing, his eyes had filled with tears, and he'd calmly got up from the table, walked through into the kitchen and closed the door.

Thorne could do nothing but sit there, hating himself for thinking that he'd have been happier at a murder scene.

The big Christmas discussion had never really materialised until Thorne was about to leave, and even then, it was just the usual tiresome dance, a frustrating bit of back and forth on the doorstep.

'So, dad . . . are you coming, or what?'

'What d'you need to know now for? It's not for numbers is it?'

'It's only a week away and . . .'

'Nine days.'

'I just want to know what's happening.'

'I don't know . . . it might be good to do something different.'

'Well it's up to you, but . . .'

'I might go to Eileen's . . .'

'Right. Have you asked her?'

'Name the last six Prime Ministers . . .'

'Dad . . .'

'Blair, Major, Thatcher.'

'Have you asked Eileen?'

'They're the easy ones. Callaghan . . .'

It was starting to get dark so Thorne flicked on the headlights. He let the Mondeo drift slowly across into the inside lane. The drive home was relaxing him, calming him down, and he was in no great hurry.

He turned on the radio and tuned it in to Radio 5 Live. The second half of Ipswich versus Leicester City. Hardly a glamour fixture, but the commentary soon engaged him as he pushed on along the all but empty motorway towards north London. Moving: out of the semi-countryside and into the unlovely and reassuring urban sprawl of Brent Cross, Swiss Cottage and Camden. Moving: from one old man's life going slowly down the tubes, to thoughts of four young women who would never even have *that* golden opportunity. Moving, towards the possibility of more . . .

Moving, away from an afternoon and towards an evening.

They rolled apart from each other and lay there, sweating, exhausted, each of them trying to think of a good thing to say. Something that might help. Eventually, Holland came up with something, but Sophie was already turning over, ready for sleep. The sex had been good, better than good, but then it usually was after an argument. They'd spent the best part of the day fighting, then fucked away the rest of it, trying to pretend the fight had never happened.

The row came at them with the slow, graceful horror of a lorry skidding on black ice. With the arse-end of a dull Sunday just around the corner, the boredom had slowly given way to irritation and finally anger. It was an anger that had been there all the time of course, like a bad smell in a locked room, and, once it escaped, it got everywhere, and into everything. It followed them around the flat, as each of them took turns in chasing the other from room to room, swearing and screaming and pounding on walls. It was still there, all over both of them, two hours later, as they cried and squeezed each other until finally, the kissing began.

Then mouths devoured each other which, only moments before, had ranted and shouted, wounding with words. Some were used far more than others. *Work, job, support, wanker, selfish, bitch, children, choice, Thorne* . . .

Sophie's breathing quickly settled into a pattern that told Holland she was asleep, but he knew that he wasn't going to follow her quickly. There were far too many thoughts rattling around in his head.

He wondered how much damage each of these weekly sessions was doing to them, and if the money they'd spent, the time and trouble they'd taken moving into a new flat, would end up being wasted.

He wondered why, considering that it was usually the other way round, he still fancied Sophie, but didn't much like her any more. Why, if he still fancied Sophie so much, had he spent most of the time they were making love thinking about Sarah McEvoy?

Jacqui had cooked lunch for seven without a word of thanks. Roast beef and the rest of it, for her husband, her mother and her sister's lot. As ever, by the time she'd finished, she wasn't actually hungry herself. Staring at her face in the dressing-table mirror, changing her mind for the second time about which shade of lipstick to go with, she decided that she'd grab something when she was out. Maybe some of the other girls might fancy a meal afterwards. If she ever bloody well got there . . .

It wasn't as if she'd expected any volunteers to help

clear up, certainly not any of her own useless lot, but it would have been nice. Her sister, as ever, sat there on her fat behind not raising a finger, so by the time Jacqui had washed up and cleared away the mess her sister's horrible kids had made in the living room, she was really late. It wasn't the first time.

For heaven's sake, it was only every other Sunday. One night, once a fortnight, when her and a few of the girls could let their hair down and talk about how shit everything was at home, and then get back to it before half past ten. She'd tried to suggest that *maybe*, every other Sunday, her sister could have everybody round to her place. The idea had not gone down well, and that had pretty much been that . . .

Mim stood in her knickers, the iron in one hand, remote in the other, channel-surfing. She stopped briefly when she got to *The Antiques Roadshow*. She knew her mother would be watching it, assuming that she wasn't sulking after the row the two of them had just had, or storming around the house taking it out on her poor father. She carried on surfing, settling finally for a documentary about sharks, and went back to ironing her jeans. It had been a row she'd known was coming, ever since term had ended and she hadn't eagerly hopped aboard the first train home. *Miriam, how could you choose to stay in that dingy bedsit rather than with your own parents in a comfortable house blah blah blah . . . ?*

She'd tried assuring her mother that she *would* be home in time for Christmas, but once the tears had started, it had been a lost cause. It wasn't like she didn't want to go home, but quite a few of the people on her course had decided to stay on for a bit and it was a laugh, just dossing about with them, going to the pub every night.

She pulled on her jeans and moved hangers back and forth along the clothes rail, looking for a shirt. It was quiz night in the pub and she wanted to get there early, make sure she was on a team with that new bloke in the first year with the nose-stud and the green eyes . . .

Jacqui was ready and waiting on the doorstep by the time her husband had got back from running her mother home. He leaned across and opened the passenger door as she came hurrying down the path. This was their routine. She pulled the door shut, placed her handbag in her lap and the car moved away, beginning their conversationless, ten-minute journey to the tube station.

Mim turned off the television before the God Squad began in earnest. There was really nothing else to do on a Sunday night than sit in the pub. Fuck, she worked hard enough, why the hell not? She pulled her door shut, jogged down the stairs and stepped out into the cold. She heard the rumble of a diesel engine and looked up to see a bus coming round the corner. Swearing enough to make her mother faint, she started to run.

Jacqui and Mim lived miles apart. They did not know each other. They would never meet. They would finally come together as two names, the latest *pair* of names, one above the other in capital letters, on a large square of white, wipe-clean plastic.

Two names.

One of them belonging to a dead woman.

*

Hendricks rang while he was feeding the cat, and Thorne quickly realised he hadn't been the only one having a shit Sunday. Mr Handy-In-The-Kitchen, who was actually called Brendan, had turned out to be Mr Unreliable-In-Every-Other-Way.

'So where's the next piercing going then, Phil? On second thoughts, don't tell me . . .'

Hendricks laughed, but Thorne could hear how upset he was. 'Not in a million years, mate. I don't know . . . I wasn't clingy, I wasn't stand-offish, I really . . . tried this time, Tom, you know?'

'Don't forget for a second that you're talking to completely the wrong person here, but for what it's worth, maybe you're trying too hard. That might be what you're doing wrong.'

Hendricks sighed, said nothing for a while, then: 'I know *exactly* what I'm doing wrong. Cutting up dead bodies, removing brains, and hearts and lungs . . .'

Thorne understood straight away. This was a conversation they'd had a couple of times before. 'Right. Another one didn't approve of the career choice?'

'Never said as much, but it was obvious. It's always difficult, but since the start of this year, it's like telling people I'm a terrorist or a murderer or something . . .'

At the start of the year, a scandal about the removal of body parts from dead children had discredited the business of organ harvesting in general and pathologists in particular. The hysteria had died down but damage had been done. Rates of organ donation had dropped dramatically. Transplant numbers were down. Pathologists had trouble making new friends.

'I tell people what I do, there's like this pause, you know?' Thorne did know, very well. Hendricks had started to ramble a little then, and Thorne could tell that he'd been smoking. The dope was something they never talked about, but Thorne had often smelled it. He could all but smell it now, as Hendricks's voice on the phone dropped to a whisper. 'I wonder if . . . what I do, is something that I carry on me. D'you reckon?'

'Phil . . .'

'Not the stink, I know how to get rid of that . . . I mean, more like a shadow or summat. No . . . more like, when you're under UV light, like at a club, you know . . . same as we use with Luminol . . . and you can see all the fluff and bits on your clothes, all that twinkly dandruff, glowing . . . shining white? Maybe it's like that . . . yeah. Little pieces of death starting to show up on me . . .'

Thorne cooked himself scrambled eggs, ate them at the tiny kitchen table. He thought about his father. Why, as the silly old bugger spiralled increasingly away into the distance, did Thorne feel so . . . buttoned up? Maybe *he* needed to do a bit of dope occasionally. Free up his thinking a little. Jan had smoked the odd joint, sometimes. Never in front of him, but he wouldn't really have cared if she had. It wasn't like he had any major objection to it; there was still far too much time and effort wasted in its criminalisation, but ultimately, it wasn't for him. He could always think of something better to spend his money on. Like beer and wine . . .

Suddenly, he could picture Jan and the lecturer she'd been screwing behind his back, skinning up, giggling, incense burning by the side of the bed. He opened a bottle of a different kind of drug and carried it through to the living room.

Abandoning the fruitless search for distraction on TV, Thorne sat for a while, considering what Hendricks had said. Remembering and thinking ahead. Thinking about bodies stabbed and bodies strangled. Thinking about a pair of cardboard coffins in the cargo hold of a plane bound for Amsterdam . . .

Were those who worked with death ever free of it?

He stood and walked across to the stereo. His fingers ran along the rows of CDs and lingered over a boxed set of Johnny Cash, before moving on. He'd treated himself to it the year before, a set of three CDs, each containing songs on one particular theme. *God*, *Love* and *Murder*. Much as he loved Johnny Cash, there was still one of them Thorne hadn't listened to.

Later, lying awake in bed, the lights turned out, the radio on, he couldn't get Hendricks's slurred monologue out of his head. It was dope-induced rubbish. It was paranoia, self-pity. It was cliché masquerading as philosophy.

It compelled him.

It had been over a year since his last relationship. No sign of another one. Was he too carrying a little of the stuff around with him? A handful of sparkling death, visible to those with an eye for it? He pictured his jacket lying across the back of the kitchen chair in the darkness. He closed his eyes and imagined them, luminescent, caught in a beam of moonlight coming through the kitchen window . . .

A few tiny fragments, glittering at his collar and in the folds of the sleeves. Like malignant diamonds.

Karen, I didn't do it.
I wish I could tell you that it was because I refused.

Because I stood up and said no to any more of it. I wish I could tell you that I was strong, that I decided not to go through with it.

The truth is, I tried to go through with it and I failed.

Thank God. Thank God, I failed. Perhaps, a big enough part of me wanted to fail, wanted it to go wrong so badly that I made it happen. Perhaps I just chose the wrong girl. Or the right one.

I sat in the pub and watched her, wanting to run, wanting to stay, counting each drink she had, listening to her laughing and feeling the thing heavy in my pocket. I sipped water and hummed along with the music and willed it all to be over quickly.

It was late when she finally left; they were virtually the last to leave the place and it was horribly perfect, Karen. They could have gone in the same direction, all of them heading home together and me needing to look again, to head into town and find a club, but she went her own way and I could do nothing but follow.

I don't often use bad language, Karen, but when I took out the gun, I was fucking terrified. It hung at the end of my arm like a dead thing and her mouth just opened so wide then, and I stood and watched her mouth and listened to her scream for a while. I don't know how long we stood there for, but instead of doing it quickly, instead of firing, instead of doing it . . . the thing I was there for, I just stared as she ran at me, and I bowed my head as she hit and hit. I backed away and I could see her bending down like she was picking something up. Then she came at me again and it started to really hurt and I know it sounds stupid but I almost laughed, because I suddenly realised that now, the sound of screaming was coming from me.

I watched her running off towards the lights and shouting and I wiped away the blood that was running from my head on to my face.

I put the gun back into my pocket and I left that place.

It has to end now, Karen.

I wish I was brave enough to come to you, but you already know that I'm not. I think the poison inside me has eaten away every ounce of courage there might ever have been.

I need to find just a little more.

2000

One phone call to the loving parents, a few weeks earlier, had been all that was necessary. He wasn't surprised that they hadn't moved. Probably never would. A bit of flannel, the charm turned full on and after a few minutes he had addresses for home and work, phone numbers, everything.

He stood outside the brasserie and peered in through the window. A fashionable expanse of exposed copper piping and deep leather sofas at the front, with tables tucked away towards the back. He couldn't see him. He'd watched him come in alone, but perhaps he'd met someone inside and they were eating . . .

His own lunch was starting to melt. He pushed the rest of the chocolate into his mouth, stuffed the wrapper into his trouser pocket and stepped through the door. The barman looked up and smiled, but Nicklin shook his head, kept walking slowly towards the back of the room, the tables out of sight around the corner.

The fluttery feeling in the pit of his stomach wasn't nerves, exactly. He didn't suffer from that particular condition, certainly not in any fearful sense. He never had. For as long as he could remember, he'd done things that he knew few others would have done, or dared to do, not because he was brave, but because he wasn't scared. He knew there was a very important difference.

What he was feeling now was excitement. The possibility of something new and more intense than anything he'd felt before. And in a way of course, he'd be picking up where he left off a long time ago. Something old and something new . . .

He reached the back of the room, glanced to his left and saw him immediately. Sitting at a table with two others – men without chins, in shirt-sleeves, guzzling wine, yapping – expense account wankers.

He began walking towards the table.

When he was ten feet away, Palmer looked up, clocked him and went back to his conversation. Of course, he hadn't recognised him. Nicklin had been almost certain he wouldn't. He would have been more than a little disappointed if he had. No fucking point if it wasn't dramatic.

He stopped. So did the conversation. He took a final step forward, his thighs flush against the edge of the table, their wine glasses wobbling.

'Can we help you with something?' One of Palmer's friends, nervous but trying very hard to sound edgy. He ignored him, his eyes only on Palmer, waiting for them to be met. When they were, and the tiny spark of recognition flared up into an inferno, it was a moment equal to anything he'd imagined in the preceding weeks.

'Martin? Are you feeling all right, mate?' The second man now, the concerned colleague, pushing back his chair, looking around.

Palmer, eyes wide, mouth dropping, yes . . . actually dropping open. Skin the colour of old newspaper.

Nicklin nodded, showed his teeth. 'Hello, Mart. This is great, isn't it?'

Palmer, struck dumb, his face frozen. Drool running from the corner of his slack mouth and dripping gently down onto the immaculate white tablecloth.

Staring, terrified, at his past.

NINE

Nearly three weeks since Charlie Garner had watched his mother die. A fortnight to the day since the case had officially begun. Eight days before Christmas.

An office full of people waiting . . .

Thorne watched as they moved around him, heads down mostly, exchanging smiles of resignation when pressed. Carrying files, answering phones, tapping at keyboards a little harder than was necessary. Frustrated, bored, some of them pissed-off for reasons of their own, others wiped out by the weekend, but all aware, to some degree, that they were doing no more than going through the motions.

The e-fit of the man seen by Margie Knight and Michael Murrell, the suspect in both the Jane Lovell and Ruth Murray murders, was on the front page of most of the papers today. But Thorne wasn't waiting for the phones to start ringing. He wasn't waiting for helpful punters, eager to pass on the news that the man in the picture might be the brother of a friend, or was like a workmate's husband, or looked a little bit like the man in the flat upstairs.

Thorne was waiting for the bodies.

Since it had become clear that they were looking for two killers, violent crime against women was being carefully monitored right across the city. Monitored and sifted. They were looking for the murder, the attempted murder, the assault perhaps . . . then waiting for its hideous mirror image to appear. Looking for both halves. Thorne remembered a kids' card game: the object was to collect as many pairs as possible.

I've got two stabbings, two stranglings . . . what have you got?

It hadn't been a particularly busy Sunday night, thank god. A lot of stuff had come in, but almost all of it was quickly dismissed. Of those cases that raised even a modicum of interest, none looked very promising. A woman attacked by another woman with a bottle outside a pub in Canning Town. A stabbing in Willesden, almost certainly a domestic. A woman threatened with a gun in Clapham, probably a botched robbery or an attempted rape . . .

The picture was also being shown on every news bulletin and it quickly began generating results. The calls came in. By mid-morning there was a list of names. None of them appeared more than once.

Brigstocke did his best to rally the troops and stop sweating. Thorne tried to stay busy. All of them, wading through treacle. Over two pints and a tomato juice at lunchtime, Holland tried, a little clumsily, to articulate the frustration they were feeling.

'It's like having sex, without ever coming . . .'

Thorne puffed out his cheeks. It was an . . . interesting analogy.

McEvoy grinned. 'Yeah, well now you know what it's

like then.' She laughed, and Thorne joined in. Holland blushed, took a sip of his tomato juice. 'I'm talking generally of course, Dave,' McEvoy added, 'I'm sure Sophie has no complaints.'

Holland said nothing. Thorne heard him say it.

'Sorry. Have I . . . ?' She looked from Thorne to Holland and back again. 'What, am I not talking like a proper lady?' She emphasised the last word comically, as if it were spelt with a 'y' in the middle and two 'e's on the end.

Thorne smiled. 'Well at least you're in a better mood than you were on Saturday. Good weekend?'

It was McEvoy's turn to redden. 'Yeah, I'm sorry about that. Just woke up feeling arsey. Weekend was . . . fine. Great, actually. Thanks.'

Before the silence had a chance to make itself uncomfortable, Thorne caught sight of Brigstocke in the pub doorway, scanning the crowd, looking for them. Thorne waved and the DCI came over. Before he arrived at the table, Thorne could tell from his face that there was news.

Simply a question of how bad . . .

'Got a fax through ten minutes ago. The description of a man who threatened a woman with a gun near Clapham South tube station last night . . .'

Thorne's shoulders lifted. A reflex as the jolt ran through him. The tingle. Not bad news at all . . .

McEvoy could see where Brigstocke was going. 'Not attempted robbery or rape then?'

Thorne answered her, quietly. 'Attempted murder.'

Brigstocke nodded. 'Sounds like our man. Tall, thickset, sandy hair, glasses. Better add *bleeding* as well. Woman he pulled a gun on says she beat the shit out of him with a high-heeled shoe.'

McEvoy swallowed a mouthful of beer. 'Fucking good.'

'When can we talk to her?' Holland asked.

'I'm trying to arrange it. She's being looked after by her family – obviously she's still upset.' Brigstocke moved to sit down. Thorne shuffled along to make room for him. 'Hopefully by the end of the day . . .' Brigstocke sighed and allowed himself the first smile that Thorne had seen for a few days.

Thorne stood up and reached for his jacket. If the man with the gun was one of the men they were looking for, then thankfully, one killer had failed. Thorne felt certain that the other one would not have done . . .

The object: to collect pairs.

Thorne disliked being the one to remove the smile from Brigstocke's face, but didn't hesitate to do so.

In his head it was a scream. It came out like a whisper.

'Somewhere, there's a woman who's been shot to death. I want to find her.'

London was a city of ghosts, some deader than others.

Thorne knew that in this respect, it wasn't unlike any other major city – New York or Paris or Sydney – but he felt instinctively that London was . . . at the extreme. It was probably down to the history of the place. The darker side of that history, as opposed to the parks, palaces and pearly kings' side that made busloads of Japanese and American tourists gawk and jabber. The hidden history of a city where the lonely, the dispossessed, the homeless, wandered the streets, brushing shoulders with the shadows of those that had come before them. A city in which the poor and the plague-ridden, those long-since hanged for stealing a loaf or murdered for a shilling, jostled for position with those seeking a meal, or a score, or a bed for the night.

A city where the dead could stay lost a long time.

Thorne had known about London's skill at concealing its cadavers for as long as he had been a police officer, but it still disturbed him. Those that died peacefully at home could lie rotting in their front rooms for weeks and months, attracting the rats and the flies, and eventually the attention of the neighbour with the well-developed sense of smell.

Those that died violently, those whose killers did not *want* them found, could lie alone and out of sight for far longer. Buried, burned or bricked up, dismembered, dumped or weighted down in water, until those that looked for them were only memories themselves. Until the dead were no more than a page in a yellowing file, or a name on a set of dental records.

Of course, such things happened in small towns and in villages, in places where they were still remarkable, but there was something about London which, Thorne felt, suited anonymous death. There were those that bleated on about how *their* particular area of the city was a little community, no really it was, friendly and welcoming . . . Thorne knew that, in reality, this meant little more than the newsagent calling you by your first name and the barman in your local *maybe* knowing what your tipple was. When it came down to it, you could still lose touch with your best friend if he lived more than two streets away, and the reaction of many Londoners to a woman being raped on their train would be to raise their newspapers a little higher.

Thorne's depressing reflections on the city where he had been born, where he lived and worked, were prompted by the simple and not unexpected fact, that by the end of the day, they had still not found the body they knew was out there. They had of course been monitoring missing persons' reports but nothing had come in. The victim had not been missed yet. There could be a hundred reasons why.

Now, as he and Holland drove towards Wandsworth to question the woman who had survived the attempted murder the night before, Thorne tried to stop thinking about the woman who hadn't. Her body, wherever it lay, might hold vital clues that even now were disappearing as the corpse changed shape, texture, consistency; popping and sighing gently.

The city would give it up when it was ready.

In the meantime, Thorne had a whole list of things to worry about.

A real cause for concern was the fact that the killings were speeding up. It had been nineteen days since Carol Garner and Ruth Murray. Jane Lovell and Katie Choi died over four months before that. A shortening of the intervals between killings was a predictable pattern, but this was dramatic. Unless of course there were murders in between the two sets that they'd missed . . . Thorne quickly dismissed this chilling thought, settling for the slightly less disturbing one that for the killers, the hunger was really starting to take hold.

The killers . . .

Thorne's other major worry. Two killers but one of them was, as yet, no more than theoretical. A shadow. They were on their way to talk to a woman who'd come face to face with one of them. The same one seen by Margie Knight and Michael Murrell. The one whose face was all over every newspaper and TV screen. Was he the careless one? The sloppy one? Or was his partner just so much better at covering his tracks, at killing and killing, and staying invisible?

The killer who had given them their only leads, the one whose blank, bespectacled face now stared out from a hundred thousand posters, was the one who killed quickly and efficiently; the single stab wound, the sustained pressure on the neck . . . the killer that wept. He was not the one who butchered and walked unseen into the darkness covered in blood. He was not the one that throttled the life out of Carol Garner, smashing and squeezing while her little boy watched.

He was not the one . . .

Thorne wanted the killer on those posters. He wanted him very badly. But he wanted his partner more.

Sean Bracher glanced at his watch as he stood at the bar waiting for the useless wanker behind it to bring his drink.

She was late.

He wasn't worried that she wouldn't come, just slightly annoyed that he'd have to get up again to fetch her a drink when she finally deigned to arrive. He handed over the money for his beer without a word, grabbed a huge handful of peanuts from a bowl on the bar and strolled across to a table.

He wasn't planning on sleeping with her tonight. Obviously he wasn't going to say no if he turned out to be wrong, but he guessed that Jo, for all her flirting, was the type to make him wait for it. Jane had made him wait too, only the one more night mind you, and it had certainly been worth waiting for. It was only ever going to be a fling of course – he'd made that clear from the word go and she was cool about it. He didn't want to be tied down to any-body, least of all a receptionist, but it certainly made the working day, not to mention the odd weekend business trip, a damn sight more interesting. She'd turned out to be kinky as fuck . . .

He stuffed a fistful of peanuts into his mouth and looked around. The place was starting to fill up with those grateful to have got another Monday over with, desperate for a quick one before the struggle home on the train or the bus. Somebody had left a rolled-up copy of the *Standard* on the next table. He reached across for it and began idly flicking through the sports pages.

Yeah, it was a nice pub. They would grab a couple here and then head off for an Italian or something. Nothing with too much garlic. He'd done exactly the same thing with Jane on their first date, over six months before.

Jo was actually better looking than Jane, but not as much of a laugh. He missed the piss-taking with Jane, the wind-ups, the crack. He'd encouraged her to flirt with that freak in the overseas section. That had been hysterical. The pil-lock had fallen for it one hundred per cent. Stammering and blushing. Went fucking ballistic when he found out he'd been had. Christ though, if you couldn't have a laugh at work . . .

He looked at his watch again. Checked his mobile for messages. Why the hell were women always so fucking late? She had been keen enough when he'd suggested meeting. He typed in a quick text message and sent it. *Where r u?* Probably still in the ladies back at the office, tarting herself up. On second thoughts, maybe he *would* end up giving her one later. Her place preferably, no reason to stay the night then . . .

He smiled, mentally in bed with her already, as he flipped the *Standard* over.

He glanced down at the front page and almost choked on his peanuts.

The young student got off the bus on Kingsland High Street. From there it was only a two-minute walk up the Dalston Road to her flat.

The evening was surprisingly mild. He took off his jacket as he went along and threw it across his arm. Walking quickly, looking through the windows of second-hand record shops and Greek cafés, thinking about the way she'd looked at him the night before.

She'd smiled a lot, raising her eyebrows, the tip of her tongue just visible against her top teeth. She had a laugh that made people on the other side of the pub stare. They'd all been a bit the worse for wear, celebrating their team's quiz win by drinking the first prize. Then the pair of them had stood at the bus stop at Highbury Corner, talking, letting three or four buses come and go before walking home – her off towards Dalston and him, in the other direction, towards the small, damp cupboard he rented in Tufnell Park.

They'd agreed to meet for lunch today at Pizza Express. He'd slept until really late and in the end he'd had to rush to get there on time, arrived out of breath and sweating. He'd waited for over an hour.

It had been a casual sort of arrangement, maybe far more casual than he remembered – he had drunk an awful lot of Guinness – but he had expected her to come. She didn't have a phone at her flat so he'd rung her mobile a couple of times during the afternoon, left messages. He was halfway through dialling her number again when he'd decided to go round. It was only ten minutes away and the bus was virtually door to door. He was sure she'd be glad to see him. Yes, they'd *both* had a lot of Guinness, but he was pretty sure she would be.

It was a dirty white door between a shoe shop and a cut-price travel agency. Three bells, her name underneath the top one.

He rang.

He put his jacket back on; she'd said she liked it last night. Looked up at the windows above him. An old man peered down at him from the first floor. Maybe they could go and have a pizza *now* – there were loads of places in Islington. Or they could just sit around, smoke a bit maybe, order something later. Whatever, it would just be really nice to see her.

He rang again . . .

'Don't let Bracher go anywhere. Just keep him there . . .'

Thorne and Holland had been heading south towards Blackfriars Bridge when Thorne's mobile had rung and he was informed that Sean Bracher was currently annoying the duty officers at Charing Cross, shouting about how he was one hundred and ten per cent certain that the man in the e-fit was someone he worked with, someone from Baynham & Smout . . .

Thorne had all but yanked the wheel out of Holland's hands. The woman in Wandsworth, Jacqueline Kaye, could wait until tomorrow. This was someone who they needed to talk to right now. They'd been to the office . . . Jesus, even Lickwood had been to the office, and the fucker had been there all the time . . .

Now, Thorne was talking to a DI at Charing Cross as well as trying to give Holland instructions on the new route they were taking.

'What's the name?' Thorne nodded solemnly as he was told, then began waving his arm in front of Holland's nose. 'Go right, we'll cut through Lincoln's Inn Fields.'

Holland smacked a palm angrily on the wheel and did as he was told, keeping one eye on Thorne, watching his reactions, desperate to be told the details.

'Has Bracher told anybody else? Anybody at work? Good . . .'

Thorne pointed some more, grunting into the phone, meeting Holland's sidelong glance and nodding. This was major.

As the unmarked Rover roared along the Strand, Thorne began to shout into the phone, as if he was losing the signal. 'We'll be there in about ten minutes . . . yes, ten.'

He punched the button to end the call and turned to Holland. 'Sean Bracher . . .'

Holland's phone began to ring.

'Fuck . . .' Holland groped inside his jacket for the mobile.

'Bet you it's for me,' Thorne said, 'I could hear the call-waiting signal on mine . . .'

'Fiver?' Holland asked, pulling out the phone. Thorne nodded.

Holland answered. 'Hello? Right . . .' He handed the phone across. 'McEvoy.'

Five pounds to the good, a smiling Thorne took the phone. Sarah McEvoy was out of breath. She'd run to make the call.

'We've got a man fitting our description, a man named Martin Palmer . . .' The smile froze on Thorne's face. It was the same name he had heard a few moments before; the name Bracher had given. 'Palmer walked into West Hampstead nick half an hour ago, dropped a gun on to the desk and confessed to two murders.'

'OK, we're on our way.'

Holland grimaced, unsure which direction to head in now. Thorne pointed north. *Keep going.*

'Slight problem,' McEvoy said. 'West Hampstead doesn't have a custody suite.'

'Fuck.' Thorne thought fast. 'Right, Kentish Town's about the nearest. Get somebody to run him over.'

'I'll call them and get straight down there.'

'Good. We should be with you in about fifteen minutes.'

McEvoy was already there by the time Thorne and Holland arrived. The three of them stood outside the room where Martin Palmer was being held. McEvoy filled them in on the details. He had walked calmly into the station to give himself up at around about the same time that Bracher had barged into Charing Cross, shouting his name out. Palmer hadn't been cautioned. He was there of his own volition.

Holland sat down on one of the green plastic chairs that were bolted in a row along the wall. 'He saw the picture too, must have. Knew somebody was going to recognise it. Thought he'd be doing himself a favour.' McEvoy looked across at him, nodded her agreement.

Thorne stared at the door. 'Maybe . . .'

'Reckon he'll give up his mate?' Thorne turned and

stared at McEvoy. She'd asked, knowing it was what he was thinking, watching the tension take hold as he glared at the scratched grey door, imagining the man on the other side of it.

Give up his mate . . .

It had been the question Thorne had been asking himself since he'd heard Palmer's name for the second time. Christ, it could be that simple. Perhaps there was a chance, if he was hit quickly, and hard.

'Is Brigstocke coming?' Holland asked.

McEvoy took a few paces back towards the main reception area, smiled politely at the small collection of gawping uniforms gathered around the desk. 'On his way.'

'Should we wait for him?'

'Probably,' Thorne said, and opened the door.

In the couple of seconds he spent marching across to the tape recorder on the far side of the room, he took it all in. The uniform in the corner, jumping slightly as Thorne slammed the door. The cold. Palmer, his white collar grubby, sitting at the brushed metal table, head bowed. The wad of bandage clumsily plastered to the top of his head, the blood dried brown.

Thorne picked up two fresh cassette tapes and began tearing roughly at the plastic packaging, his eyes never leaving the figure seated at the table.

Palmer was a big man, that was obvious, slumped and hunched over as he was. Wispy, sandy-coloured hair and metal-framed glasses. Murrell and Knight had done a good job. The picture was spot on.

'I'm Detective Inspector Thorne and I'm in no mood to piss about, is that all right with you?'

Palmer said nothing. He didn't even move.

Thorne slammed the tapes into the recorder, hit the red button and waited. Once the buzzing had stopped and the recording had begun, he cautioned his interviewee. He spoke the caution quickly, spitting out the words like pips from something gone sour. He told Palmer he was free to leave, that he was not under arrest, that he was entitled to free and independent legal advice. He said these things because he had to, without thinking about them, or caring a great deal. The only moment of hesitation came when he looked across at the uniformed statue in the corner, to ascertain his name for the tape.

The constable's eyes widened and he spoke his name as if he was confirming it from the dock.

Thorne stood opposite Palmer, his hands on the dull metal tabletop, staring hard. He was aware of Constable Stephen Legge in the corner, shifting his feet nervously. Good, Thorne thought. I'm scaring you, I must be scaring this fucker . . .

Palmer didn't look up.

'Now then, these two murders you're so courageously putting your hand up to. That's two murders out of four, if we're being accurate, isn't it? Four murders all told. There's another man, isn't there?'

Nothing. Thorne let a few seconds become thirty. Moved in that bit closer.

'Actually, we'd better make that five murders. You fucked up last night, fucked up or bottled out, doesn't matter which, but I'm bloody sure *he* didn't.' Slowly, asking it again, 'There's another man, isn't there?'

Palmer nodded. Sniffed. He was about to cry.

'Who is he?' Casual. Like asking the time. *Just give me a name* . . .

Thorne moved round the table, stood behind him. Only a cliché because it was true, because it worked. Leaning down, close enough to smell the sweat, to see the first, fat teardrop plop onto the fag-browned table edge.

'There's a woman's body . . . somewhere. At the moment, she's only missing. I'm not sure it's even been reported yet, but people are missing her. There's people somewhere who are starting to feel it in their guts about now, just *starting* to feel it. That flutter of worry, turning to concern and then eventually to panic. That's when it really starts to hurt, like a cramp that's squeezing the inside of them, making it hard to breathe. Crushing the pipes and valves, *there*, in the gut. All of them, all those people, friends and relatives, huddling together because they all feel the same, and all of them feeling like parts of them are starting to shut down bit by bit. To stop working. Feeling as bad as anyone could ever feel, ever . . .'

Palmer's head drooped slowly down until his cheek lay flush on the table. There were still tears, pooling beneath the side of his face, but no sound at all.

Thorne's voice got lower, quieter. 'But it isn't. It isn't as bad. It's nothing like. When their missing wife or daughter or mother becomes their *dead* wife or daughter or mother, that's when the real pain begins.

'Hearing the news, there's a hammer blow to the skull, and the blows don't stop coming. Identifying the body. Waiting while it's stared at and quantified and filleted. The funeral to arrange, the loose ends, the belongings to sort through. The clothes to bag up for Oxfam. To bundle up and bury your face in . . .

'The lives that have got to be carried on with, while the pain settles, inside and out. A scalding in the belly, a scab to be picked at. Rage and guilt. That's agony a long way beyond the physical, Martin.

'That's not better in the morning, or in a week's time or a month's. That's terminal . . .'

Everybody and everything perfectly still. The room, freezing but suddenly airless. Finally the question, on a slow, shallow breath.

'What's his name?'

Thorne actually flinched, as Palmer raised his head with surprising speed. His eyes were red-rimmed beneath the thick lenses, and desperate. His voice came from somewhere a long way away.

'I don't know.'

Thorne pushed himself away from the table with a roar and charged back across the room towards the door. He wanted two things, badly. He wanted to punch a hole in Palmer's fleshy face and he wanted Palmer to think that he was going to.

'You had your fucking chance . . .'

'No, *please*.' There was terror in the voice, and helplessness. Thorne stopped at the door and turned. 'You don't understand. We were at school together . . .'

Thorne shrugged, raised his palms, waiting. *And . . .* ?

Palmer turned his face slowly away from him. He cast his eyes back down to the wet tabletop. Down to his own indistinct reflection in the scarred and dirty metal.

'No . . . I don't know who he is. But I know who he was.'

PART TWO

FOR THE
CHILDREN

TEN

Detective Superintendent Trevor Jesmond smiled like he was sucking on a lemon.

'Let me see if I've got this straight. There's a double murderer sitting in the cells at Kentish Town right now, and you're suggesting that not only do we keep the fact that we've caught him to ourselves, but that we start filling the newspapers with stories of other murders that haven't even happened? Murders that we . . . make up?'

Jesmond raised an eyebrow and looked to the men on either side of him, Russell Brigstocke and Steve Norman.

The fourth man in the room rubbed at a mysterious white patch on the sleeve of his black leather jacket.

'In a nutshell . . . yes.'

Thorne was watching Brigstocke and Norman as well, looking for a reaction, trying to gauge just how much, how many, he was up against. He thought that Brigstocke looked non-committal, the slight shake of his head unreadable. Norman, the oily media merchant, just looked bored.

Thorne spoke again, thinking: I've beaten tougher opposition than this. 'We didn't *catch* him.'

Jesmond stared. 'I'm sorry?'

'We didn't catch Palmer. He wandered in off the street.'

Brigstocke leaned forward. 'Tom, splitting hairs isn't . . .'

'It makes a difference.'

The DCI leaned back again, the head movement loud and clear this time. *Don't go getting cocky and fucking up your chances, Tom. This whole idea sounds stupid enough as it is . . .*

It was two days since Palmer had walked a little unsteadily into a police station with a head wound, a revolver and a few dark secrets to whisper. The idea had lodged itself in Thorne's head from the moment Palmer had first spoken to him.

I don't know who he is . . .

The idea grew, rolled around his brain like a snowball being pushed around a field, making more noise as it gained weight, groaning, until it was massive and immovable, impossible to ignore.

Palmer had been like a man in a dream, terrified of waking up to the nightmare of an agonising reality.

He told Thorne all he knew. About the past and the messages and the terror, and *Jesus*, the excitement. He told him all he'd done. With his knife and his hands and the tears that had to be wiped away, so that he could see their faces properly as he killed them. Now, he wanted no more than to be punished for it. To be put somewhere secure. To be removed.

Thorne though, wanted much more and as soon as the plan had become fully formed in his mind, he had offered Palmer a way, surprising and simple, to make the waking up more bearable. To end the nightmare . . .

Palmer had agreed in principle to all of it.

Now, he sat waiting, as Thorne waited, for approval of what at the very least was an unorthodox move, and at the very worst, would end a career or two.

Jesmond shuffled his chair a little closer to the table, sat up straight. 'I have to tell you, I'm not convinced.'

You don't have to tell me anything, thought Thorne. It's written all over your pointless, pinched face. Spelt out in the red veins across your nose and cheeks . . .

Jesmond continued. 'Palmer is a multiple murderer, a serial killer if you want to be sensationalist about it . . .'

Norman nodded. 'Why not? It's what the press want.'

'Right. Now, we can give him to them. Now, we have a chance to ease what I assure you, Detective Inspector, is a great deal of pressure to get some results, and I must say I'm inclined to take it.'

Thorne tried to make it as clear-cut as he knew how. 'If we announce that we've got Palmer, we lose a far more dangerous killer.'

Jesmond flicked a finger across his thin lips, glanced down at the notes in front of him on the table. 'Stuart Anthony Nicklin. As was.'

Was . . .

Thorne nodded. 'Yes, sir.'

'"Far more dangerous" is a little bit over the top isn't it? Nastier, agreed, but he and Palmer have each killed twice, so . . .'

'That we know of, sir.'

Brigstocke nodded. 'I have to agree with DI Thorne, sir. Nicklin seems to be the more predatory of the two. Certainly the more violent.'

Thorne thinking, thank fuck, about time. 'Nicklin is the one that has arranged these killings. Without *him* the killings would stop. Without Palmer . . . I think he'll simply go to ground.'

There was a pause. Thorne looked over at Brigstocke but the DCI was looking at the table. Thorne shifted his gaze to the window. The sky was the colour of a long-dead fish. It was quietly drizzling.

It was Norman who spoke up. 'And that's . . . bad is it? Nicklin just disappearing?'

Thorne tried to sound informative, tried not to make Norman feel too stupid. 'He won't disappear for ever. He'll wait until he thinks it's safe, then start again. He'll do it differently. Maybe he'll move and start killing somewhere else.'

Norman nodded, but Thorne caught something in his look that told him he hadn't tried hard enough. Norman felt stupid . . .

Brigstocke took off his glasses, rubbed the bridge of his nose. Thorne had a sudden, disconcerting memory of seeing him do the same thing, right before he punched the front teeth out of a paedophile's mouth. 'I'm not sure the papers'll go for it, Tom. Knowingly running false murder stories could get them into deep shit with their readers later on. They'll only play along up to the point that their circulation gets hit.'

'Nicklin needs to think that Palmer's still out there killing for him. Can't we make the papers print what we want them to?'

Jesmond glanced at Norman. 'Steve?'

Norman looked across at Thorne. *Now who's asking stupid questions?* 'There's something in what DCI Brigstocke is saying. A balance would need to be struck. We'd have to let them feel that they were being altruistic, at the same time as offering them the big story if it works. If we get Nicklin.'

Thorne nodded. It sounded like a way forward.

Norman hadn't finished. 'There would of course be other, bigger problems. There could be . . . almost certainly *would* be, leaks from within the investigation, not to mention the odd, slightly unusual journalist with a strange compulsion to tell the truth.' He smiled at Thorne a little sadly, and shrugged.

'Perhaps I'm being a bit dim,' Jesmond said, flashing sharp incisors, 'but I'm still not quite sure why we don't just print the truth in the papers. About the failed attack on Ms Kaye I mean.'

Norman was nodding halfway through Jesmond's speech, and didn't stop. 'Right. "Twin killers strike again. One strikes out."'

'Or something of that sort,' Jesmond agreed. 'Might not reporting the failure frighten Nicklin a little? Prompt him to contact Palmer perhaps?'

All eyes on Thorne now. He seriously doubted that much would frighten Nicklin, but despite seeing some sense in what Jesmond was saying, he stuck to his guns. 'I'm convinced that the most dangerous thing would be to disrupt the pattern.'

Jesmond was stubborn as well. Stubborn, and with pips on his shoulder. 'He might know about it anyway. He might have watched Palmer mess it up. He might have seen him *fail* to kill Jacqueline Kaye. What then?'

'Obviously, we can't rule that out completely until the missing body turns up and we establish time of death, but the Lovell and Choi killings would indicate that isn't part of his pattern. I think Nicklin does his bit and then gets another jolt from sitting back later, and watching the reports of Palmer's killings on TV and in the papers. Sir.'

Jesmond shook his head, slowly. 'We must have other options. More conventional avenues of investigation. We have a description for a start and it certainly sounds as if a decent description is what got us Palmer in the first place.'

'You're right, sir,' Thorne said, thinking, *Yes, and who was that down to?* 'Unfortunately, the description Palmer has given us, based on the single meeting the two of them had in the brasserie, is hardly decent. Nicklin had a beard. For all we know he doesn't have it any more. All Palmer really has is an impression of this man, a description based on his memory of him, rather than on the way he looks now.' Thorne pictured the look of confusion on Palmer's face, as he'd tried, with very little success, to recall how the boy he used to know had looked that day he'd strolled up to his lunch table and turned his dull little world on its head. 'Palmer can describe the fifteen-year-old boy like he saw him yesterday, but he can't give us an accurate picture of the man who walked into that brasserie six months ago. We've got height and a rough idea of weight, clothes, colouring, but we don't have a face. We sat him down with the CCTV footage from Euston, but he couldn't pick Nicklin out.'

'Or *wouldn't*,' Jesmond said. 'We can't be certain he wants his friend caught as much as he says he does.'

Thorne shook his head. 'I am certain of that, sir.'

And yet . . .

There was *something* that Palmer was keeping hidden. He appeared to be co-operating fully, to be answering every question, but Thorne sensed there were secret places he was unwilling to go, pictures he was wary of painting too fully.

Thorne would keep digging. If they'd let him . . .

'What about these e-mails?' Jesmond opened a green folder and began pulling out copies of the messages Nicklin had sent to Palmer. The tech boys had printed them out from Palmer's home PC.

'They're untraceable,' Thorne said, emphatically. 'Anonymous servers. Accounts set up on stolen credit cards. He was very careful.'

Jesmond quickly re-read a couple of the mails, clenching his jaw at the most chilling – the ones that had issued Palmer with his instructions: the dates, venues and methods of the killings.

'Can't we just monitor his e-mails?' Jesmond asked. 'Have them forwarded on to one of our computers?'

Thorne leaned forward. 'We will be watching for any communication from Nicklin, of course, *and* using the description we've got, but I still don't think it's enough, sir. It's got to be all or nothing.' He pulled one piece of paper away from the others, slid it in front of Jesmond.

'Look at that one, it pre-dates the first killing by a few weeks.'

Jesmond picked it up, started to read.

```
Received: (qmail 27003 invoked by alias);
28 Jun 2001 11:35:29 -0000
Date: 28 Jun 2001 11:35:29 -0000
Message-ID:
<921065729.27000@coolmail.co.uk>
To: martpalmer@netmail.org.uk
Subject: THINKING OF SUMMER
```

From: Old Friend.
Martin. Any thoughts yet? I can see
you're thinking about it. You look miles
away sometimes and I know that you're
picturing it. Soon it will be a lot more
than a picture. I'm presuming (as I could
always presume with you) that you're on
board. I will give you details in the
fullness etc etc. Your face tells me that
you're remembering those summers. Think
about the summers to come ...

Jesmond looked up, and across at Thorne, his face giving nothing away. Stupid, or just *playing* stupid, Thorne was finding it hard to tell.

'He's watching him, sir. He says so. "I can see you", "you look miles away", "your face tells me". He's watching him.'

'It sounds like he *was* watching him, granted,' Jesmond said.

'I think he still is. He likes to be in control.'

Norman was keen to show that if his last question was a little . . . silly, it was a long way from typical. 'If he *is* watching, then what are we talking about? You've said yourself that we can't be sure he didn't see Palmer screw up with Jacqueline Kaye? He might also have watched him walk into that station on Monday. If he already knows we've got Palmer, Detective Inspector, what you're asking would be an enormous and potentially dangerous waste of time. Wouldn't it?'

It was the obvious question. The one Thorne had been most afraid of. He knew his response was hardly convincing, but it was the only one he had. 'It's a risk worth taking. It's why we need to do this quickly.' Jesmond stared down at the papers in front of him. Norman put away his pen. Thorne thought of something else. 'I'm not saying he watches Palmer all the time. He can't. He gave Palmer the impression that he had a full-time job . . .'

Jesmond started gathering up his notes, like he'd already made up his mind. 'Risk, you said. Risk is a very good word for it, Thorne. We take a murderer, a man who has killed at least two women, and just put him back on the street . . .'

Thorne sighed in frustration. 'That isn't what we'd be doing. I told you . . .'

'What would you call it, then?'

'Just leaving him . . . in vision. Not frightening Nicklin off. One way or another, when it's over, Palmer goes away.' Thorne looked back to Brigstocke, searching for backup and not getting it. He knew he couldn't rely on the DCI's support. Brigstocke was still smarting from Thorne going it alone two days earlier. Interviewing Palmer without waiting for him. The bollocking he'd dished out was still being talked about by anybody who'd been within half a mile of his office.

Back to Jesmond. 'Organised Crime do this sort of thing all the time, sir,' Thorne said. 'When they need a witness on the inside. I don't see why we can't do the same. We release Palmer on police bail, pending further enquiries. It's a common enough procedure . . .'

It was probably as close as Jesmond came to losing his temper. 'I'm perfectly aware of the procedure, Thorne, but Palmer is not a fucking loan shark. He's killed two women, and we don't normally go around releasing murderers on police bail.'

There was little Thorne could say and Jesmond quickly relaxed. The advantage was his. He took out a handkerchief and pushed one corner up a nostril, digging around, his face contorting with the effort. 'So, hypothetically, Palmer's walking about, we're watching him. Then what? Nicklin makes a silly mistake? He hasn't made too many so far has he? So, we wait for him to kill again?' Thorne said nothing. He knew it might come down to just that. 'I'm not sure you've thought this through, Inspector.'

'With respect, sir . . .' The volume rising now. Precious little respect anywhere.

Brigstocke leaned across the table. 'Listen, Tom . . .'

Thorne narrowed his eyes and opened his mouth far too quickly. 'That fence you're sitting on must be playing havoc with your arse, Russell.'

Jesmond raised a palm but Thorne carried on. He looked at each of them as he spoke, knowing he only had the one chance, if that. 'Yes, Palmer is a killer, a fucking freak, and when this is all over, whatever we decide to do, he's going away for the rest of his life. He *wants* to go away, he's not angling for anything, he's not trying to make a deal.' He stopped, took a breath, carried on. 'I firmly believe, however, that if this investigation continues *along the lines I have suggested*, he will not be a danger to anybody . . .'

Jesmond was ready to come in. Thorne didn't let him. 'I think this is our only chance to get Nicklin and if we don't take it, we'll regret it down the road. Now, as things stand, with a killer in custody, we all get patted on the back or promoted or whatever. Later there'll be blood.'

He stared at Jesmond. *Why the fuck should you care? You'll probably be long gone by then.* He had drawn the line at talking about 'taking full responsibility' but something in Jesmond's small, ratty eyes told Thorne that it would be a given; that should it prove necessary, the grip he was barely maintaining on his career would be loosened by a few strategically placed boots on fingers. Something else told him that it was all academic anyway. They weren't going to go for this in a million years . . .

Thorne stood up. 'I've said my piece I think, sir.'

Jesmond looked to his colleagues, straightening his papers like a newsreader for want of anything better to do. 'Thank you, Inspector. Obviously, this needs discussing and not just by us. I've got a conference call with the Deputy Assistant Commissioner arranged and he may want to take it even higher. So . . .'

So . . . Thorne sat in the office next door, fighting a childish urge to put a glass against the wall, and cursing the tiny strand of DNA somewhere within him that made him do . . . these things. Made him incapable of settling for anything.

He had never been one for war stories. He could prop up a bar with the best of them and swap tales, but when stories of who put who away were told, he would smile, slap backs and retreat inside himself to where he could silently revisit failure. Success did not occupy him a great deal, but failure was always around, waiting to be given the nod.

He was English, after all.

It wasn't the ones he caught that Thorne remembered. That he *always* remembered. It wasn't the ones he finally got to see in an interview room or through the peephole of a holding cell, or across a courtroom. It wasn't them.

It wasn't the Palmers.

Thorne had forgotten the faces of a dozen convicted killers down the years, but he still saw, clearly, those killers for whom he never had a face at all. He would do whatever was necessary to prevent Stuart Anthony Nicklin *as was*, taking his place in that particular gallery.

Bloody-minded, stubborn and pig-headed were easy words to use. Guilty on all three counts. Yes, yes and yes again. But they were not the *right* words.

It would have been so easy to accept the plaudits and take what had been handed to him on a plate. Easy to look at a picture of Martin Palmer on the front page, to prop up that bar for a night or two. Easy to pose with the victims' relatives, to shake hands and look into grateful faces, then turn away, ready to go to work again, to begin the next hunt.

Easy to crack on, smug and satisfied.

So hard to dismiss a small boy with a squeaky hammer. *Can* you *forget his face, Charlie? I hope so . . .*

Now Holland and McEvoy were moving across the incident room towards the open doorway of his office. He watched them getting closer, taking an age to get to him, wondering at the expressions on their faces, tight and dark, the piece of paper in Holland's hand, the fist clenched at the end of McEvoy's arm. Then they were in his office and the sheet of paper was on his desk, and he was trying to take in what it said and McEvoy was talking.

'The body of Miriam Vincent was found this morning in her flat on Laurel Street in Dalston. She's been dead a couple of days. Shot in the head.' McEvoy's tone had been professional, calm and informative. Now, in a reddening rush, she let the anger come through. 'She was a student at

North London University. She was nineteen for christ's sake . . . a fucking teenager . . .'

Holland looked at her, alarmed at the sudden display of emotion. Thorne took it, used it, let her anger clear his head. Where a few moments before he had felt woozy and disorientated, now he was suddenly bright and focused. He knew exactly what to do.

'I haven't seen this.'

McEvoy cocked her head. 'Sorry . . . ?'

'You couldn't find me. Clear?' He handed the piece of paper to Holland, pointed towards the office next door. 'Go and tell *them*.'

Holland hesitated for a second and McEvoy snatched the paper from him. 'I'll do it . . .'

Thorne held out his hand. 'No you won't, you're too . . . charged up. They've already had me.'

McEvoy handed back the piece of paper, grunted and turned away. Thorne passed it on to Holland, caught his arm, squeezed. 'Calm . . .'

Holland nodded and quickly marched out. Without looking back he walked straight up to the door of the adjoining office, knocked and went in without waiting to be asked.

McEvoy went back to the incident room and while he waited, Thorne watched her, moving among her fellow officers, fired up about Miriam Vincent's murder, blazing with the knowledge of it. He liked her anger. He understood it. He worried that lately, she seemed a little less able to control it.

McEvoy and Holland were the only people, aside from the three next door, who knew what he was proposing to do. The rest of those working on the case were still flushed with the success of the Palmer arrest. There was suddenly a lot more laughter around the building, and those not laughing were only nursing the hangovers that came from too much celebration. He knew that if his idea was to stand any chance of working, the celebration would need to stop. The lid needed to come down hard and stay on tight.

Thorne suddenly saw how unutterably stupid he was being. Stupid to think that the powers-that-be would agree to releasing Palmer and stupid for wanting them to. He started to feel relieved, light and free of it, anticipating their polite but firm refusal.

He knew that what he was planning would have gone down like a cup of cold sick anyway, for all sorts of reasons, not least the time of year. He wondered whether he owed his colleagues a chance to wind down a little, to level out, to have a life with their families.

It only took a second or two to remember that there were others, dead and alive, to whom he owed a lot more.

Those that would pull faces if Thorne got his way, those that would mutter in corners and ignore him in the pub after work, had not met Carol Garner's mother and father. They had not met her son. Perhaps he should invite what was left of that family down for the day, show Charlie around the station and sit every single officer, every member of the civilian staff, down with them for fifteen fucking minutes.

He wondered whether Carol had bought Christmas presents for Charlie before it happened. Would her mum and dad give them to him, and would they tell him who they were from . . . ?

Thorne heard a door open and looked up to see

Brigstocke emerge from the office next door, eyes scanning the incident room, looking for him.

'Russell . . .'

Brigstocke turned to look at him. When their eyes met, it was clear to Thorne that his earlier comments, which he had meant but now regretted, had neither been forgotten, nor forgiven. They would need to talk.

Suddenly, Thorne wanted it more than anything. Wanted the go-ahead. In those last few seconds, while he waited for some sign from Brigstocke, he wanted the chance to stop Stuart Nicklin, to be rid of him, and bollocks to careers, and pissing people off and celebrating a job only half done. Less than half done . . .

Brigstocke closed his eyes and nodded. All right.

Thorne acknowledged the nod with his eyes, then spoke the words quietly, but out loud.

'Oh, fuck.'

ELEVEN

The man who used to be called Stuart Nicklin was not a big fan of Christmas shopping, but these things had to be done. He'd nipped out at lunchtime and was pretty pleased with the progress so far. He wouldn't be able to face the coming weekend, the last before the big day, the crowds of zombies milling around. Everyone pretending they were happy about handing out cash for disposable shit and shiny paper. His wife would brave the crush of course, but then she had that many more things to buy. For parents and friends, people at work. *His* colleagues never really bothered. Christmas was a time to forget about work for a while . . .

He carried his coffee to a table by the window and dropped his bags down beside the seat. She would like the necklace, he was certain, and the smelly stuff, but the sweater was a bit risky. He'd got the receipt: she could always take it back. They usually spent the morning of the twenty-seventh, or twenty-eighth, queuing up with dozens of others at the M&S exchange counter, everyone silently seething, horrified at what they'd become.

This was a time of day he looked forward to immensely.

Normally he'd retire to his room about now, and maybe he'd get half an hour of peace with the papers. A chance to go through each story, each version, update or piece of breaking news. He watched the television as well, of course. He was a slave to Teletext in the days after one of his adventures, but there was nothing like getting it fresh. Seeing it laid out on the page in front of him. Feeling it on his fingertips for the rest of the day. He always bought two papers. A tabloid and a broadsheet. Needing both breadth and brevity, the detail *and* the distaste.

He'd been waiting four days now for the latest . . . coverage. The stories would always appear eventually, cheek by jowl with political analysis in the broadsheet, or jammed up against some piece of pouting, top-heavy jailbait in the Red Top. He fucking loved it all. The anticipation, as in the act itself, growing keener, almost unbearable as each day without news of what they had done, passed.

Now, the waiting was over. Today was the day, and he was really looking forward to what they had to say this time. This time it was going to be very interesting.

He took a sip of his overpriced cappuccino and reached down for the two newspapers in the purple WH Smith carrier bag. An *Independent* and a *Mirror* today. An old woman sitting opposite tore a chunk away from a pastry with her teeth and grinned at him. He smiled back as he unfolded the *Independent* . . .

There it was. There they were.

He looked at his watch. He didn't have to be back for at least a quarter of an hour. Fifteen blissful minutes in which to switch off, enjoy his coffee and immerse himself in the coverage of two brutal murders. One of which he had first-hand knowledge, of course. One was so real, was so fresh

in his memory, that he could still smell the girl's vomit.
Acrid and boozy. She'd puked the second he'd raised the
gun. Opened her mouth as if to scream and heaved
instead. He'd had to step back smartish to save his shoes,
then stretch to step over the stuff, and put the gun to her
head.

The other one, Palmer's murder . . . well, that was one
the silly bastards had gone and made up.

The detail was good, it sounded convincing enough,
but they had wasted their time. Palmer was motivated by
fear, pure and simple, always had been. He was scared
enough of Nicklin to kill in the first place, but what he was
really scared of was letting him down. Fucking up would be
the only thing that could possibly have scared Martin
enough to turn himself in. After Nicklin had shot the girl in
her flat, he'd watched Palmer all the next day. He'd seen
him come out of his flat like a man in a dream and followed
him all the way to the station. Watched him totter inside
like a drunk, failure as visible about him as the stained
bandage on his fat head.

So, now they didn't want him to know that they had
Palmer in custody. Too late. The real question of course,
was just how to respond . . .

He'd think about it more later, while he was supposed to
be working. Now he had ten minutes left to read all about
the two murders.

One true, one false . . .

He wondered which one he was going to enjoy reading
about more.

Thorne watched the rest of the world moving round him,
overwound, frenetic, going about its business. He saw

people, running around like blue-arsed flies, buying presents they didn't want to give, heaving bags crammed with food they wouldn't eat. Unable to stop themselves. Caught up in it. Peace, goodwill and socks to all men . . .

He saw some absurdly happy.

He saw those that hated it, battening down the hatches.

He saw a set of shell-shocked parents organising their daughter's funeral.

While all this was going on, Tom Thorne spent the last few days before Christmas working at his own speed. Slowly but very surely pissing off virtually everyone who knew him.

To most coppers 'overtime' was a magic word, right up there, and in some cases well above, 'conviction'.

But not at Christmas.

Coppers got a bit huffy come Christmas. Self-righteous and sentimental, and salt-of-the-earth indignant. Jesus . . . (not used in any religious sense of course) . . . didn't they deserve a break, them and their families, after the shit they waded through for the other fifty-one weeks of the year? To Thorne, it was a moot point. He didn't get overtime anyway. DIs and above had been bought out with a few grand extra on the annual salary. It was cases like this one that made it obvious how much they'd been shafted. As it was, despite gripes of his own, Thorne didn't blame anybody for feeling tired, for needing a rest from it, but there was one major stumbling block . . .

Killers didn't stop for Christmas.

Suicide was the well-known one of course, but it wasn't the only pastime which became popular once the novelty singles began clogging up the charts. Crime figures tended to go up across the board during the seasonal period and murder was no exception. Domestics, incidents involving alcohol – all increasing, all leaving victims and the relatives of victims, demanding action. None of them giving a toss if your parents were coming down from the North, or if you'd put a reservation on a cottage in the Cotswolds, or if it was your kid's first Christmas.

Especially if their own kid was not going to see another one.

Easy to think like that of course, when you were the one cancelling the holidays. No meticulously worked-out rota, no amount of overtime, was going to make the majority of officers on this case think any differently of Tom Thorne. Not Brigstocke. Not McEvoy. He wasn't even sure about Dave Holland. The simple fact was that, thanks to him, they would all be spending Christmas babysitting a double murderer.

Palmer would not be going back to work until the New Year now, but Sean Bracher had been well briefed, so that there would be no problem when he did. Palmer's absence just before Christmas would be put down to illness, and the issue of his resemblance to the man police were seeking would not be ducked. He had come forward and been immediately eliminated from enquiries. End of story. Bracher would assist in disseminating this information as well as smoothing the passage for the new Baynham & Smout employee who would be working very closely with Martin Palmer. One unhappy DC, seconded from SCG (South), would be spending *her* Christmas ploughing through *Accountancy For Idiots* . . .

Palmer's domestic situation would be easy to monitor. He lived on the second floor of a fifties mansion block in West Hampstead. There was one entrance. He would be followed to and from work, with permanent surveillance maintained outside his flat and at least one plain-clothes officer inside at all times, though at *no* time would Palmer be accompanied as he entered the building.

According to Palmer, he seldom went out anyway and had *never* invited anybody to his flat, so comings and goings shouldn't be a problem. Thorne was keen that Palmer's movements appeared normal and so, to a degree, this side of things would be played by ear. If he was asked out for a drink (which he had told them *had* happened, but not often), they'd decide at the time whether to cry off or not. Similarly, at work, he'd be accompanied to lunch by the undercover DC, with a backup team on hand should this start to become suspicious in itself. In fact, the only break from any kind of routine involved Palmer ringing his parents to tell them that he couldn't make it home for Christmas Day. This was also the only part of the whole complex arrangement that Palmer seemed remotely uncomfortable with.

Thorne wanted everything tied down tight. No mistakes. The man he was after was clever. He would, Thorne felt certain, be watching at least some of the time. He might well of course have seen enough already to tell him that Palmer was in custody. Stable doors and horses . . .

As Thorne had told Jesmond, it was a risk he felt they had to take.

There were certainly plenty of risks . . .

Norman had spotted a couple of them straight away. He himself would handle the media, but the team had not responded well to the lecture Thorne had delivered, that he felt *needed* to be delivered, on leaking ships. He'd wanted Brigstocke to do the honours, but the DCI was still in no

mood to do Thorne any favours. In terms of the bad feeling coming his way, the atmosphere that followed his
speech was pretty much the icing on the cake, but Thorne
knew that it was necessary. Besides, normally he only alienated the top brass. Now he was getting on *everybody's* tits.
At least this was a change . . .

Thorne wanted this to go right. He wanted nothing in
the public domain, *nothing*, unless it could have come from
a source other than Martin Palmer. They could, for exam-
ple, go with Palmer's description of Nicklin – they could
always invent a witness who might have come up with
that – but any avenue of investigation that could only have
originated with Palmer needed to be walked with the
utmost care and discretion.

Thorne could handle the black looks, the comments
subtle and otherwise, but the only real moment of doubt
had come at the press conference on the Saturday, less
than forty-eight hours after Miriam Vincent's body had
been discovered.

It was the *lies*, naked in the light from a hundred flash
guns and boldly sharing the stage with Miriam Vincent's
grief-stricken mother, that were hard to bear. Someone, it
might have been Steve Norman, had actually suggested
that they hire actors to play the parents of Palmer's fictitious victim. Thorne was glad he'd drawn a line and said
no to that one. This was bad enough . . .

Norman had led out an impressive looking party, consisting of Jesmond, Brigstocke, a young DC acting as
Family Liaison, and Mrs Vincent. After the predictable
rhetoric from Jesmond, Norman introduced Rosemary
Vincent. She was in her early fifties, tall and slightly awkward, with a face that had probably been open and easy to

read until two days ago, when it had become the mirror of emotions that were alien to it.

The scalding in the belly, the scab to be picked at. Rage and guilt . . .

She spoke movingly of her only daughter, clutching Miriam's picture and trying not to break down as she remembered their last conversation – a row about her not coming home. Thorne stood at the back of the room, behind the journalists, away from the cameras, unable to take his eyes off this woman. He had seen people in the same situation a hundred times, but rarely had he seen the freshly dead part of them so clearly. It was there in every nervous smile, every pull at the hair and quiver of the lip. He winced when she spoke about the grief that the parents of the other victim must be feeling. He felt the shame, like a cold hand at his throat, when she sent them her love and support, when she sympathised with their pain; an agony so crippling that they hadn't felt able to come along themselves . . .

Thorne had made a promise to himself then that, whatever happened, when it was all over he would visit Rosemary Vincent and tell her the truth, and explain why he had done what he had done.

That night, he watched the highlights of the press conference on half a dozen different channels and felt the fingers at his throat every time.

He was just about ready for bed when the phone rang.

'Yeah . . .'

'Tom? Is that Tom?'

'Who's this?'

'This is Eileen, love. Your dad's sister.'

'Oh . . .'

'Sorry if it's a bit late, but we were watching a film. You know, waiting for it to finish.'

'It's fine . . .' Thorne had actually been carrying a half-empty wine bottle and dirty glass back to the kitchen when the phone went. Now, he sat down on the sofa, stuck the bottle between his knees and yanked out the cork again.

'So how are you, love?' She spoke as if he was ill, or a little slow.

Thorne was about to fill his glass when he decided that, actually, he was in no mood to have this conversation. He knew what she wanted and he couldn't be arsed waiting for her to say it. Christ, how long had it been since he'd seen this woman? It was certainly before Jan had left. A funeral, but he couldn't remember whose. Maybe one of Eileen's husband's parents . . .

'Listen, Auntie Eileen—'

'I was sorry to hear about you and your wife . . .'

So Thorne poured the wine and made the tedious small talk, and waited for her to get to the point; to say what she'd obviously called to say. He'd warned his dad against ringing her, silly old bastard. Now it was going to be embarrassing. He started prompting her, getting tetchier, waiting to hear that she was ever so sorry but she *really* couldn't have Jim at Christmas. She had a houseful after all, and there wasn't the room to put him up and maybe if he'd given her a bit more notice . . .

Stuff you, Thorne thought. We'll be fine, the two of us . . .

'So we've talked about it and decided that your dad's coming to us this year.'

Thorne held the wine glass halfway between his knee

and his mouth. He knew he'd heard correctly, but couldn't think of anything to say. 'Sorry? But . . .'

'If you drop him at Victoria, we'll pick him up at the other end.'

Thorne felt himself starting to redden a little. 'Listen, maybe I'd better have a word with dad . . .'

'Don't worry, it's all been organised, love.'

'But you'll have a houseful. You haven't got the room . . .'

'We'll be fine. Look, we'd love to have him and I dare say it'll be a bit of a break for you.'

Then five minutes more of this and that, until Thorne heard the call-waiting signal on the line and dropped a hint. Auntie Eileen took it, announcing that now it *was* past her bedtime and telling Thorne how lovely it would be to see *him* sometime, too . . .

Thorne had told Phil Hendricks the whole thing before he'd really had a chance to decide how he felt about it. It was probably rash of Hendricks to make the invitation and Thorne couldn't decide whether it was stupidity or desperation that made him accept, but either way, two days later, here he was . . .

Christmas Eve. Playing gooseberry. Sitting in a pub and not listening.

'Tom? For fuck's sake . . .'

Thorne felt as if he were emerging at speed from a long, long tunnel. Gold, silver and red coming into focus. Cheap decorations, catching the light, dangling from fake wooden beams. He blinked. 'Sorry Phil. Is it my round, mate?'

Hendricks stared at him. 'Hello! Brendan's up there, getting them in. You haven't heard a word, have you?'

Thorne downed the last of his pint. 'Yes, I have.'

'So? What d'you reckon?'

Thorne puffed out his cheeks, just needing a second or two. He began to recall bits of a one-sided conversation. Brendan and Phil were an item again. Yes, that was it. Hendricks wanted to know whether taking Mr Didn't-Turn-Out-To-Be-A-Bastard-After-All back was a good idea.

'What's definitely *not* a good idea,' Thorne said finally, 'is having me dossing on your sofa like a spare prick at a wedding.'

Hendricks sighed. 'Look, we've been through this. It's not a big deal.'

Thorne looked around. The place was packed. It was hard to make themselves heard over the hubbub and the loud Christmas music. Slade, Wizzard, Mud. Utterly predictable and hugely reassuring. He glanced towards the bar where Brendan was handing over money for the drinks. 'Have you asked him?'

'It's fuck all to do with him. I'm not daft anyway – I know he's only back because he can't face being at home. His mum and dad don't know he's gay and he's got nowhere else to go . . .'

'None of us is exactly spoilt for choice.'

'Don't go on about it, all right? You're staying. It's either you for Christmas or some old tramp from outside the soup kitchen.'

Thorne grinned. 'Wouldn't the smell bother you?'

Hendricks gleefully supplied the punchline. 'I'm sure you can clean yourself up.'

They were still laughing as Brendan arrived with the drinks, but as soon as he put the glasses down on the table,

Thorne was out of his seat and pulling on his jacket.

'Listen, I'm going to get out of your way . . .'

Brendan held up Thorne's new pint. He looked pissed off and was about to say something, but Hendricks put a hand on his arm to stop him. He knew there was little point in arguing.

'See you later, yeah?'

Thorne said nothing. He squeezed round the table, put a hand on Brendan's shoulder. 'I'm sorry about the beer . . .'

'Tomorrow for lunch, then?' Hendricks asked.

Thorne nodded, but knew instantly that his friend could tell he didn't mean it. He took the hand from Brendan's shoulder and held it out towards Hendricks. 'Have a good one, Phil.'

Hendricks stood, took the hand and pulled Thorne into a slightly awkward hug.

'You too. Now, fuck off . . .'

So, Thorne did.

TWELVE

A DC answered the door and Thorne held up his warrant card. If the officer, who was ginger, pudgy and only an inch or so above minimum height, could smell the beer on Thorne's breath, his face wasn't letting it show. It showed only the same blank truculence that Thorne had seen on the faces of the two muppets in the car outside.

Parents coming . . . the cottage . . . the kid's first Christmas . . .

'I'll not be long.' Thorne nodded back over his shoulder towards the chair in the hallway. The officer stepped outside and sat down, muttering and disgruntled. Thorne shut the front door behind him. He probably *had* smelt the booze. It didn't matter.

Thorne noticed a copy of the *Sun* on the table just inside the door. He opened the door and offered it to the constable who took it with a grunt. *Fuck you*, Thorne thought, pulling the door shut again.

He turned and walked through into the living room. Palmer stepped out of the kitchen carrying a mug of tea. He had evidently not heard the knock on the door and started slightly when he saw Thorne.

They looked at one another for a few seconds. Then Palmer spoke, his voice deep and slightly nasal. 'Has something . . . ?' Thorne shook his head.

Palmer held up his mug, the steam fogging his glasses for a second or two. 'Can I get you one?'

Thorne said nothing, walked across to where the computer sat on a small desk near the window. It was logged on to a server twenty-four hours a day. The second Nicklin got in touch, they'd know about it.

Thorne stared at the screensaver – a series of multi-coloured clocks which swam about, bouncing all over the screen, buzzing and ticking, chiming on the hour. He leaned forwards and moved the mouse so that the clocks disappeared. He pulled the chair away from the desk, turned it round so that it faced into the room and sat down.

He hadn't taken his jacket off.

'What d'you do? Surf the Net? Chat? Play Scrabble on it?'

Palmer sat straight-backed on the sofa. He held his mug of tea in two hands against his chest. 'Yes. The Net. Sometimes.'

'And . . . ?'

'Well, with a police officer in constant attendance, I'm hardly likely to spend the hours of darkness trawling through porn sites, am I?'

'But if you were on your own?' Thorne asked, quickly.

Palmer stared down into his tea. 'I see. What would a filthy degenerate seek out? Well, I'd be looking for something perverse, almost certainly. You know, sick.' He looked up and across at Thorne. His head was tipped slightly back, his nose wrinkling slightly to stop his glasses sliding off. 'Bodies perhaps. Autopsy photographs, they're out there if you know where to look.' He started to talk faster, his voice getting louder, his breathing harsh and faintly wheezy; the best impression he could do, he could *give*, of excitement. 'Perhaps even a video or two, with sound if at all possible to pick up the noise . . . the howl of the buzz saw. You know the sort of thing, danger and dissection, the usual saucy mix for the pathetic, the sexually dysfunctional—'

'Stop.'

Palmer had. Thorne silently admonished himself. He should never have got into this. At best, it was prurient. At worst, it smacked of the kind of cheap psychology that was also to be found on the bits of paper which would spill from crackers round lunch tables the following day. He glanced across at Palmer who clutched his tea and stared straight ahead. Thorne couldn't quite read the expression. Sad? No, disappointed.

The screensaver had kicked in again, and the growing silence was now broken only by a series of distant, electronic ticks.

'I might go out tomorrow,' Palmer said suddenly. He turned to look at Thorne, his upper body leaning forward, his face now keen and animated. 'Just for a walk, get a bit of air. Going a bit bonkers in here . . .'

Thorne snorted. Palmer started to nod thoughtfully even though it was strangely comic. 'I know, I'd better get used to it. Won't be many creature comforts when all this is over. Actually . . .'

He stood up quickly. Reflexively. Thorne did the same. Palmer looked over at him, nervous. 'I've got some cans of beer in the kitchen.' He took a step forwards, then stopped. 'Have one. You could have one.'

Thorne nodded without thinking and Palmer was away towards the kitchen. 'It's bitter, I think. Is that all right?' Thorne said nothing, sat back down again.

He looked around the room. As usual, there was nothing out of place. The layout was simple, the furnishings modern and functional. The first time Thorne had walked into the place, he'd been reminded of somewhere, and then after a few minutes had shivered slightly as he'd realised that the flat was like his own. A few more books and plants maybe, an absence of family photos or souvenirs. Little evidence of a life lived with much enthusiasm. There was nothing homely . . .

Through the open kitchen door, Thorne could see Palmer moving around, hear him getting glasses from a cupboard and rinsing them out. He was a big man; a man that lumbered and loomed and yet he was oddly graceful. Considering his height and weight, he had very small hands and feet, and looked on occasion as if he must surely tumble forwards on to his pale, fleshy face.

These were observations Thorne had made in the beginning when they'd spent many hours going over it all. Getting the story. Then they'd spent days and days planning, working out how they could make it work; giving Palmer a last taste of freedom so that Nicklin might . . . *might* show his hand. All those hours in overheated interview rooms and yet they had never talked, not really.

Thorne thought about this now, as he sat in Palmer's living room, not with any sense of regret – he had no desire to get to know this man – it was just interesting, that was all, considering where they were.

And still he had that lingering sense that Palmer was holding something back. Saving something up . . .

Palmer returned with two glasses of beer, an odd look of pride on his face, as if he were delivering the heads of a pair of conquered enemies. Thorne took the glass that was offered and placed it on the floor by the side of his chair. Palmer stayed standing, staring out of the window and nodding slightly. He smiled. 'Quite lucky, actually. All these police officers everywhere, especially the one outside the door . . . at least I haven't been bothered by carol singers.'

Thorne stared up at him. Palmer was wearing baggy grey tracksuit bottoms, blue moccasin-style slippers and an orange hooded top. The clothes looked cheap, not a natural fibre anywhere. And not for the first time, Thorne wondered what Palmer spent his money on. He had a good job, but his car wasn't flashy and there were no signs of extravagance.

'Where does all the money go?'

Palmer moved across to the sofa and sat down. He looked across at Thorne, squinting at him, as if trying to grasp every nuance of meaning in the question.

Thorne tried again. 'What do you spend money on?'

Palmer shook his head, shrugged. 'I save it.'

'Holidays?'

'I save it. It's all in the building society. I send some home occasionally, well I *did*, but my parents don't like taking it, so now I just buy them things. You know, when they need them. I bought them a new boiler a couple of months ago.' He nodded again, a series of small nods, like he gave all the time. As if he was agreeing with himself, trying to confirm something.

Thorne thought again about that first meeting, when he had spoken and shouted about a disease called bereavement and Palmer had first spoken about Nicklin. Later, he'd been taken to have his head wound stitched – Jacqui

Kaye had done a fair amount of damage with that shoe –
and when he'd returned he'd talked more, and with more
ease, about Nicklin – the meeting in the brasserie, the pro-
posal, the instructions for the killings. Early on in that
conversation, when they were talking about how he and
Nicklin had first met, Palmer had mentioned a name.
Twice, perhaps three times, a girl's name had bobbed into
view. She, or at the very least, her name, had appeared
briefly, like a shape dredged up; something which you
could almost place, appearing just below the surface of
water before disappearing back into the depths. Now, that
name floated to the surface of Thorne's swampy con-
sciousness.

'Tell me about Karen.'

Palmer took a drink. He held the beer in his mouth for
a few seconds before swallowing it down. 'Karen died.'
More nodding. Thorne waited. 'She got into a car and
died. On a sunny day, she climbed into a blue Vauxhall
Cavalier – it was on the news, you can probably get the
video. That was it. She was fourteen.' He downed nearly all
that was left of his beer in three enormous gulps, put the
almost empty glass carefully down on the floor and then
looked up at Thorne. 'A blue Vauxhall Cavalier. Driven by
a murderer. Like me.'

There was only one way Thorne could fill the pause
that followed. He'd spoken the words aloud on a hundred
different occasions. He'd felt the same sour taste of loss
and longing then, hanging in the air, tart on his tongue.

'I'm sorry.'

Instinctively, he meant it. Then another instinct every
bit as strong swept over him and he felt the need to qualify
what he'd said.

'Not for you. For *her*, for her family. Not for you, Palmer.'

Then silence, and a nod or two, and the ticks and beeps from the swarm of animated clocks seemed suddenly much louder, filling the space between them.

Thorne jumped a little at the chorus of computerised chimes and turned to look at the screen. He glanced down at his watch. Midnight. Christmas day. When he looked back round, Palmer had shuffled forward to the very edge of the sofa. He was smiling awkwardly at him, holding his all but empty glass, just half a mouthful of beer in the bottom.

'Merry Christmas, Detective Inspector Thorne.'

Thorne stood up quickly, feeling as if he was going to be sick. The moment passed but he strode quickly across the room towards the door, belching the taste of vomit into his mouth and then swallowing it away again.

He opened the front door. The officer outside put down his newspaper and stood up. Thorne hovered for a second in the doorway, feeling a little woozy despite his untouched glass of beer. Behind him, in the living room, he heard the sofa creak and was aware of Palmer standing up.

'What did you come for?' Palmer asked.

Thorne beckoned the constable back inside. He leaned forward to take in a gulp of air from the hallway outside before stepping into it.

'Fuck knows . . .'

Palmer pressed his face against the window. Below him, Thorne emerged through the set of double doors and stood on the grass outside, breathing deeply.

He took a mouthful of beer from Thorne's glass and then another. As he drank it down, his enormous Adam's apple bobbed up and down and a little beer dribbled down his chin, and he closed his eyes to prevent the tears that were pricking at the corner of his eyes from forming.

When he opened his eyes and looked down again, Thorne had gone.

He'd always cried easily, even before he'd met Stuart Nicklin. Crying and blushing – he'd had little control over either of them for as long as he could remember. He recalled Stuart dancing around him in the playground, singing, chocolate smeared around his mouth.

Cherry ripe, cherry ripe . . .

And him, moving slowly towards the wall behind him, driven backwards by the heat coming off his own face, growing redder and redder . . .

He recalled the voice of an older Stuart, six months ago, that lunchtime in the brasserie; after those two from work had skulked away and Stuart had spoken to him, and it had all begun again. The voice deeper now, and weathered, but still that laugh in it, the laugh that made you want to be near him, and still that ice inside the laugh.

'Do you ever think about Karen? I never told them you know, Mart. Not everything I mean. There was no need was there? It wasn't your fault, what happened. Her going off with that bloke was nothing to do with that other business. The business with you.' He'd stopped then and leaned in close, his face creased with concern. 'Do you think it was your fault? Course it wasn't. Yes, she was upset, but that doesn't mean anything, does it? Mind you, I wonder what people would think, now, if they *did* know? Do you think they'd blame you? You know what it's like these days, everybody going on about sex and protecting the kids. People getting hounded . . .'

Palmer had tried not to let the terror show on his face as Nicklin finished speaking, but he knew he'd failed miserably.

'I'm not saying I'd ever tell anybody Martin, but you know, some people have got fucking sick minds . . .'

Sally from Glasgow: 'We only do it for the children anyway, don't we?'

Arthur from Newcastle: 'Why shouldn't it be commercial? Shopping means a damn sight more to a lot of these kids than Jesus Christ . . .'

Bridget from Slough: 'How can we celebrate anything with the world the way it is? People starving. Drug addicts. Folk living on the streets. What about the families of those two poor women shot dead a couple of weeks ago? What sort of Christmas are they going to have?'

The man who used to be called Stuart Nicklin stuck a small gold bow on to the final parcel, leaned across and turned the radio up. This was a bit more like it. Bridget, up there on her high horse, had every right to be angry of course: it was a very nasty business. Even if one of the so-called 'poor women' was completely fictitious.

Bob, the phone-in host, agreed with the caller. Absolutely. He said a big thank-you for the call, but he was keen to move on to Alan from Leeds who wanted to talk about the shocking increase in the cost of first-class post . . .

He turned the radio off, stood up and rubbed away the cramp in his legs from squatting on his heels the last half an hour, busy with Sellotape and scissors. This had become something of a tradition – Caroline in bed nice and early, and him up late, wrapping presents.

Just a few more hours now until it all kicked off. They'd have a houseful tomorrow: Caroline's parents, her sister, her sister's three kids running around like maniacs.

Maybe, this time next year, they'd have one of their own. Not if he could possibly avoid it of course, he was doing his best to duck the issue, but Caroline was bringing it up all the time. Not now though. Not yet. He had a great deal he wanted to do before he went down *that* road. When he saw himself as an observer might, when he imagined himself in his mind's eye, he was standing, straight and tall over a body, the blood fizzing through him, the light breaking over him like clouds across the wings of a powerful jet. He was cutting through life, slicing through it, capable of anything. He was mercurial. He would not be . . . lumpen. He would not potter around, hunched over a baby-buggy with milky sick on his lapel. Fucked. That was not him.

He carried his wife's presents across to the tree and slid them underneath. He straightened up, leaned forward and studied his dim, distorted reflection in a large silver bauble. He still got a shock seeing himself without the beard. He'd been a little worried shaving it off, but he needn't have been. The dramatically different hairline, the filled out cheeks and the nose-job he'd saved up for all those years ago, still gave him a face significantly different from the one he might be expected to have sixteen years on.

As it was, he could probably have kept the beard anyway. The pictures he'd seen in the papers and on TV had been so wide of the mark as to be laughable. Palmer's description must have been all over the shop. Maybe the hormone, or the endorphin or whatever, that was stimulated by fear – was it adrenaline? – maybe it fucked up the memory circuits.

Perhaps that was how dictators thrived. A line from Robespierre to Pol-Pot, all using terror to keep themselves safe. Make your enemies, and better yet, your friends, so afraid of you that they forget all the terrible things you're doing to them. The question was, did it work the other way around?

If they stopped being afraid, would they remember?

He knelt down to the plug, switched off the lights and stayed there, breathing in the gorgeous smell of the tree and thinking about Palmer.

He imagined him now, frightened and alone. Some boot-faced bobby keeping the watch, glaring at him, resentful, fantasising about hurting him and doing everybody a favour. He pictured Palmer's wide, soft, cushion face, his mournful, wide-eyed expression. Staring out into the night, thinking about Karen and waiting to be saved. Chewing on his fat bottom lip and blushing like a girl.

What do you want from Santa, Martin?

My head on a plate? My name on an arrest sheet, so that you can slope away to prison, just that little bit less guilty?

Sorry, Mart . . .

He thought about sending him a message to cheer him up. Christmas e-cards were very popular after all. Something seasonal and simple. A picture of a robin perched on the handle of a snow-covered spade and a short message.

I'm thinking about you . . .

It was a tempting idea but he knew he was just being dramatic. There was no way they could trace it, he was sure about that, but even so it was probably not the right time. He'd get Christmas out of the way first, let things settle down a bit. Then he'd decide what to do next.

Assuming that the decision wasn't made for him.

★

It was starting to rain.

Thorne flagged down a black cab on Abbey Road. He was not a million miles from the zebra crossing the Beatles had so famously strolled across more than thirty years before, McCartney barefoot and out of step.

He opened the door. 'Kentish Town . . .'

The driver didn't even look at him. 'Triple time now, mate. That all right?'

Thorne smiled at the strip of tinsel wrapped around the cab's aerial. Maybe the gesture was ironic. He nodded and climbed in. 'Yeah, whatever . . .'

'I Wish It Could Be Christmas Everyday' was blasting out of the radio. It was a song Thorne loved, one guaranteed to have him rushing out to buy holly and advocaat, but for the first time in his life, he wanted Christmas to be over and done with. Christmas *and* New Year, condensed, compressed. He wanted, no, he *needed*, to be shot of them . . .

He thought about Charlie Garner.

Would the boy be lying in bed now, listening out for reindeer on the roof, unable to sleep? Or had he been unable to sleep for the last month, and was he lying in bed now listening to his mother screaming?

The taxi rumbled through Swiss Cottage, down damp, deserted streets, towards Chalk Farm. The cabbie was talking to him, throwing meaningful glances over his shoulder, but Thorne wasn't listening.

A boy called Stuart Anthony Nicklin . . .

Thorne wished the fortnight ahead gone not because of how he was likely to be spending it, nor because of his father, nor Charlie Garner. He needed a leap forward in time to move the case on.

There was an outside chance that there *might* be a break over the Christmas period but he seriously doubted it. What he *was* sure of was that there would be pressure from Jesmond, and from Brigstocke on his behalf. The Powers That Be would demand to know what was happening. When was this stupid idea of his going to yield anything significant bar an astronomical overtime bill?

The taxi squealed to a halt at some lights. A gaggle of drunken revellers crossed the road in front of them, waving and singing. The cabbie waved back, muttering, 'Wankers.'

The cab roared away from the lights and swung right into Camden. Thorne leaned back and closed his eyes. Two weeks mollifying the PTB would at least kill the time, and he wanted it killed. He wanted it stone dead.

If he was going to get pro-active, he couldn't do it while the rest of the world was on holiday. And some people took longer holidays than others . . .

Thorne had decided that in order to move forward, he needed to go back.

He was going to go back to where it had all started.

PART THREE

THE FACE
TURNED AWAY

THIRTEEN

The school stood in a quiet, leafy part of Harrow, only a mile or so from a slightly more famous school – one with its own theatre, farm and golf course – which boasted Byron, Nehru and Churchill among its former pupils. As the car moved slowly up the drive towards the main building, Thorne knew that King Edward IV School for Boys would soon have even less reason to be proud of *its* Old Boys.

A week into 2002. The investigation in dire need of a kick up the arse.

The fortnight or so since Christmas had gone much as Thorne had feared: very little progress, lots of grief. The holidays *had* covered a multitude of sins – the inactivity in the case would have been exposed to a far greater degree at any other time, but coupled with the demands on manpower, it still drew unwelcome attention from the Powers That Be.

Brigstocke was clearly copping it from above and he seemed to take great delight in passing it on to those beneath him.

'Patience is running out, Tom.'

'Theirs or yours?'

'Same thing.'

'Right. Got it. Look, as soon as the schools go back, I'm—'

'What? Going to check Nicklin's truancy records? See if he got into detention much?'

'You got any better ideas?'

'You're the ideas man, Tom. We're just waiting to see one of them fucking amount to anything . . .'

'Is this still about the arse on the fence remark? Look, I'm getting tired of saying sorry.'

'Well I'm not tired of hearing you say it, OK?'

Pupils were moving aside to let the car through as Thorne drove slowly up the long drive and swerved into the car park. The boys looked smart in grey trousers and blue blazers trimmed with claret piping. If the school had an inferiority complex, it didn't show from the outside.

Holland stepped out of the car, widening his eyes.

'Not like my school . . .'

Nor mine, thought Thorne. He pictured a short, stocky lad jumping off the bus, thoroughly delighted with his feather cut, his new, five-button bags and his star jumper. Thorne watched him trudging up the hill singing 'Blockbuster' and 'Mama Weer All Crazee Now', wearing platforms instead of beetlecrushers, needing that extra inch or so. He smiled as the boy swaggered into the playground and chatted to his mate. Making up stuff about the weekend, swearing, talking about music and Saturday's results.

The school bell rang, and as Thorne followed Holland towards the entrance, he glimpsed the same boy again, disappearing into the distance. Thirteen-year-old Tom Thorne was hoisting his dirty green rucksack across his shoulder. The canvas was emblazoned with the names of bands and footballers – Slade and Martin Chivers – the bag crammed with games kit and Marmite sandwiches, and maybe even the odd exercise book covered in wallpaper . . .

The school secretary was like every school secretary that Thorne remembered or had ever imagined. Maybe they bred them somewhere, taught them how to put their hair in a bun and look down their pointed noses, before sending them out into the world with a pair of big glasses, a fondness for tweed and something uncomfortable up their backsides.

'Mr Marsden won't be a minute. He knows you're here.'

Thorne smiled at her. 'Thank you so much.'

He and Holland were seated on brown plastic chairs outside the headmaster's office. Opposite them sat a boy of about twelve, looking absolutely terrified. Thorne made eye contact, but the boy looked away.

'This takes me back,' Holland muttered.

'What, sitting outside the beak's office? Can't imagine you were ever in too much trouble, Holland.'

'I had my moments.'

'Come on, a policeman's son?'

Holland laughed a little but then began to think of something and the laughter quickly faded. Thorne thought about his own father. He found it hard to remember him as a teenager's dad. Jim Thorne was in danger of becoming for ever associated with worry and duty, and strange conversations.

'Happy Christmas, Dad. Is Eileen looking after you?'

'She overcooked the sprouts . . .'

'Right. Did you like the video? I didn't know what else to get you.'

'Name all the reindeer.'

'You can watch it later maybe . . .'

'There's nine of them. Nine reindeer . . .'

'Dad . . .'

'Go on. I'll give you Rudolf, that's the easy one. Dasher, Vixen, Comet . . .'

Thorne closed his eyes and searched for an image of his father from his childhood. He could smell disinfectant, taste semolina, hear the squeak of a plimsoll on a gymnasium floor, but a picture of his old man as a young man was temporarily unavailable.

He opened his eyes to find the frightened boy staring at him before quickly looking away again.

Thorne didn't see fear on the faces of kids any more. Not the ones he had cause to talk to. Maybe they just hid it very well or maybe they just weren't scared. What he saw was arrogance and scorn, sometimes even something like pity, but he couldn't remember the last time he'd put the fear of god into a kid.

Thorne looked at the clock above the secretary's door, then back to the boy. 'It's only just gone nine, son. How can you be in trouble already?'

The boy looked up at him and opened his mouth but Thorne would never get an answer to his question. At that moment the door opened and a ludicrously tall man with a shock of white hair stepped from the room.

'I'm Brian Marsden. Come in.'

Thorne and Holland did as they were told.

The next ten minutes were among the most bizarre of the entire case. Marsden knew full well why they were

there, knew about Palmer and Nicklin, and yet pro-
ceeded to treat Thorne and Holland more like
prospective parents than police officers on a murder
investigation. He handed them each an expensively produced brochure containing an outline of the current
syllabus, details of the school's impressive array of sports
facilities and even a sample lunch menu. Before either of
them could stop him, he launched into a potted history
of the school. It had been a basic state grammar until the
late eighties when it became grant maintained. This confirmed several things Thorne already knew: Palmer and
Nicklin had both earned their places at the school on
merit; Nicklin, despite being brought up by a single
parent on a nearby council estate, had passed the necessary exams to get into the best state school in the area.
He was a very bright boy.

Things Thorne already knew . . .

A knock at the door stopped Marsden in full flow. He
stood up as another teacher entered the room. This one
was short and hesitant, and Thorne thought he looked a
little embarrassed to be there at all. Marsden marched
across to the door to usher them all out again.

'Andrew Cookson is our Head of English. He'll be
showing you round, answering your questions. Perhaps
you'll pop in again before you leave . . .'

Cookson led Thorne and Holland back past the secretary's office and into the main reception area. The place
stank of floor polish mingled with a hint of sweat.

'Actually,' Holland said, 'we don't really need the tour.'

Cookson nodded slowly. He looked a little confused.

Thorne had other ideas. 'No, it's fine . . .' Holland
looked at him as if he were mad, but Thorne just shrugged.

He thought getting a feel of the place couldn't hurt and he actually quite fancied having a look round.

'Right, follow me,' Cookson said. 'There's something you'll want to see in the main hall, then we'll have a quick scoot round and then I'll hook you up with Bowles.' He held out his hands. *Fair enough?* Thorne nodded and Cookson smiled. Thorne could see instantly that he'd be a popular teacher. The smile was huge and infectious. Thorne also saw, suddenly, that Cookson's dark eyes were mischievous, and that even though he must have been in his late twenties or early thirties, he still had the energy, the vigour, of a child.

As he'd thought he might, Thorne hugely enjoyed being shown around. Cookson's wry commentary was highly entertaining, as was the look of boredom on Holland's face.

'I think your sergeant must have bad memories of his time at school,' Cookson said with a grin. 'What about you?'

Thorne shook his head. 'Sounds a bit swotty, and trust me, I really wasn't, but I bloody loved school.'

'Me too,' Cookson said. 'Still do . . .'

King Edward IV had clearly modelled itself on a public school; unavoidable probably, considering the proximity of such a celebrated one. The imitation was a good one, right down to the fives courts, the house system and even the mortar boards and gowns which, Cookson was relieved to say, were strictly reserved for the big occasions.

Speech day, prizegiving, school photos . . .

'These are the ones you'll be interested in . . .'

The entire back wall of the school hall was covered in framed photos, some dating right back to the forties. There were dozens, row upon row of them. Cookson led Thorne and Holland to a group of photos covering the late seventies and early eighties.

'Here we go. 'Eighty-two, 'eighty-three and 'eighty-four.'

Each photo was about three-and-a-half-feet long; the sort where the entire school lined up, kneeling, sitting, or standing on chairs, and the camera panned slowly down the line. Thorne remembered *his* school photos and a boy named Fox who used to take great delight in waiting until the camera had begun to move, and then legging it round the back to pop up on the other side, so as to appear on both ends of the final photo. He got detention every time, but he always did it anyway . . .

Thorne stared at the first photo. He spotted Palmer almost straight away. He was a head taller than the boys around him, with the same hair, the same thick glasses. He studied the list of names at the bottom and eventually found Nicklin. The boy had moved as the shot was taken and his face was blurry, but it looked as though he was grinning. By nineteen eighty-three, Palmer and Nicklin were standing together. Palmer stared straight at the camera, his face flat. Nicklin's head, at the level of the taller boy's shoulder, was bowed slightly, but his eyes were up, dark and full of challenge.

Thorne leaned in close to the photograph.

'Hello, Stuart . . .'

After a moment, Thorne moved on to the 'eighty-four picture, pressing his nose up to the glass. Again, Nicklin's head was looking away from the camera as he whispered something to Palmer who stood stiffly beside him wearing an odd smile.

Thorne moved on, scanned the 'eighty-five picture, but of course, neither Palmer nor Nicklin were there. He moved back, looked again at the blurred features, the face turned away. He knew that it wasn't possible, but he couldn't help imagining that seventeen years before, Nicklin had been deliberately trying to hide. Even then, as a thirteen-year-old boy, he'd somehow foreseen the day when someone like Thorne would be staring at the picture, looking at him.

Looking for him.

Cookson turned to Holland. 'Probably a stupid question, but . . . this is the first time you've seen him, right?' Holland nodded. 'Well, couldn't you have got pictures off his family?'

It wasn't a stupid question.

Nicklin's family had been traced quickly. Only the mother was still alive; nearly seventy and living in warden-controlled housing. Holland had made the call. The old woman's voice had been a little quivery, but clear. Holland had introduced himself and explained that her son's name had come up in connection with an enquiry and that he had a few simple questions. Her answers had been all but monosyllabic. Had she seen him? *No.* Had she had any contact with him? *No.* Holland had had no doubt that she had been telling the truth, but found it disturbing that she seemed to have no interest whatsoever in what her son, missing these last fifteen years, might have been doing or where he might be. She had asked nothing.

It was her answer to Holland's last question, which he had thrown in as if it were an afterthought, that had been oddest. Chilling, even. He'd asked if she wouldn't mind letting them have a few photographs, she'd get them back of course, the most recent would be best, something taken just before Stuart had left home maybe . . .

That would not be possible, she'd said. Mrs Nicklin had explained calmly that she didn't have any photographs at all of her son Stuart. Not one.

It was strange, but not the end of the world. Thorne had been unconvinced, in light of what Palmer had said, that a fifteen-year-old picture would have been a lot of use anyway.

Holland asked the teacher where he could find the nearest toilet and excused himself.

Cookson wore a moleskin jacket, button-down shirt and chinos. Thorne thought he looked rather preppy. The sound of expensive American loafers kissing the polished floor echoed as Cookson led him up a flight of stairs and down a long, straight corridor. It was a far cry from the lumbering sadists in corduroy jackets or tracksuits that Thorne remembered.

Cookson stared through the window into every classroom they passed. They were looking for Ken Bowles, a maths teacher, and the only member of staff who'd been here in the early eighties, at the same time as Palmer and Nicklin.

Thorne wondered why so few teachers from that time were still here. It wasn't much more than fifteen years, after all.

'Teachers used to stick around a lot longer in one place,' Cookson said, 'but not any more. It's easy to . . . stagnate, and money's always an issue. This is a good school. If you've done a couple of years here, there's a fair chance you can double your money in the private sector. The place up the road poaches a few every couple of years . . .'

Thorne was leading the way. He looked into the next classroom, saw an old man with tufty white hair, sitting at a desk and staring out of the window. 'What about you?'

'Been tempted, but . . . well, I'm still here. Seven years this year, and I'm already one of the old farts.' Cookson looked past Thorne into the classroom. 'Yep . . . here we go . . .'

He knocked on the door, pushed it and held it open for Thorne. 'I'll maybe see you later then . . .'

Sarah McEvoy took another swig from the bottle on her desk. She'd already got through a couple of bottles, but the water couldn't get rid of the dry mouth or the sour taste at the back of her throat any better than the cigarettes could.

She was still feeling guilty, having barked at a DC five minutes before. She was taking it out on a junior officer, as it had already been taken out on her. She'd arrived late, feeling rough, and a bollocking from Brigstocke had done nothing to help her feel better. The bad mood was being passed around the investigation like a virus, while the man who'd caused it was off at some school chasing ghosts.

They should all have been on a high since Palmer had fallen into their laps, but that would have been far too easy for Tom Thorne. It was as if he had some aversion to a morale that was anything except down in the fucking dust. As if every minute that passed without catching the second killer was their fault. As if he wanted to see shame etched onto the face of every officer and a hair shirt hanging in every locker. While he was content to let a murderer walk about, breathing the same air as normal people.

She screwed her eyes tight shut; tried to calm herself

down a little. She knew that Thorne was only doing what he believed was right.

She'd been feeling edgier by the day since the holiday. A couple of long, long days trapped in her parents' house in Mill Hill. Like she gave a toss about Chanukah anyway, with her tedious brother and his dull-as-ditchwater family. She had been desperate to get out, needing to be among strangers.

She'd found all the strangers she'd needed over New Year. The faces, strobed in white or lit up by the flashing reds and greens, had been reassuringly unfamiliar and the nights had become longer and louder, and altogether fucking fantastic, and suddenly – not in terms of the time, but in terms of her *realising* it – suddenly, dragging herself into work in the morning . . . some mornings, had become painful.

And Thorne and Brigstocke didn't fucking well like her anyway. The pair of them, commenting on her clothes and the way she looked, which she knew damn well they would never have done if she didn't have tits.

She reached for the water bottle and unscrewed the cap. Her mobile rang.

'McEvoy.'

'It's Holland . . .'

She took a mouthful of water while she waited for Holland to say what it was he wanted, but he didn't. She listened to the hiss on the line, swallowed, and wiped her mouth on the sleeve of her shirt. 'What?'

Another few seconds of hiss. 'Nothing urgent. Just touching base.'

Touching base? 'What cop show did you see that in?'

'Sorry?'

'Forget it. Just being a sarky cow. Where's Thorne?'

'Trying to track down Nicklin's old teacher . . .'

As McEvoy listened, the DC she'd shouted at earlier walked past her desk. McEvoy smiled – an attempt at an apology. The DC gave her nothing back. 'You sound all echoey.'

'I'm in the toilets,' Holland said. 'Nice to see that posh kids piss on the floor as well.'

'They're not that posh, are they?'

'I didn't see many of them playing football in the playground.'

'Yeah, but not like . . . Biscuit Game posh.'

'Eh . . . ?'

McEvoy laughed. 'I'll tell you later.'

'That's one thing they'll miss out on though,' Holland said. 'Being an all boys school . . .'

'What?'

'The sheer, unbridled pleasure of running into the girls' toilets and screaming your head off.'

McEvoy remembered the very same thing happening at her school. She suddenly pictured herself, twelve going on twenty-five, shaking her head in disgust as she listened to the whoops and cheers of half a dozen testosterone-crazed, adolescent boys. She grinned at the memory. This phone call was doing her a lot of good. 'Why did you do that anyway? I could never work it out.'

'I think it was a genetic thing. Marking your territory or something . . .'

McEvoy glanced up. On the other side of the incident room she could see Brigstocke talking to Steve Norman. Brigstocke looked across at her, then Norman. Weaselly little fucker. She wondered whether they'd heard her laughing. She took another sip of water, her mouth still sticky. 'So, anything of interest?'

'Not really, you?'

'Nothing. Derek bloody Lickwood's been on the phone again, demanding to know what's going on. He reckons he's being kept in the dark, keeps threatening to come over and make trouble. Why should I have to deal with him?'

'Short straw. Lovell was his case so we've got to work with him. The boss reckons you'd be better at it than he would . . .' McEvoy grunted. 'What about Palmer?'

'At work.' She said no more than that, but there was an edge to her voice. The unspoken bit was obvious. *At work, totting up figures and drinking coffee, when he should be sitting against a rough stone wall listening to keys turning in locks; his knees pulled tight against his chest, his heart thumping, his belt and shoelaces taken away.*

She would never criticise Thorne to Holland. Besides, she knew, somewhere, that her judgement was perhaps a little off these days. Her thinking was maybe a bit extreme . . .

'Right,' Holland said. 'Do you want to grab a beer later?'

She looked across at Brigstocke. He and Norman were still deep in conversation. 'I've never been propositioned by a man in a toilet before.' She could *hear* Holland blush. 'I'm joking Holland.'

'Yeah . . .'

She murmured huskily into the phone. 'I've been propositioned by men in toilets *loads* of times.'

Holland didn't laugh.

McEvoy puffed out her cheeks, blew out the air noisily. She reached for the bottle of water. It was empty. 'Listen, Dave . . .'

'I just meant . . . a beer. That's all.'

She tried not to snap at him, but couldn't help herself. 'I know.'

'If they were in my class it's because they had a particular aptitude for mathematics, but I don't remember either one of them covering himself in glory.'

Thorne nodded patiently. Ken Bowles didn't seem to remember a great deal about anything. He knew that teaching was a stressful profession but Bowles could not possibly be as old as he looked. He had hair the colour of confectioner's custard and leathery grey skin. Behind the wire-framed spectacles the eyes were watery, and he had big discoloured teeth, like old-fashioned sweets in a jar, which clacked noisily together when he spoke and sometimes when he didn't.

'You do remember Palmer and Nicklin being close?' Thorne asked.

Bowles pushed himself away from the edge of the desk with a small grunt and moved across to the window. His tie was askew and there were chalk marks around his crotch. 'I don't recall a great deal about them at all. I don't think I liked either of them very much but that isn't unusual. Maths is the lesson where the most disruption occurs. The taller one . . . was that Palmer?' Thorne nodded. 'He let himself get distracted by his friend. *There* . . .' He pointed to a corner of the room. 'The two of them messing about at the back. Passing notes and laughing. Palmer's homework was good, I think, but in class he was . . . somewhere else.'

'Could you not have split them up? Moved Palmer to the front . . . ?'

Bowles shrugged, stared out of the window. 'I never really had them for that long, you see. They would probably have gone into different streams anyway that September, but of course they got expelled.' He raised his hand, rubbed with a finger at a dirty spot on the window. 'An older boy, can't remember his name. They grabbed him outside the school gates, dragged him into the park, I think . . .'

Thorne knew the story. Palmer had told him. His eyes filling behind his glasses, the nodding slow and sorrowful as he looked back at himself down the wrong end of the telescope, sweating as he relived it. Each detail preserved in the hideous aspic of shameful memory. The big feet in scuffed brogues, rooted to the spot, refusing to carry him away. The thick fingers, closing slowly around the brown, pimpled grip of the air pistol.

Thorne knew then that this had been the moment when everything had changed. From then on it had been unavoidable. He thought about what Bowles had just told him. A couple more months and Palmer and Nicklin would have been in different streams, moving along different paths; Nicklin's influence on the younger boy not as strong. Would they have drifted apart then? Might a few months, all those years ago, have saved the lives of five women?

At *least* five women . . .

There was a knock at the door and Holland entered. Thorne nodded in his direction. 'This is Detective Constable Holland . . .'

Bowles peered theatrically across the room, feigning shock. 'Looks like a bloody sixth former.' Holland shrugged and smiled at the feeble joke.

'Did you follow their progress after they'd been expelled?' Thorne asked.

The teacher shook his head vigorously. 'Didn't miss either of them for a second. Nicklin was nothing but trouble and Palmer was just a big blob. Not his fault, I suppose. Boys his age can be terribly awkward, find it difficult to fit in. Like a lump of Plasticine that needs shaping. Palmer just got shaped by the wrong person, I think.'

Thorne nodded at Holland. Time to make a move. 'Thanks Mr Bowles.' Thorne handed over a card, which Bowles took without looking at it. 'If there's anything else that occurs to you . . .'

'I taught myself to juggle when I was younger,' Bowles announced. 'I'd do a bit for the class. Last day of term, that sort of thing. I can remember doing it for their class – Palmer and Nicklin's class. Cascade of five balls, six on a good day. Balancing a chair . . .' He pointed at a heavy looking wooden chair behind the desk on the platform. '. . . one of *those* chairs, on my chin. Do you know that Marsden's younger than I am?'

Thorne was itching to get away. 'Sorry, sir?'

'Headmaster. They brought Marsden in a couple of years ago, from outside. I'm ten years older than he is.' He threw his arms wide, as if the sense of what he was saying was obvious for all to see. 'Be glad to get out of here to tell you the truth. Can't even manage three balls these days . . .'

Holland opened the door, and Thorne gratefully took a few steps towards it. 'We'll be on our way, sir.'

Bowles nodded and spoke quietly. 'What's Nicklin done?'

'I'm afraid we can't . . .'

'Of course not, I'm sorry I asked. Do you know, I hadn't

thought about either of those boys in years until I was told it was them you wanted to talk to me about? I've taught hundreds of boys. I can't remember most of them to be honest. I can recall the *work* sometimes, but not faces. Ever since I heard those two names again, I've been thinking about them a good deal. Thinking about *him*. There's a look on your face, Inspector Thorne, whenever you talk about him, did you know that?'

Thorne knew it would be pointless to deny it, to express surprise. His face hid nothing. It never had. Not the scorn he felt for some, not the pity for others. The creases in his face folded as naturally into genuine expressions of horror, disgust and rage as those of a bad actor might shape themselves into their phoney counterparts. His face fell easily into darkness; the scowl more at home there than the smile. Though the smile was the rarer, it was arguably the more powerful.

Both had got him into plenty of trouble.

Bowles moved to the door to show them out. 'I suspect that now I shall be thinking about Stuart Nicklin often.' The watery eyes studied Thorne's face. 'The boy's moved on from air pistols, hasn't he?'

Thorne thought about Rosemary Vincent: the memory of an argument on the phone, the photograph turned over and over in her hand that day at the press conference. The hole in her precious daughter's head.

The shadow moved across Thorne's face as he answered the teacher's question.

'Yes. He's moved on.'

He was thinking about something that had happened a long time ago.

Years earlier, back when he'd still been Stuart Nicklin and supporting himself by tossing off sad old men and confused young ones, he'd learned about making the appropriate response to a situation. Another rent boy, a spiteful little prick who was older and uglier, had stolen some of his customers. Not his regulars, they were loyal, but some of the passing trade. The fucker was undercutting, a tenner here, twenty notes there, a bit more cash and we'll forget about the condom – poaching punters to make some last ditch money before his looks went altogether. Understandable, but very bloody annoying.

He was furious. He wanted to do something to punish the thieving toerag, the little bitch, but he knew that the sensible thing, the *appropriate* thing to do would be to ignore it. Let it go and move on. There were plenty of punters to go around and there was no need to risk trouble with the police. No need to rock the boat. That would be stupid.

He was also thinking about what was happening right now.

They were afraid he was going to disappear. Scared shitless that, with his partner taken, he would pack up and head for the hills. If that was what they were afraid of, he knew that it was exactly what he should do. It was the appropriate response. They didn't want him to melt away and then resurface when the time was right to start again. So, that was the right thing for him to do. It was simple and sensible. It was self-preservation.

It would be hard, there was no question of that. He loved what he was doing. He was very good at it and he loved that too. It was a rush like nothing he could remember, and even without the added buzz of the other, even without Palmer playing along for real, he knew that not doing it would be like dulling all his senses. Stopping would be like cutting off the oxygen to the very best part of himself. Giving it up would be like going to sleep for a while. It wouldn't be for ever, it might not even have to be for very long, but it would be very bloody hard. Still, it made sense. It was the appropriate thing to do, so he would have to try.

He would try to stop.

Years earlier, back when he'd still been Stuart Nicklin, having decided not to do anything stupid, he'd made a few calls and lured the thieving rent boy to an empty flat he sometimes used off Glasshouse Street. It was February and freezing. From the small window he could see the crowds in scarves and heavy coats, moving across Piccadilly Circus. He could just make out the icicles dangling from the bow of Eros and the frost on the steps leading up to the statue, sparkling in the multicoloured neon from the vast signs above.

When the boy arrived, Nicklin beat him unconscious with a housebrick, stuck a funnel in his mouth and poured a gallon of bright blue anti-freeze down his throat.

In its own way, an appropriate response. After all, it was a very cold night.

He was thinking.

He would *try* to stop . . .

Thorne, too, was thinking about something that had happened a long time ago . . .

The boy he'd last seen trudging towards school sporting a feather cut, though he wasn't an awful lot taller, had at least filled out a little.

It was three years later. It was twenty-five years ago.

Boxing Day. Nineteen seventy-six. A two-all draw at home against Arsenal, ground out on a snowy pitch with

an orange ball. An acceptable result in a season that was
going from bad to worse.

His dad had stayed up near the ground for a pint with his
mates, leaving him to make his own way back. He trudged
up the Seven Sisters Road, the dark slush soaking through
his boots, filling his turn-ups. The black and white scarf worn
as much for warmth as to declare allegiance.

They looked like grown men from a distance, but as
they got close, he could see that they were only a year or
two older than he was. They were bigger too, with green
Harrington jackets, and red and white scarves.

He brushed shoulders with one as they passed and a
look was exchanged. He had shrugged slightly and smiled.

Two apiece. A fair enough result, don't you reckon?

A few minutes later he heard the footsteps thumping
behind him and before he had a chance to react, the first of
them was on his back, an arm around his neck, driving him
face first on to the icy pavement.

Cars roared past, spraying water and light across the
three figures, but not slowing down.

He pushed himself up on to his knees and got the first
of several punches in the face. As the fists came down, he
deflected some with his arms, feeling something crack in
his hand at the same time as something long and heavy
smashed across his shoulder blades. He was crying and
straining to get down on to the floor so he could pull his
knees up to his chest. He could no longer tell which were
the grunts of pain and which were the dull sounds of fists
clubbing into cheekbone and shoulder.

He heard a voice and saw the shadow of an arm reaching across him. The biggest of the Arsenal fans stepped
over him, cursing, and finally, he was free to drop back to

SCAREDY CAT   225

the floor. He rolled over, moaning, and as he began to crawl away, he turned to see them laying into an older man in shirt sleeves. One of them had him by the hair while the other casually brought his forehead down into the man's face. The man was Greek, he thought, maybe Cypriot. Difficult to tell with all the blood. Perhaps he was a shop-keeper who had heard the noise and stepped out to intervene. He shouted and swore as the two thugs pushed him down into the wet gutter and drew back their feet.

Tom Thorne began to shout too, then, for someone to come. Shouting for help as the first kicks went into the groin and stomach. Shouting even louder than the man on the floor as the boots flew in again and again. Shouting for help and running away, fast . . .

He moved around the flat, turning off the lights, very ready for bed. He smiled, remembering the way his dad had ranted from the terraces: foul-mouthed and usually wide of the mark. '*Hoddle, you're fucking useless!*'

He wondered what had become of the man who'd tried to help him and got a good kicking for his trouble. He probably hadn't made the same mistake again.

He still felt guilty that he hadn't gone back. He'd scanned the papers for days afterwards but found nothing. The man was probably not seriously hurt, but the boy couldn't forget the pain and fury on his face. Twenty-five years on and Thorne could still see it, and hear the soggy thump as the man had crashed down on to his back in the slush.

Thorne closed the bedroom door, sat down on the side of the bed and started to undo his shoelaces. Twenty years a copper and he still couldn't understand why they'd attacked him.

He'd only smiled at them.

FOURTEEN

Thorne thought: so this is old age.

A heavy chair near the television, with its shit-coloured seat covered in plastic and panic buttons everywhere. Handles around the bath and piss-soaked knickers in the sink, and a woman who couldn't really give a toss, popping round twice a day to see if you're dead yet.

'Do you take sugar, Mrs Nicklin?' McEvoy stuck her head round the kitchen door.

Annie Nicklin shook her head at nobody in particular and Thorne relayed the answer to McEvoy with a more obvious gesture of his own. Though she hadn't said a lot, the woman in the heavy chair, with her clawed hands resting on top of a green blanket, was still fairly sharp mentally, but her body was on the way out. Arthritis, diabetes, angina . . . the catalogue of diseases had been reeled off cheerfully by the warden – a hard-faced article named Margaret – as she'd shown them into Annie's flat and explained that they wouldn't get a great deal out of her. Nobody ever did.

McEvoy brought the tea through, and as she handed round the mugs, Thorne continued to ponder the ques-

tion that had absorbed him since he'd walked through the
door. Which was preferable? A good brain and a body
that was fucked? Or hale and hearty flesh and bone, with
nothing left up top? Obviously, nobody ever really got
the choice, but still, Thorne couldn't help weighing it
up. Considering the options. It looked as if his old man
was heading down the second road, but Thorne reckoned that when it came to it, he'd prefer to go to pieces
upstairs *and* downstairs. At least that way, if he were sitting in his own mess, he'd be blissfully unaware of the
fact . . .

He sipped his tea and thought about meeting Ken
Bowles the day before. There was a man who could see
pain and loneliness just up ahead. He took a biscuit and
thought about the Enrights. As if the everyday agonies of
old age weren't bad enough.

He had the same old thoughts about the boy, Charlie
Garner, who was no age at all. His life still ahead of him
and already blighted. His mother taken away by the son of
the old lady sitting a few feet away, slurping tea in a shit-
coloured chair covered with plastic.

Thorne stared at Annie Nicklin. When she had looked
at her son, at Stuart, back when he was no older than
Charlie Garner, what had she seen in his future? What
had she dreamed he might become?

'That all right for you, Annie?' McEvoy asked.

Mrs Nicklin nodded again, slurped a bit more, continued to stare at the television screen, even though it wasn't
switched on.

Thorne hoisted his behind from the depths of the soft,
springless sofa and leaned forwards. 'We just wanted to ask
you about Stuart.'

Nothing. Just the noise of the drinking. The endless *beep beep* of a lorry reversing somewhere. A dog howling in one of the other flats.

Thorne looked across at McEvoy, raised an eyebrow. *You have a crack, and keep it nice.*

McEvoy, much to her annoyance, had won that morning's toss-up. Thorne had not been able to decide which would work better with the old woman – Holland's boyish, floppy-haired charm or the empathy of a younger woman? The coin had picked McEvoy and in the car on the way out to Stanmore, with Thorne driving *and* trying to coax any kind of warmth out of the Mondeo's knackered heater, she'd not been shy about why she was pissed off about it . . .

'I don't particularly feel like wheedling stuff out of a sweet old lady whose son happens to be a psychopath. You don't need to have read a lot of textbooks to figure that she might have something to do with that.'

Thorne hadn't read a single textbook and he was having none of it. 'What? Did she lock him in the coalshed? Make him wear women's clothes and lipstick? We need to talk to this woman, and frankly, I couldn't be less interested in a debate on nature versus nurture . . .'

McEvoy clearly didn't care whether he was interested or not. 'Nurture, every time. Every time.'

Thorne stopped at traffic lights and yanked up the handbrake. 'Supposing you're right. You aren't, but supposing you are . . .' – McEvoy said nothing, stared out of the window – 'what about Nicklin's father? Why can't he have been the one who beat poor little Stuart with a coathanger or whatever?' Palmer had already told him that Nicklin's father had left home when he was still a toddler.

Nobody knew, or by all accounts cared, if he was alive or dead.

For a few moments, McEvoy thought about what Thorne had said, or at least pretended to. 'No. Mothers and sons. Fathers and daughters . . .'

Thorne leaned on the horn as a white van roared away from the lights and swerved in front of him. 'You've never met my father, have you?' McEvoy didn't laugh, so Thorne stopped being nice about it. 'Listen, if there's anything this woman can tell us that might help, I want to hear it OK? You're a copper, not an amateur shrink, so go in there and do your job . . .'

McEvoy had been laying it on with a trowel ever since they'd got there.

'Maybe we could start with when Stuart left home, Annie.'

The old woman cleared her throat. Her chest rattled for a second or two after she'd finished. Then she spoke. 'That's where it starts and where it finishes. He left. The end.' It was her longest sentence so far. Thorne looked at McEvoy. *Carry on . . .*

'So you never heard from him?'

Annie Nicklin picked up an empty teacup, looked at it, put it down again. 'There was a letter once, from London.'

'Do you still have it?'

She turned her head slowly round to look at them and smiled, though she was clearly in some pain. 'I never opened it.'

'Did you not want to know where he was?' Thorne asked.

He couldn't be sure whether she was choosing to ignore him or the question. Either way, she wasn't answering.

McEvoy moved on. 'He left in September 1985, is that right?'

The old woman nodded.

'Just like that? Out of the blue?'

'I wasn't . . . hugely surprised.'

Thorne thought: *or bothered . . .*

'This was a month or so after the disappearance of Karen McMahon?' Mrs Nicklin licked her lips, stared ahead. McEvoy tried again. 'When Stuart left, that would have been about a month after . . . ?'

With a small moan, Mrs Nicklin reached for the stick that was propped against her chair and, grunting with the effort, she pointed with it to a bottle of pills on top of the television. Thorne stood up and fetched the bottle. 'These?' He opened the bottle. 'How many? Just one?' Mrs Nicklin nodded and he handed her a tablet. There was a glass of water on the tray attached to her chair and he passed it to her. She swallowed.

Thorne sat down again. Pills for Annie's body which was giving up the ghost. Still sharp up top though. Sharp enough to understand everything. To decide when might be a good moment to take a tablet in order to avoid a question she didn't want to answer . . .

'Was he upset about Karen? Was that why he left?' McEvoy was craning her head round, trying to make eye contact. 'How much was he seeing of Martin Palmer before he left?' Somewhere, the dog was still crying, and now, Annie Nicklin was avoiding McEvoy's questions as well.

Thorne pushed himself up, stepped in front of her. She began to click her tongue and tried to move her head. Thorne stood solid, between the old woman and the television that wasn't on.

The gentleness had gone from Thorne's voice. 'Tell me about Karen, Mrs Nicklin.' There was a low moan from deep in her throat but that was as communicative as she was getting. Thorne leaned down close to her, very little patience left. 'Tell me about Karen McMahon.'

The case had begun to ring a bell when Palmer had first mentioned the name. Thorne remembered it of course, but not well – a missing girl, a nationwide search – the details were vague. When he found out the date he realised why. The summer of 1985. He had been . . . absorbed by a case of his own at the time. *Johnny Boy*. Francis John Calvert, a killer of gay men, who felt that the police were getting too close. So close that he had had no choice . . .

The nightmare a young DC called Thorne had walked into . . .

'Tell me about Karen.'

He could see the pale, paper-thin flesh around her jaw constrict across the wasted muscle as she gritted her false teeth. With what little movement was left in her clawed fingers, she grasped at the blanket across her lap, pulling it close to her.

'Tell us and we'll go, Annie,' McEvoy said.

'She got into a car.' She spoke slowly and with emphasis, as if explaining something terribly complicated. Just to make sure Thorne understood, she said it again. 'She got into a car.'

'When she was with Stuart?'

'After. A bit after that. She was ahead of him and the car pulled up.'

'The blue Vauxhall Cavalier . . .'

She stared down at her blanket, clutched at it. 'You know all this.'

Thorne shook his head. She looked away. 'Stuart must have been very upset. He saw it all happen, didn't he?'

She turned back to him quickly. 'Yes. He was upset. He never stopped crying afterwards. Stuart saw everything. He saw her get into the car. He saw the man who was driving it. He told the police what the man who was driving the car looked like, you can check.'

'He told the police? Or he told you and then *you* told the police?'

'Both, both.' She tut-tutted and one liver-spotted hand began to rap lightly on the arm of her chair.

McEvoy was on her feet now, standing directly behind Annie Nicklin's chair. 'This man, the man that Stuart saw, did he grab Karen? Did he get out of the car? Force her?' McEvoy might just as well have been talking to herself. She stared at Thorne across the white hair of Annie Nicklin's bowed head. She shrugged. *Enough?*

Despite what Thorne had said to McEvoy in the car on the way over, he had an urge to shout at this old woman, to bully her. He raised his voice only slightly, but as soon as he began to speak, Annie Nicklin raised her head. She met his gaze for the first time, and held it.

'Did Stuart have any idea why? If this man didn't force her, did Stuart have any idea *why* Karen McMahon got into his car? Did he tell you that, Annie?'

Thorne could feel his hard stare being returned with interest. Then, as if the movement was painful, she dragged her eyes away from his and down towards the floor, one hand clasping the blanket for dear life and the other reaching for the walking stick.

It was only after a few seconds that Thorne became aware of what was happening and glanced down. The knocking of the stick against his shin was almost imperceptible. The impact of the rubber tip against the bone was feeble, but the impulse behind the movement was anything but. Annie Nicklin was poking and prodding, trying to push him away, to poke and push him away. Jabbing and pushing at him . . .

In time with the jerky movements of her withered arm and knotted stick, she spoke. Her voice was clear and high, and the tone of it took on a strange sing-song quality as she spoke the same five words over and over again.

'She got into a car . . .'

Urging the Mondeo back towards Hendon, along the bizarrely named Honeypot Lane, Thorne pictured a girl in a white dress – he had no idea what Karen McMahon had really been wearing, but it had been a summer's day – pulling open the door of a blue car, pushing a strand of hair behind her ear and climbing in.

At the edge of the picture stood a boy called Stuart Nicklin, blurry, with his head slightly bowed, but with those dark eyes taking in every detail. Absent, but very much there, like a phantom image or a double exposure, was a man named Martin Palmer, still utterly fucked up nearly twenty years later.

There was something wrong with the picture . . .

'So, nature or nurture?' McEvoy said, as they got near to Becke House.

Thorne smiled. 'I'm saying nothing.'

'A lot like the old woman then . . .'

Thorne had to agree. 'I've known armed robbers, rapists . . . I've interviewed axe murderers who gave it up easier.' McEvoy laughed, but Thorne was being deadly serious. 'If Nicklin's got a fraction of that determination, or that . . . cunning, we're in trouble.'

'What about Palmer's parents?'

Thorne shook his head. There was really no need, and besides, they would know what was happening soon enough. One phone call from Palmer, a day or two after he'd given himself up, had established how Nicklin had tracked him down. 'Oh yes, a nice boy you were at school with called, trying to get hold of you . . . didn't leave his name . . . wanted it to be a surprise, I think.' Beyond that, there was nothing useful to be had out of them. Eventually, it would just be about giving them the bad news.

He was intrigued, but also a little relieved that Annie Nicklin had shown no interest in news of any sort about *her* son or his whereabouts. That would have been decidedly tricky.

'*Oh yes, he's turned up . . . But . . .*'

At the Peel Centre, they pulled up to the security barrier and Thorne fished around for his ID. McEvoy leaned across him and showed hers to the officer on duty. After a moment, the barrier lifted and Thorne nudged the car towards the parking bays.

'Got plans this evening?' Thorne asked.

McEvoy turned away and stared out of the window. There were a dozen or so recruits working with dogs on the far side of the compound. 'Not really. Early night, I think. You?'

'Myself and Mr Philip Hendricks have a hot date with Sky Sports and a Chinese takeaway.'

'Sounds good . . .'

'Yeah, if you don't mind being a relationship counsellor when you're trying to watch the match.' He pulled a face for McEvoy's benefit, but really he was looking forward to Hendricks coming over.

Unwinding. Letting a little of it go . . .

Thorne guided the car into a space next to Brigstocke's Volvo estate and killed the engine. He stared up at the dun-coloured walls and peeling olive paintwork of the three-storey sixties' monstrosity they had the misfortune to work in. If management had any sense, and a desire to maintain levels of recruitment, they would have instructed the film crew to make sure they kept the cameras well away from Becke House.

'It's a phenomenally ugly building,' McEvoy said, after a few moments.

Thorne nodded, thinking: *We're in it, trying to catch people who do phenomenally ugly things.*

McEvoy pushed in the button to release her seat belt. 'What's on this afternoon?'

Thorne took a deep breath. 'Well, I'm going to make a few calls, try and find out what's going to cost more, fixing the heater or replacing the car.'

'About bloody time. I'll be spending the next half an hour trying to get some feeling back into my feet . . .' Thorne laughed. 'It's ridiculous. Why don't you use the car you've been assigned?'

Thorne shrugged. 'I don't know . . . it's brown.'

McEvoy was gobsmacked by Thorne's answer, and by how much he suddenly looked like a confused and sulky teenager. 'So, get another one . . .'

'I like this car,' Thorne said. 'It's got all my tapes and stuff.'

'Oh right, yeah. Dolly Parton and Tammy Wynette.'

Thorne sighed and opened the door. 'I'm going to kill

Holland. No, I'm going to make him listen to some proper country music and *then* I'm going to kill him . . .'

McEvoy climbed out of the car, snickering like the cartoon dog in *Wacky Races*. 'It wasn't his fault. He didn't say . . .'

'Actually, fuck that, the music would be wasted on him anyway. I'll just kill him.' Thorne turned the key in the lock, looked at McEvoy across the Mondeo's roof. 'While I'm busy killing Detective Constable Holland, I want you to do something for me.'

'I think I'm already doing quite enough keeping Derek Lickwood away from you. He knows you're avoiding him.'

Thorne smiled. 'Don't worry, it's a lot easier than that.' McEvoy waited. 'Get on the phone for me, and find out who was in charge of the Karen McMahon case.'

Alf from Stoke-on-Trent: 'Hanging's too good for these bastards. I'd happily pull the lever myself . . .'

He shook his head and broke off another big piece of the chocolate bar, thinking: *Come on, Alf, you can't have it both ways.* Still, he knew that this was how a fair proportion of the British public thought that he, and others like him, should be dealt with. This was what they considered an appropriate response.

The phone-in host, who was normally there to play devil's advocate, agreed wholeheartedly with Alf, and the two of them began to gleefully discuss whether or not, if we ever came to our senses and brought back capital punishment, we should stick to the noose or perhaps move into the twenty-first century and go for lethal injection.

He closed his eyes, tuned out the chat.

Others like him . . .

He couldn't say that he'd ever actually met *anybody* else like him. Not really. He'd run into his fair share of those for whom respect for the law was a luxury, and some whose moral framework had never existed or had been eaten away. He'd known plenty of men desperate enough to consider anything, but never an individual who was happy to consider *every*thing. This fact didn't disturb him, but neither did it give him any great comfort. He just accepted it as the way of things. He wasn't arrogant enough to believe that he was completely unique. He accepted that one day he might stare across a street, or along a station platform, or even at a television screen and recognise a look in someone's eye.

It was a look he'd certainly never seen in Martin Palmer's eye. Now it was time to get in touch with his old friend again.

He got up from the armchair and crossed the room to where the laptop computer, bought for cash in Dixons the day before, lay on the dining table. He switched it on, and while it was booting up, he fetched the freshly cloned mobile he'd picked up in south London on the way home. He'd ditch the computer and the phone the next morning on the way in to work.

He had always been careful to vary his methods. Opening up any one of a hundred free e-mail accounts was easy, and he always took care to make the hardware as near to untraceable as possible. The first few times, he'd simply walked into an Internet cafe. He preferred the smaller places – converted greasy spoons that advertised cheap photocopying, and had a couple of grubby, first-issue iMacs lined up in a back room. These places were tucked away, almost invisible between massage parlours and dodgy minicab firms: places that even the backpackers didn't know about, where no-one served cappuccino or gave a toss about what porn sites you accessed. These were places without CCTV.

He'd moved on to laptops which were, of course, ideal for his purposes, and then it had just been a case of where to plug the things in. This wouldn't be the first time he'd used a stolen mobile – he had a contact who knocked them out for next to nothing – but in the past, he'd also enjoyed the telecommunications facilities offered by a number of shitty hotels in and around central London. Just a matter of checking in, logging on and fucking off. If, and it was a very big *if*, the place was ever traced, nobody would have any memory of the anonymous businessman with the small leather carrycase.

He connected the phone to the laptop and sat down in front of it. He began to give some thought to what he was going to write. He always liked to get the wording right.

It was funny, he'd almost predicted that something like this would happen, that in some strange way his hand would be forced, his mind made up for him. Now, he had no choice but to respond. The response, appropriate or not, was pretty much the only one he could make.

He logged on and the computer began to dial. In a matter of minutes he'd opened a new account, invented a name and created a password. He enjoyed assuming fresh identities whether they lasted many years or just a few hours in a dingy hotel room. He even relished those which, like this one, he would only ever need to assume in cyber-space for the few short minutes it took to send a handful of words across the city.

Pretty much the only response he could make . . .

He wasn't sure exactly *what* Thorne had been hoping to

gain by going to the school, but there it was. He snapped off another chunk of chocolate. The Detective Inspector was clearly not a man whose actions were predictable or immediately explicable. That was all right.

Neither was he.

He laid out his instructions in the e-mail with the usual care. There was to be no misunderstanding. He had always strived to make it straightforward for Palmer, to make everything clear. Martin had always needed that.

Do this, now. Do that, only when I tell you.

What was *less* clear, at least right now, was exactly why he was bothering to do this at all. Why was he sending these details to Palmer in the first place? Why was he issuing instructions which would never be followed, except in the creation of a newspaper story about a murder that had not taken place? Mind you, once the murder that *would be* taking place was discovered, they wouldn't bother making up any more stories anyway.

So why was he going through the motions like this? Why was he playing their game?

Palmer had chosen to remove himself from the equation and in doing so had taken away with him some of the . . . mustard. Dulled that extra buzz. Maybe he could get a little of it back this way. He *needed* to get it back, to go along with their not-so-clever bit of let's pretend, and see where it led all of them.

But that wasn't the only reason.

If he was being honest, he liked his routines and only *he* would decide when they changed. So, yes, it was a refusal . . . an *absolute* refusal to relinquish control, but it was also, he had to admit, because of a perverse desire to . . . carry on as normal. Business as usual, at least for the time being. He'd always had a sneaking admiration for that very British breed of nutcase who treated flood, fire or pestilence as no more than a minor inconvenience and refused to adapt. There was never any need to move house, or see a doctor or make a scene. Stubborn and stupid. Brave and barking mad. It worked the other way round, of course. It was only ever in this country that people could win millions on the lottery and decide to carry on working in a factory. Of course, in the end, those morons always *did* adapt, and so would he, when he absolutely had to. It wasn't rocket science, after all. Go with the flow, or rot where you stood. Adapt or get caught.

For now though, he'd suck it and see.

He heard Caroline coughing in her sleep upstairs. Poor thing had been feeling rough for a couple of days. As he checked his typing for spelling errors, he made a mental note to pick up some Benylin for her the following day.

He popped the last square of chocolate into his mouth and pressed 'send'.

They rolled apart from each other and lay there, sweating, exhausted.

Holland leaned up on one elbow and whispered mock-seductively into the ear of the woman next to him.

'So, come on, tell me about this mysterious Biscuit Game.'

McEvoy was still getting her breath back and marvelling at how, just an hour and a half before, she'd arrived home to find Holland on her doorstep, clutching a bottle of wine and stammering like a poor man's Hugh Grant.

Seven thirty: awkward exchanges as keys were fumbled for. Twenty past eight: second bottle opened, lying around like students. Nine o'clock: the pair of them, smiling, naked and slippery.

She had definitely been a lot more impulsive lately.

'Come on then . . .'

Was she actually blushing? 'It's just this stupid— It's probably not even true, it's like an urban myth, about this game they play at public schools.' She turned on to her side. He was staring at her, grinning, waiting for her to carry on. 'OK, basically, all the boys stand in a circle wanking.'

'Wanking?'

'Yes, apparently. There's a biscuit in the middle, and they all come on it, and whoever comes last has to eat the biscuit.'

There was a pause worthy of a great comedian before Holland let out a groan of disgust. 'You're making it up.'

McEvoy started to giggle. 'I swear . . .'

'Whoever comes last?'

His look of confusion made her laugh even more. 'I said it was stupid . . .'

'So they're actually being trained to come quickly?'

'I know. Mind you, it certainly explains why all the public schoolboys I've ever shagged have been shit in bed.'

They lay there for a minute, saying nothing, laughing now and again and trying to get their new, rather odd picture of the world into some sort of focus. McEvoy wondered how long he was planning to stay. Holland had just decided that he should be getting home, and was thinking about Sophie for the first time since McEvoy had put her tongue in his mouth and her hand on his cock, when she spoke.

'What about you?'

'What?'

'Were you a public schoolboy?'

Holland raised his head up off the pillow. 'Was I fuck!'

McEvoy's leg slid across his, and her hand began to creep across his stomach. 'Calm down, Holland. I'm kidding. You've already made that *very* obvious.' She smiled as she hoisted herself across him and began wriggling into position.

Holland put a hand on each of her shoulders and looked deep into her eyes. 'What sort do they use?' She looked down at him, confused, so he explained. 'The biscuit. Digestive, custard cream, bourbon . . . ?'

She was still laughing when they'd finished.

Thorne had been right about the relationship counsellor bit. Within ten minutes of the kick-off, he'd learned that Brendan had not, as predicted, buggered off as soon as Hendricks had given him his Christmas presents, but had actually stuck around and was now, miracle of miracles, dropping hints about moving in.

At half time, Thorne got up and threw the remains of the Chinese takeaway into a bin-liner. There wasn't a great deal of anything left, Elvis having licked both plates clean within moments of them putting down their forks for the final time.

He returned with two more cold cans from the fridge. 'So you're happy about this, are you? Brendan staying?' Hendricks looked decidedly unsure. Thorne handed him a can. 'Oh, for fuck's sake, Phil.'

'It's just unexpected. I need to think about it a bit . . .'

'Not easily pleased, are you?'

Thorne opened his beer and slumped back into his

chair. In the studio, some bald bloke who'd won three caps in the early seventies was attempting to make the previous forty-five minutes sound interesting. Aston Villa and Leeds United grinding out a nil-nil draw in the pissing rain was proving to be far from riveting.

'So what does he make of this then? Brendan . . .'

'He's not a football fan, well, not beyond thinking Thierry Henry's got nice legs anyway, so he's not really bothered.'

Thorne took a sip, stared at the TV. 'No, I meant, you know, you coming over here . . .'

For a minute, Hendricks said nothing and Thorne wondered if, like him, he was thinking about what had happened between them a year before.

They had fallen out badly in the middle of a case. Hendricks had told him he was gay, at the same time as telling him what a selfish bastard he was being. Thorne had been gobsmacked by the confession and shamed by the accusation – he knew that Hendricks had a point. His friend had gone out on a limb for him and suffered for it. Thorne hadn't been there to speak up on his friend's behalf when he should have been.

Back then, with the bodies piling up, Thorne hadn't even been there for himself.

It was the death of strangers that had eventually brought them back together, as it had brought them together in the first place.

'You want to know what Brendan thinks about you?'

Thorne shrugged, gestured with his can towards the slow-motion replay on the screen. 'Look, he should have scored, he was clean through. Couldn't hit a cow's arse with a banjo. No . . . just, you know . . .'

'Why is it that eventually, you always get round to asking if my boyfriends fancy you or not?'

'That's bollocks.'

'Don't get me wrong, you're usually quite subtle about it, but there's always some comment, some bit of fishing . . .'

'All in your twisted mind, mate . . .'

'He thinks you're a bit chunky.'

Thorne's show of mock annoyance, the raised voice and wounded expression, barely masked how genuinely pissed off he really was. 'Chunky? What does he mean, "chunky"?'

Hendricks sniggered and reached for the remote. The teams were coming out for the second half. 'Shut up, you tart . . .'

They watched in silence as twenty-two thoroughly bored-looking individuals with bad haircuts jogged half-heartedly out into the rain. Hendricks picked up the remote again and pressed mute.

'What about you anyway? Much going on horizontally?'

'Sod all. Turn the sound back on . . .'

'You never rang Anne Coburn, did you?'

Thorne shook his head and pictured the woman he'd been involved with a year ago.

'Why don't you call her?'

A question Thorne had asked himself often enough. 'No, mate. Far too complicated.'

'Don't worry about it, you're better off on your own.' Hendricks made a wanking gesture. 'That's . . . not complicated.'

'Right, but the conversation's awful.'

Hendricks turned the volume back up, but not very

high. They said nothing for a minute or two, listened to the
pundits doing much the same thing.

'You haven't said a lot about the case . . .' Hendricks
said.

Thorne hadn't even mentioned it, but he didn't need to.
It was there all the time, the synapses sparking, the associations bursting into life in his brain and forcing themselves
upon him, in spite of his best efforts.

*Katie Choi's mother and father owned a Chinese restaurant
in Forest Hill . . .*

The programme on television, sponsored by Vauxhall . . .

*Would Charlie Garner grow up supporting Aston Villa now
that he lived in the Midlands? Or had he already begun to
cheer for a London club? Was Charlie an Arsenal fan like the
man lying on the sofa? The man who performed the post-
mortem on his mother . . .*

Thorne shifted in his chair, looked across at Hendricks.
'Not much to say.'

Hendricks nodded. 'Just waiting . . .'

'Yep, for a lot of things. Some tiny piece of fucking luck.
Waiting for them to run out of patience and hand me back
my uniform. Waiting for a body to show up.'

'Make it a warm one, will you?'

Thorne raised his eyebrows, snorted. 'We'll do our best,
Phil.'

'I want the bastard fresh on her, you know?'

Thorne did know. A warm body, a crime scene crawling
with evidence. That was what they all wanted.

He nodded at Hendricks and raised his can to him. His
friend was someone you could measure yourself against.
Someone Thorne *did* measure himself against.
Hendricks's voice was flat, and the words could often

sound harsh and ill thought through, but they sprang from somewhere deep and very clean, somewhere passionate and honest.

'Do you think he's still around?' The tone was casual, as if he was asking whether Thorne could see a goal on the cards, second half.

'Oh yeah . . . he's around,' Thorne said. 'It's just a question of whether he decides to let us know about it.'

Hendricks considered this for a moment. 'I think we can count on it. Man who enjoys slicing and dicing as much as he does . . .'

Thorne almost spilt his beer. Even for Hendricks, that was a good one. 'Slicing and dicing? Fuck, and they let you near grieving relatives?'

'Only when they're very short-staffed.'

'Turn it up.' The teams were about to kick off. They let a silence fall between them as they stared at the television, both trying to think about anything but warm bodies and cold slabs.

After about ten minutes Thorne turned to Hendricks again.

'Fucking "*chunky*"?'

The second forty-five minutes was, if anything, less entertaining than the first. This, combined with beer and central heating, and the general level of fatigue that was creeping over everybody on the case, ensured that they were both asleep at just after eleven, when the phone rang.

It was Martin Palmer.

'There's more instructions. He wants to do it again.'

It was as if Thorne had been jolted awake with a cattle prod. 'When?'

'Tomorrow.'

'Fuck.' He looked across at Hendricks who was already walking towards the kitchen mouthing 'coffee'. Thorne nodded.

'He's going to do it again tomorrow.' Palmer sounded as if he was on the verge of tears. 'Can you stop him?'

'Just shut up, Palmer, OK? Shut up. Shit . . .'

Thorne could hear the beep on the line. That would be the boys in IT trying to reach him. They were monitoring Palmer's computer and would have seen the e-mail at the same time he had.

'Palmer . . .'

The beep on the line stopped, and immediately the landline began to ring. Hendricks came through from the kitchen and picked up the phone.

Thorne could have hung up and talked to the technicians, but he wanted to hear it now, that second, from the man it had been sent to. 'Palmer, is there anything else? What does the message say *exactly*?'

Palmer held back the sobs just long enough to tell him.

FIFTEEN

Date: 9 January
Target: Male (Let's not be predictable)
Age: You're as old as you feel
Pickup: Immaterial
Site: Indoors, target's home
Method: Blunt instrument ... in
conjunction with a *sharp* mind

The man had once observed the same routine every morning. Moving from room to room and getting himself ready for the day with great care and precision. These days, the effort was all too much. Where once the clean white shirt would have been laid out ready the night before, now he just grabbed another un-ironed one from the pile and often turned the previous day's socks inside out. He put on the kettle and radio, cut himself shaving, then pulled on his rumpled cardigan in front of the heavy, free-standing oak mirror that had been a wedding present, many years earlier. He placed his battered and bulging briefcase next to the front door, made himself a slice of toast and settled down to listen to ten minutes or so of *Today* on Radio 4.

The knock at the door was puzzling, but nothing to be alarmed about. He checked his watch. It was too early for the post. Perhaps it was a neighbour, or the man to read one or other of the meters. He put down his toast, rose slowly from the kitchen chair, and moved towards the front door.

His wife had always used to tease him about his passion for routine, and the way that any disruption to the order of things could put him in a bad mood. Then, perhaps, it had been true, but not any more. These days, a surprise of any sort could be an unexpected fillip. Something to be welcomed with open arms. There was a second knock, a fraction louder, just before he reached the door.

'Just a moment . . .'

When the door was opened, the man with the leather sports bag at his feet smiled, cleared his throat, and punched the man in the creased white shirt, full in the face.

Then he picked up his bag and stepped inside.

The man on the floor held his hand to his shattered nose, but the blood ran through his fingers on to his shirt and on to the carpet. The blood felt strange and warm. It was oddly smooth against his freshly shaved cheeks. He was crying, which annoyed him greatly, and he was desperately trying to clear his head just a little, so that he might reach his shattered spectacles and work out where the noise was coming from. The noise that was like a drumming, like a thumping, like a train passing beneath the floor. The noise that drowned out the sound of the sports bag being opened.

Zzzzzzip . . .

Then a gentle rustle as something was removed from

the bag, and the man on the floor suddenly realised that
the mysterious noise was the sound of his own heart
smashing against his chest like a trapped animal. He was
pleased that he'd worked it out.

Now, there was just the pain in his face, and the
terror . . .

He glanced up and his body spasmed, and he cried out
a girl's name as he saw the long, dark shape coming down.
His eyes screwed shut and his hands flew from his face to
his head. Every one of his fingers was broken, a fraction of
a second before his skull was shattered.

The man with the cricket bat in his hand needed to get
about his business quickly and that annoyed him. It distracted him. With him, the looking . . . the *considering*, had
always been as much a part of it as anything. After he
killed, he could rarely remember the details of the act itself.
His mind had been elsewhere when that was happening.

Today, there wasn't much time for enjoyment.

With a grunt, he swung the bat.

The man on his knees seemed to jump then, and he
screamed a name which the man with the bat knew
belonged to his dead wife, and the noise of the bat making
contact was like jumping on egg boxes.

The man who used to be simply *Stuart*, lifted up the bat
which came away wet and a little sticky. He hoisted the
dripping wooden blade high above his head and brought it
back down again with every ounce of strength in his body.
He felt the shudder up his arm and across his shoulders.
He closed his eyes, and the colours and shapes that swam
about in the blackness were like the blood flying into the
dirt, and the pulped body of the frog sailing gloriously
across the blue and into the long grass . . .

The man who was variously *First Friend* and *Blast From The Past* and occasionally *Ghost Of Summer*, lifted and swung, lifted and swung, and each time he thought would be the last, but each new contact, each vibration, shook loose some new desire in him, liberated the hunger again and he felt the urge in his head and the action down his arms . . .

Finally, after many minutes, the man who had signed his most recent e-mail *Night Watchman* stopped and looked down at the swirls of bone and brain and blood making new patterns in what was already a somewhat garish carpet.

It took him thirty seconds or so to regain his breath, and then he was moving, quickly. He removed the gloves, wiped down the bat and put it back into the bag, having already taken out the fresh set of clothes. He stepped away from the body, taking care to mind his shoes. He didn't want to be walking bloody footprints all round the place for the rest of the day.

In less than ten minutes he was changed and ready to go, with plenty of time left to get to work. As he closed the front door behind him he checked his wristwatch. He tut-tutted at his carelessness.

The face of the watch was flecked with blood.

Someone, he wasn't certain who, had once said something Thorne was particularly fond of. A phrase he'd heard and never forgotten.

Knock hard, life is deaf.

It was a sentiment he did his best to live by, but there were occasions, many of them in fact, when those around him might have been happier had he tried to keep the noise down a little. Times when they seemed unwilling to discover what might be on the other side of the door.

Usually, this would only make Tom Thorne knock harder, bang louder. Today, even he was not sure he wanted to see that door opened.

Today, a man was going to die a violent death. A man who, but for Thorne, but for the course *he* had chosen to follow, might otherwise live. It was pretty much that simple, and it was not a pleasant thought to be bouncing around in your head from the second you opened your eyes in the morning.

Thorne rushed into work like a madman, but if he had imagined it might be . . . easier, with people around him, among the team – at the heart of things – he was wrong.

It was as if his colleagues, no, not just his colleagues – the woman in the newsagent, the postman, every driver he'd cut up on the North Circular on the way into work – all of them, could see his guilty thought, his dark admission. It was as though it had become visible, like a tiny spot floating across his eyeball. They all saw the terrible thought and processed it, and instantly, they all produced their own thought to keep it company:

You're right. It was/is/will be your fault . . .

Wednesday, 9 January. A wet and windy and godforsaken fucker of a Wednesday, when it was easy to see why its children were full of woe. A shitty, dreary, dry wank of a day. A day for watching clocks and losing tempers, and listening for phones.

A day for talking about it.

Thorne, Brigstocke, Holland and McEvoy. Sitting around a table, the rain beating against the windows. Talking about it.

'A man, this time. Is that important?'

'Like he said in the mail, ringing in the changes.'

'It feels like he's playing a game.'

'With Palmer, or with us?'

'What the fuck does "Night Watchman" mean anyway?'

'Like a security guard . . .'

'Or in cricket, you know? Someone they send in late on. Someone who's dispensable.'

'Sounds a bit odd. Does he think he's dispensable?'

'I doubt it . . .'

'I'm not sure how seriously we should take any of it.'

'Any of it,' Thorne said, '*except* for the killing.'

Talking about it, because that's all they *could* do. Everybody keen to make their contribution.

Jesmond on the phone to Brigstocke: 'This will probably be our only chance, Russell. Make sure you don't blow it.'

Steve Norman, who Thorne was disliking more and more each time he encountered him, on a cheery visit from the press office, annoyingly only spitting distance away above the station at Colindale: 'Well, everything's geared up at our end, Tom.' He laughed then. 'Bloody press have been making up stories for years anyway, about time *we* had a go.' Thorne neglected to laugh along, but Norman seemed not to notice. 'Just to let you know, ready and waiting when it goes off . . .'

Waiting.

To an extent of course, they were *always* waiting: Thorne, Brigstocke and the rest of them. Those at the shitty end of it. Waiting for the next call, the next case. Waiting for the one that would do their heads in, or fuck their lives up. Waiting to open the wrong door or pull over the wrong motor – the one with the mad fucker in it.

Waiting for the knife or the bullet, or if they were clever and lucky, just waiting it out. Waiting for the pension.

This was a different kind of waiting though. This was far crueller. Now they had been given . . . parameters.

They knew when, sort of. They knew the sex of the victim. Christ they even knew *how* he was going to be killed – the death to which this man, whoever he was, had been doomed. They had been shown what few have seen, and yet, at the same time they were powerless to change the picture. It was like being some not quite all-knowing, not quite all-seeing force, hamstrung by the missing pieces of the jigsaw. Omnipotent and impotent.

Like being God with Alzheimer's.

It was just a matter of *exactly* when and *exactly* where. Then, yes, then, they would move. Then, the springs tightened beyond endurance would be released and they would move like streaks of fucking lightning, blazing to wherever this man's violent compulsions led them, praying that it would turn out to be worth it.

Thorne sat at his desk wondering whether *anything* could be worth this, remembering the conversation he'd had a few short hours earlier. He stared out through the rain-streaked windows into the glowering, grey sky. Into the face of Phil Hendricks, those dark eyes lit up.

Make it a warm one, will you?

At lunchtime, a fleet of mopeds delivered a mountain of pizzas. Thorne and Brigstocke shared an extra large Spicy Meat Feast, but not equally. Brigstocke's reply when this fact was pointed out was not one Thorne felt like arguing with, even if the DCI did have a broad grin plastered across his greasy chops as he spoke.

'If I'm going to sit on fences, I'll need a fatter arse, won't I? So stop moaning.'

Thorne wasn't very hungry anyway.

The small talk didn't feel forced or awkward, just a little inappropriate. Like a bad joke at a funeral where everyone's turned up way too early and they're standing around waiting for the body to arrive.

Which was, of course, exactly what they were doing.

'How're the kids?'

Brigstocke's eyes widened as he slurped up a string of red-hot mozzarella. He had four kids under six and was often to be found spark out at his desk in the middle of the afternoon. Often, but not during this case.

'Little bastards,' Brigstocke mumbled. 'Glad to be here if I'm honest, whatever the circumstances.'

Thorne knew what he meant. He'd come into work more than once for pretty much the same reason, except that in his case, the only person he was escaping from was himself.

'Everybody reckons it gets easier, but fucked if I can see when. The time they're old enough to start making their own breakfasts and sticking on Cartoon Network, so you can stay in bed for a bit longer, is just about the same time they start bunking off school and doing crack. Just a different set of things to worry about. Do you want that last bit?'

Thorne shook his head and watched as Brigstocke pushed the entire slice of pizza into his mouth. He grunted with satisfaction, then started looking around and waggling his oily fingers.

'I'll grab some paper towels from the Gents,' Thorne said. He could hear Holland and McEvoy laughing about something in the adjacent office as he moved across to the door.

He stopped and turned, his hand on the metal door handle. His palm slippery with sweat and grease. 'I know this was what I wanted. Flushing him out.' He took a deep breath. 'It still feels shit though.'

Brigstocke swallowed the last of the pizza, pushed up his glasses with a clean knuckle. 'Course it does, and you're not the only one feeling bad.'

'I know, but . . .'

'I'm the only DCI in this room, Tom. Nobody's got a gun to my head on this one. Jesmond gave me the chance to say no.'

'Why didn't he just say no himself?'

Brigstocke stood, jammed the pizza box into the wastepaper basket and crushed it down hard with a size eleven brogue. 'Fear.'

Thorne opened the door. 'I'll get us a couple of coffees while I'm out there . . .'

All day at work he thought about what the police might be doing.

He imagined them in their offices, in their incident room. Some of them staring at the carpet, waiting for the news to come in. Others reacting differently, scurrying about the place, trying to feel useful, keeping themselves busy. Just another day on the investigation.

He pictured them in their toilets. The joshing, pudgy types at the stinking urinal, heads bowed and cocks out. Other less experienced, alone in cubicles, elbows jammed on knees and legs going to sleep after too long on a warm lavatory seat. Staring at a cracked tile floor, breathing heavily. The shit pouring out of them like water. Arseholes red, raw.

Plenty of lame jokes to ease the tension. The bog door kicked as their colleagues took the piss, the echoing sound of jeers and hollow laughter to chase away the feeling of dread.

Hopefully, yes, a feeling of dread . . .

He saw the pale and puffy faces of these men and women who were so very desperate to catch him. These police officers – fat and unhappy, skinny and dried-up, soft as puppies or hard as housebricks. He saw them all, as they sat at their desks and stared out of windows, and spoke into the grubby mouthpieces of grey telephones. As they passed in corridors and shared illicit cigarettes by open windows. The smell of the fags never quite managing to cover up that sour smell of sweat, trapped, rich and rank in the weave of cheap shirts and rumpled jackets.

All day at work he imagined it, alone or with colleagues, at his desk or about the place. Each new thought, each fresh image, entertaining the hell out of him.

He couldn't quite conjure up an image of Thorne, though.

His face, yes, but not its expression. Not the *set* of him. Thorne was definitely not the headless chicken type, but neither was he the sort to brood and wait, powerless and hog-tied. He knew that Thorne would be the one to feel it the most when the body was found. When the call came through and the sparks started to fly.

That certainly couldn't be too far away.

For him, the day was just rushing by. He doubted that it was passing quite as quickly for Tom Thorne.

*

'Fuckfuckbollocksfuck . . .'

On the way back to his office with two steaming cups of coffee, Thorne had been ambushed by the lethal corner of the desk that hated him. The pain of a bloody graze across an already existing bruise along with the scalding to both hands was intense. For a second, he felt as though he was going to be sick.

'Hand me that fucking Sellotape.'

The passing uniform did as he was told while Thorne grabbed a handful of paper from the desk and sank grimacing to the floor.

Brigstocke, alerted by the industrial-strength exclamations, emerged from his office to find Thorne on his knees, screwing up wads of A4 and taping them clumsily across the corner of the offending desk.

'I'll get my own coffee then, shall I?'

'Bollocks!'

Brigstocke laughed. This was a piece of slapstick that would probably do them all a lot of good. 'I hope you've checked that isn't important . . .'

'What?'

Brigstocke pointed to the corner of the desk. 'That paper. Six months from now we don't want the prosecution case collapsing because a vital witness statement is taped to the corner of a desk in Hendon.'

'I don't care . . .'

There was more laughter, this time from Holland and McEvoy, who stood giggling like children in the doorway of the smaller office. Thorne stood up and threw them a filthy look. He rubbed his leg.

Christ it hurt . . .

Thorne realised abruptly that this pain, laughable though the cause of it might be, was actually the first thing he'd really *felt* in hours. The agonising stab woke him up and reminded him where he was. All at once, the sting of the graze, the tingle of the burn, shook something loose in his brain and shoved it roughly into focus. A jumble of indistinct words and blurred images formed themselves into a question. Something slippery became graspable and he seized upon it.

Suddenly, Thorne was knocking hard.

'Keeping Palmer on the outside, keeping him visible, was so as the pattern wouldn't change. So that the other killer wouldn't panic and bolt. So that he might carry on as normal. Now he's changed the way he does things. Why?' Gritting his teeth, Thorne marched back into his office. Brigstocke, Holland and McEvoy followed him.

'He hasn't changed it really,' Brigstocke said, shutting the door behind them. 'I mean the details have always changed, from one killing to the next. The murder weapons, the locations . . .'

Thorne crossed to the far side of the office. He leaned back against the window, looked hard at the other three. 'Always a woman though.'

Holland shrugged. 'Three times, yeah. I suppose that's always.'

'Yes, Holland, that's always.' He spoke slowly, emphatically, his next sentence as complete a description of the man they were after as he needed or cared about. 'He kills women. He got Palmer to kill women. So why a man suddenly?'

McEvoy sniffed, then replied, her voice casual, her answer much the same as it had been earlier. 'I think he likes to vary things, keep them fresh. He makes that stupid joke about being predictable in the e-mail . . .'

'That's another thing. The joke feels wrong. The tone of the whole thing is forced. None of what he's doing is casual. He wants us to think it's random, like it's whimsical, like it doesn't matter to him who he targets. He doesn't want us to know that maybe, for the first time, he's got an agenda.' He made eye contact with each of them. 'I think there's a good reason for this, for today . . .'

McEvoy was the first to see it. 'Fuck!'

Brigstocke and Holland looked at her, desperate to know what she was thinking, annoyed they weren't already thinking it.

'We were too late,' McEvoy said.

Thorne nodded, pushed himself away from the window and moved quickly across to his desk. 'He's pissing around. He knows we've got Palmer.'

Brigstocke stiffened. 'What?'

Thorne grabbed his jacket from the back of the chair and headed quickly for the door. The pain in his leg was gone. 'I got it wrong. He knows all about Palmer. We need to get him away from work *now*, get him home. It's Martin Palmer who Nicklin's planning to kill today . . .'

Brigstocke picked up the phone, shouted after him. 'Hang on, Tom. There must be at least half a dozen officers there . . .'

Thorne walked out without looking back.

'*I'm* not there.'

SIXTEEN

Thorne thought that Palmer looked scared, then realised it was the way he always looked. Certainly, Palmer's laughter when Thorne told him what was going on – why he'd been forced to take the rest of the day off 'sick' – seemed genuine enough.

He'd taken off his thick glasses, wiped his eyes and squinted at Thorne. 'Whatever else he is, Inspector, he's still my friend. I'm sure he still thinks of himself that way at any rate. He wouldn't try to kill me . . .'

Thorne had said nothing, dragged a chair across to the window.

That had been many hours ago. Since then they'd sat, or moved slowly around each other, saying virtually nothing as it grew dark, Thorne occasionally talking on the radio to the officers in the unmarked cars at the front and rear and to those on foot. Six officers were present, seven including Thorne. Still, the sudden crackle of static from the radio, the shrill ring of the telephone or a shout from an adjacent flat were enough to tighten something momentarily in his guts, to increase the beats per minute by a couple.

'What do you think of me, Mr Thorne?'

Palmer had been perched close to the television. Thorne had turned the sound right down. Palmer leaned forward, switched the set off and swung round to look at Thorne who was sitting straight-backed on the sofa, eyes closed. He had his mobile in one hand, his radio in the other.

He spoke without opening his eyes. 'Nothing. I think . . . nothing of you.'

'Sorry, I'm being dim. You think nothing of me or you don't think of me at all? It's confusing. Which do you mean?'

Now Thorne opened his eyes and his voice was tight with what might have been irritation. 'Either. Both. Turn the television back on . . .'

Palmer got up and moved across to take the chair opposite Thorne. As he sat down, Thorne stood and stretched, produced a yawn from somewhere. 'I'm going to get another coffee . . .'

'You must have seen a lot of killers, Inspector.' Palmer's voice was quiet, a whisper almost, but as always, he sounded like he had a heavy cold: nasal and laboured, the chest faintly wheezy between phrases. 'You've been in rooms with plenty of people who've done the same as me. Breathed the same air as a few who've done a lot worse I should think. I don't know, kids . . . what have you.' Thorne said nothing, but the coffee seemed forgotten. He wasn't going anywhere. 'So why do I make you so uncomfortable?'

Thorne took a step towards Palmer, annoyed suddenly that he seemed so relaxed. Palmer drew back in his chair a little. 'You know that I'm here to catch *him*. Not to protect *you*. You do fucking well know that, don't you?'

Palmer nodded. Thorne stayed angry, groping for

words. 'By the way, my dodgy knee makes me uncomfortable, one or two of my superiors often make me
uncomfortable, *wind* makes me fucking uncomfortable.
You . . .'

'What? I make you sick? I make you want to hurt me?'

Thorne turned away and walked towards the window.
He checked his watch as he went. It was a little after half
past nine.

He stared down at the courtyard outside, at the high
green fencing and the quiet street on the other side of it.
He could see one of the cars sitting a hundred yards or so
away, could just make out the figures of the two officers
inside. He imagined their tiredness, their irritation, and his
own began to vanish, like dirty water down a drain. He
waited a minute or two. 'I'm impressed you waited so long.'

Palmer pushed up his glasses, shook his head a little.
'Waited for what?'

'To give me the "I'm not like him" speech.'

'I wasn't . . .'

Thorne didn't take his eyes from the street below. He
held up his hand to cut Palmer off. 'If that's what you're
building up to here, you needn't bother. I don't care,
and for what it's worth, I think you're actually worse.' He
turned to see Palmer lowering his head, clasping his
hands to his chest. 'Nicklin, you know, the one you
reckon still thinks of himself as your friend, is a maniac.
Psychopath, sociopath, whatever. I don't know why he
kills. Not exactly. He likes it, he gets off on it, it's the
only way he can express himself, sad little fucker. And
he gets an extra kick out of getting you to do it as well.

'So, with you it's a bit easier isn't it? We know exactly
why you kill.' Palmer raised his head, blinked slowly behind

his glasses. Thorne acknowledged the small plea he saw in Palmer's eyes.

'All right, past tense, we know exactly why you *killed*. You killed because he told you to. Pure and simple. To my mind, that makes you worse than he is.'

Thorne turned back to the window. 'He slaughters women in front of their children, and you're worse.'

It was several minutes later that Thorne heard the sigh of the armchair as Palmer stood up, and a few moments after that when he saw the shadow creep across the floor at his feet, and felt the presence of the man behind him.

'Have you ever been really afraid, Inspector Thorne?'

Outside it was cold and clear, but as he stared out at the night, the thoughts came against his will.

Thorne saw the rain suddenly begin to come down in sheets, and he was driving too fast along the dark, wet streets of south-west London, following a car with tail-lights like the eyes of a monster . . .

He was moving through the corridors of a house full of whispers, the voices of those for whom it had been the last place they'd spent any time alive.

He was climbing, blind into an attic, rising up through the floor of a room that would soon be drenched in blood. What he saw when his eyes adjusted to the bright light stopped him dead like a palm pressed hard into his chest, took the breath out of him as effectively as any fist . . .

Now, one year on, the night was cold but clear, and as the memory receded, Thorne felt his heartbeat start to slow. While his breathing grew less shallow, he watched unmoving as the reflection of the man in the window grew larger and a killer drew closer to him.

Palmer spoke slowly, the deep nasal voice emotionless,

almost robotic. He gazed straight ahead, as if talking to the distorted image of himself in the windowpane. 'Whatever it is you're thinking, however bad it is, or *was*, imagine living with it. Not now and again. Not when you've had a few too many and it comes rushing at you out of nowhere. Not in the middle of the night when you wake up sweating and you thank God or whoever as mercifully it drifts away from you, but *all the time*.

'I'm talking about living with something that paralyses you, that turns your skin to something wet and unknown, even to your own touch. Something that makes your bowels boil and your blood freeze, that ties you up and cuts you off utterly, from *every* person but the one who frightens you, the one who generates the power of the fear itself, the one to whom you are bound and beholden.

'Now, imagine living with it to the point where, in spite of how much you hate and dread it, eventually it becomes something that you cannot bear to be without. It becomes a thing that you crave – the tightening in the chest, the rush as it hits you, the jolt as it does its work. The spidery touch of it, delicate and deadly, climbing up your body, from your toes to somewhere just behind your eyes, and yes, in your groin, always down there . . .

'By now, you need to be afraid to feel alive. The fear is the worst feeling in the world, the very worst, until it isn't there any more and you realise that there's a worse feeling.

'These aren't excuses, though I'm sure they sound like it. It isn't as simple as I'm making it sound, I'm not saying it is. What I did was not just . . . a reaction. There was obviously some foul and desperate part of me that wanted to turn the tables, that wanted to make others afraid.'

Palmer shook his head, as if arguing politely with the

other him on the dark side of the glass. 'No. No, I didn't do the terrible things I've done *just* because I was afraid. I don't even know if it was him I was afraid of, or whether I was being afraid *for* him, on his behalf.

'He was frightened of nothing, you see. He *is* frightened of nothing . . .'

Thorne did not want to turn to look at Palmer. Instead he looked hard at the reflection: the mouth turned mournfully down, the tears obvious despite the dirt on the window and the low light. At that moment, and Thorne would always be amazed by this, Palmer reminded him of nothing so much as one of those giant bears in some eastern European shithole. A lumbering thing, de-clawed and degraded, dancing in a collar and chain while idiots threw coins and those who watched it on the news at home threw bigger ones to try and put a stop to it.

Thorne was equally surprised by his own tone of voice when he spoke. It was, if anything, *reassuring*, so at odds with his anger of a few minutes ago. He was speaking for Palmer's benefit, as much as for his own.

'If he's out there,' Thorne said, 'he *should* be frightened.'

Palmer moved slowly forwards and placed a huge hand against the window, the fingertips whitening as he pressed against the pane. Thorne glanced sideways and watched Palmer staring out into the darkness at his past: distant, recent and somewhere in between.

'He's out there. He's always been out there.'

Holland woke and looked at his watch, panic-stricken.

'*Fuck . . .*'

He'd told himself he needed to get up an hour and a half ago but it had been so easy to drift off. Now he'd have some explaining to do. He needed to get showered and get the hell out of there.

He needed to get home.

When he opened the bathroom door and saw her bent over the sink, his first thought was that she was being sick. He moved towards her, an arm outstretched.

'Sarah . . .'

She turned, the white powder obvious above her top lip.

They stared at each other for a while. He was naked, goose-pimply, his arms wrapped around himself. She was wearing a white towelling dressing gown, her hair wet, her mouth hovering somewhere between two very different expressions.

Finally, she smiled. 'Want some?'

Holland barked out a laugh. His mouth formed itself into a question, a *why* or a *what*, but it wouldn't come out. He just wrapped his arms tighter, gritted his teeth and stared hard at the tiles around the bath, at the grout greying and flaking off, until he had something to say.

'Well, looks like I'll be making Sergeant a lot quicker than I thought . . .'

McEvoy's smile vanished and she turned away from him. She looked at herself in the mirror, leaned in close and blinked. In one quick, practised movement she wiped away the coke around her nostrils and slid the powdery finger into her mouth. She ran her tongue around her gums and spoke to his reflection, the anger not far below the surface.

'I don't need a fucking lecture, Holland. All right?'

'You're not going to *fucking* well get one,' he said. 'I just want a shower and I'm away . . .'

The smile came back then, of a different sort entirely. 'Right, back off home to her indoors, once you've washed the smell of me off your cock . . .'

Holland reached for a towel, wrapped it around his waist. 'Yeah, right. Change the subject, whatever.' He reached into the shower, turned on the taps, held his hand under the water waiting for it to get hot. 'Do you get high at work?'

McEvoy laughed and coughed at the same time. She spat something out into the sink. '*High*? Jesus, Holland, you sound like my dad . . .'

The water was suddenly red-hot. Holland pulled his hand away quickly. He wanted to hit her. He wanted to shout, so he shouted. 'OK . . . slaughtered, wankered, off on one, monged, fucked up . . . whatever bit of stupid, fucking druggy jargon is the most current. Fair enough?'

'Well, we have been reading our pamphlets haven't we?'

'Answer the question.'

'What do *you* think? Do you think I take drugs at work? Do you not think I can do my job?'

'Not if you're using at work, no.'

McEvoy cocked her head, as if she was thinking about his answer. For a few moments they stood there, saying nothing, the small bathroom starting to fill with steam. She ran a hand through her wet hair and sniffed. 'So, now what happens, Constable?'

Holland had no answer. Her dressing gown was starting to gape and his eyes dropped, just for a second, to her breasts. He felt himself harden immediately. She saw it at once and smiled, opening the dressing gown completely.

'Well, I'm still up for it if you are. I mean cocaine doesn't make you *quite* as horny as ecstasy but still . . .'

Before he could stop himself, Holland was moving across the bathroom, ripping the dressing gown from her shoulders and pushing her down on to the floor.

It was far better than when they had done it an hour earlier, better than it had ever been. Their voices, as they moaned and shouted and swore, echoed off the tiles. The hiss and spatter of the shower was not loud enough to drown out the noise.

In Martin Palmer's bathroom, Thorne stared at himself. Weighing up his options if, *when*, he walked away.

Thorne the pub landlord. Quite a few went down that road anyway, why not sooner rather than later? A couple of extra pounds and a beard maybe. Early mornings, changing the barrels, a free bottle or two for the local uniforms. Piece of piss . . .

Thorne the shopkeeper. Why the hell not? The greying hair slicked back and someone else to do the accounts. No need to kowtow either. Curmudgeonly, characterful, with a faithful clientele . . .

Thorne, forty-one and fucked. The copper who was fooling nobody.

He leaned forward slowly until his forehead was flat against the cool mirror. Opening his brown eyes wide, he stared at the long, thin snakes of blood crawling across the whites, the creamy crumbs of sleep still trapped in the lashes and the lines underneath, up close, like the skin of an old man.

Like his father's skin.

Thorne opened his mouth. A long, low moan escaped

and was swallowed by the splash of the cold water that poured into the sink. The breath he pushed out to follow it rose and fogged up the mirror. He pushed himself away from the glass, raised a hand to wipe away the condensation and looked at the face of a man who was dead-on-his-feet tired. Tired of waking up and needing a minute or two. Of bodies in baths and in student bedsits, of chit-chatting to killers and of needing to remind himself who and what they were.

Tired of being on his own. Tired of being so fucking angry. Tired of waiting.

The noise of the running water faded away until it was no more than a faraway hum, and for a moment his mind was wonderfully clear and empty. It was just a moment . . .

Then, in a rush: the gulp and rumble of the plumbing, the shock of the ice-cold water on his hands and face, Charlie Garner still there, hammering when he closed his eyes, and somewhere, the sound of a phone ringing . . .

When Thorne ran back into the living room, Palmer was holding out the chirruping mobile like an extremely bright dog with a stick of dynamite in its mouth. As Thorne reached for it, the ringing stopped.

'Shit . . .'

He snatched the phone, punched at it, called up the last number received. It wasn't one he recognised.

The voice that answered was terse, professional. A man's voice. A police officer's voice.

'Yes?'

'This is Tom Thorne. You just . . .'

'Oh, right. This is DS Jay from Harrow Station here. I'm in attendance at a murder scene, and I know some of your lads are on their way, but I thought I might as well try

you, because my victim has got your card in his jacket
pocket.'

Thorne's mind began to race. 'Have you got an ID on
the body?' He looked across at Palmer whose fingers were
entwined across the back of that thick neck, his head shaking, his eyes glassy.

'Yes, nice easy one,' Jay said. 'Everything here in the
wallet, which is handy. The poor bastard's head has been
battered into the middle of next week. Looks like he was a
teacher at a local grammar school.'

The realisation was instant then, and dreadful.
Something that did not belong, dropping, slapping,
crunching into place. Like a coffin toppling from the
shoulders of pallbearers and smashing onto a concrete
path. For no particular reason, Thorne saw the smiling
face of the English teacher who had showed him and
Holland around the school.

'Cookson . . . Andrew I think . . .'

'What?'

'Medium height, dark hair, mid-thirties.'

'Sorry. This bloke's a damn sight older than that . . .'

The telephone line crackled, but Thorne heard only the
terrible noise of the coffin hitting the ground, the deafen-
ing sound of the wood splintering as it hit. Before DS Jay
had a chance to speak the name of the dead man out loud,
Thorne knew that Ken Bowles had been right to be afraid
of the future.

Now, so was he.

SEVENTEEN

This time, Thorne wasn't even allowed at the meeting . . .

There are dozens of pubs in London with what can only be described as a less than salubrious past. Places where strong drink and acts of violence have come together, often infamously, to create moments of history.

The Ten Bells in Spitalfields, which used to be called The Jack the Ripper. Where the man himself is thought to have drunk, where several of his victims plied their trade, where, over a hundred years after five local prostitutes were butchered in three months, you could buy Jack the Ripper books, mugs and baseball caps and, most bizarre of all, you could watch strippers a couple of lunchtimes a week.

The Blind Beggar in Bethnal Green, where, if people are to be believed, at least a hundred thousand East Londoners saw Ronnie Kray shoot George Cornell, allegedly for calling him a 'big fat poof'.

And the Magdala Tavern in Hampstead, where Ruth Ellis put five bullets into the pointless prick of a man who told her he loved her, three months before she became the last woman in Great Britain to go to the gallows. The

Magdala Tavern, where Tom Thorne was sitting, early on a Monday evening, nursing a pint, waiting to hear what *his* sentence would be.

It was a pub he was fond of anyway; somewhere to pop into after spending an hour tramping across the Heath and marvelling at the stupidity of grown men wanting to spend their free time flying kites. The beer was good, the landlord was amiable enough and the food was passable. It was the dark history of the place though, its associations, that drew Thorne, that engaged him. He could never resist putting a finger into those bullet holes that still cratered the tiling on the wall outside. It made him feel connected somehow. He would incvitably turn then, and imagine her.

Always in black and white.

The bleached hair, the pale, powdered skin tight against those perfect cheekbones, her long nails scraping against the heavy Smith & Wesson revolver. Twenty-eight years old and nowhere left to go. Fingers in the bullet-holes – as spiritual moments go, it was hardly thrusting a hand into Christ's wounds, but fuck it, when you've had a few of a lunchtime . . .

Easter Sunday, 10 April, 1955. A moment of madness, of judgement, on a Hampstead pavement: the first step on a journey to the long drop in the execution chamber at Holloway Prison. Forty-seven years later, nearly half a century after they hanged Ruth Ellis, and life for those who kill for pleasure didn't always mean life.

Now, Thorne sat and waited for DCI Russell Brigstocke, wondering just how tight they were going to tie the noose around his neck. Staring into his glass and looking at a few highlights of the past few days.

The pre-sentence proceedings.

The early hours of Thursday morning: gazing down at bits of a teacher's brain on the carpet, Jesmond making his grand entrance, his face set in a reasonable facsimile of horror and grim determination. The smile that the Detective Superintendent had saved just for him. 'I think it might be best if you took things easy for a couple of days . . .'

'Best for who?'

Thursday evening: Hendricks ringing with the results of the post-mortem. As usual, nothing of any real use, but a reference finally explained. 'The tiny wooden splinters embedded in what was left of Bowles's skull. They were willow.'

'A cricket bat . . .'

'Right. Night Watchman. Ha, fucking ha . . .'

Friday afternoon: His father. 'Oh . . . I didn't think you'd be there. I was going to leave a message on your machine . . . I need a bit of info. By body count, who were the three greatest killers in British history?'

'Greatest? Jesus, dad . . .'

'It'll be a trick question see, to wind up some of the lads down the Legion. I ask them for the greatest killers. They say Christie or whoever, and I tell them the greatest killers were actually bubonic plague or smallpox or what have you. See?'

'Right . . .'

'But I need the names. I reckon Shipman's got to be first hasn't he . . . ?'

Saturday morning: Holland with an update. 'Nobody knows what the hell's going on to be honest. There's one or two new faces around, but everything's all over the place. There's a meeting on Monday, the DCI, Jesmond, you know . . .'

'Right, thanks. McEvoy OK?'

'How the fuck should I know?'

Thorne looked up to see Brigstocke walking quickly towards him. He downed the rest of his pint. What had Holland been so tetchy about anyway?

Brigstocke slid in next to him, leaned in close. The quiff had looked better. His breath smelled of the cheap cigars he was so fond of.

'You owe me a drink. You owe me *lots* of drinks.'

Fighting the urge to punch the air like a goalscorer, Thorne nodded, made his way to the bar and bought them both a couple of pints each. Halfway through the second, Brigstocke gave Thorne the headlines.

'You're still on the case. Just.'

'Why do I get the feeling that's the only bit of good news?'

'Depends how you look at it. People are very pissed off.'

'I assume you're including Ken Bowles's family?'

Brigstocke struck a match, held it to the end of one of his cheap cigars. 'I'll ignore that, but strictly as a mate, shut your silly mouth, Tom.'

'Sorry, Russ.' Thorne was. He knew that Brigstocke had stuck his neck out for him. He would try to remember it. 'So, what's next?'

'Damage limitation.' Thorne opened his mouth, remembered, shut it again. 'The case proceeds as normal,' Brigstocke said slowly. 'Emphasis on *normal*. No more fucking about. We work crime scenes, we make enquiries, we gather evidence. It proceeds, as in *procedure*.'

'What about Palmer?'

'Martin Palmer was taken into custody and charged

with the murder of Ruth Murray this morning. Highbury
Corner Magistrate's Court this afternoon. Belmarsh or
Brixton by teatime. By the numbers, Tom.'

Thorne had no argument. There simply wasn't one.
Nicklin had killed Bowles as a warning. He must have. He
knew that Thorne and Holland had gone to the school and
that they could only have been led there by Palmer. There
was no point in any further pretence.

Having said that . . .

'Why did he send the e-mail to Palmer, when he knew
we had him?' Thorne asked this question of Brigstocke, as
they had all asked it of each other, as he had asked it of
himself a hundred times in the last few days. The reply he
got was pretty much the best that anybody could come up
with.

'He's playing some kind of game. Dicking us about.'

'Dicking *me* about. It was me that went to the school.
Me he must have been watching . . .'

Brigstocke leaned forward to flick ash into a vast plastic
ashtray. He shook his head. 'He's a clever sod, that's all. He
wants us to be doing this, to be asking these questions.'

Thorne shrugged, picked up his pint, looked at it. He
couldn't help feeling that in killing Ken Bowles, somebody *he* had spoken to, Nicklin had been sending him
some sort of message. He wasn't sure whether thinking
this was ego or instinct. He'd confused the two before.

He emptied his glass, put it down. He didn't know
whether he wanted to stay at that table and swallow down
beer until he couldn't feel anything any more, or rush
home and shut the door tight. 'Are they giving Palmer to
the press?'

'That's still being decided. Jesmond and a few higher up

are in with the press office. It would be a good move in some ways, you know – killer in custody, get a few old dears worked up, ready for a bit of banging on vans outside the Bailey come the trial. Do us all a bit of good, so soon after . . .' He left an appropriate pause which Thorne filled in in his head.

. . . *I got Ken Bowles killed.*

'It's hard, without admitting we fucked up.'

Thorne scoffed. 'Thanks for the *we*.'

'Don't blame yourself for Bowles, Tom.'

'Why not?'

Brigstocke blinked, reached for his drink. He hadn't got an answer. Thorne asked the only appropriate question. 'Another pint?'

Brigstocke finished off the one he was drinking, shook his head as he swallowed. Thorne reached behind for his jacket. It looked like he was going home.

'You're off the hook for the same reason they let you get on it, you know,' Brigstocke said. Thorne raised his eyebrows, asking the question. 'Fear. They were afraid of being wrong, afraid of fucking up. Now they're afraid of being *seen* to fuck up, which is a thousand times worse.'

Thorne stood and pulled on his jacket. Brigstocke stayed seated, his cigar down to nothing. 'They've got sod all to be afraid of. I'll be taking responsibility.'

Brigstocke ground out his nub-end. 'Oh, don't worry, you have.'

They both laughed, a little louder and longer than was necessary. 'What happened to being off the hook?'

'You are,' Brigstocke said. 'But it's only a matter of time until you're on it again . . .'

'A stay of execution.'

Brigstocke looked at him, smiling, not understanding the reference. Thorne was already wondering how many more he would need to drink. How much before he would be able to wrap himself inside his duvet and crawl deep down into the darkness without seeing Ken Bowles, eyes open and swimming in blood, hands clawing at the carpet, bits of his own cerebellum beneath his finger-nails.

Without seeing Martin Palmer, huge and hunched against the white wall of a cell.

When the adverts came on – cheaply made soundbites for pension or blame-and-claim companies – he got up and went to make himself tea. The show wasn't very interesting tonight anyway, which was a shame. He'd been looking forward to the calls even more than usual.

He'd had a pig of a day at work. It was a busy time: lots to do and he, as usual, the one to do most of it. It was his own fault if he was honest. He was something of a control freak. While he complained of the workload, he didn't trust anybody else to do it as efficiently as he would, so he got on with it himself.

He'd actually been glad of the extra work. He'd needed something to focus his mind a little for the past few days. He'd been struggling to adjust, to adapt to the new way of things.

Palmer was gone: it was just him again.

However much he'd wanted to be in control, to be the one to change things, he couldn't be too angry about what had happened. Palmer was always going to be taken out of circulation after this last murder, and that, after all, had been his choice. He had decided to kill Bowles. Just when he'd been getting into Thorne's little game, enjoying it even, it had become necessary to change direction and now he had to live with the repercussions.

Back on his own. He liked it like that, yes, but *still*, he'd have to find some other way now to up the ante. He couldn't bear to be bored, to be still. Stillness meant sinking, and he'd do anything to avoid that. He needed to find the next thing quickly, the something, the *new* thing, the bright spot on the horizon. He'd found it with Palmer, but now, with him out of the picture, he'd need to find some different way to jack up the rush a little. While he waited for inspiration, he got his head down at work.

Work work work, home, chat, dinner with Caz, and then an hour or two next to the radio with a bottle of wine, enjoying the wit and wisdom of the country's more opinionated insomniacs. Later, he might wake Caz up and fuck her. Stick it in and move it around, while he closed his eyes and thought about Bowles's brain like undercooked porridge, or the nice neat hole in the student's head, or perhaps the way the woman with the little boy had stiffened when he put his hand over her mouth.

While the kettle boiled, he thought about Thorne.

He wondered how the Detective Inspector relaxed after a tough day. After a tough *few* days. It couldn't get harder than a fresh body could it? The body of someone he'd connected with. How quickly did a man like Thorne get over that, especially when it was . . . unnecessary? Who did he talk to about those things? Family? Friends? He was suddenly hugely amused by the idea of turning on his radio and hearing Thorne himself phoning in.

'*We're going to Tom in London, who has a problem. How can we help you Tom?*'

Then that voice, recognisably London. A little rough around the edges, just like the man himself. Deep and impressive, certainly. Soothing or stentorian, depending on his mood, or the impression he was trying to create. Tonight though, the voice a little higher, nervous, a catch in it . . .

'*Well, Bob, it's a bit embarrassing.*'

'*Tom, are you a first time caller?*'

'*Yes, I am, sorry . . .*'

'*Just relax, you're among friends.*'

'*The thing is, I was wondering if any of your listeners might be able to help me. I'm trying to catch a multiple murderer you see, and it isn't going at all well . . .*'

He picked up his steaming mug of tea and carried it back into the sitting room, still chuckling to himself. On the radio, a new caller was broadcasting to the nation. Not Thorne of course, but he sounded equally interesting.

Leonard from Cheshire: 'This bloke who was battered last week, this teacher? They say on the news it was that pair, the ones who've been doing all these murders, but I reckon it was just some little bastard, pardon my French, what hadn't done his homework. I mean it could have been, couldn't it, you know what they're like now in some of these schools . . . ?'

He was laughing so much, he had to hold on to his tea with both hands.

When Thorne arrived at work the next morning, the last thing he was mentally prepared for was a bust up with Steve Norman. The press officer, on the other hand, who was waiting for Thorne in his office, seemed well up for it.

'You've made us all look very stupid, Thorne.'

Thorne cocked his head and crossed to his desk, thinking, *how hard can that be?*

Norman followed him, standing at his shoulder as Thorne, without looking at them, picked up a pile of reports from his desk. 'Alienated most of your fellow officers already, now you're making a pretty good job of pissing the rest of us off as well.'

Thorne carried the sheaf of papers across to the window and began pretending to read them. He wasn't sure why Norman was here and why he was in such a bad mood, but he *really* wanted him to leave and guessed that it might be a good idea if when he did, it wasn't with a broken nose or any teeth missing.

He dropped the paperwork down onto the window ledge and turned to face him, trying his damnedest to look tired rather than angry. 'What's your problem, Norman?'

'No problem. I just wanted you to be aware just how much trouble you've caused. We worked our bollocks off, liaising with the press, getting close to the journos . . .'

'That must have been hard. All that expense account wine to get down your necks . . .'

Norman laughed in mock confusion. 'Sorry, don't you remember whose idea this was? An idea which, for the record, most of us thought was half-arsed at the time.' Thorne shrugged. He hadn't forgotten. 'Yeah, well this time it was people like me at the sharp end of it. You wanted false stories planted in the press, you needed a lie perpetrated and we did it. Brilliantly. Now, it's all gone tits up because *you* were wrong, and we've got to sort the mess out.'

'Let me get this straight,' Thorne said, starting to fray a little round the edges. 'You're shouting your mouth off, because basically, you've got to do your job.'

'I'm not . . .'

Thorne took a step closer to him. 'Well, why don't you shut up and go and do it?'

Norman showed no inclination to retreat. He raised a finger, jabbed it towards Thorne's chest. 'I will, and you'd better be bloody thankful that someone round here's good at their job. I might, *might*, just be able to put things right with the press. I might be able to get this operation out of the mess it's in with half a decent reputation left.' He turned away and strolled towards the door, stopped when he got there. 'When I say *this operation*, I'm not including you of course. You're already down the shitter and there's no way to get you out again . . .'

Thorne laughed, moved to the chair behind his desk. 'Listen Norman, I'm busy, and if you're just going to stand there stating the obvious . . .'

Norman opened the door. 'Later, Thorne . . .'

Thorne spoke calmly, straightening things on his desk, lining up the pens. 'Oh, just to let you know, if you point that finger at me again, I'll break it. Fair enough?'

Norman turned around. Thorne saw the colour rise to his cheeks and was quietly delighted to see a little of the cockiness disappear from around the eyes. They looked at one another, unblinking, for a few slow seconds.

'There's a theoretical equation of ranks between officers and civilian staff. Did you know that, Thorne?' Thorne did, but said nothing. 'It's a courtesy thing really, but most people tend to observe it. A press officer on my team equates with a Detective Inspector such as yourself. I'm a *senior* press officer, which if I'm not wrong, *and I'm not* . . . equates to a DCI – the rank immediately superior to yours. Are you listening, Thorne?'

Thorne looked up, the desk nice and tidy, the eyes nice and dead.

'Like you said, it's theoretical. Now fuck off.'

Norman did as he was bid, and was replaced almost immediately by a far friendlier face. Holland leaned against the doorframe and watched Norman as he made his way across the incident room.

'Cheer me up,' Thorne said. 'Tell me the Desk of Doom has got him, gouged a big hole in his leg. Better yet, taken one of his bollocks off.'

'Sorry, no luck. You padded it with all that paper anyway.' Thorne grunted. He'd completely forgotten doing it. 'What was all that about?' Holland asked. 'I could hear it from next door.'

Thorne got up and walked across to join Holland in the doorway. 'Your guess is as good as mine. Something got up his arse though.'

'Well, whatever it is, it looks like it's gone now . . .'

The two of them watched as Norman stood talking to Sarah McEvoy. He was smiling, gesturing with his hands. She smiled back, leaned towards him, briefly placed a hand on his arm. Her eyes darted towards Thorne and Holland. Half a second later, they were looking at the floor in front of her.

Holland moved into the office. Thorne followed him.

'Oh, listen, I'm sorry about the other morning on the phone,' Holland said. 'You asked about McEvoy, how she was doing, or something, and I was a bit stroppy. Didn't get much sleep . . .'

Thorne had been wondering if Holland would say anything. His reaction had been so out of character. He shrugged. 'I don't know what you're on about.'

Holland breathed in, let it out. Like he'd got something out of the way. 'Norman got it in for you then?'

'Looks that way,' Thorne said. 'Buggered if I know why though. Worst thing about it is, I can't really argue with him. Most of what he was saying was spot on.'

Holland opened his mouth to argue but Thorne cut him off. 'He's a little tosser, don't get me wrong, but he knows what he's talking about.'

'No need to make it personal though, is there?'

Thorne sat down. 'He's a small man, you know? All got big chips on their shoulders.' Holland looked at him, eyebrows raised, a grin threatening to appear. Thorne's face crinkled, sarcastically, in return. 'He's smaller than *me*, OK? I'm average . . .'

Holland held up his hands. 'I'm not arguing. What about chips though?'

Thorne thought for a second, then smiled, like he'd suddenly remembered an old friend.

'Me? More than Harry Ramsden, Dave.'

Holland laughed loudly, and at that moment, Thorne would have been happy, Jesus, he would have been deliriously happy, to just close his eyes and listen to the sound of it all day. He would have been delighted to shut the door and do fuck all of any use to anybody and just sit and wait for the darkness outside the window. To let the night come and grow thick around him. To sit in his office and drink tea and talk to Holland about nothing: about Sophie, his girlfriend and his last holiday, and Tottenham's pointless push for a place in Europe, and what films he'd seen lately and how bloody awful they both thought public transport was . . .

Whatever.

But he knew that every few seconds, his voice, even as he spoke, would grow quiet to his ears, as if the Mute/Fade button on his brain's remote control were being fingered, and a new sound would take its place. A sound that he had to invent. One that could only exist in his imagination. A sound that very few people, very few people *living*, could ever have heard. The dull, wet smack of a bat striking a skull.

Over and over again.

I got Ken Bowles killed.

The phone rang. Thorne reached for it absently, picked it up without looking, said nothing.

After a moment or two, a voice. Tight, impatient, a faint Midlands accent.

'Is this Thorne?'

'Yes . . .'

'This is Vic Perks. You've been trying to get hold of me.'

'Have I?'

Perks sighed. 'Well *somebody* there has. Ex-DCI Vic Perks. I was in charge of the Karen McMahon investigation in 1985.'

Thorne grabbed a notepad and began to write . . .

As he jotted down details, as he and Perks made arrangements, an image began to form at the back of Thorne's mind. There one second and gone the next. Then back again, like the picture glimpsed in a cloud formation or an odd arrangement of shadows.

He saw a stranger leaning down and reaching out a hand to pull him up – to drag him from the cold, dark water at the very moment he was about to go under.

EIGHTEEN

They met in a pub called The Mariners' Arms on the Isle of Dogs.

It was a basic kind of place. Thick nylon carpets, a dart board, beer. Wednesday lunchtime, and aside from Thorne and Perks, there were only two people in there: the barman – a student by the look of things with dyed blond hair and bad skin – who stared intently at the small television above the bar; and a wizened old man in a battered brown trilby who sat in the corner with a newspaper, half a Guinness and a fierce-looking Alsatian at his feet.

While they worked their way through their beers and waited for two cheese rolls to appear – there must have been *somebody* else there, in the kitchen, because the rolls materialised eventually – they talked about their respective journeys. The pub had been Perks's idea. He hadn't wanted to travel too far from the small flat in Epping to which he and his wife had retired. When the older man mentioned where he lived, Thorne had glanced up from his pint, only for a second, but Perks still knew what he was thinking. That part of the world did have something of a reputation.

'That's right. Retired to the same place where most of the villains I spent all those years chasing ended up. I see one or two of them now and again. Buying the paper or down the garden centre. We say hello . . .'

Thorne had been right about the Midlands accent: Birmingham was his best bet, or Coventry maybe. Perks was a tall man. His face was thin and deeply lined, but Thorne guessed that laughter was probably just as responsible as worry. He was in his early sixties, with his grey hair cut short and a neatly trimmed moustache, a collar and tie beneath the padded car coat.

Perks finished his last mouthful of cheese roll, wiped the crumbs from around his mouth with a wax-paper serviette and looked Thorne in the eye.

'You haven't found her. You haven't found Karen, else you'd have said by now.'

Thorne was still eating. He swallowed quickly. 'No. But I intend to.'

Perks stood up, scanned the room for the entrance to the toilet. He looked down at Thorne before making a move.

'So did I . . .'

Later, they walked east, along the river. The fine rain was annoying more than anything – not enough to warrant an umbrella, but enough to necessitate screwing up the eyes and hunching the shoulders. The Thames was wide here. They walked within feet of cheaply built sixties' council housing, drab and depressing. On the other side of the river, at the top of the hill was Greenwich Observatory, the Royal Naval College and the *Cutty Sark*.

They walked slowly; Thorne moving a little slower than he might normally have done. The river belched and slid and slurped beneath them, oily and gunmetal grey. Ahead and across from them, the bizarre monstrosity that was the Millennium Dome rose up through the drizzle, rusting and ridiculous. A million and more a week, so they reckoned, just for it to sit empty.

'That's a decent hospital every couple of months,' Perks said. 'A school every few weeks.'

'Did you think she was alive?' Thorne asked. 'When you were looking for her?'

Perks turned his face away towards the river, towards the wind. When he finally spoke, Thorne had to strain to hear the words. 'For a week, perhaps a fortnight, we hoped. I probably thought so longer than anyone else. That was my job I suppose.'

Thorne went another step or two before he realised that Perks had stopped. He turned and walked back towards him. 'There were sightings weren't there?'

'Several. Always plenty of sightings though. People are well-meaning or else they're being plain malicious. Hard to tell at the time. One though in particular . . .'

'Carlisle?'

Perks nodded, wiped rain from his face with the back of a brown leather glove. 'A few miles outside actually. Three days after she went missing. That one was hard to ignore. The clothes were spot on – we never released everything but the description was perfect. Hair, clothes, the car. That one felt right.' Perks said something else but it was lost as a screaming gull passed just overhead, its cry mingling with the clatter of a nearby helicopter. Thorne looked up and saw a bulky, tomato-red chopper swooping down towards City Airport.

Perks moved past him. Thorne followed, but kept an

eye on the helicopter, unable to explain the sudden, morbid thought, but not wanting to miss a moment should it burst into flame and plunge into the river.

'So that's why you never searched locally?' Thorne asked.

'We searched everywhere . . .'

'Sorry, I mean . . . looked for a body, looked for it in the area where she disappeared. The country park, the railway line . . .'

'The sightings were one reason, certainly. Didn't make sense for whoever took her to kill her and bring her back to dispose of the body. Not that these animals do anything normal . . .'

Perks's gaze was steady but despite the disgust in his voice, Thorne thought that there was something missing from the eyes. It was something Thorne saw in the bathroom mirror every morning, flickering into life. On a good day he might call it passion. On a bad one, panic.

'Then there was the lad's statement,' Perks said. 'The boy that saw her get taken. We had an eye witness who watched Karen get into that car.'

'Stuart Nicklin.'

Perks's eyes narrowed for a moment. 'Yes. Nicklin.'

They walked on in silence for a few minutes. A varied panorama of heavy riverside industry moved slowly past them on the other side of the water, some of it flourishing, some of it long dead. All of it pig-ugly. A disused power station, a grain processing plant, the scrapyard where the *Marchioness* was finally broken up and melted down, wharves piled high with gravel and aggregates, rusting cranes poking skywards.

The sky, the shore, the water, the buildings. Black, grey and brown . . .

'Tell me about Nicklin.'

'He was a strange kid . . .'

Thorne nodded, thinking, *Jesus* . . .

'You don't know how much things like that are going to affect kids down the road, do you? He was really upset. Seeing her get into that car. He knew it was wrong, you see. I think he knew he should have done something to try and stop it. He never said that but . . . he knew. Seeing her taken like that, it shook him. They were close, not boyfriend and girlfriend, but close. Best friends, you might say. Actually there was another kid, Martin Palmer. They were a bit of a threesome. They'd all been together earlier that day, but then they'd had some kind of falling out and Palmer had gone home.'

'Any idea what they'd fallen out about?'

Perks squinted at him, his mind racing ahead, aching to work it out. 'No . . .'

'You knew that Nicklin had been expelled from school before this? Him and Palmer?' The look on Perks's face – the confusion, the desperate desire to know – made Thorne feel suddenly guilty. He was going round the houses. Pissing a decent ex-copper around for no good reason he could think of. He should have just said what he had to say back there in the pub, told Perks what he wanted – what he wanted *confirmed*.

Thorne put a hand on Perks's arm. 'I wanted to talk to you about Stuart Nicklin. Palmer as well, but really . . . this is about Nicklin. I wanted to check that his statement was the only reason why you didn't look for Karen closer to home; how much what he said to you at the time had to do with that . . .'

They couldn't walk any further. They'd reached

Saunders Ness, the end of the riverside walk. A spit, or *nose*, of land formed by the huge curve of the river as it swept round the Isle of Dogs and out towards the estuary.

Perks leaned on the handrail and stared out across the river. 'The Thames was more or less dead a couple of years ago. Did you know that? Bugger all could live in it.' Thorne was not surprised. All manner of shit got dumped in the river and most people didn't know or didn't much care. To the average Londoner, the Thames was just something you had to cross sometimes. Perks looked at him as if reading his thoughts. 'The few people who gave a toss did something about it though. There's nearly a hundred different types of fish in there now – sea trout, salmon, jellyfish. They found seahorses up past the Dartford crossing. They've brought this thing back to life. Nice you can do that, isn't it?'

Thorne nodded, acknowledging that yes, it was nice.

Perks smiled and pointed towards the water. Thorne peered at the shoreline and saw what he was so pleased about; his tale of life after death being illustrated for him, right there. White against the dark water, a heron, standing motionless in the shallows, looking for lunch.

Thorne took a breath, and started. 'Stuart Nicklin has murdered at least four people. He . . . manipulated Martin Palmer into killing another two. I'm sorry if this is hard for you to listen to. I can only say that I want to catch him, every bit as much as you wanted to catch the man you thought abducted Karen McMahon. Nicklin, whatever he calls himself now, whoever he is . . . he's a man who kills for pleasure.' He waited just a second or two before saying the hardest thing of all. 'That said, you won't be surprised when I tell you that I don't think he told you the truth about what happened to Karen.'

Thorne stopped, waited. It was impossible to gauge exactly how Perks was going to react. In most cases, being told, however sensitively, that something you had done was wrong, or at the very best, a touch misguided, was likely to provoke a defensive reaction. Thorne remembered Lickwood's anger: a predictable response to allegations of incompetence. This was far from that, but still, a similar reaction would be entirely understandable.

Perks turned and looked at him, looked at his eyes. Thorne had been wrong in thinking he'd get an angry response. The tone was gentle, comforting almost. Vic Perks did no more and no less than voice thoughts that were familiar to him. These were words that passed through his mind daily: simple and straightforward words he'd heard many years before, and now spoke easily and without hesitation. As Perks talked, Thorne knew that he'd been wrong about something else. The passion wasn't missing at all.

'She got into a blue car, sir. A Cavalier, I think they're called. Blue with rust on the front bumper and a sticker on the back window, and a six and a three in the number plate. She had a strange look on her face. I remember wondering what she was thinking, but she didn't seem frightened. Just before her head disappeared, down behind the door, I think she might even have waved at me. Just a little wave. Either that or she might have been pushing the hair back behind her ear. She did that a lot. It was hard to tell because the sun was in my eyes . . .'

Perks stopped, screwed up his own eyes. He was trying to remember something else, or perhaps he was simply recreating the face of the boy who'd first spoken these words. Thorne couldn't be sure.

'He was fourteen, Thorne. A few weeks older than she was, that's all. Karen had just turned fourteen. 17 July, 1985.' He blinked twice, slowly. 'Karen would be thirty-one this year.' Thorne nodded. It was clearly a calculation Perks could do in his sleep. 'He was still a child. I had no reason not to believe him.'

'I know.'

'Christ, people saw the car. Bloody idiots thought they saw the car, thought they saw Karen . . .'

Thorne was a fraction of a second from reaching out a hand and placing it on the old man's arm, when Perks turned away, shaking his head. He leaned on the wall, fixed his gaze on the shoreline.

The tide was almost fully out. Thorne stared down at the assorted detritus revealed by the retreating water, squatting in the sludge. Tyres, dozens of them, broken crates and of course the ubiquitous supermarket trolleys. How the hell did these things get here? He couldn't imagine anybody unloading the weekly shop into the back of the car and then merrily hoiking their trolley off the nearest bridge. Yet here they were, probably deeply symbolic of something or other, but to Thorne, right at this minute, just a bunch of old trolleys stuck in the mud.

This was a fairly typical bankside treasure trove, though Thorne had often come across more exotic items. A number of artificial limbs. A 1968 Harley-Davidson. A dead white bull-terrier, bloated and snarling like a hideous spacehopper.

And of course, the occasional body.

Every so often the river gave them up. Gently laid them

out on a sandy bank, coughed them up into a tangled bed of weeds or spat them onto the mud. Most were never identified, never claimed, remaining as anonymous as the supermarket trolleys. Many still waited to be discovered, moving up and down the river far below the surface. Their eyelashes and fingernails, the flakes of their skin, snacked upon by sea trout, salmon and seahorses.

Thorne wondered how quickly, if at all, the body of Karen McMahon would be given up, released into his care so that he could learn things from it . . .

'Two things,' Perks said suddenly. Thorne turned to him, waiting. 'I know I won't be the first person you call, or the second. Probably won't be high up on the list at all. Get to me as quickly as you can though, will you? When you find her?'

Thorne nodded. He hadn't needed to be asked.

'What's the other thing?'

Perks turned to him, shivering, tucking his scarf down inside his car coat. 'I want to be the one that tells Karen McMahon's mother.'

Holland stood in the doorway, blocking it. McEvoy moved to go past him. He moved to prevent her.

She laughed without a trace of humour. 'This is stupid.'

'Yes, it is,' Holland said. 'If you come into the office and I'm here, you turn around and leave. I come in when you're already here, you get up and go . . .'

'So, ask the DCI if you can move offices.'

'Right. What am I supposed to tell him?'

'Anything you like.'

'. . . that we're suddenly not getting on?'

Holland sighed and stepped forwards, giving McEvoy

little choice but to move back a step or two. He closed the door.

'We're not doing our jobs properly, Sarah.'

McEvoy narrowed her eyes and lowered her voice. 'You're on that one again, are you?'

'I said *we*, Sarah. Both of us need to sort this out before it goes too far.'

'Is that a threat? Going to grass me up, Holland?'

Holland brushed past her, sank into a chair. 'Jesus, Sarah, you're so paranoid.'

'Yeah? Well you should see me when I've done a few lines.' She glared at him, standing her ground but wanting more than anything to throw open the door and run. Wanting to bolt into the toilets and open her bag and sniff up a little confidence . . .

It was almost as if Holland could see the need in her face. 'And have you? Done a few today?' McEvoy said nothing, but felt the burning start behind her eyes. 'Where do you keep it? When you're here I mean. In your bag is it? In here somewhere . . . ?' Holland's eyes scanned the room. 'Better pray none of the trainee sniffer dogs ever gets loose in here . . .'

She cried easily these days. The tears could come at almost any time. They were just gathering in the corners of her eyes, only a drop or two, and easily pressed back with the heel of her hand, but still enough to stop Holland dead in his tracks.

'Sarah . . .'

'*No!*'

Her hands dropped back to her sides and she raised her head. Not a trace of softness remained in the set of her features. The anger always followed the tears and she welcomed it. She was on safer ground then. A clenched fist and a tightness in the chest felt more comfortable than the taste of saltwater in her mouth.

'Listen, I don't want your help and I don't need your advice. I certainly don't need telling what's good for me, work-wise or any other fucking-wise.'

'Nobody's trying to tell you . . .'

'A few fucks and a grope in the car park does not give you any rights at all, OK? And I didn't hear you complaining the other day when you were giving me one on the bathroom floor. Grunting and pushing me into the side of the toilet . . .'

'I only want . . .'

'Just leave it alone. I don't do it at work.'

The single knock was followed instantly by the noise of the door opening and they both turned at the same time. McEvoy instinctively took a step towards the door. Neither she nor Holland had a clue whether the man in the sharp suit with the slicked-back hair who was walking into the office had heard any of their conversation, but it was all either of them was thinking during the exchange that followed.

'I'm looking for McEvoy.'

'I'm DS McEvoy. Do you not know how to knock?'

'I knocked.'

'You knock, you wait, you get asked to come in, you come in. It's pretty bloody straightforward.'

'Who's got time? I'm DCI Derek Lickwood from SCG east.' He dropped an overcoat on to a chair, held out a hand. 'You're nothing like you sound on the phone.'

Thorne got on to the Docklands Light Railway at Island Gardens which straddled the Greenwich Meridian. Here, a tiled Victorian walkway ran right under the river, connecting with the south shore near the *Cutty Sark*.

In no time at all, the train was rattling through the heart of Canary Wharf; the view as breathtaking to Thorne as any he had just seen staring across the Thames.

It was a bizarre journey. A matter of minutes separated one of the oldest parts of London from the brand new developments that were changing the skyline for ever: from nineteenth-century tea clipper in Greenwich dry dock to forty-foot yacht in Limehouse Basin; from the classical elegance of the Queen's House to the very different beauty of the new skyscraper, days away from becoming the tallest building in the city; from stucco and slate to steel and mirrored glass in a couple of minutes.

The DLR was as close as the city got to a time machine.

Now Thorne needed to make a far shorter journey back in time. Just the tiniest hop back, seventeen years to the summer of 1985.

A hot summer. Live Aid, French nuclear testing, Brixton ready to boil over. DC Tom Thorne, newly married, standing in a stuffy interview room with a man named Francis Calvert, everything about to change.

And a young girl who, while Thorne was fighting to get the smell of death off his clothes, may or may not have climbed into a car. A girl whose picture grew smaller and finally dropped off the front pages as bigger stories exploded on to them. A girl who almost certainly died alone and afraid on a warm night when perhaps people danced at Wembley stadium or threw petrol bombs on Electric Avenue, or sat at home like Tom Thorne, trying to keep the rest of the world well away.

Thorne put his head back and looked out of the

window. Walls and windows and endless stretches of spray-painted metal moved past him in a blur. Seventeen years ago when Karen McMahon had disappeared, he'd been somewhere else. Now, perhaps they could finally help each other.

The train rumbled on towards Bank where he would change: Northern line back to Hendon and a few hours in the office before driving back out to south-east London again later on.

He closed his eyes and pictured himself twenty years down the road – being sat down in a grotty pub or walked along the river by some spunked-up wannabe; a fast-track thirtysomething DI only too eager to tell him how he'd got it so very wrong all those years before, how he'd screwed up and how they were re-opening the case and how, finally, now, they could put his mistakes right . . .

He pictured himself smiling and saying, fair enough mate, but you'll have to tell me which case you're talking about. Which particular fuck-up.

It's a bloody long list . . .

Later, approaching HMP Belmarsh, Thorne's mind turned to DIY or gardening as it usually did. The place couldn't help but put him in mind of a B&Q, or any one of those other shop-cum-warehouse monstrosities he could see from his office window, if he was unlucky and it was a clear day. Belmarsh looked as if it had been modelled on an American-style penitentiary: utilitarian, functional. Though the big old Victorian prisons like Strangeways and Brixton were doubtless grimy and overcrowded, Thorne couldn't help thinking that they had a little more . . . character.

Not that character was really the point, of course.

That bizarre London mix of old and new was there again, sandwiching Thorne on his drive south, from the Greenwich marshes, through Charlton towards where the prison squatted, somewhere indistinct between Woolwich and Thamesmead. It was a straight road running alongside the river, and though the scenery on either side was hardly picturesque, it was certainly contrasting. On the right, set back from the road, were a number of converted Victorian barracks and army buildings. Dark and dirty, and on land most probably poisoned by a hundred years of oil and ord-nance. To Thorne's left as he drove along beneath a sky already dour and darkening at four o'clock, stood plot after plot of new housing developments. They were the sort that used to be advertised by that bloke with the square chin and the deep voice who swooped down in a helicopter. Red bricks and green roofs, which would almost certainly fall down long before the somewhat darker buildings on the other side of the road.

Then there was the prison itself. Its security level was as high as anywhere in the country. Home at one time or another to Jeffrey Archer, Ronnie Biggs and any terrorist worth their salt. Nobody had ever escaped. Low and grey and grim, and itself overlooked by yet another housing development. Thorne wasn't sure who had the worst view: the unhappy families in their lovely new red-brick houses, or the prisoners . . .

It took a little over half an hour from when Thorne first showed his warrant card at the desk in the visitors' centre to when he was sitting in the Category-A legal visit room, waiting to see Martin Palmer.

It was a drawn-out and regimented procedure. From the visitors' centre, where Thorne had to leave all personal belongings in a locker, on to the main building where his authorisation was checked again and an ultraviolet mark stamped onto the back of his hand. Then out into a court-yard where his pass was re-checked, through an X-ray portal, a maze of glass and air-lock type passages – one door shutting before the next one opened. And then the wait for the van that transported visitors to the separate Category-A compound. Once there, a third check on cre-dentials, another X-ray machine and a good deal more grunting and staring before Thorne was finally ushered into the small, rectangular visit room.

Then another wait that depended on nothing but the mood of the prison officers concerned. It was always the same and it always pissed Thorne off. Police officers and prison staff were old enemies. The finders and the keepers resenting each other. Screws were seen as failed coppers. Coppers were thought of as delivery boys with smart suits and clean hands. On a prison officer's territory, if any-thing could be done to make things that little bit more tedious and difficult, it usually was.

Ten minutes later, a heavily tattooed and deeply depressed prison officer led Martin Palmer into the room. Palmer walked across and took a seat at the table opposite Thorne. The prison officer, who Thorne thought looked like a shithouse with right-wing leanings, left to take up his position behind the door from where he could observe through the window.

Palmer was pale. He was wearing the orange hooded top that Thorne had seen him in at his flat on Christmas Eve. He stared at Thorne, blinking slowly. He looked more like a man who'd just woken up than one who, as a matter of policy, would be on suicide watch.

Despite the time and trouble he'd taken to get there, Thorne wanted to keep it quick and simple. He was only really there to deliver a message.

'I'm going to find Karen,' he said.

PART FOUR

NEED

NINETEEN

Palmer looked lost.

He stared around in search of something that might anchor him, some familiar landmark from which he could navigate, but everything felt alien and unknown.

Thorne watched, trying to imagine the man as a boy in this place when the world was very different, but he was no more successful than Palmer at recapturing the past.

It was understandable, of course. The embankment was unrecognisable compared to how it must have been almost twenty years earlier. This stretch of line, which a mile or so further on ran past the bottom of the King Edward's playing fields, had been disused for years. It had been earmarked for a development which, luckily for this operation, was never quite funded properly. The railway buildings – maintenance sheds and equipment stores – had long been demolished. The track was overgrown and in pieces. In patches, the grass was over eight feet high. Palmer was a stranger in this place he had once known so well.

The handcuffs he was wearing hardly helped.

Thorne moved across to him, stood at his shoulder.

'Something tells me this isn't going to be easy.'

'It's not the same place. It's completely different.'

'Nowhere's ever the way we remember it.'

'I know. But this . . .' Palmer began to move towards a clump of trees. Thorne went with him. The sky was clear, but it had rained heavily overnight and the wind, which had picked up, blew water off the brown ferns and grey sycamores. The long grass clinging to their legs as they walked was heavy and wet. Thorne was wearing water-proof over-trousers and Palmer's jeans were already soaked.

'The curve of the bank, maybe,' Thorne said. 'A partic-ular arrangement of trees. Anything that might at least narrow it down for us.'

Palmer nodded. 'I'm looking.'

Thorne saw the confusion etched across his face, but beneath it, Palmer wore the same base expression, his *key* expression, that Thorne had seen often. The one he had seen staring out at him from the front page of most of the papers that morning. Palmer, six months earlier, blinking and blurry, cradling a soft drink at some doubt-less horrendous office party or other. Snapped hiding in a corner, his eyes wide, the pupils reddened by the flash; doing his best to look as if he was enjoying himself and failing dismally.

Thorne's money was on Sean Bracher as the source of the photo. If the slimy wanker had been in front of him at that moment, he might have given him a dig, but he couldn't summon up the energy to be too pissed off about it. Bracher, like that cleaner in the hotel, cashing in on killing, making a little something. One person's tragedy and all that. One dog-eared snap. One nice new sports car and a couple of weeks in Antigua with the girlfriend. It was only a picture. Fuck it, why not . . .

Palmer with that same expression now as he stared around him.

All at once, Thorne recognised the expression for what it actually was: embarrassment. Embarrassed to be at that party. To be walking into a police station confessing to murder. Embarrassed to be here. Palmer was, Thorne realised, embarrassed to be pretty much wherever he was.

Palmer let out a small groan, his disorientation growing, and it struck Thorne that even the seasons were conspiring against him – against both of them. Palmer would have remembered this place as it was in summer. Then the trees would have been heavy with fruit and flower. Today they dripped, dark and skeletal.

'It might help to think of the place in relation to the houses,' Thorne suggested. 'Can you remember which estate Nicklin used to live on?' They both looked up towards the top of the embankment. A healthy crop of TV aerials and satellite dishes blossomed, just visible, beyond the treeline.

Palmer shook his head. 'They're different. Newer.'

'What about the bridge? Can you get your bearings from that?'

Palmer looked up at the metal footbridge, a quarter of a mile away, high above the embankment valley. 'That wasn't even there. They were still building it. I can remember the noise . . .'

Thorne suddenly felt wetter and a damn sight colder as the thought hit him. How devious and clever could the fourteen-year-old Stuart Nicklin have been? Was Karen McMahon buried under a hundred tons of concrete bridge support? If she was, they'd almost certainly never find her. Not that Jesmond or those above him would even agree to looking. He'd had enough of a job getting a search on *this* scale organised. The three magic initials had done the trick in the end. Having spoken to Hendricks he was far from sure whether it was even possible, but the outside chance of the killer's DNA being salvageable had swung it. They'd got nothing from any of Nicklin's recent victims, but maybe he'd not been quite so careful back when he was still a beginner.

DNA – a huge breakthrough in the struggle to catch and convict murderers. A useful weapon when it came to getting the better of one's dimmer superiors . . .

Palmer's eyes moved from the bridge to the slopes that rose up on either side of them. He studied the small troop of uniformed officers, positioned at various points along the bank on his right-hand side. Some stood perfectly still, radios in hand, and some of them were moving slowly, their steps mirroring those of himself and Thorne.

'What's going to happen?' Palmer asked. 'How's this going to work?'

'As soon as we get a fix, whenever you can give us somewhere to start, a team will come in to clear the area – get the grass cut, bring in machinery to make it a bit more manageable. For a while, it'll be more like *Ground Force* than anything.'

Palmer nodded quickly. This wasn't what he wanted to know. 'I mean what about afterwards? The actual searching. The digging . . .'

Thorne puffed out his cheeks. Not having been involved in an operation like this for a number of years, he wasn't a hundred per cent sure himself. 'A team of specially trained officers. With dogs probably . . .' Palmer flinched. Thorne wondered how on earth they trained dogs for this . . . speciality. It wasn't something he bothered to think about for long. Sniffing out drugs was one thing, but sniffing out death? 'Cadaver dogs' they called them in the States.

A vivid image caught him off guard for a second, took a little breath away . . .

Lolling, leathery tongues, and paws scrabbling away at soil. Tearing through delicate cobwebs of skin and pressing down through chalk sticks of powdery bone.

Thorne waited a few seconds. 'Then, if we find a body, we'll bring in a forensic archaeologist . . .'

Palmer cut him off. 'You won't find anything.' He stopped and looked down at Thorne. His wrists were cuffed in front of him and his naturally stooping gait had become almost absurdly exaggerated. He looked like a hunchback. 'Why would she be here?'

The question, seemingly genuine and heartfelt, prompted Thorne to ask one of his own. One he'd asked before. Why had Palmer not considered the possibility that Nicklin might have had something to do with Karen McMahon's disappearance? 'Not back then, maybe,' Thorne said. 'That's fair enough. But *now*, since he came back, and the killing began, now that you know about him. Don't you at least think it's possible?'

Something like a smile appeared on Palmer's face, as it had when Thorne had pressed him on this before, and he more or less repeated the only answer that he seemed prepared to give.

'Anything is possible, I suppose. If either of us was responsible for what happened to Karen that day, it was me . . .'

'Tell me why.'

Palmer leaned forward as if he might fall, but at the last second he took a huge step and his momentum carried him away. Thorne watched him go for a second or two, thinking. Was it something about Karen, the thing which Palmer seemed to be keeping back? Or was there something else? Something he wasn't saying about Nicklin?

Thorne moved off after him, following in his wake as Palmer noisily stamped down a path. The rust-coloured couch grass wind-whipped and sopping. Sharp enough to draw blood. The ground itself was sodden underfoot. Muddy water squelched up and into Thorne's boots as they walked.

'I talk to her sometimes,' Palmer said suddenly. 'I know that sounds very stupid.'

Thorne didn't think so. He'd enjoyed, or more accurately, endured, a number of conversations with the dead down the years.

'What do you talk to her about?'

'I don't so much now, but before, I used to tell her what I'd done.'

'Confessing?'

Up ahead, Palmer grunted. 'She knew anyway, of course.'

'Did she forgive you?'

'You could never be sure what Karen was thinking. I don't think even Stuart knew a lot of the time . . .'

Palmer began to move well ahead of Thorne. He veered off sharply to the left, away from the embankment that climbed steeply up to the new housing estates and towards the gentler slope on the other side. At the top, high metal fencing separated this wild, untended patch of wilderness from a shiny new industrial park. Thorne glanced towards the embankment on his right. The officers were still tracking their movements, one or two moving gingerly down the slippery bank.

'She knew what *I* was thinking all the time, of course. All the time . . .' He said something else. Thorne strained to hear, but it was lost on the wind.

Palmer's strides were getting bigger, the distance between himself and Thorne growing with every step. Thorne started to move a little quicker, but they had come through the grass now and were heading into an area where progress, for him at least, was rapidly becoming far trickier. Though the ground was suddenly drier, the undergrowth was denser, his feet heavier. He couldn't raise his legs high enough to step over the huge expanses of bracken and briar. He stumbled through masses of bare bramble, across a tangle of spiky dead thistle-heads. He swore as he caught his hand on something sharp, and bringing it to his mouth, he lost sight of Palmer for a second or two. He looked round quickly, in time to see a uniformed officer a hundred or more yards away, sliding down the embankment on his backside. He was on the verge of calling out, when he heard Palmer's voice . . .

'That's because I loved her, I suppose. I always loved her . . .'

Thorne pushed aside the overhanging branches of a dead blackberry bush, and saw him standing thirty feet away. Thorne was breathing heavily. He suddenly felt rather stupid. He looked at Palmer up ahead of him, stock still. What on earth had he been worried about?

He followed Palmer's tracks through a shin-high patch of dried-out ferns until he was standing alongside him.

'Was Karen the only woman you ever loved?'

'Yes. The only *woman*.' He turned to Thorne and smiled sadly, like an idiot. 'I always loved Stuart, of course.'

Palmer raised his handcuffed wrists and pointed as best he could towards the gnarled black roots of a sorry-looking oak tree a few yards away.

'This is it. I found a baby bird here once.' He turned around and began looking excitedly in different directions. 'The sheds we used to mess about in were over *there*. Stuart's house was up *there*.' He looked at Thorne, nodded. 'It was around here, where we used to come, the three of us. This was the last place I saw Karen.'

Thorne turned around. After a few seconds, he made out the figure of Dave Holland at the top of the embankment, talking to two uniforms, drinking tea. Thorne stuck two fingers in his mouth and whistled loudly to attract Holland's attention. When he had it, he started pointing.

Holland waved and began to speak into his radio.

Checking in his rear-view mirror, Thorne saw that Palmer's head was bowed, as if he was looking down at the metal around his wrist and around that of Dave Holland who was sitting next to him, and quietly reminding himself how the handcuffs came to be there. How *he* came to be in the back of this particular car. The detective driving the Vectra behind them caught Thorne's look and flashed his lights. Thorne raised a hand in acknowledgement.

The small convoy turned left off the southern approach to the Blackwall Tunnel and made for Woolwich, heading back towards Belmarsh Prison.

Palmer spoke casually, as if he were asking to have a window opened, but even over the rattle of the Mondeo and the roar of other cars on the road, Thorne could hear the need in his voice.

'It will be life, won't it? I'll not be coming out . . .'

Thorne always tried to put the trial to the back of his mind. He'd need to give evidence of course, but his real job, if he'd done it properly, was over by then. He was usually on to the next one. Occasionally, *more* occasionally in the last few years, some moron of a judge – some fossil, who didn't know what rap music was and thought that women in short skirts were asking for it – might fuck things up for everybody: make headlines and undermine months, maybe years, of police work by sentencing a murderer as if he'd neglected to take his library books back . . .

'It will be life?' The emphasis on *will*. 'Do you think . . . ?'

A glance in the mirror told Thorne that, now, Palmer's head was raised, his eyes fixed straight ahead. Thorne gave the only honest answer he could. 'I hope so, yes.'

Palmer nodded a few times to himself, to Holland. Thorne thought he looked relieved. 'The other thing is, they'll separate me as well, won't they? When I'm in there? They do that, I read it somewhere, for prisoners who've killed women. They isolate them, because the other inmates, the honest, *decent* thieves and armed robbers, and contract killers will hurt the likes of me inside, if they get the chance. That's true isn't it?'

Thorne saw little point in denying it. 'Sometimes, yeah. It's normally sex-offenders, stuff with kids . . .'

'I know, but I would be a target though.' It wasn't a question. Thorne shrugged, let Palmer continue. 'There's no way they can keep you apart all the time though, is there? Even if you're with . . . other prisoners who are the same as you, the special ones. There's a pecking order of some sort, I imagine. If you're a pervert who's killed a schoolgirl, you're obviously worse than the animal who killed the old age pensioner. The man who's battered his wife to death is not quite as hated as the one who's murdered two women he didn't even know . . .'

Thorne did not want to listen to any more of this. In the beginning, it had sounded like an attempt at self-assurance. Now, it was sounding like self-pity. 'Listen Palmer, if you want me to tell you it's going to be tough inside, I'll tell you. Yes, you're going to hate it. Then again, you're not a stupid man are you? Isn't that sort of the point?'

'Yes, of course . . .'

'If you're asking me to feel an ounce of anything like fucking sympathy . . . ?'

'No. Absolutely not.'

'Good.' Thorne stuck his foot down, gambled on amber and roared across a mini-roundabout onto Woolwich Church Street, the river to the left of him. He checked in the mirror to be sure that the Vectra had made it through the lights behind him. His eyes flicked across to Holland who'd said next to nothing since they got into the car. He stared out of the window, lost in thought. Just a body to handcuff a prisoner to.

'Something else you need to think about, Palmer. Yes, you're quite right, you'll be hated because you killed women. Doesn't matter *why* you killed them, the ones who'll want to hurt you for it will think it was a sex thing, whatever. They haven't really got a lot of time for psychology. Well they *have*, of course, loads of time, but they just can't be arsed. They'll just make presumptions.'

Palmer raised up his wrist, Holland's moving with it,

and scratched the side of his head with a thumbnail. 'I suppose it would be stupid to ask if anybody ever puts them straight. Tells them the truth.'

'Very stupid. It gets a lot worse as well. They'll have two reasons to hate you.'

'What . . . ?'

'Two reasons to smash your face into a sink. To push you down a couple of flights of stairs, or knock something up in the tool shop to stick into you while you're queuing up for your dinner. Don't get me wrong, these people have *got* a moral code, it's just not a normal one.' Thorne caught Palmer's eye in the mirror and held it. 'They hate men who hurt women, or *pretend* to hate them, doesn't much matter which, and if you're lucky, they might only piss in your tea. But if there's one thing they really *do* despise even more than that, it's a grass. With you, they'll be getting two for the price of one.'

Slowly, in the mirror, a clear view of the Vectra emerged, as Palmer's head dropped and he slumped down in his seat. Pleased as he was with his little speech, Thorne couldn't help but feel like a grown man who's played games with a small child and refused to let him win.

Ten minutes later, Thorne swung the car round and pulled up at a T-junction. The Vectra came alongside him, the four officers exchanging looks, both cars waiting for a gap in the traffic coming from his left. A thousand yards away on the other side of the road, across the expanse of reclaimed saltmarsh, lay the prison. The slouching concrete warehouse . . .

Cons R Us. Kingdom Of Killers.

The driver of the back-up car gave Thorne the thumbs up and accelerated away into the stream of traffic heading back towards the city. Thorne pulled across the road and drove slowly towards the prison's main entrance, feeling the first twinges of a headache kicking in behind his eyes.

He looked at the clock on the dashboard as he rolled up the drive towards the barrier. It was just after half past one. He began to think about where he was due to be in less than an hour.

The day was not going to get any better.

TWENTY

If someone told Thorne that he had a nice singing voice, chances are they'd be wearing black . . .

He *did* have a good voice, surprisingly high and light for someone who looked and spoke like he did, and usually coming as a shock to anyone who heard it for the first time. As he sang, it struck him, as it usually did on these occasions, that such events were actually the only time that he ever really sang, the only time *most* people sang properly: weddings, or more likely in his case, funerals.

They finished singing 'The Lord Is My Shepherd' more or less together, and sat down. As Brian Marsden, the headmaster, made his way to the lectern, Thorne looked at the people around him.

It was a large congregation. Sixty-five or seventy people maybe. The majority were friends and colleagues, several generations of teachers and ex-pupils, but a number of those who sat shuffling feet and orders of service were there in an official capacity.

There were more police than family.

Thorne and McEvoy were there, representing the key investigative team. Malcolm Jay, the DS from Harrow, was in church, and Derek Lickwood. Steve Norman was around somewhere, to liaise with any unwelcome reporters who might try to grab a few words with grieving relatives.

While respects were being paid, the mourners were being closely watched in case the killer himself decided to pop along and sprinkle soil on the coffin of his victim. He wouldn't be the first, but as always, Thorne thought it unlikely that he or anybody else would be able to spot him if he were to show up. He would hardly be the one dressed in bright colours or sniggering during the eulogy. He was unlikely to be looking shifty or coughing nervously when the vicar talked about the deceased being 'taken from us'. Nevertheless, it was a useful thing to do. They would ask discreetly for a guest list and, even more discreetly, some-one would be filming those guests as they filed out of the church.

Thorne craned his head round. There was a row of six or seven schoolboys in the rearmost pew. They were sixth-formers probably, sitting stiffly and wearing what in Thorne's day would have been called 'lounge suits'. One of them caught his eye and smiled. Thorne inclined his head non-committally and turned away. The teachers, at least fifteen or twenty of them, sat together on the left-hand side. Some were wearing gowns and mortar boards. All of them watched the tall, white-haired man at the lectern. The headmaster's voice echoed round the church, as it did every morning round the main hall at King Edward's. Thorne looked at the sombre expression on Brian Marsden's thin face and guessed that he looked the same every day in assembly.

The family sat on the front row. The teenage nephew and niece. The sister in her forties. The father . . .

Thorne looked at the old man and saw the shadow of Charlie Garner's grandfather. Thirty years older perhaps, and a sight more frail, but with the same haunted expression. Like he'd been hollowed out and there was nothing of substance to hold the bones in place any more.

The congregation was rising to sing again, the organist playing the opening bars of 'Abide With Me' badly. As Thorne stood, he caught the eye of the headmaster who had just returned to his place, his tribute to Ken Bowles paid. Thorne opened his mouth to sing and realised that he hadn't heard a word of what had been said.

Later, outside the church, people watched the coffin being loaded into the back of the hearse. With McEvoy away somewhere re-applying make-up, Thorne was joined by Malcolm Jay and Derek Lickwood. They both lit cigarettes hungrily and the three of them stood around, not knowing what to do with their hands and trying not to look too much like police officers.

'Inspector Thorne . . . ?'

Thorne turned at the familiar voice and found himself face to face with a smiling Andrew Cookson, the teacher who'd shown him around the school. The teacher who, two weeks earlier, Thorne had mistakenly assumed to have been the body they had today come to bury.

'Here mob-handed then?' Cookson said, laughing.

Thorne nodded and turned to his colleagues. They had obviously not been doing a great job of blending in. 'DS Jay, DCI Lickwood . . .'

'Andrew Cookson. I worked with Ken.'

While handshakes were exchanged, Thorne looked at the man who was hovering at Cookson's shoulder. His head was completely bald and spotted with brown patches.

He leaned on a walking stick and stared at something in the distance, his lower jaw moving constantly, as if he were chewing something everlasting.

He turned his head suddenly, looked at Thorne. 'Thank you for coming.'

'I'm sorry about your son,' Thorne said.

Cookson stepped back and took the old man by the elbow. 'This is Leslie Bowles, Ken's father.'

Thorne saw Jay and Lickwood exchange an uneasy glance. Before they had a chance to mumble an awkward response, the old man spoke.

'Very kind of Andrew here, to look after me . . .'

'Don't be silly,' Cookson said.

'Doesn't know me from Adam.'

'I knew Ken . . .'

'Not as well as some.'

Cookson shrugged and shook his head. Bowles took a slight step towards Thorne and the others. 'It's supposed to stop isn't it?' he said. 'Everybody says it switches around when you get old and they have to look after you. The parent becomes the child . . .' He sounded well educated. The voice was surprisingly strong and deep. Thorne knew that the old man was a lot tougher than he looked. 'It's non-sense though, it really is. Even when they're cooking for you and getting your shopping in, you know? Even when they're doing up the buttons on your pyjamas and pretending to listen to your stupid stories, even . . .' His eyes twinkled and he lowered his voice conspiratorially. '. . . Even when they're wiping your arse, you're still the father—' His voice faltered suddenly. He swallowed, took a breath and continued, the sentences now shorter, the words spoken between gulps of air. 'It never stops, never. You're still the father and he's still the son. Still the son . . .' He turned his head away from them. His jaw began its chewing movement again.

'Dad. They're ready . . .' Leslie Bowles's daughter appeared behind him. Thorne watched them move slowly away towards the line of cars, and saw McEvoy pass them on the narrow gravel path, walking towards him.

'He's amazing,' Cookson said, looking towards the old man. 'He must be pushing ninety.'

McEvoy arrived. She nodded to Lickwood and Jay, stepped in close to Thorne. 'Lippy re-applied. All's right with the world. What's happening?'

Thorne caught a look from Cookson and made the introduction. 'Andrew Cookson, he teaches at King Edward's. This is Detective Sergeant McEvoy . . .'

McEvoy and Cookson shook hands. 'I was wrong,' Cookson said. 'You don't all look alike.'

'Oh, you've noticed that, then?' McEvoy said, smiling sarcastically. 'And you're a *teacher*, are you?'

The cars were rolling sedately away from the church. The mourners began to drift after them, putting up umbrellas as a light rain began to fall. Thorne was pleased. He was still damp anyway from tramping about on the railway embankment and his feet were freezing, but he thought that, all things considered, it *should* rain at a man's funeral. There should be flurries of black umbrellas and rain hammering down on to the lid of the coffin, and a mysterious woman who nobody can identify, weeping . . . and a dirty great shitload of alcohol.

Maybe he was just thinking about his own funeral . . .

'Come on,' Thorne said, and he and the others began to move towards where the cars were parked. It was three or four miles to the cemetery. Graveyard of course, never crematorium. Always burial, in case the body should ever need to be exhumed and looked at again.

'*I mean what about afterwards? The actual searching. The digging.*'

He remembered what he'd been doing that morning, thought about the dogs again. Barking, howling, pawing at the ground, sniffing out the stench of something long-dead below the Coke cans and the fag ends and the weeds.

The rain was really starting to come down by the time they reached the cars. Thorne and McEvoy climbed into the Mondeo. He started the engine, remembered that he still hadn't got the heater fixed, flicked on the squeaky wipers. He pulled the car out on to the main road and followed the line of bigger, blacker cars up ahead.

I got Ken Bowles killed.

And Thorne knew that he *had* – that he would always be sorry for it, that he would catch the man who had done the killing. He knew that standing at the graveside, he would feel his guilt, hot and heavy inside him, curling round his innards and settling down to sleep fitfully in his gut.

He also knew that as he watched the coffin going down into its grave, he would be thinking about Charlie Garner's mother Carol, in *hers*. About Katie Choi and Miriam Vincent in *theirs*. As they lowered Ken Bowles down, he would be thinking about Karen McMahon, in a grave as yet unknown and never tended.

A grave a good deal shallower.

He sat there shaking. Across the table from him, Caroline was crying, and in truth he wasn't far away from it himself . . .

She had cooked pasta. They'd been sitting and talking

about their respective days, neither of which had been particularly easy, and suddenly, she'd brought up the subject of kids again. It surfaced every few months, and for him, it was usually just a question of making the right noises. He'd nod and smile, and point out how far she could still go career-wise. He'd question whether now might be *exactly* the right time and squeeze her hand, and assure her that yes, of course he wanted children too, but that they needed to be sure. They needed to decide *together* . . .

Tonight he'd been unable to conjure up even that piss-easy piece of flannel.

His mind was racing, as it was every second of the day. There was so much to consider, so many avenues to explore. He was still searching for the idea that would excite him, that would fire his imagination. He knew what he had to do, but he had yet to succeed in visualising it. The big idea. The concept that would replace the short-lived adventure with Palmer.

Caroline was talking about crèches and maternity leave . . .

It would involve creating a new scenario. A new backdrop to the act itself, which after all was the easy bit, the unsophisticated part. He *had* toyed with juicing up the killing. He'd visualised new and interesting ways of doing it, but it ended up like the script to an old Hammer movie, with Vincent Price knocking off people who'd upset him in the manner of Egyptian plagues or Shakespearean tragedies.

No, he needed to mould the context, to shape his environment in a way that would stimulate and spark, that would challenge and charge him.

Above all, he needed to keep moving forward. Never still and never back.

This was what *should* be occupying him, but there was

anger in the way. He couldn't think creatively while that was clouding his thoughts, preventing any real focus.

He was furious that they were looking for Karen.

Caroline leaned across the table and took his hand. Would there be a better time than this? Their jobs were secure, there was enough money coming in. It wouldn't be plain sailing, of course not, there was bound to be a period of adjustment, but they could make it work . . .

He'd watched Thorne and Palmer down by the railway line. Thorne cajoling, suggesting, Palmer looking forlorn in his handcuffs. He'd watched them strolling along the embankment like a pair of old poofs with a taste for S & M. What the fuck did Thorne think he was going to gain, even if he did find her?

Her family would help. Giving them stuff, babysitting. They would still be able to go out, have their own lives . . .

It was *his* past and he wouldn't have it messed with. He didn't want it altered. When, *if*, he wanted things discovered, he was the one who would lead them to discovery. He was the one that controlled things.

It was about working together, supporting each other . . .

He needed to put the anger aside, in one part of his brain. Yes, that might do it. Let the other side concentrate on the future – on finding a new motor.

Caroline didn't want to leave it too late. She wanted to enjoy being a mother while she was still young . . .

He would find it, course he would, if he just had some space to work it out, but Thorne and the rest of them were really starting to needle him.

A child would bring them close, bring them closer . . .

He could see it in his mind's eye, almost – unformed and not quite reachable.

Didn't he want a child? He'd said he did.

Like something on the tip of his tongue, nearly there, nearly . . . but what the fuck did Thorne think he was up to?

Didn't he love her any more . . . ?

He leaned forward and slapped her.

It wasn't his fault. She wouldn't shut up, wouldn't be quiet for just a few seconds so that he could compartmentalise. Probably not her fault either, course not, she didn't know, did she? She couldn't see past the smile, the face that gave nothing away, but even so, I mean *bloody hell* . . .

He just needed a bit of space to deal with things. To separate the anger from the creativity.

He looked at her. The handprint was clear, a livid scarlet across her jaw and the top of her neck.

Silly bitch. Waffling on about babies. When he needed a bit of peace and quiet so that he could think about death.

For Thorne, the mug of tea before bed had become something of a ritual. The stroll down to the late-night grocers, after discovering he'd run out of milk, was not uncommon either.

He was in this shop half a dozen times a week, minimum. The three brothers that ran it were Turkish, he thought, maybe Cypriot. He didn't know any of their names. They smiled, sometimes, when he bought his bread, paper and beer, but they didn't seem that interested in getting to know him.

As Thorne reached into his pocket to pay for the milk, he imagined finding that he'd left his wallet at home. He wondered if they'd let him owe them the money until next time. Seeing as he'd been in their shop six times a week for the past eighteen months. Would they? Probably not. Maybe if he produced his warrant card, showed them he was a policeman.

Outside the shop, Thorne stood waiting for the lights at the pelican crossing to change, studying the adverts in the window. The one that caught his eye was scribbled in red felt-tip on the back of a postcard. It was misspelled, but the services offered were plain enough.

It had been a long time.

Thorne took out a pen and scribbled down the number on the side of the milk carton.

TWENTY-ONE

They'd found Karen McMahon within twelve hours.

From the top of the embankment it was obvious where the team was working. The white tented-off area around the grave stood out starkly against the browns and dark greens of the long grasses and tangles of fern. A white square billowing above the bones.

Holland began to move down the hill towards the site, McEvoy ten feet or so away. The two of them had driven there together, along with another DC and a trainee detective. The conversation in the car had been sparse and far from sparkling. Now they moved slowly down the slope, their white plastic bodysuits rustling. Aliens descending, unsure of their footing.

The grave had been found in one of the drainage ditches that ran alongside the embankment at the foot of each slope. Once the overgrown and overhanging greenery had been cut back, it had not been hard to see or to reach. The ditch was about four feet wide but movement was restricted. The sides were muddy and in danger of collapse, and hours of hard work which had revealed the remains of Karen McMahon could be undone by one clumsy step.

Holland and McEvoy pulled up their masks and ducked down inside the tent. It was cramped and crowded. There were already half a dozen people in there, crouched or stooping, the tent not high enough to stand up straight in. The sun had not been up long and the morning wasn't warm, but the heat beneath the canvas was stifling. Though the lamps had been turned off outside the tent, there were still two powerful ones inside and the temperature was climbing all the time. Inside the bodysuit, Holland could already feel the sweat trickling down his back as he stepped carefully past Phil Hendricks who was on his haunches at the graveside, and moved towards where Thorne was deep in conversation with Doctor James Pettet.

Thorne glanced towards Holland and McEvoy as they entered the tent. Instantly, and for a second or two, he wondered if something might be going on between them. There was an atmosphere . . .

He dismissed the thought, and returned to a conversation about death and decay.

As forensic archaeologists went, James Pettet was probably as good as they came, but he was no great shakes as a human being. If Thorne never saw him again, he wouldn't lose a great deal of sleep.

'. . . moisture is the enemy of composition. Moisture and heat together is just about as bad as it gets. Or good of course, depending on which way you look at it.'

Behind his mask, Thorne let out a long slow breath and very quickly took another one in. *Which way you look at it?*

'Buried in a drainage ditch, as you say, at the height of summer, it's remarkable we have anything at all.' Pettet's voice was deep and he spoke as if he was constantly on the verge of nodding off, worn out by the effort of explaining things to idiots. 'There is a complete absence of fleshy matter and you can see that the bones themselves are mushy.'

Thorne had never met Pettet before and could only guess at what lay beneath the plastic hood wrapped tightly around the face and the mask that covered the nose and mouth.

'The non-organic material has been better preserved of course.' As Pettet catalogued it, an assistant moved carefully around the grave, occasionally dropping to his knees or onto his chest to gather up a fragment with long forceps and drop it into a plastic evidence bag. 'The material of the dress, the refuse bags, what's left of the carpet she was wrapped up in. The rope, or cord, around the neck remains remarkably intact . . .'

Thorne imagined Pettet to be balding, perhaps with a Bobby Charlton comb-over and very bad skin.

Thorne turned away and looked down into the grave, the buzzing arc lights casting a harsh and unforgiving light across its grisly contents.

Mushy was about right. Tea-coloured bones sunk down into mud and slime. Tattered remnants of a blue dress, *not white, thank heavens*, and matted clumps of carpet, all floating in a brown soup. Tufts of hair, plastered to the bobbing skull like worms.

The white bleached bones of the human skeleton existed nowhere but under the skin, where they belonged, and in the imaginations of television scriptwriters. *Dem bones dem bones*, hanging, grinning and unreal in doctor's surgery sketches.

Not like this. This human stew.

At the foot of the grave, Hendricks stood back to let one of the team come in close, to stoop down and pluck something long and greasy from the mud. Thorne caught his eye. Hendricks winked at him. He turned back to Pettet.

'What about DNA?'

The archaeologist puffed out his cheeks. 'Don't hold your breath.'

Thorne grunted – as close as it was possible to get to a laugh. The smell inside the tent was overpowering, and, masks or not, holding their breath was exactly what everybody around the grave was trying to do. Everybody but Pettet, anyway. The archaeologist failed to see any irony in what he'd said. 'The victim's DNA, yes, perhaps. Get me some comparable material – hairs, fingernail clippings. Sometimes the parents hang on to those things for sentimental reasons.'

Of course they'd go through the motions, run the tests, but Thorne knew he was looking at what was left of Karen McMahon. 'Any chance of anything from the killer?'

Pettet almost managed a smile. 'Always a chance. There's a chance you'll win the lottery isn't there? Only possibility is the rope. Bits of skin caught in there, perhaps, but any cellular material will have been destroyed by the creosote.'

Thorne turned, raised his eyebrows.

Pettet explained, slowly. 'Creosote is used to weatherproof the railway ties. Same stuff you put on your garden fence. Over the years it's leached into the water running along these ditches. Ironically, if she'd been buried on higher ground, somewhere drier, the creosote in the soil might have acted as a preservative and we might have had a lot more of her left.'

To Thorne, the disappointment in Pettet's voice sounded strictly professional. Not sentimental like those silly parents with their jewellery boxes full of hair and fingernails . . .

Thorne glanced over to the other side of the tent where a small pile of dirty rocks stood in the corner. Pettet caught Thorne's look. 'At least all the bones are there. The killer took the trouble to make sure the foxes didn't get at them.'

A layer of rocks laid carefully on top of the grave. Rocks too heavy to be shifted by the snout of something hungry. Rocks, then a layer of mud two feet or so thick and underneath it all, the body of a 14-year-old girl shrouded in bin-liners, rotting beneath an old carpet. Safe from foxes.

Safe from everything.

A few minutes later outside the tent, Thorne dropped a hand on to Phil Hendricks's shoulder. 'Don't get big-headed, but it's a treat to talk about death with someone who doesn't behave like he's suffering from it . . .'

'Wish he was,' Holland muttered. 'Miserable sod.'

Hendricks grinned. 'He *was* hard work, wasn't he?'

'Like I don't know what fucking creosote is!' Thorne shook his head, the wounded expression just what was needed to set them off. They all laughed then, as they desperately needed to. They laughed and shook their heads as they stepped clumsily out of their bodysuits. McEvoy lost her footing and her hand reached out to Holland for support. The laughter stopped quickly after that, and they all stood in silence for a few moments, taking in lungfuls of wonderful dirty London air.

'I don't understand,' Hendricks said, looking around. 'He obviously didn't want her disturbed, you know, by animals . . .'

Holland nodded. 'Must have taken him ages to find all those rocks. There's not many of them anywhere round here.'

'. . . but he didn't seem to much care where he buried her. She wasn't very well hidden.'

'She wasn't hidden at all,' Holland said. 'She wasn't hard to find. Nobody'd ever bothered to look for her, that's all.'

McEvoy lit a cigarette, spoke as she exhaled. 'Obviously he didn't think anyone *would* look for her.'

'Oh, he *knew* they wouldn't,' Thorne said. 'He made sure of it.'

She got into a blue car, sir. A Cavalier I think they're called . . .

'He did this when he was fourteen,' McEvoy said. 'Then he disappears, and pops up again over fifteen years later. Fifteen years.'

Thorne nodded. He knew what was coming. He asked the question out loud, the one he'd asked himself as he'd stared down at Karen McMahon's remains. 'How many more bodies are there out there?'

It was warming up. There was no wind at all where they stood at the foot of the embankment and the smoke from McEvoy's cigarette rose straight up, blue against the con-crete-coloured sky.

'No chance on the DNA then?' she asked.

Thorne shook his head.

'I told you,' Hendricks said.

Thorne shrugged. *Worth a try.* It was all academic anyway. They knew who it was lying back there inside the tent, in a hole they dignified with the word *grave*, and they knew who had put her there. There would be nothing in the way of concrete evidence on the Palmer–Nicklin case, on the *Garner* case, to present to anybody. But they had found a body. Bullseye. Thorne had a corpse to offer up to his superiors. He saw himself rather like a cat, dropping a dead bird at the foot of its master. *Stroke me. See? Look at how clever I am.*

Thorne had never felt less clever in his life.

They turned at a rustle of canvas from behind them, and saw Pettet emerge from the tent carrying a small plastic evidence bag. He pulled down his mask and strolled across to them. Thorne was pleased to see that he had been right about the bad skin.

'I thought you might want to see this.'

He held out the bag, and Thorne and the others clustered around, staring at what was inside. Whatever it was had once been a bright colour, but was now faded and thick with black mud. It was Holland who first made sense of the broken down and barely legible lettering.

'Bloody hell, I used to love those. Can you still get them?'

Hendricks leaned in a little closer, peering at the plastic bag. Its sides were streaked with muck. The bottom filled with dirty water, gritty with tiny stones and traces of bone marrow. 'What is it?'

'It's the wrapper off a chocolate bar,' Thorne said. 'And no, I don't think you *can* get them any more.' He guessed not anyway, unless Nicklin's tastes had changed. It wasn't the same brand as the one they'd found licked clean and clutched in Charlie Garner's hand, but its presence chilled him every bit as much.

Thorne took a few steps up the slope of the embankment towards the cars, stopped and looked back. He spoke to Pettet, staring over his head at the small white tent. 'Be careful taking her out of there, will you?'

Pettet opened his mouth to reply, but Thorne was

already turning and climbing away up the hill. He clutched the white plastic bodysuit in his fist, wondering just how much protection it provided against what Hendricks had called the little pieces of death. Back in that tent, there would have been millions of them floating around, settling unseen against the bright white material. Some would have got through and ended up sitting on the skin, nestling in the cuffs and trapped on the soles of shoes. Waiting to sparkle when the time was right.

When it was dark enough.

Thorne took a breath and started to climb faster. He was starting to feel the ache in his thighs as he took out his phone and dialled Vic Perks's number.

He would have liked to have stayed and waited until they brought her out. That would have been interesting. He wondered how she would look. Probably just one more stain on that manky old carpet he'd wrapped her up in and tossed across his shoulder. The outline of her reduced down and imprinted on it. Bodily fluids marking out her skinny frame in the cheap nylon pile.

He would have liked to have stayed, but he needed to get to work.

He was annoyed but he was not letting it get to him. He was angry that his past was being disturbed, examined, when he had taken such great care, *always*, to ensure that to all intents and purposes, it had never really existed. He was in control of what lay behind him, every bit as much as he was of what lay ahead. It wound him up to see them taking a little of that control away. He felt usurped.

But he wasn't going to let it spoil things.

Let them uncover a small piece of who he used to be. It

wouldn't do them any good at all. He was about to take another leap into the future.

He'd felt close to it the night before. It had been there, almost within his reach when Caroline had been going on about kids. Then afterwards, as she had sobbed and shouted, as he'd reached out to draw her into an embrace, it had come to him.

The way forward.

Two major changes to the way he was going to go about things, now that he was working alone again. Two. And each *on its own* enough to ratchet up the excitement, to get whatever it was that spewed out adrenaline working overtime. Even as he considered what he had decided to do, his exhilaration was tempered by the thought that he would never be able to top it. How could he?

He was being far too modest, of course. Hadn't he thought the same thing with his hands around a woman's neck, imagining Palmer's hands around another doing as he'd been instructed? When he'd put the gun to that young girl's head and pictured another gun being raised? A gun, as it turned out, in somewhat shakier hands.

Now, things were about to change. He had his new motor.

Never stay still and never go back.

This time, the victim would not be chosen at random. She, and it would be a *she*, would not be plucked from the crowd. She would be carefully selected.

The second change was the breathtaking one – the part of his plan that really raised the stakes. It was so beautifully brazen.

The woman who he was going to kill next would be *invited* to die.

Now it was just a question of deciding on a guest list.

★

Sarah McEvoy slammed the door behind her with such force that Holland braced himself, waiting for the sound of shattering glass, which thankfully never came. The windows were equally lucky to survive the onslaught of McEvoy's fury, which moved in front of her like a swinging bludgeon as she stomped across the office.

'*You wanker!* You self-righteous, tight-arsed little wanker!'

'Listen . . .'

'What was it? WD40? Motor oil?'

Holland felt like he'd been punched in the stomach, winded by the force of her anger, sick because of what had caused it. Gutted that what he'd done had been proved to be necessary. 'It was cooking oil. Just cooking oil . . .'

A thin layer across the top of the cistern in the Ladies, invisible unless you were looking for it. The cocaine gone in a second. A trick they used in some of the more drugs-conscious clubs. He'd picked up the oil on the way to work. He hadn't wanted to be seen taking the bottle from the cupboard at home . . .

'Think you're clever, don't you?'

'No.'

'Any idea what it costs? Come on smartarse, you've got your finger on the pulse, haven't you? Any idea how much it is a gram?'

Holland had had quite enough of being lectured at. He stood up, took a step towards her. 'Listen to yourself . . .'

'I can't afford to waste it . . .'

'I don't think you can afford not to.'

McEvoy laughed. It wasn't a pleasant sound. 'Which fucking seminar did you pick that one up at?'

Holland looked at her. She was shaking her head, breathing heavily. Her speech had been machine-gun fast. Though the oil had stopped her, it clearly hadn't held her up for very long. She'd probably just done a line off the back of her hand.

'You said you didn't do it at work.'

'You really think I've got a problem, don't you?' She was laughing again, looking anywhere but at him. 'You go on like I'm some fucking junkie. It's just an occasional thing. Just now and again, *Jesus* . . .'

'You said you didn't do it at work, Sarah.'

She coughed, wincing a little as something came up into her mouth. 'Yes, well, it hasn't exactly been a normal sort of day, has it?' She pushed past him and dropped into the chair behind her desk. 'I needed something after spending all morning staring into that hole, all right with you?'

Holland realised that at that moment there was almost nothing about this woman, whose body he knew intimately, that he recognised. 'No. It isn't all right.'

She glanced up, threw him a twisted smile. 'Are you still here?'

'That is the sickest piece of self-justification . . .'

'Bollocks! I don't need to justify what I do to you.'

'No, but you obviously need to justify it to yourself . . .'

McEvoy picked up a sheet of paper and studied it. 'The gun that Palmer failed to shoot Jacqui Kaye with. He says that Nicklin delivered it, left it outside his door. The boss thinks that's bullshit, reckons Palmer's lying for some reason . . .'

'I know. Sarah—'

'So we don't know why Palmer's not telling us, but he

must have got the gun from somewhere. From somebody who made it very clear that he better keep the *whos* and *wheres* to himself.'

Holland wasn't listening. He wasn't sure she was. 'This is stupid—'

'If there's a connection to Nicklin we've got to start chasing it, so this is a list of known, or suspected dealers which I've divided up, A, because it's depressingly long, and B, because we should probably work separately, I mean, I wouldn't want to compromise you . . .'

'You need to talk to somebody.'

Her look was one he would remember. 'Or *you* will?'

There was a small knock and Paul Moorhead, a trainee detective, poked his head round the door. His expression said that he knew full well it was about to be bitten off.

'Sorry . . .'

'What for?'

'DCI Lickwood on the phone for you. Do you want me to put it through?'

'Yeah, thanks.'

McEvoy put her hand on the phone, picked it up the instant it began to ring.

'Derek.'

She laughed at whatever it was Lickwood said, placed a hand across the mouthpiece and stared at Dave Holland until he left.

'There's something else I want to tell you.'

On TV, half a dozen dull, unattractive people sat about in a house, each trying to avoid being voted out. Thorne bit unenthusiastically into a sandwich and prayed for something interesting to happen. Like a meteor striking the house, or maybe a knife fight. He thought it was ironic that this was called fly-on-the-wall television. The morons that enjoyed it would have got as much entertainment out of capturing a real bluebottle in a jam jar; watching it smack into the glass over and over again.

The sound was turned down. *Folsom Prison Blues* provided the soundtrack.

Thorne was almost certain that there would be nothing jaunty about Belmarsh Prison Blues. No *boom-chicka-boom* two-beat. Just feedback. A tuneless dirge screamed over the monotonous thumping of boots on stairs and heads against walls. Martin Palmer had walked into the visiting area a few hours earlier looking like it was a song he'd been hearing a lot in the last week.

Thorne had said nothing. He'd put the plastic bag down on the table, slid it across. Palmer had leaned forward and stared at the wrapper, much as Hendricks and the others had done earlier. Palmer had seen what it was straight away. He'd recognised it.

'Nicklin killed Karen, Martin. He killed her and buried her in a ditch, then told everyone she'd been abducted.' Thorne had only glanced away for a second but when he'd looked back, Palmer's face had been wet. 'Come on, did you never even consider it?'

Palmer had reached forward and put his hand over the plastic bag. Obscured it.

'Karen was his first,' Thorne had said. 'At least, I think so. There isn't much of her left to test, so we'll never know for sure, but I'd guess he assaulted her as well. Some kind of sexual activity before he killed her . . .'

Palmer had looked away, poking two fingers behind his glasses to wipe his eyes. 'How did he do it?'

'He strangled her. Wrapped a rope around her neck. Stuart, who you loved.'

'I don't believe he did anything to her like that. Anything sexual, I mean.'

Thorne had scoffed. 'You're right, I'm only guessing. We'll just stick with murder and dumping the body in a shallow grave, shall we? Did you ever ask yourself how many more he might have killed, Martin? How many more Karens there might be?'

Palmer had turned back to him suddenly. 'I want to see where she was.'

'You know where she was. At the embankment. I told you, we found the body in a drainage ditch . . .'

'I want to see exactly. I'd like to see exactly where he put Karen.'

Thorne had heard similar requests before from friends and relatives of victims. *Show me where he died. Take me to the spot they killed her. Where did the accident happen?* Location was important to people. Somewhere to leave a marker, to visit. Increasingly, thanks to Diana and the emergence of a shrine culture, a place for complete strangers to leave bunches of flowers or teddy bears.

Palmer was not a victim though. Palmer was on remand, charged with murder.

'Sorry, no. What's the point, anyway? They've taken the body away, she's not there any more. There's nothing there any more . . .' Thorne said this, but didn't know for sure. The body would probably have been removed by now, but he didn't know what else might be happening at the site.

'I don't care. I want to see.'

'Forget it.' Thorne stood up, took a few steps in no particular direction. 'Before, you were helping us locate the body, fair enough, but this is pointless. Even if I was in favour of it, which I'm not, I couldn't get it authorised.'

'Please.'

'Shut up.' With Palmer, it always seemed to go the same way. He made Thorne feel something that was *almost* like sympathy, whatever it was turning quickly to something that was *definitely* anger. 'Why the fuck should I try to . . . ?'

Palmer shoved back his chair and stood up fast. Through the window at the far end of the room, Thorne could see one of the prison officers moving to check that everything was all right. He had been about to signal that there was no problem when Palmer had said what Thorne had been desperate to hear since those first few days after he'd handed himself in.

'*There's something else I want to tell you . . .*'

Now, in his flat, the phone was ringing.

Thorne got up, turned off the television and stereo en route and fetched the phone from the table by the front door. Stepping sideways to avoid the unfinished sandwich on a plate on the floor, he dropped backwards over the arm of the chair leaving his legs dangling, and hit the button.

It was his dad. They hadn't spoken for a week or so.

'Tom . . .'

'How's it going?'

'Fine, you know.'

'Gags tonight, or quizzes?'

'Tom, it's Dad.'

'I know.' Thorne laughed. 'You all right?' His dad breathed heavily down the phone at him. 'Listen, you never told me how it went down the Legion.'

'What?'

'The trick you were going to pull. You called me and asked me about the worst killers.'

There was a pause. 'I didn't . . .'

'That smallpox thing. It was a joke to play on your mates. Remember? It was a couple of weeks ago, I think.'

'No. Sorry. No idea what you're on about. Smallpox?'

'Come on, yes you do. You asked me for the names of the worst killers . . .'

'What, you mean diseases?'

'Yeah, that was the point, I think. Forget it. Wasn't one of your best anyway.'

'Is this a wind-up?'

Thorne laughed again, pulled a face. 'Well if it is, it's not me that's doing it . . .'

'Just piss off, all right . . .'

'Dad . . . ?' Thorne swung his legs over the arm of the chair, sat up straight.

'Who the hell d'you think you're talking to? Talking to me like that . . .'

Thorne was suddenly concerned, but tried his very best not to sound it. 'Look, calm down, Dad. It doesn't matter OK. OK?'

There was silence then, save for the laboured breathing. Ten, fifteen seconds . . .

'Dad, I—'

'Go to hell, you little fucker!'

An explosion of rage, then the dialling tone.

TWENTY-TWO

Karen McMahon's parents hadn't been informed about the finding of a body, at least, not officially. That wouldn't be done until tests had been completed, but being asked to provide material for a DNA comparison must have given them a fair idea. A call out of the blue fifteen years down the line, and suddenly they would be thinking about finally laying their daughter to rest.

Karen McMahon's parents would not yet have visited the site of this, her first grave. When they did, they wouldn't have a great deal of trouble finding it.

Over forty-eight hours now since they'd found the bones, the bin-bags and the carpet. The equipment, the paraphernalia, was already long gone. Now it was just a muddy hole, its location marked by footprints, a few scraps of crime-scene tape, and the small pile of rocks which Nicklin had used to keep the animals away which now stood like some parody of a headstone.

They'd probably come down with Vic Perks, the parents, when they came . . .

Perks had been very clear about wanting to visit. He'd

sounded grateful when Thorne had told him – grateful and devastated.

'Would it have been quick, do you think?' Palmer had been staring down into the drainage ditch for several minutes, saying nothing. The sudden question took Thorne a little by surprise.

'To bury her?'

'To kill her.'

Thorne pictured the rotten black rope hanging loose around the bones of the neck where once it had bitten tight against the flesh. He remembered Carol Garner's post-mortem report. 'Not quick enough,' he said.

Palmer stepped back from the ditch and turned away. He looked up towards the top of the embankment where the back-up officers sat in their car – the Vectra parked up next to Thorne's Mondeo. It was raining gently. Both cars were splattered with mud. At the foot of the slope, Holland, in a yellow waterproof jacket, wandered up and down, glancing across occasionally at Thorne and Palmer, looking like he'd rather be anywhere else.

'Stuart lied to me,' Palmer said.

Thorne had heard stranger things said, but he couldn't remember when. 'Did he?' he said, thinking: *he did a lot more than fucking lie to you . . .*

'Something happened the day Karen went missing.' He cleared his throat, corrected himself. 'The day she was killed. When the three of us were together down here.' He began to move, each step taking an age, as though he were walking in slow motion.

Thorne moved after him, taking two steps to each one of Palmer's. They'd cut the grass and the earth felt spongy beneath his feet. He was aware of Holland away to his right at the edge of his vision, the bright jacket vivid against the dark bank behind him.

'It was a trick,' Palmer said. 'I don't know for sure whether they were both in on it. It doesn't matter now anyway. I thought Karen . . . wanted me, and I felt excited. She wanted *me*, you see. Not Stuart.' His voice was a little higher than usual, as if the memory were forcing it closer to the way it had sounded fifteen years before. He shrugged. 'Like I say, it was a joke. I was being made a fool of, but I didn't know that then. I was excited, more than I'd ever been, more than I *have* ever been. What happened wasn't intentional. I'd tell you if it were, you could hardly think any worse of me, but it genuinely was not.' He took a breath. 'I exposed myself to her.'

Palmer had stopped moving and turned to look at Thorne as he arrived at his shoulder. 'I'm well aware of how . . . insignificant this sounds now. Then, *at that moment*, I would have taken my life in a heartbeat if I'd had the means. If I'd had the courage. When I turned round I saw the joke, I could see that they had probably been conspiring, but the look on Karen's face was horrible. She was disgusted. Not comic disgust, real horror, like she was reminded of something . . .

'I've wondered since if perhaps she was being abused, if the sight of me brought something back.' He nodded to himself. 'Useless to speculate now, I know . . .

'Whatever, I ran from that place, from *this* place, terrified that I had done something to Karen that day. Later, after she had disappeared, Stuart did his best to confirm it.'

Thorne looked down. He saw that Palmer's fists were clenched. They bobbed in front of his groin, forced forwards by his elbows, pressed tightly together by the handcuffs.

'He told you that it was your fault she got into the car, didn't he?'

Palmer nodded. 'Like I'd disturbed her so much she needed to get away. He told me he would keep it secret. He told me he was protecting me. He reminded me of it, that day when he walked into the restaurant. Hinted at things . . . made threats.'

'He was using you to protect himself.'

'Yes I know that now,' Palmer said, irritation creeping momentarily into his voice. He lowered his head for a second, raised it. The irritation had gone. 'I'm sorry.'

Thorne said nothing.

'Over the years I gave it all a slightly spooky twist. I thought about it all the time, and it got hammered into this bizarre shape in my head. I convinced myself that what I'd done to Karen had somehow contaminated her. Like I'd put the smell of it on her. The victim smell. Something . . . powerful. The perversion of it lingering around her, attracting that man in the car, drawing him to her . . .'

Thorne waited a few seconds, making sure the story was finished.

'What else did you want to tell me about Nicklin, Martin?'

Palmer's eyes slowly closed. His head drooped. As Thorne watched, he half expected to see Palmer's bulk begin to sink into the soggy ground, pushed into it by the force of the invisible weight that was pressing down on him.

'What else were you going to tell me?'

Thorne turned and signalled to Holland, shaking his head. It was getting dark anyway. They might as well try and beat the rush hour.

Martin Palmer wasn't saying anything else for the time being.

Two cars driving nose to tail from north-west London in a long diagonal down to the south-east. In the dirty blue Mondeo, three men, lost for the majority of the journey in their own thoughts. Looking for solutions.

Nursing desperate ideas.

Martin Palmer. Remembering lies, considering the nature of betrayal, praying in advance for forgiveness.

Dave Holland. Weighing up his options and finding each of them in their own way unpleasant, sickening. Beyond him.

Tom Thorne. Running out of time and ideas. Wondering if this was to be one of the ones he'd be doomed to remember. Would Stuart Nicklin's be a face he'd never see and so never be able to forget?

For each of them the answers would come sooner than they could have guessed.

'I want this sorted before we get back to Belmarsh, Martin.' Thorne spoke casually, as if resuming a conversation. They were passing through Maida Vale, down towards Paddington. Twenty minutes without a word and he'd had about enough.

'I took you to see Karen's grave. Believe me, I went to a great deal of trouble . . .' Brigstocke's face had been a picture. Thorne couldn't begin to imagine the rictus that must have distorted Jesmond's deathmask features when the request was passed on.

'You led me to believe there was something else you wanted to say. That's what I told people. Something about Nicklin.'

Palmer sat handcuffed to Holland, unmoving.

'I want to hear it, Martin. It felt like an agreement to me.'

'*Quid pro quo*, Doctor Lecter,' Holland whispered.

'Right,' Thorne said. Fuck knows what it meant, but he'd seen the film. He turned and threw Palmer a look. *Well?*

If Palmer knew what it meant, it didn't appear to make a great deal of difference.

Five minutes later, just past Victoria Station, Thorne yanked the wheel sharply to the left and put his foot down. Behind them, the Vectra flashed its lights.

'Sir,' Holland said, 'Vauxhall Bridge, Camberwell, Peckham, New Cross. That was the agreed route . . .'

Thorne raised a hand, acknowledging the Vectra. He raised his voice a little to answer Holland. 'Lambeth Bridge, Elephant & Castle. That's the new route. I've changed it.'

'The Elephant?'

'Dropping you off home, Dave.'

Holland leaned forward looking concerned. Palmer did likewise and not just because of the handcuffs. 'I appreciate the gesture, but in terms of the amount of shit we're all likely to be in, this really isn't one of your better ideas. Sir.'

'Probably not, but there's no need for anybody to know about it, is there?'

'No, but I still think . . .'

'Look, we're virtually driving past your place anyway. Besides, I think Martin's come over a little shy.'

Holland looked at Palmer, looked behind to the back-up car. One of the detectives raised both his palms. *What the fuck are we doing?*

They drove on through Victoria, across the river and past the huge twin guns outside the Imperial War Museum. Ten minutes later they were cruising slowly up Holland's road.

'Get the handcuffs off, Dave. Unless Sophie wants an extra body for dinner. Second on the left isn't it . . . ?'

Thorne watched, amused, as Holland slammed the door and walked back to the Vectra. The two detectives were out of the car before he got there. A couple of minutes of shrugging and headshaking later, they were back inside, waiting.

Holland came round to Thorne's window, leaned down. 'Are you sure, sir?'

'Go inside, Holland.' He nodded towards the back seat. 'Look at him. I don't think he's going to be giving me a great deal of trouble. We're just going to be chatting . . . hopefully.'

Holland stepped aside as the Mondeo pulled away and sped off towards the Old Kent Road.

Inside, Thorne was playing cabbie. 'Look at this traffic, not even four o'clock and it's mental. I bet it's already snarled up round Deptford. You've got about fifteen minutes I reckon, twenty, tops.'

Thorne checked the rearview mirror. Palmer was staring at the back of his head, breathing hard. Was what he had to say *so* difficult to spit out?

'A quarter of an hour until we get back to the prison, Palmer. That's all. Now fucking speak up . . .'

Nearly going-home time.

The place was starting to empty but he was staying behind. He had one or two things to catch up on. Above all, he wanted to sit alone for a while and enjoy his cleverness.

He never thought about what he did as being particularly clever. What he did with his knives and his hands and his friends. It was something he needed to do, it felt more instinctive than anything else. Yes, of course there was planning, more when he was manoeuvring Palmer, but none of it was really difficult. It was straightforward stuff, mostly. Surviving was easy. It was making it interesting that was the tricky bit.

This was clever though, no question. He wondered whether it had been lodged in his subconscious for a while, waiting to pop out, fully formed. It was so perfect. *She* was so perfect. She fitted the plan and the plan fitted her, so snugly that he wondered if perhaps it was her, the idea of her, the things she made him think, that had been responsible for it in the first place.

He had finally selected his guest and really, there could never have been any other.

He could not be certain of course, not yet, that she would come, or if she did, that she would do precisely as she was invited to do. Whatever happened, he was protected. That was the brilliance of the scheme. As things stood, he was quietly confident. He knew he had made a wise choice.

A wise choice. Like ordering an expensive bottle of wine in some up-its-own-arse restaurant. A wise choice if I may say so, sir . . .

It quickly became apparent to him that he was not going to get any work done. He could concentrate on nothing but the enterprise ahead.

How was he going to kill her? Where? Jesus, so much

excitement ahead, so many brilliant bits of it all left to work out . . .

No wonder he couldn't be bothered with paperwork. That had always been his way though: scan the horizon, find the source of the new adventure and then forget everything else. Throw yourself into it, take others with you if they had the bottle to come, wring each last ounce of life out of it, every drop of juice . . .

He'd pick up a nice bottle of something on the way home, Caroline would like that. She'd forgiven him for Monday night, suggested that maybe he was working too hard, getting stressed out. He'd agreed, said that yes, perhaps he *had* taken on a bit much, laughed to himself about that when he was alone.

Dinner and some TV, and then the radio later, after Caroline had gone up to bed. He was thinking about it already, but later, alone, he'd decide on the final wording. The wording of this first part at any rate. It wasn't going to happen immediately, of course. He'd need to make it irresistible and that would take time. The time frame was still a little vague. He only had a provisional date in mind for the big event itself, but he would start tonight.

Sending out the invite.

'We'll see the fucking prison in a minute, Palmer. It's less than half a mile.' Thorne was trying not to shout. 'Once I pull up to the barrier, that's it. You can forget anything else you might want to say to me, ever. If I don't hear something from you in the next few minutes, I stop listening. Do you understand?'

Thorne wasn't sure he understood himself. He wasn't certain what he was threatening Palmer with. All he knew was that Palmer had seemed keen to tell him something. He always had. He suddenly wondered if all this time it had simply been the confession about exposing himself to Karen McMahon. That was certainly something about which he'd been obsessed. Thorne's hands were clammy on the wheel. Had he seen salvation or inspiration in what was nothing more than a teenager's guilt about getting his cock out?

No, there had to be something else. Something that could point Thorne towards Nicklin.

'What is it, Palmer?'

Palmer, bouncing his handcuffed wrists on his knees, those annoying little nods . . .

'For Christ's sake, you walked into a police station with a gun. You walked in bleeding. I saw how desperate you were, how fucked up. You said you were sick of it, you said you would do anything to help. You said you wanted to stop him.'

'I do.'

Thorne almost jumped. Palmer's first words since the railway embankment.

'So tell me, then. What is it? What was it you were talking about in the prison the other day?'

As Thorne asked the question, the car turned a corner and Belmarsh came into view, the lights of the perimeter fence just a thousand yards away, dancing as the light dimmed.

'Here we go, Palmer, home sweet home.' Palmer made a noise, something like a growl. 'Not very nice is it? Why not go back in feeling like you've done something useful. You can't make up for the women you killed, but you can help me try and stop any more dying . . .'

Palmer shaking his head, wrestling with something. Thorne no longer trying not to shout.

'Come on!'

They slowed down, stopping at the point opposite the main drive, the T-junction where they had to wait before crossing the main carriageway. Headlights sped towards them from their left, a gap in the traffic maybe half a minute away. The Vectra pulled out to come up alongside them.

'I fucking mean it. I'm walking away . . .'

The driver of the Vectra looked across at Thorne, waiting for the confirmation that everything was hunky-dory, looking for the signal that they could go.

'Give me something on Nicklin. I know there's something you aren't saying . . .'

Just a couple more cars.

Thorne glanced to his right. 'How much more guilty do you want to feel? How much more fucking guilty?'

Thorne waved. The Vectra nosed forward, waiting for the gap.

Palmer's body tensing, reaching for something.

'Tell me about Stuart. Tell me what you're thinking. Please . . .'

The Vectra sounded its horn, the detective nearest Thorne's window raised an arm.

'*Come on!*' Thorne shouted, as the car alongside him roared away to the right. Thorne watched it go, slammed his hands on the dashboard, took his foot from the brake. 'Too late . . .'

The voice from the back of the car: '*I think he might be a police officer.*'

Thorne's left foot slipped from the clutch. The car

stalled and lurched forward. He rocked back in his seat, and was about to turn round when his head was pushed violently forward.

Thorne was still conscious as his face bounced off the worn vinyl of the steering wheel, but not for very long.

Might be seconds . . . might be minutes . . . how long?

Thorne looked at the clock on the dash, waited for his vision to clear.

Minutes. Just a few . . .

He turned round slowly. He felt like cement had been poured in through both his ears. Palmer was gone. The back door was open.

Where . . . ? What was it he said . . . ?

Thorne looked around wildly, each eye movement like a punch as he scanned the area, desperate to see Palmer lurching away into the distance. Headlights from the cars that continued to rush past lit the darkening stain down his shirt, the string of scarlet snot that dripped from the steering wheel.

A hundred yards behind the car was a fence maybe six or seven feet high. Up onto the telephone junction box there and over. Away into the building site.

Piece of piss. Could he climb the fence with cuffs on? Probably. Taken the key anyway. Away and gone . . .

Thorne opened the door and all but fell out onto the road. He stood up and stumbled a few feet forward. He raised an arm and waved at the oncoming traffic.

Nobody stopped.

Nobody gives a fuck. No trust in anyone these days. Six days a week, for the past eighteen months in that shop. Maybe if I produced my warrant card, showed them I was a policeman . . .

The Mondeo's headlights were still on. Thorne winced as he brought a hand to his shattered nose and stepped into their beam. The car that rushed past him blared its horn as Thorne staggered across the carriageway through a tunnel of light, towards the prison.

TWENTY-THREE

'Jesus, Tom. Do you feel OK?' Brigstocke looked shocked and concerned.

The nose had swelled grotesquely almost immediately, and now, two days later, the rest of Thorne's face had caught up. He had huge dark rings under his eyes and blue-black bruises along each cheekbone.

'I feel fine,' Thorne said. 'I look like a fucking panda, but I feel fine . . .'

The concern vanished from Brigstocke's face. 'That's very fitting, because pandas are an endangered species as well, aren't they? What the fuck did you think you were doing?'

There had been occasions in the past when Tom Thorne would have fought his corner a little at this point. Stood his ground and made a speech about ends and means. Today, he couldn't be arsed.

'I fucked up.'

Brigstocke had stood up on Thorne's appearance in the doorway. Now, he slumped back down behind his desk. 'Listen, I've got to serve you with this.' He handed Thorne a piece of paper. 'It's a Regulation 7 notice. The DPS want to see you . . .'

Thorne had expected nothing less. The Directorate of Professional Standards – another stupid American name for what had used to be the CIB, the Complaints Investigation Bureau: the team that was there to root out corruption, to weed out the bad apples. The same organisation that had recently been involved in a well-publicised operation to deal with officers moonlighting as extras on *The Bill*, and were currently investigating a complaint that an officer had broken wind during a raid and failed to apologise.

'I can't wait,' Thorne said.

'What about the nose?'

'No picking, no sneezing. I go back in a week or so when the swelling's gone down. Depending on how it looks, they either do nothing, or break it again, re-set it.'

'Do they need volunteers?'

Thorne crossed to the other desk and sat down. 'What are you doing about Palmer?'

'What are *we* doing? You're priceless . . .'

'Sorry. I know that sounded . . .'

'We're doing what you'd expect, which is more than you did, isn't it? The media are all over this and we'll have to play along a bit if we want to use them. Somebody knows where Palmer's gone and the only way we're going to find them is through the papers, the TV . . .'

As if on cue, Steve Norman strolled into the office.

'Russell . . . DI Thorne . . .'

Brigstocke stood up. Thorne, for no good reason, found himself wearily doing the same. 'I'm going to get coffees,' Brigstocke said, moving to the door. 'Everybody want one?'

Thorne nodded. Norman grunted his assent as he

dropped a pile of newspapers onto the desk. He picked off the top one and turned to Thorne, holding it up.

'You certainly know how to generate a good story, Thorne.'

The front page of the tabloid was almost filled with a photo of Martin Palmer. The headline was simple and dramatic. What the Americans called a 'scarehead' . . .

KILLER ON THE RUN.

Thorne stepped around the desk. He was tired, in pain and in no mood for another shouting match. 'Listen, Norman . . .'

Norman raised a hand to stop him and looked surprised when it did the trick. 'Look, before this kicks off, I want to apologise for the argument the other week. I was being an arsehole, OK? I've been meaning to come in and sort it out, but work's been piling up.'

Thorne was completely on the back foot. 'Right . . .'

'Things had been a bit tricky at home to tell you the truth, and I was just on a short fuse. It was out of order, and I know we're not going to be best mates but there's no point us being at loggerheads, is there? Especially not now. Fair enough?'

Thorne nodded, wondering if he was suffering with delayed concussion.

Norman thrust a finger at the front of the paper. 'Actually, *this* is exactly what we need. The phones have been ringing all morning. We'll probably have him back in custody by tea time.' Norman's expression darkened a little as he pulled out another paper from further down the pile. 'Did you see yesterday's?'

Thorne shook his head. He'd been lying in a darkened room most of the day, waiting to stop feeling like somebody had their boot on his face. This time the picture on the front page of the paper was far more indistinct. Two figures, shot with a zoom probably, from hundreds of feet away, like one of those blurry photos of Bigfoot or the Beast of Bodmin.

Thorne and Palmer at Karen McMahon's grave.

'This one we *didn't* give them,' Norman said. 'Somebody did though. Somebody who's getting a bit too pally with the press.'

Distasteful as it was, Thorne had to agree. Bracher was probably responsible for the early stuff the papers had got hold of, but this had to be down to someone on the team. 'I'll find out who it is.'

'Good. I have to say, though, that it's doing us more good than anything else at the moment. We've actually started feeding them a bit more on Karen McMahon.' Thorne looked slightly confused. 'They formally identified her thirty-six hours ago. Around the time this was taken.'

Thorne needed to catch up fast. He'd been out of the loop since he'd put Palmer in the back of the Mondeo on Thursday afternoon and driven him back to the railway embankment.

'*I think he might be a police officer . . .*'

'There's a lot of human interest there,' Norman said. 'Which they love of course. Fifteen years of torment for the parents, all that. Plus, the simple fact that a murder's been solved. Finding that body has done everybody a lot of favours. We can claw back a bit of lost ground.'

The stabbing pain that ran across Thorne's face cranked up a notch. He reached into his jacket pocket for the painkillers. 'I found one body, then lost another.'

Norman laughed, a wheezy snicker. 'Right. But they

kind of cancel each other out.' Norman had a newspaper in
each hand. He held them up in turn to illustrate his argument. 'Thanks to the brownie points we earn for finding
Karen McMahon, we can let them go to town with
Palmer's escape, and hopefully we can keep one or two of
the less impressive procedural details out of it.'

Less impressive procedural details?

'Right,' Thorne said. 'Obviously I'd be grateful . . .'

Thorne poured himself a glass of water. He needed it to
swallow the pills and to take a very unpleasant taste out of
his mouth. As he threw his head back, he caught sight of
Brigstocke heading towards them across the incident room
with three plastic cups.

'Coffee's here . . .'

'Great.' Norman's mobile rang. He looked at the screen.
'Excuse me, I need to take this . . .'

Thorne watched as Norman took the call, turning away
and murmuring into his phone. He was finding it hard to
distinguish between the pain and disorder colliding in his
head like a pair of very long trains, ploughing endlessly into
each other. Norman apologising . . . one body lost, one
body found . . . a leak on the investigation . . . the DPS . . .
Palmer's tone of voice in the car when he said what he said
about Nicklin.

Then, there was the one less-than-impressive procedural detail he hadn't told them about at all . . .

McEvoy was logged on to the Internet. Holland hadn't
recognised the page she'd had up on screen, but the glimpse
he'd caught before she saw him and quit, gave him the idea
it might be a mail server. They were not supposed to use the
system to send or receive personal e-mails, but Holland said

nothing. In the scheme of things it was pretty trivial, and besides, he knew how any comment of that sort would be taken.

'At least you're not leaving when I come into the office. We must be making progress.'

McEvoy shrugged, not looking up. 'Can't let you accuse me of not doing my job properly.'

Holland saw no point in pussyfooting around the issue. He opened his mouth and said it. 'I think one of us needs to transfer off this team.' Her face told him that he'd shaken her. 'Come on, you must have been thinking about it, it's—'

She cut him off. 'Well *I'm* not fucking going.'

'Sarah . . .'

'Right, course. By *one of us*, you mean me. Well?'

Now would be the time to walk away if he was going to; to forget he'd brought it up and make the best of it. He hesitated. 'Yes.'

'Forget it.'

'You're the one with the problem, not me.'

'Are you sure?'

'Don't psychoanalyse me. I'm not the one snorting away my wages, fucking everything up, putting the lives of my colleagues at risk . . .'

The colour sprang into McEvoy's face. She could feel tears pricking at the corners of her eyes. 'When? Tell me when?'

'Maybe never. Maybe half an hour from now . . .' Holland wanted so much to cross the five feet of space between them, right then, and take hold of her. He couldn't.

'Nobody else knows about this, Dave.' McEvoy watched

herself, feeling like a ditzy blonde trying to avoid a speeding ticket. Loathing it. 'Let's just forget all the shit that's happened. Dave . . . ?'

'Nobody else knows for now. I don't think you're doing a very good job of hiding it.'

McEvoy changed tack in a second. 'You go to Brigstocke and I'll be right behind you. I'll tell him you've been harassing me. They'll think you're making it up because I wouldn't fuck you . . .'

Holland could see that she was desperate, backed into a corner. He knew that she was clinging to the ledge by her fingernails, saying things she didn't mean and would never carry through, but still his temper got the better of him. He marched across the office, picked up the newspaper from the top of a filing cabinet and threw it down in front of her.

McEvoy stared down at the picture of Thorne and Palmer at the drainage ditch.

'You talk to *anybody*,' Holland said, 'and you'll be opening a major can of fucking worms.'

McEvoy looked up at him, confused. 'You think I'm the leak?'

'*I can't afford to waste it*, you said.' Holland snatched up the paper, screwed it into a ball. 'Shit, this is easy money, isn't it? A tip here, a photo opportunity there, that's you sorted for the week. For all I know, they probably fix you up with the coke themselves, save messing about with cash.'

'Dave . . .'

'Just admit it, you did, didn't you? Just fucking well admit it . . .'

Holland saw McEvoy's eyes flicker, saw her body tense. He turned to see Thorne standing in the doorway. There was no awkward pause, no meaningful silence. McEvoy was up and moving towards the door, wisecracking to Thorne on her way out as if nothing had happened.

'Some people around here are obviously feeling as shitty as *you* look . . .'

Then there was a silence.

Thorne closed the door, moved into the room. 'Dave, is there a problem between you and Sarah?' Holland said nothing. Thorne felt hot and hassled. He did not want any more uncertainty, any more disorder. 'DC Holland, is there a problem between yourself and Detective Sergeant McEvoy?'

Holland looked at Thorne. Later, standing at bars or staring up at a striplight, he would remember this moment. In the months and the years to come, sitting on the side of the bed in the middle of the night, Sophie stirring next to him, he would look back and picture this instant. He would recall every detail of Thorne's bruised face, every nuance of his bruising voice. He would remember, and wish to God that he'd told the truth.

Holland looked at Thorne. 'No, sir.'

Thorne let out a long slow breath and moved across to the window. He looked down, hoping to see something that might raise his spirits. Some cadets marching badly would do the trick. Better yet, a group of them forming a human pyramid, mounted on the back of two motorbikes like they used to do on those displays when he was a kid . . .

There was just a pair of civilian staff smoking in a door-way.

Thorne turned and walked back across the room. He was feeling aimless, untrusted, unnecessary. He opened the door of the office, looked out across the incident room. In the far corner he saw Norman standing over McEvoy's desk. She said something that made him laugh.

'McEvoy and Norman are getting friendly, aren't they?'

'He's probably trying to talk her into going on to the next press conference,' Holland said. 'He's been telling her she should get some media training. Says he thinks she'd come across well on camera.'

Thorne turned back into the room. 'What about me? How camera-friendly am I looking?' Holland said nothing, trying to decide how diplomatic to be. 'Does it really look bad?'

'Once the bruising's gone it'll be fine. A broken nose is quite cool actually. Women go for that sort of thing . . .'

'Please, God . . .'

'I should look on the bright side,' Holland said. 'Fact is, with all due respect, sir, you were quite an ugly fucker before.'

No picking, no sneezing. The pain told Thorne that they definitely needed to add laughing to the list.

Thorne waited until the office was quiet before making the call.

His heart was pounding as he dialled, as it had each time he'd tried the number from home. A dozen times or more since getting back from the hospital. A dozen times or more, he'd got the answering machine.

He waited for the connection.

He should have told them about this, there were things they could have done – traces – but he felt instinctively that their efforts would be fruitless, that this was the right thing to do.

The phone rang.

This was the way he *might* make up for his mistake . . .

Ten, twelve rings as usual, then the familiar message. 'Shit . . .'

'*This is Tom Thorne. Leave a message or try my home number, which is . . .*'

Then suddenly Thorne remembered the call he'd seen Steve Norman take earlier. He pictured the press officer as his phone was ringing. *Looking* at the screen before answering.

Caller ID . . .

This number, the office number, was withheld, as was his own at home. Both would show up on the screen as private numbers. The calls would go unanswered. He needed a number which was registered, which would show up and give the man who had his phone a good idea who was calling.

Thorne opened the door, scanned the incident room, hoping that Dave Holland hadn't left yet.

Minutes later he was dialling the number again on Holland's borrowed mobile. The name would show up on his phone. He had programmed it in himself.

The phone began to ring . . .

Whoever was holding it would be seeing HOLLAND MOB come up on the small screen and would surely be able to guess who was calling. Would perhaps risk taking the call.

The phone was answered.

'Palmer. This is Thorne.'

Fifteen seconds. Thorne was starting to wonder if maybe it wasn't Palmer on the other end. Then that voice, the nasal tones even more pronounced over the phone. 'I'm really sorry, Mr Thorne . . .'

'You broke my fucking nose . . .'

'I'm sorry, I didn't mean to.'

Thorne moved across to the window, stared out at the lights of Hendon, the cars speeding north on the M1. 'Why did you take my phone?'

'I won't be on long enough for you to trace this. I presume you're tracing this . . .'

'Did you take it to give yourself more time to get away, or because you knew I'd call?'

Thorne could hear Palmer breathing, considering the question. 'A little of both, probably.'

'This is so stupid you know. We'll find you. You've given yourself up once, you should do it again.'

Palmer laughed, but it sounded desperate. 'Why? Is it going to make a difference to my sentence?'

'Why should you care about that? You wanted to be locked up for life anyway. What's changed, Martin? Why are you doing this?'

'I should go . . .'

'Is it because of what I said about what might happen to you in prison?'

'Not really. Yes, sort of . . .'

Thorne looked at himself reflected in the blackness of the window, the bruises dark shadows across his face. For half a second he forgot that he was chatting to a murderer. He felt like a character in some noirish pop video, his mouth miming these disconnected sentences – strange snippets of conversation dropped into a dark ballad about loss or the impossibility of forgiveness.

'What did you mean in the car? What did you mean about Nicklin being a policeman?'

'I didn't mean anything. I was just saying it. I needed to distract you . . .'

'That's bollocks, Martin. You could have done anything, said anything. Why did you say *that*?'

'I had a feeling, that's all. It was just an impression, like he was used to people doing what he told them . . .'

'Wasn't he always like that?'

'I told you, it was just a feeling. Something about him that day in the restaurant. It's nothing I could put into words. I have to go now . . .'

'Wait. I want you to think about stopping this. Wherever you are, we'll find you. What's the point of it?'

'I really can't talk to you any more . . .'

'Wait a minute. I'll call again. I'll let it ring three times first, and then hang up, so you'll know it's me. Three times, Palmer. OK?'

The line was dead.

McEvoy lay on her back, holding her breath, staring up at the mirrors.

Her heart was going bonkers in her chest. Her face was tingling, the gorgeous numbness spreading across her mouth and teeth, the buzz dancing its way up into her skull.

She froze as she heard a car pull up outside. Every muscle tensed, waiting for the footfall outside the door. She could get to the mains switch in ten seconds . . .

She was flat on the floor beneath the window ledge in the living room, out of sight. She'd moved the free-standing mirror in from the bedroom, positioned it to the inch, tilted it until it gave the optimum view. Now she could lie here safely and watch the back garden. She would see any of them coming immediately. There was another mirror halfway down the garden – a big one she'd hung from a fence post. From this position, she could see around the side as well.

When she'd first bought the flat, the garden had been great. She'd enjoyed sitting out there on summer nights, with a man sometimes, sharing a bottle of wine before bed. These days it was a bloody liability. It would be the way they would come. It was the place they watched her from most of the time, though the officer in the cherry-picker pretending to fix the lamp post on the street outside was a clever idea. But she was cleverer. She knew all the tricks, didn't she? The surveillance game. She knew the car that was following her was probably the one in front. She knew all the tricks because she was one of them.

Holland must have been talking. Everybody knew, she was certain of it. She'd caught two people at it in the space of five minutes, earlier in the day. Talking about her, clamming up when she came into the room. Watching her and judging. Well she was watching *them* as well. As she re-applied make-up using the small mirror she kept in her bag. She could see what they were thinking. Same as Holland. Same as everybody. All of them thinking that she couldn't do the job.

She froze. A shadow moved across the garden. She could be at the mains switch in less than *five* seconds at a push, plunge the place into darkness, turn everything off. She'd done it before when she'd heard them coming. It was a pain to spend the time re-programming the video and re-setting clocks, but she'd had no choice.

They were out there, listening. The bastards weren't going to hear or see anything tonight. She slid across the floor until she was away from the window before standing up and inching her way around the wall. She dropped into the chair by her desk, woke up her computer.

There were those she could talk to who *knew* how good an officer she was. Who thought she was probably better at the job than anybody else. Who challenged her to prove it.

She had e-mail.

The ringing phone punched its way into Thorne's dream where it became the bark of a hungry animal, scrabbling at a door, digging its way beneath it. Behind the door stood a small boy, rooted to the spot, terrified, until a girl arrived and took him by the hand. Thorne woke then and leaned across, fumbling for the phone.

'Palmer?'

'Thorne? It's Colin Maxwell. You in bed?'

Thorne blinked hard and looked at the clock. It was just after eleven. He'd been asleep less than half an hour. 'I was reading. Trying to get an early night . . .'

Maxwell. The hotel killings. More bodies . . .

'Which hotel is it?'

Maxwell sounded surprised. 'The Palace, in South Kensington. How the hell did you know?'

Thorne was wide awake now. He needed some more painkillers. 'Why else would you be calling? How many dead?'

'Nobody's dead. Listen, I think we've got our wires crossed here, mate. This is good news, and I reckon you could do with cheering up. Our man isn't as bright as we thought he was.'

The painkillers could wait. 'You've got him?'

'He delivers bar supplies. Drives a fucking beer wagon. Delivery once a month, gets friendly with the catering managers, chats up a few waitresses. Who've you got staying? Who's throwing their money about? Bungs them a few quid for the right bit of information . . .'

'What's the Palace hotel got to do with it?'

'A witness comes forward, a cleaner, gave the suspect information last year when she was working at the Regency, back when our murderer was still just a thief. The suspect approaches this girl again last week, only now our cleaner's read the papers hasn't she? She knows all about him. We've told her she's in the clear if she plays along.'

Thorne was growing irritated. They could go over it all in detail later. 'Colin, just tell me about the Palace hotel . . .'

'That's the best bit, mate. What are you doing next Tuesday night?'

TWENTY-FOUR

Thorne looked down at his new phone. It was smaller than the one it was replacing and flashier. He'd spent most of the day making sure that everyone who mattered had the new number. He hadn't discontinued the account on his old phone. He wanted that number active for the time being.

While it was quiet, while they were waiting, Thorne messed around with some of the new phone's features. This one had a predictive text function. He had never been one for sending text messages, it always seemed easier and quicker to make the call. This might be fun, though. He typed the message. There were probably all manner of symbols and shortcuts he could be using – he knew this stuff was hugely trendy with kids – but he just kept it straightforward. He pressed the send button and looked up, smiled at a couple of the others. Nobody was saying a great deal.

Thorne was pretty sure that what he'd sent would be read. There was no risk in opening it, even if the number that sent it wasn't familiar. It was a simple enough message.

GIVE UP . . .

A stomach rumbled, breaking the silence, dispersing the tension. They all had a good laugh. Somebody suggested calling room service, ordering up a bit of dinner on expenses.

Holland and McEvoy pushed through the revolving door and made their way across the lobby towards reception. Holland was wearing a blue suit. McEvoy wore a soft leather jacket over a black dress.

They were hand in hand.

'Room 133, please,' Holland said.

McEvoy took a small hand mirror from her bag and checked her make-up.

The woman behind the reception desk plastered on a fake smile that was almost, but not quite, the same fake smile she plastered on the rest of the time. The tremble in her hand was almost imperceptible as she handed over the key.

'Do you need a call in the morning?' she asked.

McEvoy shook her head.

'Would you like a newspaper?'

Holland smiled. She was very good. 'No thanks. Goodnight . . .'

They waited for the lift. McEvoy stared at her reflection in the metal doors. Holland turned round casually, had a quick look. A man smoking a cigar on the armchair by the main entrance, fifty-ish, waiting for someone. A party of noisy business types spilling out of the bar. A younger man on the phone.

The lift arrived, bringing with it half a dozen more jabbering businessmen. Holland and McEvoy stepped inside. Holland pressed the button for the first floor.

It was only when the doors had closed fully that they stopped holding hands.

Jason Alderton moved quickly along the corridor, his feet in soft black training shoes that made no noise on the deep carpet. A woman came around the corner. He grinned as they passed each other, got a smile in return.

He stopped outside the door and readied himself. He placed the bag soundlessly at his feet, looking left and right every few seconds, pulling on the gloves. It was important to step up close to the door, to get your face right up against the spyhole. The clothes were utilitarian enough anyway, but up close all anyone could see was the smiling face that looked away unconcerned, whistling.

Jason breathed in and out very fast a dozen times, then knocked. It gave him a little kick that inside the gloves, his palms were perfectly dry. He was getting very good at this.

Footsteps from inside the room. He tensed up, ready for it. It was the surprise that gave him the edge. They were always so completely stunned. He saw that expression on every face. They'd felt safe.

'Who is it?'

'Hotel maintenance, sir. Problem with one of your radiators . . .'

When the door was opened, in the half a second before he struck, Jason took in every detail necessary.

Fucker in a suit, about thirty, here for the conference like the girl had told him . . . average size, not big . . . fit-looking, but that wouldn't matter . . . full of himself most probably, but he would cry like a baby when it came to it . . . the look on his face, the shock, starting to sense much too late that something isn't right . . . a woman, the wife or girlfriend, behind him, sitting on the edge of the bed . . .

He raised both hands and pushed the man in the suit hard in the chest, shoved him back down on to the floor. He was moving in then, picking up the bag and shutting the door in one clean, quick movement, and the man in the suit was on his hands and knees moaning, and as Jason stepped forward to kick the fucker in the stomach, he saw the woman on the bed jump up, *really jump up in the air*, just like the old Dutch woman had done.

She jumped up in the air and screamed . . .

McEvoy screamed.

The scream of the terrified wife. The scream of the good copper giving the signal for everyone to move.

Thorne stepped quickly out from his hiding place behind the right-angle formed by a line of built-in wardrobes. He saw the look of sudden panic on the suspect's face, watched it grow as he turned, looking for a way out, only to see two more men bursting out of the bathroom behind him.

It would be five seconds, no more, from the moment Thorne stepped out into plain view, to the moment he would find himself staring down at the man on the floor, amazed at the fact that he wasn't punching him into unconsciousness.

As Thorne moved towards him, the suspect tried to run but Holland moved fast from his hands and knees, tackled him around the waist and drove him back across the room. McEvoy moved out of the way, and Holland and the suspect crashed down onto the edge of the bed. Thorne and Maxwell were right behind them, and together they lifted the suspect clear off the floor and threw him across the bed into the wall on the other side.

Before the suspect had hit the carpet, Thorne was stepping round the bed after him.

Up for it.

Ready to do some damage to that face.

The face not hidden by a balaclava, because the fucker hadn't been planning on leaving anybody alive to identify him. The bag over his arm – the bag that contained the knife and the tape, and Christ alone knew what else . . .

Thorne remembered the last time he'd been in a hotel room. He thought about the bodies in the bath and on the bed. Now he was ready to kick and punch and smash away a little frustration. Half a yard behind him, Maxwell and Holland moved just as quickly, reading the look on Thorne's face, ready to stop him.

They wouldn't have to.

Thorne saw something like amazement on the face of the man lying crumpled on the floor between the wall and the bed. In the tussle, his trousers had got pulled down to the top of his thighs, exposing grey underpants. A livid scratch ran across his forehead. His hair, thick with gel, lay plastered to his scalp like the legs of fat black spiders. Beneath, a thin, bland face, the small eyes wide, the mouth hanging open as he panted for breath. Thorne came around the bed at him, his fists clenched, his discoloured face a disaster area. Thorne could see the man on the floor wondering if *his* was going to end up the same way . . .

Thorne stopped dead. He stopped and stared down at the pig-shit-thick piece of pond scum, who'd more or less handed himself over to them. The vicious moron who wasn't quite careful enough and who would grow old in prison thinking about it. A tick in a plus column, a feather in a commander's cap. A killer caught for the same simple reasons that most of them got caught.

Blind luck and stupidity.

Sutcliffe, West, Nielsen, Shipman. Virtually everybody on that list his father had asked for. All of them tripped up by a piece of good fortune, or coincidence, or carelessness. Not just the big ones either: Killer A and Rapist B too. Everyday maniacs on any street corner, and the majority of them a long way from the bright, refined psychopaths of popular fiction. All killing for ordinary, dull reasons. Anger, envy, lust, greed. Malign individuals, yes, but also every bit as stupid as some of those that hunted them . . .

Thorne and the rest of them stumbling around, having good days and bad. Hot streaks and shitty patches. Following procedure or not following it, depending on who they were and how much they gave a fuck. Detectives hoping that *this* one wanted to get caught and failing that, praying for the sharp-eyed witness, the conscience-stricken relative, the dim-witted accomplice.

Needing all the help they could get.

Thorne knew it, of course. He knew it very well, but once in a while it would slap him in the face. A moment, an image, would remind him. How lost he was. How much he was reliant on fortune and fuck-ups.

Detective? They needed to invent a new name for it.

Thorne couldn't remember the last time he'd detected anything but the smell of bullshit or beer on a colleague's breath.

It was five seconds, no more, since he'd stepped out of his hiding place. Thorne felt an arm on his sleeve, heard something high-pitched and unpleasant. Came out of it . . .

The man on the floor was not looking at him, but *past* him, across the room at something else. The arm on his was pulling him away – not from the suspect, there had been no violence – but towards something else, something that demanded his attention.

Thorne turned at the same time as he started to really hear it. He turned, wincing, and looked in the same direction as everybody else in the room. They had their hands over their ears. They stared at where Sarah McEvoy sat slumped against the wall near the door.

She was still screaming.

TWENTY-FIVE

When she lifted her head up to look at him, Holland could see that his shirt was sopping, with snot, and tears.

McEvoy had been crying for over an hour.

She'd kept it together until moments after they'd climbed into his car and driven away from the hotel. She'd been hysterical from there, all the way back to Wembley, and when he'd pulled up outside her flat, she'd leaned across, crying so hard she was almost unable to speak, and demanded to be held.

They hadn't moved since.

At the hotel, the two of them plus Thorne had moved downstairs once Jason Alderton had been taken away. They'd gone silently down in the lift and moved to a sofa and chairs in the deserted reception area. Thorne had found somebody, ordered coffee and then looked at them, demanding answers. Holland had been gobsmacked at how quickly McEvoy had recovered her poise, how easily she was able to look Thorne in the eye and lie to him. She told him that her mother was ill, that she was finding it hard to cope. She laughed and said that the business up in the hotel room was probably just down to her subconscious getting a lot of pent-up shit out of her system. Just a one-off thing. A bit of a wobbler, sir . . .

Thorne had fucking believed her. Talked about her taking a bit of time off. Asked a bit more about her mother.

Or maybe he hadn't believed her. Holland had looked in the rear-view mirror as they'd pulled out of the hotel car park and seen Thorne standing there, watching them leave. It struck him then, watching Thorne standing with his hands in his pockets, *that look on his face* . . . perhaps he was just leaving it all for another day.

Holland tried to shift his position a little. McEvoy was all but on top of him, her weight making him uncomfortable, but every time he tried to move, she began wailing again. It had started and stopped half a dozen times since they had arrived at her flat, unbearably loud; the noise dredged up from somewhere deep down in her guts. An emotion so raw and unformed that it screamed when it met the fresh air. Each time, the sobbing seemed to tear through her whole body, and through *his*, for long minutes at a time until it finally settled down.

With the engine off, the clock on the dashboard wasn't lit, but it must have been well after midnight. A man walking his dog looked into the car and quickly looked away again. Holland didn't know if he understood what he was seeing.

'Sarah . . .'

She moaned and raised her head. She looked like she'd been dunked in paint-stripper. When Holland opened his mouth, she pushed her tongue into it and he felt the stirring in his groin. It took a major effort to pull away from the kiss.

'Sarah, let's get you inside.'

'No . . .'

She squeezed his neck so hard that he had to fight not to cry out. He reached up and wedged a hand between her fingers and his skin. 'You need to stop this. You need to get to bed and go to sleep.'

Her voice was hoarse and punctuated by desperate, absurd intakes of breath. 'Was it nice . . . to be proved right? To see me . . . fuck up at work . . . ?'

'Don't be stupid.'

'In front . . . of everybody . . .'

'What you said to Thorne was . . . good enough.'

'If he believed me . . .'

Holland realised that he'd been stroking her hair for a while. 'Listen, what you said about me being proved right. I don't give a toss about that, but maybe it's enough of a warning for you to want to do something about it . . .'

She burrowed her head deeper into his shoulder. She might have been nodding, but he couldn't be sure.

'Sarah?'

She whimpered. It sounded like there might be another attack of hysterics on the way. His hand stopped stroking her hair, grabbed a handful of it. 'This might be the last chance you get, you know?'

She raised her head and stared at him, with something strange in her bloodshot eyes which he couldn't come close to reading. She looked up at him for maybe fifteen seconds. Challenging . . . apologising . . . accepting . . . saying *something* without words; something he would spend a long time afterwards trying to interpret.

Then, in the early hours of the morning, with the first few drops of rain crashing onto the windscreen, he could say very little which didn't sound pat and pointless. 'I'll be here to help you, if you try and change things . . .'

He pulled her head gently back down on to his shoulder, and the two of them sat there, holding on to each other for all the wrong reasons.

McEvoy needing to go through this but wanting him to go. Wanting to get inside, on her own, and turn on her computer.

Holland shushing her like a child. Changing his position ever so slightly, moving his arm just a little to get a look at his watch.

Mary from Rickmansworth: 'He should never be let out. What about the life sentence the parents have been given? What about the parents of that little girl?'

Alan from Leicester: 'It isn't about vengeance, Bob, it's about justice. It's just too soon.'

A child jailed for the murder of a little girl now a grown man eligible for parole. The debate had raged eight months before, over the parole for the boys that killed Jamie Bulger. It was raging again. The phone-lines, as Bob kept reminding everybody, were red-hot . . .

Susan from Bromley: 'That boy should be kept in prison for his own good. If he comes out, someone will find him and kill him.'

That one was his favourite. Let's not talk about releasing our own demons back into society. Let's not say we want them locked away for the rest of their lives because it makes us a bit less guilty about not protecting our children. Let's pretend we're concerned for the safety of the murdering bastards. Priceless.

He weighed up the arguments, as he always did, and in the end, he was firmly with the majority on this contentious issue.

The man should never be set free. Killing kiddies was evil.

Caroline had gone to bed nice and early, and he'd had most of the evening to sit and think, and assure himself that he'd thought of everything.

He'd considered abandoning the whole thing when Palmer had escaped. He thought about trying to find him, starting their little partnership up again. He bore him no ill will for weakening the last time, for turning against him. That was the way it went with characters like Martin. The fear could be harnessed, but it was sometimes a bit unpredictable.

After due consideration, he'd decided to press on. Never still and never back. Palmer was part of his past now, let him flounder and drown. *His* future was far more exciting. It did give him a laugh though, Palmer escaping the way he did. Thorne was so arrogant. Thorne, who never suffered fools. Now he'd fucked up very badly.

Now, Thorne was the fool.

He poured himself another glass of wine. He wondered if McEvoy would fuck up. It wouldn't be the end of the world if she did – he'd be covered – but it would be disappointing after the effort he'd put in so far. On balance, he decided he had good reason to be optimistic.

She was the perfect choice after all.

The first time he'd met her, he'd recognised something. He'd seen a need, and not just the obvious one. He'd spotted the drug dependency immediately, of course: he'd seen it many times when he was on the street. It was probably the coke that had first put the idea in his head, but he quickly found out that McEvoy's need ran far deeper.

So, all being well, they would *both* get something out of

it. He would know if he had made the right choice very soon, but if all did not go well, he had already decided that he would kill her later anyway.

He leaned across to the radio and turned it up. Some idiot was wittering on about how it would be impossible for this boy to hide who he used to be, even if he was released. They'd said the same things about Venables and Thompson. They'd have to become different people; they'd need to hide their past from everyone. They'd have to lie, for ever, to close friends and future spouses. It wasn't possible. *Someone* would find out, surely. How could you keep your past so secret?

He smiled at that. He knew it could be done.

Thorne pressed the *Play* button on the answering machine, and a day that had ended badly got even shittier.

'Hello . . . Tom, it's Eileen. Auntie Eileen, from Brighton . . . I hate these things. Listen, we need to have a chat about your dad. I've been in touch with him a fair bit, you know, since Christmas and, well . . . it's not good. You wouldn't really remember, but your grandad was the same . . . later on. Sometimes I think he forgets to eat anything. Anyway, I've been nagging him and he says he's going to see the GP. I think he'll probably get referred, you know, for proper tests, but anyway, give us a call and we can put our heads together. You should tell him yourself as well, make sure he keeps the appointment . . .'

He hit the *Stop* button and went to put the kettle on.

He banged down the mug on the worktop. It had been a week since the row with his dad. He should have called him back the next day, sorted it out. What was Eileen getting involved for anyway? She'd never been arsed before.

Christ, they always came out of the woodwork when there was something to get worked up about. Busybodies like that loved a fucking crisis didn't they?

That KFC he'd picked up on the way home had been a mistake. He was starting to feel a little sick.

Proper tests? What did that mean . . . ?

He looked at his watch. It was far too late to call his dad now. He tore at the milk carton roughly enough to spill milk everywhere. Fuck it, the tea would only keep him awake anyway. Wasn't there supposed to be more caffeine in tea than coffee?

He stomped back into the living room and sat there in silence, cradling his phone.

Who was he kidding? If he slept at all it would be a miracle. The adrenaline that had rushed through his bloodstream in the hotel room earlier was still around, looking for something to do. The feelings that had taken hold of him, knocked him around a little, as he'd looked down at Jason Alderton, had gone back to wherever it was they hid most of the time, but he was still feeling bruised.

And McEvoy . . .

What the hell had all that been about? He'd need to talk to Brigstocke about it in the morning. Maxwell would probably write it up in his report, but Thorne knew it would be good if he could get in first. He hadn't a clue what he was going to tell Brigstocke though. Probably the same bollocks McEvoy had given *him* . . .

He'd need to talk to Holland as well.

He looked at his watch. Only five minutes later than the last time he looked.

He let it ring three times, hung up, dialled again. It rang for a very long time.

'Palmer?'

'I was asleep . . .'

'Give me an address.'

'What . . . ?'

'Give me the address where you are, and I'll come and get you.'

'I can't.'

Thorne hadn't expected it to be that easy, but he was still genuinely annoyed. 'Why don't we just get this over with, Palmer? You're not someone who escapes. You're not even someone who runs. You're just a fuck-up, you're just weak.'

There was a pause long enough for Thorne to get up and move through to the bedroom. He lay down on the bed. Then Palmer spoke again.

'I know . . .'

'So what do you think you're doing?'

'I'm not sure.'

He wasn't the only one. Thorne stared up at the ceiling and asked himself why an escaped killer was the only person he could think of ringing at half past midnight. There was no need to answer the question of course – it was bollocks. He was tired and thinking all sorts of strange shit. Holland wouldn't have minded, he was probably still up anyway. Hendricks as well. He could have called Hendricks . . .

'Is there any news on Stuart?' Palmer asked.

'Worried he might find you before we do, Martin?'

'No . . . just, you know, any news?'

Thorne grunted. 'Only if you've got some.'

'Sorry . . . I don't know anything about him.'

'Except that he might be a policeman.'

'I did say, before, that it was just a feeling. It was nothing I can back up with anything. I've never lied to you, Inspector Thorne.'

'I'm supposed to be impressed with that, am I? Supposed to think that counts for something?'

'I never said that.'

'You've stabbed one young woman, strangled another . . .'

'Please . . .'

'But deep down you're pretty honest!'

'I'm sorry if I don't fit into a convenient pigeonhole for you.'

'Bollocks . . . shut up. That's crap.'

Thorne could hear the distant rhythms of an argument from somewhere down the street. A man and a woman. He couldn't tell if they were getting closer or moving further away.

'You aren't the only one who would like to know,' Palmer said. 'What I am.'

'Don't make any mistake about this, Palmer, I *know* what you are . . .'

'I'm sorry if I got you into any trouble . . .'

'And stop fucking apologising. It's pathetic.'

Thorne needed more of his painkillers. He took a deep breath and swung his legs off the bed, the undigested chicken rising up his throat.

'Inspector Thorne . . . ?'

He stood and walked slowly across to the wardrobe. He kicked open the door, stared at himself in the full-length mirror on the back of it.

'Jesus Christ . . .' He hadn't meant to say it out loud.

'Inspector Thorne . . . ?'

The swollen distorted face looked back at him and reminded him of what he was supposed to be. It asked him, politely but firmly, what the fuck he thought he was doing.

'Are you all right, Inspector Thorne?'

Then the explosion of rage. The one that ran in the family.

'Don't talk to me. Not like that, do you understand? Not *are you all right*? Not *sorry . . .*'

'I don't . . .'

'Talk to me like a murderer.'

TWENTY-SIX

Thorne arrived at work feeling hollow, certain that little would happen during the day that could fill the empty space.

The sleep following his conversation with Martin Palmer had been surprisingly deep – a welcome side effect of the painkillers. This time, the animal had worked longer and harder at the space beneath the door. Digging down, forcing its snout into the gap. This time, behind the door, Karen McMahon had not been there to take Charlie Garner's hand.

The day ahead would, Thorne knew, be almost surreal considering the state of the case.

The hunt for Palmer was going nowhere.

The hunt for Nicklin was going backwards.

Thorne and the team would probably spend the day celebrating . . .

A bottle or two and a backslap or three to put the lid on last night's result at the hotel. A session of whistling in the dark that would only be interrupted – right after lunch, according to his Regulation 7 notice – by Thorne's initial meeting with officers from the DPS.

A day when nothing was going to happen. A day when *everything* was going to be settled . . .

Tom Thorne was not the only one arriving at work, and in the head of the man who used to be Stuart Nicklin, a clock was ticking.

Thorne's assessment of how the day would pan out was pretty much bang on. The only thing he hadn't foreseen was quite how early the party was going to start. The word had gone out: a bit of a drink at lunch-time to toast a job well done. Morale, however, was not exactly through the roof anywhere in Serious Crime. Not among Team 3, not among the team that had taken over the hotel killings, nowhere. A couple of pints in the pub at lunch-time would certainly be welcomed, but there was always going to be a need to push the boat out a little further than that.

The first bottle of scotch had appeared before the morning cups of tea and coffee were finished.

Thorne and Brigstocke watched from their office as paper cups were filled and the stories that had filtered back about the events the previous night were exaggerated and passed around.

'It's a bit early isn't it?' Thorne asked.

Brigstocke raised his eyebrows theatrically. 'Bugger me, are you feeling all right, Tom? Maybe that smack in the face did more damage than we realised.'

Thorne said nothing. Looking out, he noticed that Holland was nowhere to be seen. He wasn't joining in the celebrations.

Brigstocke shrugged. 'I think we need this to tell you the truth. As long as it stays controlled, it's no problem. As long as nobody's too shit-faced when Jesmond pops over to bask in his bit of reflected glory . . .'

The volume of noise from the incident room dropped.

It was clear which bit of the hotel story was being repeated.

'I spoke to McEvoy first thing this morning,' Brigstocke said.

'How did she sound?'

'Half-asleep. Embarrassed about what happened. Said she was fine to come in, but I've told her to leave it until the end of the week. What do you think?'

Thorne nodded; that sounded about right. 'She's got some personal stuff to sort out.'

'With Holland?'

Thorne wasn't surprised that Brigstocke had noticed something – he always had a good handle on the relationships between the members of his team. 'Holland says not,' Thorne said.

'It's not the end of the world. Shift one of them across to Belgravia or the West End . . .'

'Make it McEvoy.'

'Problems?'

'No, not really.' *Not really*. Nothing beyond a loyalty to Dave Holland, and a slight unease about Sarah McEvoy. Nothing he could even name, beyond a vague suspicion he had no intention of voicing.

'Anyway,' Brigstocke said, 'if Holland says not . . .'

'Right.'

'Hello . . . your best mate's here.'

Thorne watched as Steve Norman strolled into the incident room, a slim leather bag slung across one shoulder. He greeted the officers like old friends and held up a hand to gently turn down the offer of a drink.

'What's he doing here? Doesn't he have his own office?'

'I think he's one of those that likes to feel part of the team, you know?'

'Oh fuck . . .'

Norman was on his way towards the office. There was nowhere to hide.

'Hi, guys. Just stopped in to say well done for last night. More work for *me* . . . but that's the nature of the beast, I suppose. Right . . . I'll no doubt see you for a quick one at lunch-time, but I'd better be off. On the move a lot today, loads to do . . .'

He patted his shoulder bag as he turned to leave. Thorne realised that it contained a laptop computer. Norman was clearly one of those that liked to remind others just how important he was. Just how *very* busy. He probably used it a lot on the train.

'Tosser,' Thorne muttered as Norman closed the door behind him.

'I think DCI Lickwood said he might stick his head in later on, just to say hello and have one on our team's tab.' Brigstocke grinned at Thorne's expression. 'Thought you'd be pleased.'

'So no chance of trying to catch any murderers today, then?'

'Come on, Tom. People will be coming and going all day, and we had a good result last night. It's the first one for a while.'

Thorne didn't need reminding.

'Business as usual, of course,' Brigstocke said. 'But with a good feeling round the place for a change. A positive atmosphere. Don't you remember what it was like, last day of term?'

Thorne knew what Brigstocke meant, but it still felt wrong somehow. He walked out of the door, grumbling.

'I'll fetch the party hats . . .'

Then the desk got him.

Thorne swore loudly and kicked at the offending corner – the ball of screwed-up paper he'd taped to it long gone. As he rubbed his thigh, he decided that while the rest of the place was celebrating the end of term, he was going to do something useful. He shouted to no-one in particular:

'Right, get me a fucking saw . . .'

A couple of regulars sat up at the bar, nursing grudges and pints, moaning to the landlord and throwing dirty looks over their shoulders, but the place belonged to Serious Crime. There were a hundred or more officers and civilian staff crammed in to the back bar. Though it was officially just a lunch-time thing, Thorne was pretty sure, based on the morning, that there wasn't going to be a fat lot of work done in the afternoon.

'Fancy a drink, big boy?'

Thorne actually started slightly. Despite the noise and the crush, he'd actually drifted away for a moment, thinking about the generations either side of himself. Young boys and old men . . .

'Only you've been stood here with that half for twenty minutes,' Hendricks said. 'Wishing you were somewhere else.'

'That obvious, is it?'

'I was going to say you've got a face like a smacked arse, but, looking at it, *kicked* arse would be a bit more accurate.'

Thorne raised his glass, took a sip and then gestured with it, pointing at nothing in particular. 'This is fucking nonsense though, isn't it?'

Hendricks shook his head, leaned on the bar. 'Don't

agree, mate. We all need to let our hair down, this lot more than most. You as much as anybody . . .'

'A copper with a pint pot in his hand is not my idea of a good time. Christ, it's rough enough *working* with them.'

'Not been flattened in the rush for a matey chinwag then?'

Thorne finally smiled. 'Most of them stay away . . .'

'Are you having another one?' Thorne shook his head. Hendricks turned to the bar and raised his hand to attract the attention of a barmaid.

Most of them. Steve Norman had marched straight up and bent Thorne's ear for ten long minutes. Keen to impress upon him just how hard he was working. Delighted that after the depressing weeks on Nicklin and Palmer, he finally had some positive material to work with – the McMahon discovery and the hotel murders. He'd drunk two tomato juices before rushing away, as he told Thorne excitedly, to prepare a press release detailing the brilliant operation that had resulted in the arrest of Jason Alderton.

Hendricks was back at Thorne's elbow with a pint of Guinness and a disgruntled expression. 'We've got to *pay* for these now. How much did Brigstocke put behind the bar?'

'Two hundred and fifty. It lasted about fifteen minutes.'

The two of them said nothing for a minute or two. They stood and watched as police officers of all ranks and ages enjoyed a momentary triumph. Battered bomber jackets and fleeces with bottles of lager. Shirts with grimy collars and Christmas ties, spilling pints of bitter. Sharp suits on spritzers. Women who were harder than they looked and men who were a damn sight younger. Old stagers from the squads, a squeak away from their pensions, and West End wannabes with Audis on double yellows and dialogue from a Guy Ritchie movie.

A couple of hours to pretend, to forget. Then back to it.

The Met was haemorrhaging. It was losing officers at the rate of five a day. Thorne was surprised it wasn't ten times that number. He was amazed he was too stubborn, or stupid, or scared, to be one of them.

'It'll all still be there tomorrow, Tom,' Hendricks said. 'A couple of hours on the piss isn't going to make a blind bit of difference. Have a drink, catch the fucker another day . . .'

Thorne smiled and finished his drink, thinking: *Tomorrow is another day nearer the next body. A couple of hours might make all the difference in the world.*

Lunch-time was excruciating. Talking to people, and eating and smiling. Looking like he was interested in their pointless drivel. It was so hard today, when such excitement was so close.

He managed it every other day of course, but that was just routine. And didn't everyone dissemble to some degree or other? Saying you're not bothered about getting the stupid job when you'd happily kill for it. Saying that you just want to be friends when actually you're already fucking somebody else. Wearing a mask. Pretending to care.

On the days he killed, though, it was always like this to some extent. He remembered the tedious meeting at work on the day he'd killed the Chinese girl; the expression of concentration stuck on to his face when all he could think about was what she might look like, how it was going to feel. He could still feel Caroline's mouth against his freshly shaved cheek as she kissed him goodbye on the morning he'd paid his visit to Ken Bowles. He'd smiled and kissed her back, they'd talked about what they might have for dinner later, and all the time he could feel the wonderful weight of the bat in his bag . . .

This one was going to be even better. This time, he was having trouble keeping himself from grabbing people and shouting into their faces. Telling them exactly what he was planning to do, how brilliantly he'd arranged everything, how superb it was going to feel. The buzz was already building. He could almost feel the mask beginning to slip.

Somebody spoke to him. He said something back. He stuck something tasteless into his mouth, glanced at his watch.

He needed a little time on his own. Just half an hour or so, for a coffee and a bar of chocolate. To gather himself before the adventure started.

Thorne looked up to see Holland pushing through the tables towards him. He could see by his face that Holland was having about as good a time as *he* was. The fact that he'd been stuck in a corner with Derek Lickwood couldn't have helped.

'Thanks for that,' Holland said, squeezing in between Thorne and Hendricks.

'Privilege of rank, Holland. I get to inform the next of kin, you have to talk to DCI Dickwood. Did he do that thing of looking over your head while he's talking to you?'

Holland smiled and shook his head. 'He's *such* a wanker. Kept having little digs about Palmer escaping. Asked if you'd ever worked for Group 4.'

Hendricks snorted into his Guinness. Thorne turned to him. 'Shut it.'

'He's off,' Holland said. Thorne looked across in time to see Lickwood at the door on the far side of the room. Just before stepping through it on to the street, he turned and cocked his head towards Thorne. It was a hard expression to read, but Thorne would have put good money on smug.

'I've got a good idea why he was here, though,' Holland said. 'He seemed very disappointed that DS McEvoy wasn't around. A bit confused . . .'

Hendricks enjoyed this sort of intrigue hugely. 'What? Lickwood has the hots for McEvoy?'

'Oh yeah, fancies the pants off her.'

'What did you tell him?' Thorne asked.

'I just sort of ducked it really, made out like I didn't know where she was myself. He was pissed off about it, though, definitely.'

Hendricks downed the rest of his Guinness. 'She's a popular girl is McEvoy.'

'That's true,' Thorne said. 'Problem is, I'm not sure she likes herself very much.'

If Thorne had had a problem reading the expression on Lickwood's face, the one on Dave Holland's at that moment was well beyond his reach. He stared at it for a second or two and then turned away, his heart sinking at the screech of feedback from across the room. Some idiot had got hold of a microphone.

'It's Jesmond,' Hendricks announced.

Thorne knew a cue to leave when he heard one. 'Come on, Holland. Let's get the hell out of here.'

'Where are we going?'

'Happily, I have a pressing engagement in Colindale

with the Directorate of Professional Standards. You can hold my hand.'

As the first distorted platitudes rang across the bar, Thorne and Holland pushed their way towards the exit. Thorne wondered whether the beer on his breath might count against him at his meeting.

Behind him, Holland was remembering how cold it had been at half past three that morning. Sitting naked on the edge of his bed. Whispering into his mobile with Sophie stirring next to him, disturbed by the phone, but not fully awake yet.

McEvoy's voice had been strained, garbled . . . raised just enough to reach him over the noise in wherever the hell she was calling from; as heartbreaking a mixture of helplessness and arrogance as he could ever have imagined.

'I'm fine. OK? I just wanted to tell you that. I really am absolutely fine.'

TWENTY-SEVEN

The voice was getting quieter, line by line.

She hadn't slept in nearly thirty-six hours. She hadn't been straight for a good while longer. It was hard to work out exactly which of these things was responsible for the various things her body was now subject to every few minutes. She was overtired. She was shaking. She was out of it. She was wired, hysterical, comatose, terrified, buzzing, fearless . . .

The night before, as soon as Holland had gone, she'd done the last of the coke in the flat and rushed to her computer. She'd written a few e-mails, received a few and then she'd gone out to score. Walking, running most of the way, she hadn't stepped on any of the cracks in the pavement, as per usual. That way she knew that her dealer would be there, that he'd have something for her.

For the rest of that night she'd been awake – drinking and chain-smoking, opening up the wrap made from a folded lottery ticket, chopping out a line every half an hour or so. Since the sun had come up, she'd been doing one every fifteen minutes.

The fucker was ripping her off, must be. She'd always got

four lines out of a quarter, and now, suddenly, she was getting no more than three. She was needing to make the lines thicker. The bastard must be cutting her stuff . . .

Still, cut or not, the stuff was doing the trick. It was silencing the voice. The voice in her head – so much posher and more attractive than the one that came out of her mouth – had been growing quieter with each new line. The voice that told her she was stupid, that what she was planning was insane, that she was risking her life. Each hit was turning it down another notch.

There were other voices she could still hear, that she *needed* to hear. Holland's voice, telling her she couldn't do her job any more. Her mother's voice. The voice she had never heard, but which she imagined when she read the e-mails. These were the voices that, for the time being, she didn't want to tune out, that were making her do this thing, that she would soon silence once and for all.

A wave of rage swept over her as she imagined them all taking the credit for what she was going to do; praising her initiative and then taking all the glory. Fuck that. She imagined Holland coming back to her, walking out on his dim girlfriend and trying to start things up again . . .

She moved to the table. The empty vodka bottle. The empty wrap.

Fuck, fuck, fuck . . .

She opened up the lottery ticket, pressed it flat on the table and licked. She got down on her knees and began dabbing at specks on the carpet, rubbing equal amounts of cocaine, dirt and dead skin into her gums.

Christ alive, how much had she got through? Bastard must have cut it half and half. Must have . . .

She lit a cigarette, put on her coat.

There wasn't a great deal of time. There was still that one crucial piece of information she needed. The one thing he'd held back while he was sending his cryptic little messages. He thought he was being so clever this last week or so, but he had no idea how good she was. None of them did. She was one step ahead of them, all the time. And she was one step ahead of *him*.

She sent an e-mail, and when she didn't get an immediate reply, she sent another, telling him she had to go out. Telling him how he could contact her. It was the only thing she could do, other than sit and wait until lunch-time which was when he usually came on line. She couldn't wait another second.

She grabbed her bag, and after making sure there was nobody on surveillance outside, she closed the door behind her, shivering as she stepped into the cold air.

McEvoy walked quickly away down the greasy pavement, making quite sure she didn't step on any of the cracks.

'How did it go?'

Holland had been waiting for Thorne in reception, chewing the fat with an old mate on duty behind the desk. He waved goodbye as he and Thorne pushed out through the doors and started the ten-minute walk back to Becke House.

What little sun there was up there was having no luck breaking through a solid blanket of cloud. The sky was the colour of pewter. There were already one or two cars with sidelights on.

It was a little after three o'clock.

'How was it really?'

'I think I got lucky,' Thorne said. 'A pair of rubber-heelers with a sense of humour.'

Holland smiled. Rubber-heelers. *You couldn't hear the buggers coming.* 'What was it that they found funny . . . ?'

It hadn't begun well.

DCI Collins (short and overweight) and DI Manning (tall and overweight) did not look like they enjoyed a laugh. Both had that strange expression – a mixture of boredom and seething resentment – which Thorne had previously seen only on the faces of men standing on Oxford Street with signs reading GOLF SALE.

Manning had shuffled papers while Collins had leaned forward across the table to deliver the caution. It had begun and ended with much the same words that Thorne had used to caution Martin Palmer. In the middle, they had detailed the neglect of duty – the procedural lapse that had allowed Palmer to escape – speaking slowly and seri-ously. These officers were doing their job of work so much better than Thorne had done his.

'I'd like a number of other serious incidents noted for the record,' Thorne had said. 'Incidents where I neglected my duty.'

Manning had thrown a sideways glance at Collins and then at the tape recorder to check that the spools were turning. 'Go ahead, Inspector.'

Thorne had cleared his throat. 'I have, on a number of occasions, farted without apologising, and though I have never actually *appeared* in *The Bill*, a woman who was drunk told me I looked a bit like the bloke who plays DI Burnside . . .'

Manning and Collins had looked at each other and then pissed themselves.

'So, how did it finish up?' Holland asked. They were approaching the pub where, doubtless, Serious Crime was still busy inside, pursuing various lines of enquiry.

Thorne wasn't certain what would happen next, but for a change he had decided to think positive. 'I'm not exactly off the hook, but I don't reckon they're sorting me out a uniform just yet.'

Holland stopped and nodded across the road towards the pub. 'Are we going back in?'

Thorne kept on walking, shouted back over his shoulder. 'You can do what you like, Holland, I'm going to go and pick the car up. I thought I'd go and see how McEvoy's getting on. Find out if her mother's any better . . .'

At three thirty, they pulled up outside Sarah McEvoy's flat in Wembley.

Thorne got out of the car and walked up the steps to the front door. He turned and looked at Holland who was still sitting in the passenger seat, staring forwards. 'Come on, Dave . . .' Holland got out while Thorne rang the bell. He arrived next to him as Thorne rang again.

Nothing.

Thorne took a step back, peered to his left at the dark blue curtains drawn across the bay window. 'Is that her flat?' He'd picked McEvoy up outside the place on a few occasions, dropped her off on a couple more, but he'd never been inside.

Holland's answer was non-committal. 'Maybe she's in bed,' he said.

Thorne shrugged, thrust his hands into his jacket pockets and trudged back down towards the car.

Holland watched Thorne moving away, wrestling with it, knowing how easy it would be to jog gently down the steps after him. His voice when he spoke was louder than he'd intended it to be – more urgent.

'I think we should go in . . .'

Thorne turned, twirling the car keys around a finger. 'I don't think I want the Funny Firm doing me for breaking and entering as well, Dave . . .'

'I've got a key,' Holland said.

Thorne came up the steps two at a time and took hold of the arm that was already reaching forward to push a key into the lock.

'We'll need to talk about this, Holland . . .'

It was as dark and gloomy inside the flat as it was outside on the street. As well as the curtains at the front, in McEvoy's bedroom there was a blind pulled down over the back window, the one that looked out on to the garden.

'Well, she's not asleep,' Holland said, coming back into the living room.

Thorne wasn't listening. He was staring at a dozen reflections of himself. He counted at *least* a dozen of them. Mirrors were suspended from the ceiling, propped up on the floor, leaning against the walls at a variety of strange angles. Heavy and ornate, plain and unframed, round, square, all highly polished . . .

'What the fuck is this . . . ?'

Holland moved past him to the window, raised the blind, then turned around. He opened his mouth to answer the question but nothing came out.

Thorne moved slowly around the room, every glance bringing some new reflection, some bizarre perspective on himself. The back of a leg, the top of his head. His fading bruises appeared straight on and profiled at the same time.

On the table, Thorne saw another, smaller mirror, and the creased lottery ticket. He knew at once what he was looking at.

'How long have you known about it?' he asked.

'About three weeks.'

'You're a fucking idiot . . .'

Holland raised a hand to shut Thorne up. Yes, he *was* a fucking idiot, he was much much worse, but he had to stop Thorne going off on one. Not now. He could bow his head and accept the bollocking another time. Now, there was something else . . .

'Sir, I think McEvoy's in some sort of trouble.'

'*Some sort* . . . ?'

'Real trouble.' Holland couldn't say why he was worried. He didn't know what it was that was nagging at him, couldn't explain where the feeling came from. It made him shiver and it kept him awake, and he needed to tell someone. It was there in McEvoy's eyes and the things she said, and the way she'd been acting for a while.

It was as if she had a secret. *Another* secret . . .

'What?' Thorne said.

Holland shook his head, looked around the room, searching desperately for something that might bring this indistinct unease into sharp relief. His gaze settled on the computer.

The look on McEvoy's face a few days before, when he'd walked in to the office and found her on the Internet. Panic, and something else. Defiance? Triumph . . . ?

Thorne watched Holland walk across, pull up a chair, hit the button to wake the machine up.

'What are you doing?'

'I'm going to check her e-mails.'

'You think she's been ordering drugs by e-mail?'

'No . . . maybe. I don't think this is about the coke . . .'
Holland began moving the mouse, clicking, opening windows.

'Don't you need some sort of password?'

'I would if I was actually going to sign on to her account, but I should be able to check her filing cabinet – see what she's been sending out, what she's received . . .'

Thorne nodded, letting Holland get on with it, whatever it was.

Cocaine. Thorne had suspected as much. He'd known a few coppers who liked a sniff. It was usually the older ones who should have known better, the ones that couldn't be doing with Ecstasy because it involved dancing. Whatever their reason for doing it, some of them got seriously messed up.

Thorne wondered how far into it McEvoy had got. He looked up and saw the answer reflected around the room, from one mirror to another . . .

'Fuck . . . oh fuck, no.'

'What?' Thorne felt the change in his body straight away. He sensed a livening in the nerve endings, a heightening of the senses as he moved rapidly across the room, reacting instinctively to the panic in Holland's voice. 'What is it, Dave?'

Holland ran his fingers through his hair, scratching hard at his scalp, staring in disbelief at the screen. Thorne leaned in and looked over his shoulder. He couldn't immediately work out what he was looking at.

'I can't . . .'

'She's been getting e-mails from the killer,' Holland said. 'From Night Watchman . . .'

Thorne felt something prickle around the top of his shoulders, heard his heartbeat quicken. 'Getting them, or getting them and replying? How long . . . ?'

'Wait . . .' Holland clicked, sorting the mails by date. He began to scroll slowly through them, and Thorne watched it move down the screen in front of his eyes. A correspondence between a woman on his team and the man they were trying to catch. A man who killed more brutally than anyone Thorne had ever lost sleep over.

'A week or more,' Holland said. 'Shit, there's fucking dozens of them . . .'

It had begun tentatively, like an exchange of letters between lovers-to-be. He told her he thought she was special, that there was something about her. He wondered how far across the line she would go to get the right result. His words were cryptic, teasing. Thorne could tell that, at least initially, he had been fishing, trying to find out how much she knew, how much any of them knew about him. He was wooing her. Thorne could see it, clear as day. He wondered if McEvoy had seen it. Her responses were open and forthright. She had fallen for it, or was letting him *think* she had. Thorne couldn't tell which.

'What the fuck is she playing at . . . ?' Holland's panic was increasing with every minute that passed, with every e-mail opened.

As Thorne read on, the answer became horribly apparent. The round-the-houses stuff had given way, in the last day or two, to something specific. An invitation. Did she want to meet him? Was she the individual he thought she

was? McEvoy had replied. She was *everything* he thought
she was, and more.

'When? There's got to be something that gives us a
time . . .'

'Got it,' Holland said, opening another mail. 'Jesus, it's
today. Four o'clock . . .'

Thorne looked at the time flashing at him in the top
right-hand corner of the screen. Whatever the hell McEvoy
thought she was doing, she probably had about twenty-five
minutes to live.

'Where?'

Holland clicked, scrolled, jabbed viciously at the keys.
'His last e-mail was . . . just after one this morning.' He
opened the file and they stared at the killer's words on the
screen.

```
Let's make it the place where Martin
was told the Jungle Story. Looking
forward to it, Sarah ...
```

'What the hell does that mean?' Holland put his finger
against the screen and pressed hard, as if he was trying to
push through it, rub out the words floating on the other
side.

'What about McEvoy's last mail?'

Holland called it up. 'She sent two, one after the other,
just before midday today . . .'

```
No idea what that means. Should I? If
you want me
to come, you'd better spell it out.
```

'Let's see the second one.' Thorne dared not hope. He already knew there was no reply from the killer, nothing that spelled anything out. Would McEvoy's final message be to cry off, to suggest they rearrange? She would have no choice, surely. She didn't know the place he was suggesting . . .

```
Going out now. Not sure when I'll be
back. Need
to know where to meet.
```

Then, two words that jumped off the screen, sent the guts shooting up towards the throat.

```
Text me.
```

Holland's body spasmed. 'Shit. He's sent a text message telling her where to meet him.'

'We don't know if he contacted her at all,' Thorne said. 'We don't know anything. She might come breezing back in here any second, off her tits with a bag full of Charlie.' Holland's look told Thorne that he didn't believe it any more than he did.

Thorne grabbed at the phone on the corner of the desk, thrust it at Holland. 'Call her mobile.'

He walked away, across to the window and stared out into the garden. The wind was coming up. He watched the overgrown grass sway slightly, and the long, rusty mirror bump gently against the fence post. Watching, hoping to hear Holland's concern translate into anger when he got through. *Where the fuck are you?* Hearing instead a long, frustrated breath, the crack of the phone going down, two more words he could really have done without.

'Switched off . . .'

Thorne turned around, walked back to the desk and picked up the phone himself. He dialled, waited, then hung up.

'Who are you calling?'

Thorne said nothing, his hand never leaving the receiver. He snatched it up again and dialled the number. He looked away from Holland, waiting for an answer . . .

'It's me. Tell me about the Jungle Story . . . never mind that, *just tell me*! Listen, Palmer, there isn't time for this, tell me what it is. No . . . forget that, just tell me *where*. Where was it . . . ?'

Holland couldn't believe what he was hearing. *Palmer?* What the hell was Thorne playing at . . . ? He stopped thinking about anything at all when Thorne's face changed. Even the bruises on his face seemed to grow momentarily pale. He thought that perhaps Thorne let out a long, low moan, though it might actually have come from him . . .

Thorne hung up with his finger. Gently but quickly he passed the receiver to Holland.

'It's at the school. He's meeting her at King Edward's.'

'Where are you . . . ?'

Thorne was on his way to the front door, his voice getting louder as he moved further away. 'Get on the phone and get it organised, right now. Tell Brigstocke I want an armed response unit. Keep trying McEvoy's mobile, or get somebody else to.'

'Sir . . .'

By now Thorne was shouting.

'And get a message through to the school . . .'

TWENTY-EIGHT

McEvoy walked into the playground in slow motion.

Stop. Just move backwards. Out of here the way you've come. Only he will ever know you bottled out. You don't have anything to prove, Sarah . . .

It was that strange time between darkness and light, the half an hour or so that can't quite make its mind up. As McEvoy pushed herself through the air, she felt like she was wading through a sticky, viscous liquid.

Adults and children milling around. Their movements impossibly fast. Their voices ringing through her, setting her teeth on edge. The squeals of the younger children, the honking voices of those a year or two older, the shouting of teachers. A braying cacophony fighting for space in her head with the voice.

The voice was back with a vengeance.

She thought about turning round, getting away to somewhere she could do a line and shut herself up. Getting away was just what the voice was telling her to do, though, so she kept moving forward. Maybe, if she just dived inside the school, found the toilet . . . She couldn't do it out here, not with children around. It would only take a minute. The teachers had to have their own toilet, surely . . .

What the fuck do you think you're doing? Think why you've come here. Worrying about where you do your next line is neither here nor there, considering.

She just kept walking. She'd decided that when she reached the far side of the huge playground she would turn around, walk slowly back again. They hadn't agreed on anywhere more specific. His text message hadn't narrowed the location down.

Silly bitch. Hard-faced bitch. Hard-faced as you like . . . not going to do you any good now. What's he going to do to you?

Her bag was over her shoulder. She pulled it in close to her body. Was there anything in there she could use against him if it came to it?

Run. Get out. Call Thorne . . .

Most of the boys smiled as they walked or ran past her on their way out. In a hurry to get home, but still polite as they had been taught to be. Deferential to adults, well-mannered, especially with ladies.

He was a pupil here, wasn't he? He isn't very well-mannered with ladies.

She raised her head and looked up at the school building on one side of her, the trees in the park high up in the distance on the other. Was he watching her from somewhere? Would there be some sort of signal? The weight of all the things she didn't know felt suddenly unmanageable. She felt stupid. Trapped and stupid. Even fifteen minutes before, she was so in control, so ready for this.

Now she walked across a playground, her grip loosening with every step.

★

He could see that she was scared.

Probably nobody else who saw her would have spotted it. She looked like she was out for a stroll. Adjusting her route to avoid collision with a burly sixth-former, turning side-on to miss a gaggle of first-years. She looked like she was in control.

He knew what to look for, though. He recognised fear. He would have seen it even if he'd been a long way away. He could see it coming off McEvoy like a heat-haze.

Her being scared was good, but it was less important than the fact that she was here. And that she'd come alone.

That had been the gamble all along, and it was one he couldn't really lose. He'd been able to watch her arrive. From his vantage point he'd been able to verify absolutely that she'd done as he'd asked. If she hadn't, if at the last moment she'd double-crossed him, gone to Thorne, he'd have known it. Even if they'd sent her in *as if* she'd come alone, using her as bait, he'd have seen it. He'd have spotted them, however well hidden they were.

They would never have recognised him.

Even if she'd stood him up he would have coped, taken her to task over it later.

But she was here, as ready for him as she was ever going to be. He felt a surge of pure excitement that, but for these moments just before he killed, he hadn't felt since he was a child.

He grinned. He could still taste the chocolate. Was that what all this was about? Getting in touch with his inner child?

cu @ 4 @ plygrnd :o)

The text message had been simple. The childish short-hand was proof, if she needed it, of his sense of fun.

Now it was time for the real fun to start.

Driving like an idiot through Wembley Park, horn blaring, lights flashing; one eye on the dashboard clock, and a speech forming itself in his mind. The words tumbling into sentences with each busy junction, every queue at traffic lights. The speech he would be giving to Sarah McEvoy's parents if he was too late . . .

Why had the killer targeted McEvoy? *How* had he targeted her?

Thorne leaned on the horn, swerved inside to accelerate noisily past a Transit van. He knew he wouldn't get the answers to these questions, not yet. Not until the fucker was in a chair opposite him, shitting himself in an interview room in the early hours of the morning.

There were other questions, though. Questions a little closer to home that got into his head and stayed there like a jingle he couldn't shake. Why hadn't he noticed? Why hadn't he seen a senior member of his team getting into this? The drugs, the lies, the descent into something warped and deadly . . .

He drove north across Fryent Country Park, the school now maybe less than five minutes away. The minute hand moving another notch past the vertical. The speech almost fully formed.

DS McEvoy was a fine officer, who gave her life in the line of duty . . .

Thorne hammered the Mondeo across a roundabout and turned left towards the centre of Harrow. He bellowed at the windscreen as the car that should have had right of way missed him by a matter of inches, the face of its driver murderous. Thorne returned the look with interest and stamped on the brakes, catching his breath through gritted teeth as a line of stationary vehicles appeared in front of him.

All of those who worked with her, of whatever rank, will miss her dedication and good humour . . .

The school was no more than a quarter of a mile away. Thorne's knuckles were white on the steering wheel, his foot pumping the accelerator as he raced the engine in neutral. The shriek of the complaining engine was almost as loud as the scream inside his head.

Nothing was moving. There were no lights ahead, no sign of an accident. Nobody was going anywhere.

The fucking school run.

McEvoy reached the far side of the playground, turned and looked around, thinking *come on you fucker, where are you?* Moving back towards the centre now, saying it out loud, like a madwoman on a bus. *I'm here, why the hell aren't you? There's a big surprise coming your way, coming everybody's way . . .*

Then a few words from the voice, and she stopped, because she needed to evacuate the playground. Of course she did. After all, she had no idea what was going to happen. There were still plenty of kids around – the slower ones, the stragglers, a group kicking a ball around. Christ he'd used a gun before, hadn't he? Thoughts of Dunblane, of Columbine High . . .

How messed up are you? Protecting the public should have been your first thought, would have been a few months ago. If this is about showing how good you are at your job, it's not going very well so far . . .

She reached into her jacket pocket for her warrant card, opened her mouth to start shouting . . .

What if they panicked? If he was nearby, it might provoke him into something. No, she might scare him off. She needed to do what they'd agreed. Besides, if he *was* nearby, she was going to take the fucker before he could hurt anybody.

That was her last thought before she felt the knife in her back and heard the voice, close to her ear.

'You are alone, aren't you, Sarah?'

'Yes.'

'You're not lying. That's good. Walk with me, and please be sensible . . .'

She gasped as the point of the knife pressed through her jacket and shirt, and into her skin. A hand was placed in the small of her back and began to guide her forwards towards the exit.

His voice. Did she recognise it? Yes, maybe, couldn't remember. Fuck it . . .

McEvoy almost laughed. *She was going to take the fucker.* She knew exactly what she wanted to do, *needed* to do, but couldn't for the life of her remember how. She was suddenly all but asleep on her feet. Helpless. If she hadn't felt as weak as a baby already, the words whispered into her ear would have taken away any last vestige of strength in her body.

'If you scream or try to run, I will kill a child.'

Thorne thought that from somewhere a few streets back he could still hear the horns that had blared at him as he'd got out of the Mondeo and begun to run. Now they were being sounded in pure rage and frustration at the abandoned car.

Oh Christ . . .

He began to slow down, his hands flying to his head, legs suddenly leaden.

Fuck . . .

Where were they coming from? Which direction would the back-up vehicles come from? Brigstocke, Holland, the Armed Response Unit? The traffic had been impossible before. Now, thanks to him, it would be gridlocked. If the cars were coming the same way he had . . .

Suddenly, Thorne was aware of schoolboys moving past him: in ones and twos at first and then in bigger groups. Jabbering and clowning around. Blue blazers, trimmed with claret. The ties taken off for the journey home.

He was nearly there.

He took a painful breath and picked his legs up again, drove himself forward.

We can only hope that more young women of her calibre will come forward and offer their services to the public . . .

The tree-lined streets around the school now thick with blue and claret, alive with shouts and taunts, and boasts.

Hitting the ground. Dragging his knees up . . .

His stomach began to burn, the judder of each step sending an agonising shockwave through his shattered nose and up into his forehead. His chest rattled and clattered. Beneath his jacket, the sweat had plastered his shirt to his back. It froze as it met the cold air blowing down his collar.

Christ they were big, some of them. A pair of lumbering teenagers, striped ties wrapped around their foreheads, blocked the pavement ahead of him. Thorne put his head down and charged at them, ignoring the shouts and jeers as he crashed through the middle and began sprinting for all he was worth up the school drive.

As he ran, as his feet smacked the ground beneath him, he remembered the car crunching slowly over the gravel. He remembered the last time he'd come up this drive. He and Holland comparing educations in the car.

Then inside the school, the first time he'd got a look at Stuart Nicklin. The face turned away.

In making the ultimate sacrifice, this brave officer has increased the determination of those she leaves behind, to continue the fight . . .

Was he about to see that face in the flesh?

He was only a hundred yards or so away. The drive curved sharply to the left and then narrowed suddenly, a bottleneck forming at the high, narrow gate that was the main entrance to the playground.

He began to slow down as he approached it.

Everything seemed normal. Kids coming out smiling. There was no noise, no *abnormal* noise. He slowed to a jog and then a fast walk. Getting his breath back. Everything *seemed* normal, but he had no idea what was waiting for him inside that gate.

He was suddenly very worried – sweating every bit as much as he had been when he was running.

If the message, whatever it was, however it had been worded, had got through to the school, then surely things would *not* have been so normal. Wouldn't the kids be inside? Kept away from any danger, held inside the building?

Thorne put out an arm, brushed past a boy hovering at the gate and stepped through.

He stood there, his guts churning, his eyes flicking across the expanse in front of him, trying to take it all in quickly. The main building to his right. The huge windows of the gymnasium, lined with wallbars. Up ahead, the newer buildings – the sixth-form block, the music rooms – and beyond them the playing fields. Still plenty of kids about. Singing coming from somewhere. A few teachers moving around . . .

McEvoy . . .

He took a step in her direction and then stopped. Her eyes bulged, terrified, out of a bloodless face. What little breath Thorne had left was gone in a moment.

'Sarah . . .'

Then Thorne got his first look at the face of the man immediately behind her. The man who was guiding her gently but firmly towards him. The man who stopped and looked straight at him, scowling, as if he were no more than a hindrance.

Then Thorne knew exactly why Ken Bowles had been killed.

TWENTY-NINE

'You're out of breath,' Cookson said. 'What *have* you been doing?'

It was a moment of terrible clarity. The sort that only ever comes hand in hand with terror, or great pain. Thorne embraced it as he would the sting of the flame that cauterised a wound.

Andrew Cookson . . .

'You killed Bowles because he recognised you,' Thorne said. 'It wasn't random. It wasn't a message. You *needed* to do it . . .'

Cookson casually placed a hand on McEvoy's shoulder. 'Silly old sod should have retired years ago. Could barely do his sums any more. Then after half an hour with you he takes one good, hard look at me without the beard and . . . bang! Cobwebs well and truly blown away. Corners me in the staff room. Pointing his finger and making melodramatic speeches. *I know who you are.* Fucking idiot . . .'

Thorne pictured the chalk on Bowles's crotch, the soil dropping down on to the lid of his coffin. Why hadn't he called the police? Why, when he'd recognised Cookson as

Nicklin, hadn't he used the card that Thorne had given him, the one that Jay had found in his jacket pocket?

The answer was a painful one to acknowledge. It wasn't heroism, it was desperation. It was Ken Bowles's last chance. A crack at balancing that chair on his chin one final time.

'Enjoyable as this is,' Cookson said, 'the situation is a little tricky, wouldn't you say? I think we need to resolve it quickly. So, any bright ideas?'

His tone was easy and faintly amused. Not hard when you were the one with a knife in a woman's back.

'Not really,' Thorne said.

'I thought not.'

There was a silence that should have been heavy with threat and danger, but with children filing past smirking, it felt no more than awkward or embarrassing. Thorne wondered what the three of them looked like. Cookson and McEvoy might have been lovers, and he the ex-boyfriend, bumped into at an inopportune moment . . .

Cookson smiled, as if working something out that pleased him enormously. 'You've come on your own as well, haven't you?'

Thorne thought about lying but wasn't quick enough. Cookson leaned forward, ready to move on. 'Well, you have somewhat gatecrashed things, but we're not going to let it spoil our enjoyment, are we, Sarah?' McEvoy winced as the knife nudged through another layer of skin. Thorne was close to rushing at him, hammering fists into his face. 'So, we're just going to carry on as if we never saw you. Excuse me . . .'

There was nothing Thorne could do. He had to step aside to let Cookson walk away. He didn't have a shred of doubt that he would push the knife into McEvoy's spine at the slightest provocation. He turned side-on, giving Cookson the room to get past, to manoeuvre McEvoy through the gate and away. Thorne noticed that in his free hand Cookson was carrying his briefcase with him. His cover was perfect. This was territory he'd felt safe on. Just a tired teacher heading home with a friend at the end of a long day . . .

Cookson froze suddenly, looked right and left. Then Thorne saw what was happening. Children were moving back towards the building, some running. Teachers had appeared silently around the edge of the playground and were gathering in those pupils still around.

The message had got through.

Hissing instructions, beckoning, gesturing, the teachers emptied the playground in as orderly a way as they could. Following the directives that they had been given – that were standard in such situations – they were trying to do it without alarming anyone, least of all the killer they'd been told might be nearby.

He was nearer than they realised and he *was* alarmed. Thorne could see the hesitation, the tension in Cookson's face and in the hand that squeezed the back of Sarah McEvoy's neck.

'Please,' McEvoy said. It was more of a moan than a word.

'I think we're stuck with each other,' Thorne said. 'Half the Met is waiting for you out there. Plenty of them are armed and looking for an excuse . . .'

Cookson shook his head, and in an instant he had brought the knife round to McEvoy's throat. Smiling, he began to move backwards, towards the centre of the playground. Thorne followed slowly, praying that what he'd just told Cookson was, or would very soon be, true. As they neared the middle of the playground, McEvoy's eyes locked on to Thorne's. He couldn't begin to guess what they were trying to tell him.

Cookson stopped and took a deep breath. He adjusted his position, leaving the knife exactly where it was, the blade biting into McEvoy's neck, but moving round a little to stand next to her.

'You know I'll kill her, so why don't we stop pissing about. One way or another, I'm leaving here. If I'm in the back of a squad car, then she'll be leaving in a body bag.'

'Fuck you,' McEvoy said.

Cookson opened his eyes wide in mock surprise. 'It speaks,' he said. 'I was wondering where you'd got to. I reckon your blood must be about ninety-eight per cent Colombian.' He laughed, and McEvoy grunted as a line of blood an inch or so long sprang onto the flesh of her throat and began to drip.

'Sorry,' Cookson said. 'Accident . . .'

Thorne twitched and Cookson's look told him to keep very still. It told him that the next time there would be a lot more blood.

'What did you do with the boy when you killed Carol Garner?' Thorne said. 'Did he see it happen?' Cookson narrowed his eyes and pursed his lips as if confused by the question. 'Did you make her son watch while you killed her?'

Cookson shook his head, blew out a breath through tight lips. 'Sorry, you'll have to help me. Which one was Carol Garner again?'

Thorne knew then that as things stood, none of them

were likely to leave that playground alive. He was willing his feet to stay where they were, but he knew that at any moment he would fly at this man, that rage would simply stop him caring any more. He knew that McEvoy's throat would open and cover the two of them with blood as she dropped away while he and Andrew Cookson murdered each other with cuts and clutching hands on the cold asphalt . . .

Thorne became aware of a low buzzing noise. He realised that the sound was coming out of McEvoy's mouth.

'I'm sorry . . . I'm sorry . . . I'm sorry . . .'

'McEvoy . . .'

Thorne's voice just seemed to activate some switch in McEvoy's brain. Now the words gushed out of her. She shook her head violently as if trying to dislodge something, shake it out of there; her neck moving back and forth across the blade of the knife, the blood running down Cookson's fingers.

'I'msorryI'msorryI'msorryI'msorryI'msorryI'msorry . . .'

Thorne could have sworn that the scream that followed came from him, or was at the very least inside his head, but if it *was*, why was Cookson spinning round? Why was he looking so astonished . . . ?

The figure came running from around the side of the main building, shouting and waving. Thorne blinked, looked again.

The figure was waving a gun.

Martin Palmer lumbered towards them, and the things that Thorne was seeing seemed to happen in slow motion at the same time that the thoughts in his head started coming faster than he could make sense of them.

Cookson pushing McEvoy away, dropping the knife . . .

McEvoy turning, running straight at Palmer . . .

Cookson bringing up his hands to protect his head as the first shot rang across the playground . . .

As Thorne went down hard, he heard the second shot, and at the edge of his vision he saw McEvoy stumble and crash heavily to the ground. An instant before he closed his eyes, he saw the look of astonishment frozen on Cookson's face, and a look there were simply no words to describe on Martin Palmer's.

It was no more than a few moments, but when Thorne opened his eyes, it seemed to have become considerably darker. There were a few spots of sleet in the air.

Thorne raised his head. Twenty-five yards away, McEvoy lay on the floor. He had no idea where she'd been hit, how badly she was hurt. He heard her moan as she tried to move the leg that was twisted awkwardly beneath her.

She was moving at least.

Thorne slowly got to his feet. His eyes, and those of Andrew Cookson, never moved from the figure of Martin Palmer. He stood no more than a few feet from them, his head bowed, the hand that held the gun twitching spastically.

'What the fuck are you doing, Palmer?' Thorne said.

Palmer looked up. His eyes seemed huge behind his glasses. The gun was smacking against his leg. 'I'm sorry.'

Behind Palmer, McEvoy cried out. Thorne couldn't make out whether it was pain or anger.

'Sorry?' Thorne shouted. 'Fucking sorry . . . ?'

'You're full of surprises, Martin,' Cookson said. 'I *tell* you to shoot someone, you throw a wobbly and run to the police . . .'

Palmer shook his head. 'Shut up, Stuart . . .'

Cookson didn't even draw breath. 'Then up you pop out of the blue, and fuck me if you don't put a bullet in one of them.'

Palmer raised the gun and pointed it at Cookson's chest. 'I told you to shut up.'

'Not deliberately, of course. I think we know who the bullets were meant for.' He nodded his head towards McEvoy. 'She was just a lucky accident.'

Thorne looked at Cookson, no more than two paces away, and promised himself that whatever else happened, he was going to hurt him.

A noise came up from Palmer's throat, a low growl which erupted out of his mouth as a roar. His knuckles were white against the grip of the gun, his finger twitching against the trigger. He nodded once, twice. Those little nods. Urging himself to do it, telling himself to shoot.

Cookson looked unconcerned. 'I always had to get you riled up, didn't I?' he said. 'Do you remember? There was a small window of opportunity if I was going to get you to do something, because you never held it together for very long. So, what's got you so excited now? Specifically?' He asked the question casually, as if checking some trivial fact. 'Was it Karen?'

Palmer swallowed hard. He brought his left hand up to steady the gun.

'Yes, of course it was.' Cookson smiled. '*Was* is right, isn't it, Martin? You've lost it already. You *want* to kill me, but whatever made you brave enough to actually *try* has vanished, hasn't it? Run out of you like watery shit. Now you're just scared again . . .'

Thorne looked at McEvoy. She was getting harder to

make out clearly. The clouds were lower now, and blacker. The light was dirty, diffuse. The whole scene seemed lit by a thousand dusty, forty-watt lightbulbs.

He had to make a move. 'I need to get to my officer,' he said. Palmer didn't appear to be listening. Thorne took a step forwards, and in a second the gun was levelled at him.

'*No!*' Palmer shouted.

Thorne was genuinely surprised. 'What are you playing at, Martin?' Palmer said nothing. He looked lost. Lost, confused, and with a gun pointing at Thorne's belly.

Thorne tried to keep his voice low and even. 'There are armed officers watching us right now. They're slightly better at this than you are. Do you understand, Martin?'

Palmer nodded slowly.

Thorne knew damn well that there was nobody watching them – not yet. If the Armed Response team had been there, then Palmer would not be standing and pointing a gun. He would almost certainly be dead by now.

'Throw the gun away and let me get across to my sergeant. Martin . . . ?'

A light came on to Thorne's right. His eyes flicked across and he saw that there were children at the windows of the gymnasium, watching.

The sleet started to get a little heavier.

'Martin?' Thorne said.

Cookson shrugged. 'It's a toughy, Mart . . .'

Thorne's head whipped round and he spat gobbets of spittle and hatred into Cookson's face. 'Shut your fucking stupid cunt's mouth. *I* will kill you, is that clear? *I'm* not afraid, certainly not of you. I don't care what happens. He can shoot the pair of us, I don't give a fuck. But if I hear so much as a breath coming out of you before this is finished, a single poisonous whisper, I'll rip your face off with my bare hands. I'll take it clean off, Nicklin. I'll make you another nice, new identity . . .'

Cookson's face was blank. He was very still. Thorne thought he'd shaken him, but he couldn't be sure whether the stillness was that of the prey that seeks to protect itself, or the predator that is conserving its energy, preparing to strike.

Palmer spoke and the thought was gone.

'I'm sorry about your officer.' His voice was lower than usual, certainly calmer than it had been a few minutes before. 'I need to tell you something,' he said. 'I got the gun from a man in a pub. The first gun I mean.' He pointed with the gun to Cookson. '*He* knows, he can tell you. It's a pub in Kilburn, I'm sure you could find it . . .'

Thorne stared at him. *What the hell was he on about?* 'We don't have to do this now, Martin . . .'

'I got this gun from the same man. I followed him from the pub. He's got a lock-up garage in Neasden, near the railway works, just across from the tube station.'

Thorne was confused, but his mind raced, made connections. *Neasden, four or five stops from where they were on the tube. Fifteen minutes, no more. Palmer, easily able to get here quicker than he had.* 'Martin, this isn't important . . .'

'Please, you have to listen. I took the gun, and there was a great deal of cash . . .'

Cookson snorted. 'He'll fucking kill you.'

'He's dead.' Cookson's eyes widened. Palmer's looked like they were ready to bulge out of his head as he craned his neck towards Thorne. 'He was a bad man, though, so maybe I did a good thing. I had no choice anyway.' He glanced at the gun in his hand. 'I needed . . . this. I needed somewhere to stay for a while. I stayed in the garage. With the body. It was starting to really smell in there . . .'

Palmer blinked slowly, his eyes closing almost, but not for quite long enough for Thorne to think about lunging . . .

'We can sort all this out later, Martin. There'll be loads of time. Just get rid of the gun. You must get rid of it . . .'

Palmer lowered his arm.

'That's good, Martin, but you have to drop it. Let it go.'

Palmer shook his head. Thorne sensed movement away to his right, and turned his head to see the children in the gym being led away from the windows. One by one the faces disappeared.

Thorne blinked. The last face pressed up against the window, eyes wide and full of doubt, belonged to Charlie Garner . . .

There was other movement, indistinct and fleeting, somewhere above and to the right of him. Finally, Thorne knew that back-up had arrived. Positions were being taken up, targets identified, sights fixed. A momentary glance told him that Cookson had seen it too.

'I don't want you to be afraid,' Palmer said suddenly.

Thorne looked away from the rooftop. As he brought his gaze back round to Palmer, he checked out Cookson, who was standing stock still, arms by his sides, eyes narrowed.

Palmer's expression was bizarrely earnest. 'Really. You don't have to be afraid.'

'Guns make me afraid, Martin. Throw it away.'

'You know fear has a taste, don't you? It's actually the taste of your adrenal gland. That's what you can taste, that's the flavour of it . . .'

Thorne saw Palmer's fingers moving. He watched, afraid to breathe, as the finger moved away from the trigger.

Should he move now? Go for the gun . . . ?

'It's a very strange taste. Like chewing on a bit of tinfoil. That suggestion of metal in your mouth. It's actually the chemical that's in adrenaline . . .'

Palmer slipped his finger out of the trigger guard. Rested it against the outside. Safe.

He needed to do it now. He wasn't sure he'd seen McEvoy move for a while . . .

'It's called adrenochrome. Did you know that?'

Thorne shook his head. He didn't know the name, but he knew the taste very well.

As Palmer screamed and raised his arm, Thorne saw what was happening. As Palmer levelled the gun at him, Thorne saw exactly what he was trying to do.

He saw everything, far, far too late.

The bullet from the marksman's rifle had ripped through Palmer's throat before any of them had even heard the shot.

Palmer dropped to his knees with an odd slowness, but then pitched forward fast on to his face. Thorne thought, or perhaps imagined, that he could hear nose, cheekbones and glasses shattering as the face hit the ground.

Thorne went down quickly, put his hands on the gun that was lying a foot or so away from Palmer's corpse. He looked across towards McEvoy, hoping . . .

'Congratulations on being alive, Thorne.' Cookson smiled, slowly raising his hands into the air. 'Being alive's the easy bit though, isn't it?'

From somewhere behind them, a distorted voice

boomed through a loudspeaker. Cookson took a step towards it, his arms high and straight. 'It's *feeling* alive, that's the hard part . . .'

In one smooth movement, Thorne stood up and whipped his arm round hard, smashing the butt of the gun across Cookson's mouth. He could feel the lips burst. He saw the teeth shatter and split the gums an instant before the hand moved to stop the gush of blood.

Thorne heard the thump of feet behind him. He turned to see officers pouring in through the gate, and Dave Holland sprinting across the playground towards Sarah McEvoy's body.

THIRTY

The pitch was frozen. A lot of mistimed tackles, flare-ups, silly mistakes. All the game needed was a dubious penalty and a sending-off, and Thorne would feel that this month's subscription to Sky had been justified.

He wondered whether his dad would be watching, shouting at the screen as if he were still on the terraces. His dad who had taken him to his first Spurs game over thirty years before, back in the days of Martin Chivers and Alan Gilzean. Thorne wondered how much longer his old man would be *able* to watch, able to follow the game.

The call had been typical of him. He'd dealt with the situation in a predictable way.

'Remember the joke I told you about the bloke who goes to the doctors?'

Thorne laughed. There had been plenty. 'Which one?'

'The doctor says to him, "Bad news I'm afraid. You've got cancer *and* Alzheimer's disease . . ."'

Thorne felt something tighten. 'Dad . . .'

'So the bloke looks at the doctor . . .' The voice on the phone, starting to waver a little. 'He looks at the doctor and says, "well, at least I haven't got cancer."'

'What are you on about, Dad?'

There was a long pause before the old man repeated the punchline, said what he'd called to say.

'*At least I haven't got cancer, Tom.*'

Then Thorne had understood what it was his father *did* have.

The hiss of a ring-pull brought Thorne out of it, and he turned to look at Hendricks. He was stretched out as usual, shoes off, feet up on the sofa.

'You said something interesting once,' Thorne said.

'Only once?'

'You said you thought the smell of formaldehyde put people off. You don't reckon your feet might have anything to do with it?'

'Piss off,' Hendricks said.

Things were pretty much back to normal.

Nearly a month since Thorne had walked away from the playground at King Edward's. Watching the stretchers sliding into ambulances. The arms of teachers wrapped around crying children. The look on Dave Holland's face . . .

Nearly a month since he'd walked back up that long drive, wondering idly what might have happened to his car.

How long it would take to scrub blood off asphalt . . .

Palmer had known exactly what he was doing, when he'd pointed that gun. Thorne should have seen it coming earlier – when Palmer had been so keen to tell him where the gun had come from. A last attempt at a good gesture, before the most desperate one of all.

Was suicide, which is what it was, the act of a coward or a brave man? Thorne thought, in the end, that Palmer had done what he did, not out of self-disgust, but simply because he knew, emotionally at least, that he would never survive prison.

The school's former Head of English, on the other hand, was made of sterner stuff. Of far stranger stuff.

Andrew Cookson would do very nicely. While the true-crime cash-ins were being scribbled, he would carve out a niche for himself in Belmarsh or Broadmoor. Number one nutter in the nick. Fear was all-important in prison. In a place where getting through a day unscathed was hard enough, robbers and rapists would probably scare just as easily as Martin Palmer had done.

Palmer, scared stiff all his life, whose one act of anything like bravery had gone so tragically wrong.

The words of the speech, the platitudes that had rattled around in his head that day, were close enough to those that were needed. To those that were eventually used.

'*All of those who worked with her, of whatever rank, will miss her dedication and good humour . . .*'

The faces of Lionel and Rebecca McEvoy had joined those of Robert and Mary Enright, Rosemary Vincent and Leslie Bowles. The flaking portraits of those that had lived to bury their children.

Leslie Bowles had put it simplest, and best.

It never stops. Never.

'By the way,' Hendricks said. 'If Brendan rings, I'm not here . . .'

Thorne turned and stared at the scruffy article sprawled on the sofa, at the open and expectant face of the man who had performed the post-mortem on Sarah McEvoy.

Who afterwards had somehow managed to misplace the toxicology report.

'Oi . . . I'm not here. If he rings. Is that OK?'

'I see another piercing coming,' Thorne said. 'What's happened now?'

Hendricks swung his feet on to the floor and sat up. 'You remember when I thought he was freaked out by the job, yeah? Well, it turns out he actually quite likes it.'

'So?'

'So, now *I'm* the one that's a bit freaked out . . .'

'You're never happy.'

'Me! What about you?'

Thorne stood and strolled towards the kitchen to get a couple more beers. 'I'm fine.'

Hendricks leaned back grinning, his hands behind his head. 'Yeah, well, so you should be. Fantastic mate like me, beer, Spurs one-nil up away from home. It doesn't get much better than this really, does it?'

With his back to him, Hendricks had no way of knowing if Thorne was smiling as he spoke.

'Christ, I sincerely hope so . . .'

EPILOGUE

23, Dyer Close
Kings Heath
Birmingham
B14 3EX
West Midlands

28 February, 2002

Dear Inspector Thorne,

I know it's taken a while to drop you a line, but I'm sure
you appreciate that there's a lot going on and that it's
been quite difficult for us since the arrest.

We were very sorry to hear about Detective Sergeant
McEvoy. She must have been about the same age as Carol.
Please pass on our condolences to her family.

Charlie is really starting to do well now. He's settled in
very well at school and is sleeping a lot better. The child
psychologist is very pleased with him. My wife thought
you'd like to know.

The real reason I was writing, was to say a belated 'thank
you' for the tool set you sent Charlie at Christmas. It was
thoughtful. I hope you don't mind, but we didn't tell him
that the present came from you. We're not sure if he
remembers you anyway and we thought it best, considering, to just tell him it was from us. I'm sure you
understand.

Yours sincerely,

Robert Enright

Robert Enright

*An extract from Mark Billingham's
exciting new thriller*

Lazybones

Available in Little, Brown hardback from 3 July 2003

PART ONE

BIRTHS, MARRIAGES AND DEATHS

10 August 1976

He inched himself towards the edge, each tightening of the sphincter muscle moving him a little further across the narrow breadth of the banister's polished surface. He twisted his wrists, wrapping the towel once more tightly around them. Not giving himself the get-out, knowing his body would look for it. Knowing he would instinctively try to free himself.

His heels bounced rhythmically against the banister spindles below him. The blue tow-rope that he'd found at the back of the garage was itchy against his neck. He smiled to himself. Scratching it, even if he could, would have been stupid. Like dabbing at the skin with disinfectant before slipping in the needle to administer a lethal injection.

He closed his eyes, bowed his head and let his weight tip him forwards and over and down.

It felt as if the jolt might take his head off, but it was not even enough to break a bone. There hadn't been time to do the maths, to set weight against height. Even if there had been, he wasn't sure he'd have known what the relationship between them was. He remembered reading somewhere that the proper hangmen, the Pierrepoints or whoever, could do the calculation, could figure out the necessary drop, based on nothing more than shaking the condemned man's hand.

Pleased to meet you – about twelve feet I reckon . . .

He clenched his teeth against the pain in his back. The skin had been taken off his spine by the edge of the stair-rail as he'd dropped. He could feel warm blood trickling down his chin and he realised that he'd bitten through his tongue. He could smell the motor oil on the rope.

He thought about the woman, in bed, not ten feet away.

It would have been lovely to have seen her face when she found him. Her liar's mouth falling open as she reached up to stop his body swinging. That would have been perfect, but of course he would never see it. And she would never find him.

Somebody else would find both of them.

He couldn't help but wonder what the authorities would make of it all. What the newspapers would say. Their name would be spoken, would be whispered again in certain offices and living rooms. His name, the one he'd given her, would echo around a courtroom as it had done so often before, dragged through the mud and the filth that she'd spread before her like an oil slick. This time they themselves would be mercifully absent as others talked about them, about the tragedy, about the balance of their minds being disturbed. It was hard to argue with that now, this very moment. Him waiting to die, and her upstairs, thirty minutes ahead of him, the blood already soaking deep into their mushroom-coloured bedroom carpet.

She had disturbed both their minds. She had asked for everything she'd got.

Half an hour before, her hands reaching to protect herself.

Eight months before that, her hands reaching, her legs spread, on the floor of that stockroom.

She'd asked for everything . . .

He gagged, spluttering blood, sensing a shadow preparing to descend, feeling his life beginning, thankfully, to slip away. How long had it been now? Two minutes? Five? He pushed his feet down towards the floor, willing his weight to do its work quickly.

He heard a noise like a creak and then a small hum of amazement. He opened his eyes.

He was facing away from the front door, looking back at the staircase. He shifted his shoulders violently, trying to create enough momentum to make himself turn. As he spun slowly around, seconds from death, he found himself staring down, through bloodied and bulging retinas, into the flawless brown eyes of a child.

ONE

The look was slightly spoiled by the training shoes.

The man with the mullet haircut and the sweaty top lip was wearing a smart blue suit, doubtless acquired for the occasion, but he'd let himself down with the bright white Nike Airs. They squeaked on the gymnasium floor as his feet shifted nervously underneath the table.

'I'm sorry,' he said. 'I'm really, really, sorry.'

An elderly couple sat at the table opposite him. The man's back was ramrod straight, his milky blue eyes never leaving those of the man in the suit. The old woman next to the old man clutched at his hand. Her eyes, unlike those of her husband, looked anywhere but at those of the young man who, the last time he had been this close to them, was tying them up in their own home.

The trembling was starting around the centre of Darren Ellis's meticulously shaved chin. His voice wobbled a little. 'If there was anything I could do to make it up to you, I would,' he said.

'There isn't,' the old man said.

'I can't take back what I did, but I do know how wrong it was. I know what I put you through.'

The old woman began to cry.

'How can you?' her husband said.

Darren Ellis began to cry.

On the last row of seats, his back against the gym wall-bars, sat a solid-looking man in a black leather jacket, aged forty or so with dark eyes and hair that was greyer on one side than the other. He looked uncomfortable and a little confused. He turned to the man sitting next to him.

'This. Is. Bollocks,' Thorne said.

DCI Russell Brigstocke glared at him. There was a *shush* from a red-haired squaddie type a couple of rows in front. One of Ellis's supporters by the look of him.

'Bollocks,' Thorne repeated.

The gymnasium at the Peel Centre would normally be full of eager recruits at this unearthly time on a Monday morning. It was, however, the largest space available for this 'Restorative Justice Conference', so the raw young constables were doing their press-ups and star jumps elsewhere. The floor of the gym had been covered with a green tarpaulin and fifty or so seats had been laid out. They were filled with supporters of both offender and victims together with invited officers who, it was thought, would appreciate the opportunity to be brought up to speed with this latest initiative.

Becke House, where Thorne and Brigstocke were based, was part of the same complex. Half an hour earlier, on the five minute walk across to the gym, Thorne had moaned without drawing breath.

'If it's an invitation, how come I'm not allowed to turn it down?'

'Shut up,' Brigstocke said. They were late and he was walking quickly, trying not to spill hot coffee from a polystyrene cup that was all but melting. Thorne lagged a step or two behind.

'Shit, I've forgotten the bit of paper, maybe they won't let me in.'

Brigstocke scowled, unamused.

'What if I'm not smart enough? There might be a dress code . . .'

'I'm not listening, Tom . . .'

Thorne shook his head, flicked out his foot at a stone like a sulky schoolboy. 'I'm just trying to get it straight. This piece of pondlife ties an old couple up with electrical flex, gives the old man a kick or two for good measure, breaking . . . how many ribs?'

'Three . . .'

'Three. Thanks. He pisses on their carpet, fucks off with their life savings and now we're rushing across to see how sorry he is?'

'It's just a trial. They've been using RJCs in Australia and the results have been pretty bloody good. Re-offending rates have gone right down . . .'

'So, basically, they sit everybody down pre-sentence, and if they all agree that the guilty party is really *feeling* guilty, he gets to do a bit less time. That it?'

Brigstocke took a last scalding slurp and dumped the half-full cup in a bin. 'It's not quite that simple.'

A week and a bit into a steaming June, but the day was still too new to have warmed up yet. Thorne shoved his hands deeper into the pockets of his leather jacket.

'No, but whoever thought it up is.'

In the gym, the audience watched as Darren Ellis moved balled-up fists from in front of his face to reveal moist, red eyes. Thorne looked around at those watching.

Some looked sad and shook their heads. One or two were taking notes. On the front row, members of Ellis's legal team passed pieces of paper between them.

'If I said that *I* felt like a victim, would you laugh?' Darren asked.

The old man looked calmly at him for fifteen seconds or more before answering flatly. 'I'd want to knock your teeth out.'

'Things aren't always that clear cut,' Darren said.

The old man leaned across the table. The skin was tight around his mouth. 'I'll tell you what's clear cut.' His eyes flicked towards his wife as he spoke. 'She hasn't slept since the night you came into our house. She wets the bed most of the time.' His voice dropped to a whisper. 'She's got so bloody thin . . .'

Something between a gulp and a gasp echoed around the gymnasium as Darren dropped his head into his hands and gave full vent to his emotions. A lawyer got to his feet. A senior detective stood up and started walking towards the table. It was time to take a break.

Thorne leaned across and whispered loudly to Brigstocke. 'He's very good. Where did he train? RADA?' This time, several of the faces that turned to look daggers at him belonged to senior officers . . .

Ten minutes later and everybody was mingling in the foyer outside. There was a lot of nodding and hushed conversation. There was mineral water and biscuits.

'I'm supposed to write a report on this,' Brigstocke mumbled.

Thorne waved across the foyer to a couple of lads he knew from Team 6. 'Rather you than me.'

'I'm trying to decide the right word to use to describe the attitude of certain attending officers on my team. Obstructive? Insolent? You got any thoughts . . .?'

'I *think* that was one of the stupidest things I've ever seen. I can't believe people sat there and took it seriously, and I don't care *what* the results were in sodding Australia. Actually, no, *not* stupid. It was obscene. All those silly bastards studying every expression on that little prick's face. How many tears? How big were they? How much shame?' Thorne took a swig of water, held it in his mouth for a few seconds, swallowed. 'Did you see *her* face? Did you look at the old woman's face?'

Brigstocke's mobile rang. He answered it quickly, but Thorne kept on talking anyway. 'Restorative Justice? For who? For that old man and his skeletal wife?'

Brigstocke shook his head angrily, turned away.

Thorne put his glass down on a window-sill. He moved suddenly, pushing past several people as he walked quickly towards the group he'd seen emerging from a door on the other side of the foyer.

Darren Ellis had taken his jacket and tie off. He was handcuffed, a detective on either side of him, their hands on his shoulders.

'Good show, Darren,' Thorne said. He raised his hands and started to clap.

Ellis stared, his mouth opening and closing, an uneasy expression that had definitely *not* been rehearsed. He looked for help to the officers on either side of him.

Thorne smiled. 'What do you do for an encore? Always best to finish on a song I reckon . . .'

The officer to Ellis's left, a stick-thin article with dandruff on his brown polyester jacket, tried his best to look casually intimidating. 'Piss off, Thorne.'

Before Thorne had a chance to respond, his attention was caught by the figure of Russell Brigstocke marching purposefully across the room towards him. Thorne was hardly aware of the two detectives leading Ellis away in the other direction. The look on the DCI's face caused something to clench in his stomach.

'You want to restore some justice?' Brigstocke said. 'Now's your chance.' He pointed at Thorne with his mobile phone. 'This sounds like a good one . . .'

It was called a hotel. They also called MPs 'right', 'honourable' and 'gentlemen' . . .

The sign outside *said* 'Hotel', but Thorne knew full well that certain signs in less salubrious parts of London were not to be taken too literally. If they all meant exactly what they said, there would be a lot of frustrated businessmen sitting in saunas waiting for hand-jobs they were never going to get.

The sign outside should have read 'Shithole'.

The room was as basic as it could get. The maroon carpet, once the finest offcut the warehouse had to offer, was now worn through in a number of places. The green of the rotting, rubber underlay beneath matched the mould which snaked up the off white anaglypta below the window. A long dead spider plant stood on the window-ledge, caked in dust. Thorne pushed aside the grubby orange curtains, leaned against the sill and took in the breathtaking view of the traffic inching slowly past Paddington Station towards the Marylebone Road. Nearly eleven o'clock and still solid.

Thorne turned round and sucked in a breath. Opposite him in the doorway, DC Dave Holland stood chatting to a uniform, waiting, like Thorne, for the signal to step in and start. To sink both feet deep into the mire.

In different parts of the room, three Scene-Of-Crime Officers crouched and crawled – bagging and tagging and searching for the fibre, the grain, that might convict. The life sentence hidden in a dust-ball. The truth lurking in detritus.

The pathologist, Phil Hendricks, leaned against a wall, muttering into the new, digital voice recorder he was so proud of. He glanced up at Thorne. A look that asked the usual questions. Are we up and running again? When is this going to get any easier? Why don't the two of us chuck this shit in and sit in a doorway for the rest of our lives drinking aftershave? Thorne, unable to provide any answers, looked away. In the corner nearest him, a fourth SOCO, whose bald head and bodysuit gave him the look of a giant baby, dusted the taps of the brown plastic sink with fingerprint powder.

It was, at least, a shithole with en suite facilities.

Altogether, seven of them in the room. Eight, if you counted the corpse.

Thorne's gaze was dragged reluctantly across to the chalk-white figure of the man on the bed. The body was nude and lay on the bare mattress, the spots of blood join-ing stains of less obvious origin on the threadbare and faded ticking. The hands were tied with a brown leather belt and had been pushed out in front of him as he lay prostrate, his knees pulled up beneath him, his backside in the air. His head, which was covered in a black hood, was pressed down into the sagging mattress.

Thorne watched as Phil Hendricks moved along the bed, lifted the head and turned it. He slowly removed the hood. From behind, Thorne saw his friend's shoulders stiffen for an instant, heard the small, sharp intake of breath before he laid the head back down. As a SOCO moved across to take the hood and drop it into an exhibits bag, Thorne took a step forward so that he could see the face of the dead man clearly.

His eyes were closed, his nose small and slightly upturned. The side of the face was dotted with pinprick-size blood-spots. The mouth was a mask of dried gore, the lips ragged, the whole hideous mess criss-crossed with strings of spittle. The stained, uneven teeth were bared and had gnawed through the bottom lip as the ligature had tightened around the neck.

Thorne guessed that the man was somewhere in his late thirties. It was just a guess.

From somewhere above them, Thorne became aware of a rumble suddenly dying – a boiler switching itself off. Stifling a yawn he looked up, watched cobwebs dancing gracefully around the ceiling rose. He wondered if the other residents would care much about their morning hot water when they found out what had happened in here. Thorne took a pace towards the bed. Hendricks spoke without looking round. 'Bar the fact that he's dead, I know bugger all, so don't even ask. All right?'

'I'm fine. Thanks for asking, Phil, and how are you?'

'Right, I see. Like you only came over here for a fucking chinwag . . .?'

'You are *such* a miserable sod. What's wrong with exchanging a few pleasantries? Trying to make all this a bit easier?'

Hendricks said nothing.

Thorne leaned over to scratch at his ankle through the bodysuit. 'Phil . . .'

'I told you, I don't know. Look for yourself. It seems pretty obvious how he died but it's not that simple. There's . . . other stuff gone on.'

'Right. Thanks . . .'

Hendricks moved back a little and nodded towards one of the SOCOs, who moved quickly towards the bed, picking up a small toolbox as he went. The officer knelt down and opened the box revealing a display of dainty, shining instruments. He took out a small scalpel and leaned across, reaching towards the victim's neck.

Thorne watched as the SOCO pushed a plastic-covered finger down between the ligature and the neck, struggling to get any purchase. From where Thorne was standing it looked like washing line, the sort of stuff you could get in any hardware shop. Smooth, blue plastic. He could see just how tightly it was biting into the dead man's neck. The officer carefully cut away the line in such a way as to preserve the knot that was gathered at the back of the neck. This was, of course, basic procedure. Sensible and chilling.

They'd need it to compare with any others they might find.

Thorne glanced across at Dave Holland who raised his eyebrows and turned up his palms *What's happening? How long?* Thorne shrugged. He'd been there more than an hour already. He and Holland had been over the room, taking notes, bagging a few things up, getting a feel of the scene. Now it was the technicians' turn and Thorne hated the wait. It might have made him feel better were he able to put his impatience down to a desire to get stuck in. He wished he could say, honestly, that he was itching to begin doing his job, to kick off the process that might one day bring this man's killer to justice. As it was, he just wanted to do what had to be done quickly and get out of that room.

He wanted to strip off the plastic suit, get in his car and drive away.

Actually, if he were being *really* honest with himself, he would have had to admit that only *part* of him wanted that. The other part was buzzing. The part that knew the difference between some murder scenes and others; that was able to *measure* these things. Thorne had seen the victims of enraged spouses and jealous lovers. He had stared at the bodies of business rivals and gangland grasses. He knew when he was looking at something out of the ordinary.

This was a significant murder scene. This was the work of a killer driven by something special, something spectacular.

The room stank of hatred and of rage. It also stank of pride.

Hendricks, as if reading Thorne's mind, turned to him, half smiling. 'Just another five minutes, OK? I'm not going to get anything else here . . .'

Thorne nodded. He looked at the dead man on the bed – the position of him, as if he were paying homage. Had it not been for the belt, for the livid red furrow that circled his neck, for the thin lines of blood that ran down the backs of his pale thighs, he might have been praying.

Thorne guessed that, at the end, he probably had been.

The room was hot. Thorne raised an arm to rub a sore eye and felt the tickle as a drop of sweat slid down his ribs then took a sudden, sharp turn across his belly.

Down below, a frustrated driver leaned on his horn . . .

Thorne was not even aware that he'd closed his eyes and when he heard a phone ring, he snapped them open, convinced for a few wonderful moments that he'd woken suddenly from a bad dream.

He turned, a little disorientated and saw Holland standing next to the bedside table The phone was an off-white seventies' model, the dial cracked, the grimy handset visibly jumping in its cradle. Thorne was now fully alert but he was still somewhat confused. Was this a call for them? Was it police business? Or was it possible that whoever was down at what passed for a reception desk had not been told what was happening and had put a caller through from the outside? Having met one or two of the staff, Thorne could well believe that even knowing exactly what had happened, they might still be dim enough to put a call through to the occupant of room six. If that was the case, it would certainly be a stroke of luck . . .

Thorne moved towards the ringing phone. The rest of the team stood frozen, watching him.

The victim's clothes – it had to be presumed they *were* the victim's – lay strewn about the floor nearby. Trousers – minus their belt – and underpants were next to the chair. Shirt, crumpled into a ball. One shoe under the bed up near the headboard. The brown corduroy jacket slung across the back of a chair next to the bed had contained no personal items. No wallet, no bus tickets, no crinkled photographs. Nothing that might help identify the dead man . . .

Thorne did not know if the phone had already been dusted for fingerprints, and he had no time to check. He reached out to grab a plastic evidence bag from the fat, babyish SOCO and wrapped it around his hand. He held the hand up, wanting silence. He didn't need to ask.

He took a breath and picked up the receiver. 'Hello . . .?'

"Oh . . . hi." A woman's voice.

Thorne locked eyes with Holland. 'Who did you want to speak to?' He was holding the phone an inch or so away from his ear and didn't hear the answer properly. 'Sorry, it's not a very good line, could you shout?'

'Is that any good?'

'That's great.' Thorne tried to sound casual. 'Who do you want to speak to?'

'Oh – I'm not really sure actually . . .'

Thorne looked at Holland again and shook his head. *Fuck*. It wasn't going to be that easy. 'Who am I talking to?'

'Sorry?'

'Who are you?'

There was a short pause before she spoke. The voice was suddenly a little tighter. Confident though, and refined. 'Listen, I don't want to sound rude, but it was somebody there who called me. I don't particularly want to give out . . .'

'This is Detective Inspector Thorne from the Serious Crime Group . . .'

A pause. Then: 'I thought I was calling a hotel . . .'

'You *have* called a hotel. Could you please give me your name?' He looked across at Holland, puffed out his cheeks. Holland was poised, notebook in hand, looking utterly confused.

'You could be anybody,' the woman said.

'Listen, if it makes you happier I can call you back. Better still, let me give you a number to call so you can check. Ask for DCI Russell Brigstocke. And I'll give you my mobile number . . .'

'Why do I need your mobile number if you're calling me back?'

The conversation was starting to get faintly ridiculous. Thorne thought he could detect a note of amusement, perhaps even flirtation, creeping into this woman's voice. Pleasing as this was on an otherwise grim morning, he wasn't really in the mood.

'Madam, the phone I'm speaking on, the phone you've called, is located at a crime scene and I really need to know why you're calling.'

He got the message across. The woman, though suddenly sounding a little panicky, did as she was asked.

'It was on my answering machine. I got here . . . I got into work this morning and checked my messages. This one was the first. The man who called left the name of the hotel and the room number for delivery . . .'

The man who called. Was that the man on the bed, or . . .?

'What was the message?'

'He was placing an order. Bloody funny time to be doing it though. That was why I was a bit – cautious about calling. I thought it might be a joke – you know, kids messing about, but kids wouldn't give you the right address, would they?'

'Did he leave a name?'

'No, which is one of the reasons I'm calling. And to get a credit card number. I don't do cash on delivery . . .'

'What do you mean, *bloody funny time?*'

'The message was left at ten past three this morning. I've got one of those flashy machines that tells you the time, you know?'

Thorne pressed the mouthpiece to his chest, looked across at Hendricks. 'I know the time of death. A tenner says you don't get within half an hour either side . . .'

'Hello?'

Thorne put the phone back to his ear. 'Sorry, I was conferring with a colleague. Can I ask you to keep the tape from the machine, Miss . . .?'

'Eve Bloom.'

'You said something about placing an order?'

'Oh sorry, didn't I say? I'm a florist. He was ordering some flowers. That's why I was slightly freaked out I suppose . . .'

'I don't understand. Freaked . . .?'

'Well, to be ordering what he was ordering in the middle of the night . . .'

'What exactly did the message say?'

'Hang on a minute . . .'

'No, just . . .'

She'd already gone. After a few seconds, Thorne heard the click of the button being hit and the noise of the tape rewinding. There was a pause and then a bang as she put the receiver down next to the machine.

'It's coming up,' she shouted.

Then a hiss as the tape began to play.

There was no discernible accent, no real emotion of any sort in the voice. To Thorne it sounded as if someone was trying hard to *sound* characterless, but there was a hint of something like amusement in the voice. In the voice of the man Thorne had to assume was responsible for the bound and bloodied corpse not three feet away from him. The message began simply enough. 'I'd like to order a wreath . . .'

SLEEPYHEAD

Mark Billingham

His first three victims ended up dead. His fourth
was not so fortunate . . .

Alison Willetts is unlucky to be alive.
She has survived a stroke, deliberately induced by
a skilful manipulation of pressure points on the
head and neck. She can see, hear and feel; she is
aware of everything going on around her, but she
is completely unable to move or communicate.
It's called Locked-In Syndrome. In leaving Alison
Willetts alive, the police believe the killer's
made his first mistake.

Then DI Tom Thorne discovers the horrifying
truth: it isn't Alison who is the mistake, it's
the three women already dead. 'An appropriate
margin of error' is how their killer dismisses them,
and Thorne knows they are unlikely to be the last.
For the killer is smart, and he's getting his kicks
out of toying with Thorne as much as he is
pursuing his sick fantasy . . .

Thorne must find a man whose agenda
is terrifyingly unique, and Alison, the one person
who holds the key to the killer's identity,
is unable to tell anybody . . .

ICARUS

Russell Andrews

Icarus. The boy who flew too close to the sun.
The boy who fell to his death. It is a story that
captured the imagination of ten-year-old Jack
Keller, but one that is also eerily prescient. For a
vicious assault resulted in the murder of Jack's
mother, sending her plummeting seventeen storeys
to her death – right in front of her son's eyes.

Thirty years later, and history is repeating itself
in the same horrific manner. Kid Demeter,
a physiotherapist Jack helped raise as a teenager,
has fallen to his death. The police think it was
an accident, but Jack doesn't believe them.
For Kid had confided in Jack about his ongoing
relationships with a string of women, women
he gave a series of intriguing nicknames.
The Mortician. The Mistake.
The Destination. The Murderess.

As Jack delves into Kid's world and realises just how
high the stakes really are, he knows only one thing
for certain: he must find the killer before the killer
finds him, and makes him the final victim . . .

THE NATURE OF THE BEAST

Frances Fyfield

Amy Petty is dead. But Amy Petty is alive . . .

Different people react to disasters in different ways.
When an intercity service travelling from Kent
to London joins Paddington, Hatfield and Selby
in a deadly list of notoriety, it isn't only fate
that decides who is killed: one passenger uses
the opportunity for argument to spill over into
murder; while another – blond, beautiful Amy
Petty – sees the train crash as an opportunity
to leave her life behind.

But why would Amy Petty want the world
to presume her dead? Is it because of her
husband, currently embroiled in a libel action
against a national newspaper? Douglas Petty,
a former barrister, is rich, charismatic and evil-
tempered: he runs a dog sanctuary – inherited from
his father – in his brutally eccentric manner.
Amy was to be his star witness: without her,
his reputation faces ruin.

Or maybe it isn't the present day that Amy
is running from. Maybe it is the past
from which she cannot escape . . .

ANIMOSITY

David Lindsey

With the violent end of his latest love affair,
the renowned sculptor Ross Marteau decides
to leave Paris for the reassurance of his American
home, only to find himself drawn into a world
of dark secrets and deadly deception . . .

Ross is famed for his sensual depictions of women,
and when the charismatic and attractive Celeste
Lacan asks him to sculpt her young sister Leda,
he can't help but accept the commission: Leda's
body is as startlingly repellent as her face
is beautiful.

Before he knows it, Ross is obsessively in love with
Celeste and obsessively intrigued by Leda. Then a
sudden, violent murder draws him deeper into their
world. Too late, Ross will learn that his bond with
the women is older, deeper – and more explosive –
than he could ever have imagined . . .

MAN AND WIFE

Andrew Klavan

Cal Bradley is living the good life. A man of
decency and integrity, he is loved by his children,
respected by his patients, and has a marriage that is
the stuff of romance. For fifteen years he has
shared his life with Marie, a sweet, simple woman
whom he passionately adores.

Then one evening, a troubled teenager named Peter
Blue unleashes a night of madness that will change
Cal's life for ever and send him on a journey into a
world of fear, deception and murder.

As taut as it is tense, *Man and Wife is* a gripping
psychological thriller about what happens when you
no longer believe the one you trust the most.

<u>SIX DAYS</u>

Brendan Dubois

A week is a long time in politics but six days can
destroy democracy.

It should be the happiest of days for former special
forces agent Drew Connor. Out walking in New
Hampshire's White Mountain range with his
girlfriend Sheila Cass, he has butterflies in his
stomach and an engagement ring in his pocket.
Then a thunderstorrn hits, and they take shelter in
what Sheila thinks is a relay station for a state utility.
But when Drew enters the building, he realises they
have stepped into something far more sinister.

Bullet-proof checkpoints. Telephone hotlines. A
sign by a map that reads 'Internment Centres'.
Drew's instinct is to get Sheila out as quickly as
possible, and when they stop at a general store and
the police open fire without asking questions, his
worst fears are confirmed.

Someone wants them dead for what they
have seen . . .

Other bestselling Time Warner Paperback titles available by mail: